Wreck Me

By A.J. Blaze

Wreck Me

By A.J. Blaze

Published by A.J. Blaze
ISBN (ebook): 979-8-9930309-0-6

Table of Contents

A.J. BLAZE

Dedication

For the girls who like their men dirty, dangerous, and just emotionally unavailable enough to make it interesting.
And for the boys like Ghost.
You are the chaos and the calm—wrecked and wrecking.

A Special Thank You

To Jody—

Thank you for your endless patience while I lived in this story, for understanding when my mind was tangled up in a fictional world. Thank you for sharing me with these characters, for letting me pour so much of myself into them, and for always giving me the space to create.

Wreck Me would not exist without that gift.

Content Note

This book contains content that might not be a preference for some readers.

I've included a list of content notes in the back of the book. DO NOT touch this link or go to the back before reading this book if you don't want spoilers.

Content Warning

Chapter 1

H ave you ever been to an illegal fight before?

        Neither had I... until now.

We were obviously on someone's land, but I wasn't sure whose. There was a lake, and the entire property was surrounded by trees. It was a hidden, isolated stretch of land where rules didn't exist, and blood wasn't spilled by accident. It was expected.

The only rule? There were no rules.

My friends Drew and Josh were the ones with the hookup for the fight. They did this on the regular, whereas this was the first one I'd agreed to attend.

And honestly? I had to remember to stop giving in to peer pressure.

I could have been at home, curled up on the couch with a blanket, a pint of ice cream, and the remote right now instead of standing ankle-deep in questionable grass with my friends, watching a bunch of muscle heads with no brains beat the crap out of each other for a rank and a payday.

A collective cheer erupted around us, followed by the unmistakable wet sound of flesh on flesh.

I turned toward the fight to see two massive men locked in a brutal brawl.

Neither of them was attractive, at least not to me. One had a shaved head and cauliflower ears, his nose already split open and leaking blood. The other was just as big, but somehow uglier. His face was swollen, and his knuckles dripped blood from fresh cuts.

They weren't strategizing. They were brawling. It was all fury and brute force, no technique, no control, just rage and fists flying.

I winced as yoga pants guy (yes, that's what I was calling him) straddled his opponent and started pummeling his face into the dirt.

"Jesus," I said. "How hasn't this been broken up by the cops yet?"

Josh smirked. "It moves every week."

That made sense. Keep it moving, keep it hidden.

The brutality was enough to make my stomach turn. It was hard to watch.

"Isn't it so hot?" Jen sighed dreamily.

I gawked at her. "Not the word I'd choose at this moment."

Jen just shot me a grin.

"So gross. Is someone going to stop that psycho?" The guy's face looked like bloody ground chuck.

Then, thankfully, yoga pants guy finally stopped, jumping up from his near-unconscious opponent and throwing his bloodied fists into the air.

The crowd exploded, screaming his name as if he were a god.

"I'm so turned on right now!" Jen said.

I blinked at her, horrified. "I don't think I can watch this."

Jen rolled her eyes. "I told Drew not to invite you. I told him you couldn't handle it."

I exhaled slowly, trying not to lose it. "I'm not sorry that violence doesn't turn me on."

Niki nudged my shoulder. "They're not all that brutal," she assured me.

I wasn't convinced.

Chapter 2

The sea of bodies parted, making way for the next two fighters as they stepped into the circle.

Then, I saw him. The second he emerged from the crowd, the spectators erupted into a frenzy, their voices a chaotic mix of cheers, taunts, and drunken shouts.

I couldn't look away. He was beautiful. Bigger than I usually liked, but undeniably hot and built like a machine. His body looked like it had been chiseled from a lifetime of violence and discipline.

His presence was commanding, and his frame was broad and packed with solid muscle. His jeans clung to his thick thighs. The white T-shirt he wore outlined his sculpted chest and arms in a way that made my stomach flip. His hair was trimmed short on the sides and back, with the top longer, thick, and swept back. And his beard... God, his beard was thick, the kind of beard a man earns, not just grows.

He was soaked in sweat, his skin glistening under the blistering sun. He cracked his neck, rolling his built shoulders as he stood on the grass. The man looked like he belonged in another time, like some Viking warlord who got bored with pillaging and decided to beat men half to death for fun instead.

"There you go. This one will be fairly quick," Drew said, nodding toward the fighters.

"Who is that?" I asked, my eyes still glued to him. "The one with the beard."

"That's Ghost. The guy's a legend. He wins, he gets paid. He loses... Well, he doesn't lose. At least I've never seen him lose."

Jen practically moaned beside me. "He's built like a freaking god."

I refused to agree with her out loud, but yeah. Yeah, he kind of was.

"Yes, Daddy!" Jen moaned dramatically.

That totally deflated my lust buzz. "Ew! No," I said.

Jen turned to me, confused. "What?"

"That's disgusting."

"There's nothing disgusting about that man. He's gorgeous."

"I'm talking about the name. Why would you say 'Daddy' toward any guy that isn't your dad?"

Niki laughed. "Because she's twisted."

I snickered.

"Because it's sexy," Jen defended.

"No, it's not sexy. It's incestuous," I told her.

Niki snorted, barely holding back laughter.

"It's because you're a good girl," Jen threw out, rolling her eyes.

I shrugged. "No, it's because I don't have daddy issues."

Jen smiled, then licked her lips suggestively. "Call me Mommy."

I groaned, exasperated. "Could you try to look less lustful toward another man in front of your boyfriend?"

She shrugged unapologetically, and Drew just shook his head.

That's when the ref... if you could call him that, started in with the announcing. He introduced Ghost, and the crowd went crazy with cheers, screams, and even some wolf calls by clearly horny women.

His opponent, Gator, stood across from him, a thick-necked beast of a man with fists the size of wrecking balls. He grinned, showing off a missing tooth, his knuckles already bloodied from his last fight.

"You look like you were conceived behind a dumpster during a prison riot," Ghost taunted. "Must be why your mama never taught you to fight," he added.

The crowd broke out in fits of laughter at his teasing.

Gator cracked his knuckles. "You talk a lot for a man who's about to get his face rearranged."

Ghost chuckled, rubbing his jaw. "I like my face just the way it is, but thanks for the concern. You're sweet. You should get that tattooed on your ass: World's Nicest Guy."

The crowd went wild again.

I had to admit; I laughed too. He was a smartass. Now, let's see if he could fight as well as he talked.

The ref raised a hand and let it drop. The fight was on.

Gator charged first, a freight train with fists, but Ghost was quick. He dodged left, coiled back, and landed a sharp right hook to the guy's ribs. The impact was like hitting a wall, but Ghost was relentless, following up with a brutal uppercut that snapped Gator's head back.

The crowd roared, the air thick with adrenaline.

Ghost stalked him like a predatory animal, his muscles flexing as he moved.

What made my breath catch wasn't his sheer size or intimidating presence. It was his eyes. I wasn't close enough to make out the exact color, but they were sharp, calculating, as if he was already five steps ahead of the fight.

This wasn't mindless violence. This was strategy. He moved with purpose. He wasn't just swinging, hoping to hit something like some of these guys.

The two men traded blows, the crowd going wild, and for the first time since arriving, I felt the unmistakable pull of adrenaline mixed with... Yes. It was pure, unfiltered lust.

The fighters squared off again, circling each other.

Gator came at him again, but Ghost dodged like a predator playing with its prey, landing a devastating right hook into Gator's ribs, who was more jacked but clearly less skilled.

Gator suddenly dove headfirst into Ghost's stomach.

I winced. "Seriously? Come on! Even I know better than to dive into someone like that."

Drew nudged me, grinning. "See! It's easy to get into."

I just smiled at him. Yes, Drew was Jen's boyfriend, but he was the total opposite of her in every way. He was laid-back, observant, down to earth, and much less horny in public.

Gator threw wild punches, but Ghost dodged them effortlessly. His speed was shocking for someone his size, moving with a grace that made little sense.

I was mesmerized.

Then Gator lunged forward again, Ghost grabbing him mid-motion, and with one powerful shove, he knocked Ghost into the lake, going down with him.

The crowd went wild.

For a split second, I thought that was the end, that the ref would call the fight right then.

My stomach dropped as Gator, like the complete psychopath he was, gripped Ghost by the hair and held him under the water.

I clutched Niki's arm.

"Oh, shit," Josh muttered. "That bastard is trying to drown him."

I couldn't breathe.

The water was too dark to see beneath the surface, but the violent thrashing gave everything away. Ghost wasn't just fighting anymore. He was fighting for his life.

I gasped. "Is that allowed?"

Josh smiled. "Technically, this is an underground fight. There aren't really any rules."

I turned to Drew. "Why would anyone want to enter a competition that's so brutal?"

"The money is good. Especially if you're undefeated like Ghost."

"Guys and their testosterone," I muttered, scanning the lake for any sign of life from Ghost.

My heart pounded wildly. Seconds ticked by. Too many seconds.

A sick, uneasy feeling crept over me. "Is anyone going to help him? That guy is going to kill him!"

I took a step forward, instinct telling me to do something, but Drew grabbed my arm before I could move. "He's got this."

"Are you sure?"

Drew just laughed. "You gonna go give him hell?"

"If I have to jump in, I will."

"That's why I love you," Drew said, throwing an arm around my shoulders, grinning. "That's the one reason there's always a referee. He'll step in and call the fight if he's under much longer."

Before I could respond, Ghost exploded out of the water, his right arm swinging up in a vicious uppercut that clipped Gator under the chin.

Gator went down, sinking into the water.

The crowd lost their minds.

I exhaled, realizing I'd been holding my breath, relief washing over me.

And then... Ghost emerged from the water with Gator in tow. Gator was limp, his body drenched and lifeless as Ghost hauled him onto the grass and dropped him like dead weight.

For a second, I thought he really was dead.

But then Gator coughed violently, sputtering up water, gasping like a man who had just seen the afterlife and was rejected back to Earth.

Ghost, standing over him, soaked and completely unfazed, ran a hand through his dripping hair. Then he grinned and said, "If you wanted me to get wet, you could've just bought me dinner first."

The crowd erupted, laughing, whistling, screaming, clapping.

My eyes stayed locked on the man who had just won.

And as Ghost disappeared into the crowd, water dripping from his skin, something inside me shifted. I had walked into this place disgusted, unimpressed, and ready to leave.

The fight was over, but the adrenaline still pounded in my chest, the lust still swimming through my veins.

What the hell had I just witnessed?

Chapter 3

"Why do they call him Ghost?" I asked, my eyes scanning the crowd for any trace of him.

Drew grinned at me. "Because he has the ability to pass through solid objects."

I shot him a flat look. "Be serious."

He laughed. "Not literally. He's just fast as hell. Gives off the impression that he moves right through you."

I frowned. "He was so... big."

Drew shot me a knowing smirk.

I flushed pink. "I mean, muscular. Bigger guys are usually slower."

Josh leaned in. "Some are, but Ghost is pretty damn fast."

"Surprisingly so," I agreed.

"He's famous for his one-two knockout," Josh added.

I raised an eyebrow. "What's that?"

"It's his signature move. A hit of some kind, like a jab to the ribs, or a knee, followed by a punch or elbow, maybe a spin kick to the jaw."

Josh's smile widened. "The first is a distraction. Then he hits you with the follow-up."

Drew smirked. "Then it's lights out."

"Exactly."

Drew downed the last of his beer. "He watches people. Studies them. He knows your next move before you do."

"Like a chess player," Josh said. "Only bloodier."

I chewed my lip. "I noticed he wasn't just throwing wildly out there. He's... strategic."

"Deadly and smart," Drew said with a grin. "That's what makes him dangerous. Most guys come out swinging. Ghost? He waits. And when he moves..."

Josh whistled low. "You don't even see it coming."

"And with women?" Jen asked.

Josh let out a dry laugh. "Let's just say Ghost isn't in the habit of making friends with women."

"He doesn't like women?" I asked.

Josh nodded. "He likes women."

Drew smirked. "He likes them well enough to fuck them. Just don't expect any contact from him after that. One night. No repeats. No exceptions."

My stomach dipped. That was disappointing. "Wow."

Josh glanced at me. "He doesn't do relationships. Just damage control. But he's not a bad guy."

"He was seriously hot," Jen sighed.

"Yeah, but you could never date him," Drew told her.

"Why not?" she asked.

"You'd be a one-night stand. Less than, actually."

"He sounds like a real jerk," Niki said.

Josh shrugged. "Who says? Just because he wants to get laid without baggage?"

"Sometimes I think he has the right idea," Drew said.

Jen pushed him playfully. "You know you'd rather be with me than screwing random women."

Drew grinned. "Of course I would. When you give me some, anyway."

Everyone laughed. Except for Jen.

"So, would Halston be his type?" Niki asked suddenly.

"My t–type?" I sputtered. "Because I'm the single one here?" I shot her a look. "Oh, no. I don't want that. I'm not interested in that."

"Not interested in him?" Niki asked, raising an eyebrow.

Oh, I was interested in the man himself. But I wasn't willing to admit it out loud. "Not interested in hit-it-and-quit-it sex."

Drew shook his head. "Don't worry. I love Ghost, but I wouldn't try setting the two of you up. I'd hate to see your spirit broken when he screwed you, then ghosted you."

I smiled my thanks to him.

"Halston isn't the type of girl a man like that would go for," Jen added.

Drew scowled. "That's rude, babe."

He gave me an apologetic glance, and I just smiled at him. I was used to Jen's insults. She was convinced the world revolved around her and that she was the only woman who existed when men were around. To be fair, that was usually true. She had long, perfectly straight, bleach blonde hair, sharp features, and the kind of confidence that made men flock to her. I had seen it happen a thousand times.

And me? I wasn't that girl.

She shrugged, completely unapologetic. "I'm sorry, Halston, but you know it's true. You're too shy for someone like him."

I took exception to that. "I speak my mind."

Jen shrugged. "But not where it counts."

My brows furrowed. "What? What does that even mean?"

Jen let out a long sigh, like I was a lost cause. "That's half your problem, Halston. You don't even know."

I crossed my arms, irritated. "Half my problem?"

"In bed, Halston. A man like that wants a bad bitch in bed."

I had nothing to say about that. Because, well... she wasn't wrong. I wasn't a bad bitch in bed. I hadn't even had enough experience with anyone to know if I had a wild side. My sexual resume consisted of one guy, and that was over six years ago. I hadn't dated since.

Jen grinned like she had proven her point. "See? She knows I speak the truth. Now, me? I'm an animal in bed, right, baby?"

Drew laughed, rubbing the back of his neck. "Yes, baby, you are."

She grinned with satisfaction, her chest puffing up. "He probably likes kinky stuff in bed, like choking you out."

I rolled my eyes. "Just because you're into that doesn't mean everyone else is."

Jen gave me a knowing smirk. "Well, I know you're not."

I snorted. "Damn right. Proud of it, too."

Drew laughed, but Josh chimed in. "I like a bad girl in bed sometimes, but I still don't want that kind of kink."

"Me either," Niki agreed.

Jen rolled her eyes. "Pussies. I'll try anything once."

Drew shrugged. "Ghost would still kick you to the curb after screwing you, kink or not."

Jen flipped her hair. "You don't know that."

Drew raised an eyebrow. "Are we seriously having this debate right now? I know the guy. You've never even met him."

Jen tilted her chin up. "It still stands. Men love kinky girls. I'd leave that man wanting seconds and thirds."

At times like this, I couldn't understand what Drew saw in her. She was so conceited. She didn't care about his feelings, and that pissed me off. Which always led me to wonder why I was still her friend. I never had an actual answer for that, except for the fact that she befriended me when I had just lost my parents and needed a distraction from the loss.

Josh let out a short laugh. "Good luck. He'd still kick you to the curb."

Jen flicked her hair back. "I'd fuck him so good he would beg me to stay the night."

Drew's jaw tightened.

"Oh, my God! Would you stop?" I practically yelled. I wasn't even sure how Drew could listen to it.

Jen waved me off. "I'm just joking."

"No, you're not joking. And it's a really fucked-up thing to say in front of your boyfriend."

Jen rolled her eyes. "You're so sensitive. What? Do you have a thing for Drew?"

Drew snorted. "Don't be stupid. She doesn't like me. She's just sticking up for me because she's a friend. And sometimes, Jen? You say pretty shitty stuff. Like now."

Jen folded her arms. "Wow. Neither of you can take a joke."

Drew rubbed a hand down his face, clearly frustrated. "Yeah, well, let me know when your jokes get funny, and then maybe I'll laugh."

Jen's expression darkened. "What the fuck ever."

Then she turned and stormed off.

Chapter 4

"I better go talk to her," I muttered, sighing.

Drew put a hand up to stop me. "No. Just let her go. When she gets like this, there's no talking to her."

I hesitated, but... he was right. She would just escalate the fight. It was better to let her cool off. "I'm going to go grab a couple of beers. You guys want?"

Drew nodded. "Yes."

"Yes," Josh said.

"Yes, please," Niki said.

I returned with four beers, holding the plastic cups close to the bottom, two in each hand.

That's when I saw Ghost.

I watched as he rolled his shoulders. His jeans and t-shirt still clung to his soaked, sculpted body, those tattooed arms flexing as he ran a hand through his damp hair.

I swear to God; he looked like a walking wet dream.

He was surrounded by people, mostly women, wanting his attention. And he looked utterly unaffected.

And for some reason… I wondered what it would take to shake him.

Jen was still MIA, no doubt sulking somewhere, or off flirting with random guys.

As I approached my friends, Ghost had my full attention. He was walking up to Drew and Josh, greeting them in guy speak. It was that half-handshake, half-hug thing men did when they respected each other, but didn't want to seem like they cared too much.

His back was to me, and I finally got an actual sense of just how big he was up close. He was built like a fortress. The man was broad, muscled, and tall enough to make my five-foot-two frame feel microscopic.

Then, out of nowhere, he took a sudden step back and crashed into me.

I gasped as plastic crunched between us, the ice-cold liquid drenching my front, my arms falling helplessly to my sides as the ruined cups tumbled to the ground.

I shivered, looking down at my stained white t-shirt.

He turned toward me.

And that's when I got hit with his unsettling, crystal blue, intense gaze. For a second, I forgot how to function. Up close, he was even hotter. His body was a work of art, every inch of him screaming power and raw masculinity. His full beard framed his sharp jawline, running seamlessly into his sideburns, adding to the Viking warrior aesthetic he had going on.

And I might have been a little mesmerized…

Until he opened his mouth.

"Nice tits."

My sexual high was obliterated in the blink of an eye, replaced by pure disgust. "Nice manners," I shot back.

He laughed as if I had just amused him.

Drew rushed forward. "Oh, shit. Halston, are you okay?"

I forced a tight smile. "I'm good." I threw a pointed look at the Viking god turned jackass. "I just lost all the beer, and my shirt is soaked."

He laughed again. "Which one of you does she belong to?"

I cut my eyes at him. "I don't belong to anyone."

Drew shook his head. "Neither. She's a friend."

Ghost's grin widened as he looked back at me. "A friend with benefits?"

I felt my blood pressure spike and my jaw tighten.

"I've got some free time if you wanna go bang one out in my truck," he added casually, like he was offering me a ride to the airport.

My jaw dropped. "That's repulsive."

He just laughed again. "Really? That usually works."

"I bet it does. On your Instagram sluts, no doubt."

His laughter deepened, like he thrived on pissing me off. Then, without missing a beat, he switched gears like he hadn't just propositioned me with all the finesse of a frat boy on spring break.

"You still with Jen?" he asked Drew, turning away from me.

Drew smirked. "Still together. She's here somewhere, pissed at me."

Ghost nodded once. "I'm not surprised. Can't let her walk all over you forever."

As much as I thought he was a cocky asshole, I couldn't exactly disagree with that. Jen had been treating Drew like a doormat for years. At least Ghost had no problem calling it how he saw it. He was direct, unapologetic, and entirely too bold.

Niki handed me some napkins, and I took them with a grateful smile. "Thank you."

I tried to pat myself dry, but it was useless. I was soaked. My white t-shirt clung to me like a second skin, now practically transparent and drawing more attention than I cared to notice. My jeans were sticking to my thighs, the beer smell seeping into the denim.

Ghost watched me with zero remorse, an amused smirk playing at his lips—like he was taking in a show he didn't pay for. I had expected a helpful hand, or at the very least, an apology. Instead, I got an obnoxious ass.

He was staring at me with those smug blue eyes and that infuriating grin, like this was just another Saturday night for him.

"Last chance," he said, grinning like the devil with a fight schedule. "I got a couple of minutes before my next fight."

I didn't miss the way his eyes dragged over me again, like he already knew exactly what he'd do with those couple of minutes.

I raised an eyebrow, grabbed another napkin from Niki, and dabbed at the front of my soaked shirt. "A couple of minutes?" I echoed. "If that's all you've got to offer, you should be embarrassed."

Josh choked on his beer. Niki turned her face away, laughing into her arm.

Ghost's grin flickered, then deepened into something darker. Like I'd just poked the tiger, and he was thrilled about it.

"Damn," he said with a wicked glint in his eyes. "You've got claws, sweetheart."

I rolled my eyes. "Keep talking, and I'll use them."

He chuckled again, shaking his head. "You're a mouthy little thing."

"Better than being a caveman with a concussion kink," I muttered.

He actually laughed at that, giving a half-shrug like he couldn't even argue. "Damn, Tits. You might just be my type after all."

"Good," I said with a smirk, turning my attention back to my soaked shirt. "Too bad you're not mine."

He grinned wider. "Suit yourself, Tits."

I shot him a glare that could've melted brick, but he only winked, turned back to Drew and Josh, and slapped a hand to Drew's shoulder. "I'll check you guys later."

"Later!" Drew called after him, still cracking up.

I stood there, beer-soaked, flustered, and wildly confused as to why my entire body still tingled from the interaction.

Drew looked at me like he was holding back another laugh.

"What?" I said. "You think it's amusing he called me 'Tits'?"

"I think you flustered the shit out of him. And that was more entertaining than anything else happening here."

I shook my head, letting out a slow exhale. "He's—"

"Something," Drew finished, grinning.

"Yeah. Something offensive."

But later that night? That didn't stop me from stalking Ghost online.

I found his Instagram first. And wow. It was a sea of women. Women who bent to his every whim, just like in real life, no doubt. Comment after comment littered his posts, most of which were from thirsty women begging to be his cum receptacle.

"Yes, please, Daddy."

"So, are you stopping by my place later?"

"I'll let you do whatever you want to me."

It was endless. Too many Jens in the world. And all of them seemed to be following him on Instagram. I scrolled through his photos, trying to understand the hype, and it didn't take long.

It was because he was hot. Frustratingly, ridiculously hot.

But after what happened tonight? I knew exactly who he was. And I knew I wanted nothing to do with him.

Chapter 5

A few days later, I was on speakerphone with Drew. Josh and Niki were with him in the car.

"Ghost invited us to his ranch to shoot some guns," Josh said. "Come on, meet us there."

See the wet dream guy again? As hot as he was, he wasn't exactly someone I wanted to spend more time with. "I'll pass."

"He got some new AK-47s," Drew added. "He's gonna let us shoot them."

"That doesn't sound like fun to me," I admitted. "But you guys go have fun. I know you like that kind of stuff."

"I don't want to be the only girl there," Niki whined. "You have to come."

"What about Jen?"

"She's still pissed. She said she has better stuff to do."

I wanted to say me too, but I didn't actually have anything to do. And I knew if the roles were reversed, I'd want Niki to come with me. I sighed. "Fine."

I was sure I was going to regret it.

As I pulled up to the ranch, the sign caught my attention. It had clearly once read Legacy Ranch, but now only Legacy remained. The rest was broken off and leaning against the stone wall to the right. I wondered what had happened there.

Pulling up to the speaker, I pressed the button and waited.

A second later, Ghost's voice came through. "Didn't know you were coming, Tits."

I glared into the camera, not remotely amused. "You're making me sorry I did."

He laughed just as the gate began sliding open.

I parked next to Drew's car, leaving my purse inside before stepping out.

That's when I heard the barking. Not just random yapping, but deep, furious barking that shook the air like thunder. And the sound of running. Fast, heavy paws pounded against the dirt like an oncoming storm.

I turned to see two massive German shepherds charging straight at me.

I let out a yelp and bolted back toward the car, reaching for the handle like my life depended on it.

"Stopp!" Ghost's command cut through the air, sharp and dominant.

I froze, my fingers still gripping the car handle, my heart in my throat. I turned just in time to see both dogs skid to a stop with terrifying discipline.

"Komm!" The dogs immediately turned back, flanking Ghost's sides with military precision.

I stood there, panting, my heart racing like it was trying to beat its way out.

He turned slightly. "Sitz!"

The dogs immediately sat at his side, alert but still, like statues that could murder you.

"You coming?" Ghost asked, smirking.

"Nope. I think I'll head back out. A drive-thru ranch tour sounds safer."

"Fuß!" He started walking again without looking back, the dogs moving perfectly in sync with him.

"What does that mean?" I asked cautiously, finally inching forward.

"Heel," Ghost said. "It's German. That's how they were trained. Catch up," he tossed over his shoulder.

"I'm not walking anywhere near those things." But I followed anyway, carefully keeping a car-length of distance.

Now that I wasn't fearing for my life, I could finally look at them.

Two stunning, muscular German Shepherds with dark fur, intelligent eyes, and sharp alertness. They were terrifyingly beautiful. "Do they attack everyone?"

"No," he replied simply. "Only if I tell them to. Otherwise, they just put the fear of God into people."

"Yeah, no kidding," I muttered, still trying to calm my pulse.

"That's kind of the point. They're not poodles, Tits."

I rolled my eyes. "So how do you get them to not terrify people?"

"I tell them that person's a friend."

I raised an eyebrow. "Did you tell them I'm a friend?"

"No."

I stopped walking. "Why not tell them that so they don't rip my face off?"

He looked back at me as if it were obvious. "Because you're not a friend. You haven't earned that respect from me, so you haven't earned it from them."

My mouth fell open.

I wasn't sure what offended me more—his words or the fact that he said them like they were law carved in stone. "And how exactly does one earn your respect, oh mighty dog lord?"

He gave a half-shrug, his tone maddeningly casual. "I rarely use that word. It's reserved for my guys. People I trust. People who work the ranch and bleed for me, if I ask."

"So... I need to watch my back the whole time I'm here?"

"No." He stopped and looked at me, his eyes serious now. "They won't hurt you. I meant that. But if you come back next time, yeah... we'll probably go through this little chase scene again."

I scoffed. "Don't worry. There won't be a next time. Niki begged me to come so she wouldn't be the only girl. This whole cowboy-patrol vibe isn't really my thing."

Ghost grinned wide. "Big surprise."

My eyes narrowed. "What's that supposed to mean?"

He shrugged, walking again like he hadn't just poked me with a stick. "Nothing. Just... you're a little high-maintenance for dirt and dogs."

I stopped dead in my tracks, my jaw tightening. "I am not high-maintenance," I said through gritted teeth. "I'm not Jen."

That made him glance back.

His expression didn't change. But something flickered in his eyes. Amusement maybe. Or curiosity. But not remorse. "Didn't say you were," he said simply, with just enough edge to let me know he didn't regret the comparison—even if he clearly wasn't a fan of Jen either.

He kept walking, and the dogs followed, leaving me in his dust, fuming.

I muttered under my breath. "Asshole."

I was still standing there, arms crossed, watching the dogs like they might turn back and lunge at me just for fun.

Ghost turned back when I still didn't follow. He rolled his eyes like I was the problem. Then, with a glance at the dogs, he muttered, "Lass sie in Ruhe."

They didn't move a muscle. They just sat there like perfect soldiers.

I narrowed my eyes. "What did you just say to them?"

Ghost gave me a slow smirk. "Told them to leave you alone." He paused, then added under his breath, "Just for today."

I scoffed. "Gee, thanks. That's so reassuring."

"Don't get cocky," he said, already walking ahead again. "You're still not a friend."

I followed Ghost, keeping a respectable distance from his dogs, who walked beside him like silent bodyguards.

When we reached the back, I saw the others gathered at a shooting range setup. There were multiple targets lined up in the distance.

Josh was already firing off rounds, looking way too happy. "Hell yeah!" he cheered as he lowered his gun. "This is insane!"

Drew grinned at me. "Glad you decided to show up."

"Yeah, yeah," I said.

Ghost walked past me, grabbing one of the AK-47s from a gun rack, checking it with expert ease before handing it to Drew. "Your turn."

Drew took the gun, looking like a kid on Christmas morning.

I sighed, already regretting this trip.

Ghost glanced at me. "You ever shot before?"

I shook my head. "Nope. And I don't plan to."

He shrugged. "Your loss, Tits."

I rolled my eyes, refusing to take the bait.

Niki nudged me. "Just try it once. It's not so bad."

I sighed, already knowing I was gonna cave.

Ghost lifted an eyebrow. "Want a lesson, Tits?"

I turned to him, deadpan. "You call me that one more time, and I swear to God, I will shoot you."

He laughed.

Chapter 6

I rolled my eyes at Ghost's boast to Drew. They were talking about women again, more specifically, Drew's situation with Jen.

"I have plenty of women I can have sex with," Ghost said, loading a magazine into the AK-47 like he was talking about ordering food off a menu.

Drew barely looked up. "True. But how many can you trust with your heart?"

Ghost laughed, like the idea itself was a joke. "Is that what you think it is with Jen? Love?"

"Hey!" I shot out.

Ghost turned his head, his unsettling blue eyes landing on me.

"That's his girlfriend you're talking about."

"And?"

Damn it. He had a point. It wasn't like Jen treated Drew with love. She barely respected him, using him as a placeholder to pay her way until she found something better.

Still, I crossed my arms. "It's rude."

Ghost grinned at me, flashing a genuine-looking smile. And damn it, he had a really nice smile. When it wasn't accompanied by horrible remarks.

"There's nothing wrong with love," Niki told him.

"Exactly," I said.

Ghost gave a chuckle. "Fuck that. Love is for pussies. The only pussy on this body is when she's sitting on my face or on my cock."

The guys laughed.

I rolled my eyes. "That's... charming."

Ghost glanced back at me, and before I could recover from his vulgar mouth, he shot me a wink.

A white-hot bolt shot through me, my breath catching in my throat. I went from grossed out to turned on in a split second. What the hell was that? He talked and acted like a barbarian, but that barbarian was undoing me with one damn look.

Ghost casually adjusted himself, and I realized what he was doing at the same time he lifted the AK-47, aiming at the target.

I leaned in toward Niki. "The man is playing with himself."

She laughed. "He's adjusting. There's a big difference."

I raised an eyebrow. "Please enlighten me, so maybe he'll repulse me a little less."

Niki grinned. "I've been dating Josh for almost a year, so I've learned quite a bit about men and their mannerisms. They have to adjust themselves. It's crammed into a small space. Sometimes they have to move it around a bit to get it in a comfortable position."

I made a face. "Oh. I had no idea."

Niki lowered her voice. "Apparently, it's bigger than average."

"What is?"

She gave me a knowing look.

It took me a second. "Oh! Really?" I whispered back.

"Apparently."

I raised an eyebrow. "As in, you don't even know if it's true?"

"I mean, the man is always adjusting. So, I asked Josh, and he told me that several women told him and Drew that he's carrying a little extra."

I stared at her. "A little extra what?"

She laughed. "You know…"

I rolled my eyes, laughing too. "Right, I got that. I just meant… Never mind. Stupid attempt at a joke."

Niki smiled at me.

"Maybe it's all a rumor," I offered. "Maybe it just feels good to play with himself."

"I'm sure it does," she said, making me laugh harder. "Are you less repulsed?"

"Less repulsed? No. More intrigued? Yes."

"How do we find out?" Niki asked.

I shrugged. "I'm certainly not asking him to drop his pants."

She laughed, then sent me a devious grin. "You could bite the bullet and sleep with him."

I shot her a look. "I'm not that intrigued."

We both laughed again, but our giggling must have been too loud because Ghost turned toward us. "Having fun back there?"

I shook my head, trying to compose myself, but Niki burst out laughing, which set me off all over again.

My eyes involuntarily darted downward to the bulge in the front of his jeans, then shot lower to his black motorcycle boots. If stereotypes were to be believed, the man had a definite advantage.

"You ladies want a turn?" Ghost asked.

Niki vehemently shook her head.

"How about you, Tits?"

Everyone laughed.

I let out a frustrated groan. "Seriously? I have a name. It's Halston."

He acted like he was considering it, then smirked. "I like Tits better."

I rolled my eyes.

He laughed. "Come, give it a try."

His large hand shot out, palm up. And damn it all if I didn't take it.

His long fingers curled around mine, easily tugging me toward him. I swear, it was like a damn tractor beam pulling me to him. His large hand was rough and warm against mine, sending a shiver up my arm.

Ghost helped me put earplugs in before sliding safety glasses onto my face, his touch lingering just a few seconds longer than necessary. Then he turned me toward the target, stepping right behind me.

I had to remind myself that he was crass, even though his hard body against mine caused a warmth to spread through me.

He positioned my hands on the 9mm pistol, his arms around me, cradling my body like it was natural. "Only aim at the targets," he said.

I breathed him in, my eyes rolling back involuntarily. What the hell did he smell like? Like cologne or body wash, and something distinctly male.

I was distracted. Very distracted. And I hated it.

Ghost lifted the gun, his beautiful, muscular arms flexing. "Like this."

He squeezed the trigger. The loud sound so close made me jump with a small yelp. The shot tore through the red bullseye, punching a perfect hole in the center of the target.

He did it again and again, each shot perfect, effortless. Then, he finally dropped his arms to his sides.

"I thought earplugs were supposed to block the noise. That scared the crap out of me."

He laughed. "I noticed by the way you damn near jumped outta your panties."

I rolled my eyes.

He grinned. "Cute noise, though. Might have to make you do it again." Then he leaned in closer, his voice dropping low, taking on a sinful tone. "See? I can get you out of those panties without even touching you."

Heat shot up my neck. A shiver ran through my body, and my nipples immediately hardened.

I managed to fire back a response. "I'm sure your fighter groupies hand their panties over without hesitation, but you'll never get me out of mine."

He grinned a cocky smile, his voice still low. "If I wanted you, I could make you beg me to tear them off."

White-hot heat shot through me, torching my face, my breath catching in my throat.

His grin deepened, like he could see exactly what his words did to me.

"The ego on you."

He smirked, then stepped away. "Go on, Tits. Give it a try."

I narrowed my eyes at him as he handed me the gun and pointed me toward the target again.

I focused on aiming, blocking out the fact that my body was still buzzing from his filthy words.

Just as I was about to squeeze the trigger, he leaned in and whispered, his mouth grazing my ear. "Squeeze it."

The sound of his voice, the feel of his hot breath on my ear, caused my finger to twitch involuntarily and shoot prematurely, the bullet going way over the target.

Ghost laughed.

I turned my head, glowering at him. "I wasn't ready."

"I see that. Looked like you came early."

My jaw dropped.

Niki choked on a laugh behind me.

I glared at him.

He grinned, lifting a hand in surrender. "Go again."

This time, he positioned himself even closer, his arms wrapping around mine again. His chest pressed against my back.

His hands steadied mine, guiding my aim. His voice was rough; his breath warm against my cheek. "Relax."

And suddenly, the gun wasn't the only thing locked and loaded.

Chapter 7

It was dark by the time the buzz of the evening faded and everyone finished off the last of their burgers. The fire pit smoldered in the distance, casting an orange glow over the gravel as I walked toward my car, ready to head out.

That's when I noticed a tall, black-haired man standing near the front of the garage, arms crossed, posture relaxed, but observant. He looked to be in his late forties. He was rugged in a practical way, the kind of guy who probably fixed things before most people knew they were broken.

He glanced at me and offered a nod. "Your tire's low. If you pull into the garage, I'll top it off for you."

I looked down, frowning. Sure enough, it was sagging a little. "Oh. Yeah, thank you."

I slid into the driver's seat and pulled into the garage right next to him. He already had the air compressor in hand.

Stepping out, I tucked my hands into the back pockets of my jeans, watching as he crouched beside the tire. "I'm Halston," I offered.

He looked up and gave me a polite smile. "Nice to meet you, Halston. I'm Henry. I manage the ranch for Ghost."

"Very nice to meet you, Henry."

He checked the pressure with a small analog gauge, squinting in the garage light. "You should always keep an eye on this. Low pressure can mess with your control on the road."

I gave a sheepish smile. "Yeah, I didn't know. I'm not exactly mechanically inclined."

He chuckled. "Nothing wrong with that. Your dad never taught you?"

I stiffened slightly, caught off guard. "No."

It came out short. I didn't elaborate.

Henry didn't press. He clipped the hose back in place and stood. "All set. Should ride smoother now."

"Thank you so much. That was really sweet of you."

"Not a problem. Drive safe, yeah?"

He gave me another nod and turned to walk back across the garage.

"Thank you again, Henry!" I called after him with a smile.

And that's when a voice slid through the air behind me. "Are my guys your personal pit crew now?"

I turned sharply. Ghost had just stepped into the garage, head tilted slightly like he was sizing me up and not entirely thrilled with what he saw.

His blue eyes locked onto mine, unreadable but cutting.

"My tire was low. Henry offered to help," I said, confused at the sudden shift in energy.

"Henry, huh?" Ghost echoed, one brow arching. "We're on a first-name basis with my crew already?"

I furrowed my brows. "I introduced myself. He introduced himself back. That's how people interact, in case you've forgotten."

Ghost's mouth curled into a half-smirk. "Mmm. Women always know how to work their angles when they want something."

I froze, blood rising to my cheeks in rage. "Did you really just say that to me?"

He tilted his head with mock curiosity. "Did I hurt your feelings?"

"No," I snapped. I crossed my arms tightly across my chest. "Henry offered. I accepted. End of story. I didn't bat my lashes or twirl my hair, if that's what you're implying."

Ghost didn't blink. Didn't move. Just stood there looking smug and infuriating.

"Have I done something to offend you?" I asked, my voice clipped.

Ghost chuckled low, and his eyes dropped to my chest before crawling back up to my face with absolutely no shame. "Nah. Just saying, you do have a substantial asset that men go stupid for."

My eyes narrowed. "My brain?"

He grinned. A full, unrepentant, I'm-enjoying-every-second-of-this grin. "I like your sense of humor, Tits."

"Thanks," I deadpanned, sarcasm practically dripping from my mouth.

He laughed again. Full-on this time, like I was the best entertainment he'd had all week.

And then, like some demon possessed me, I blurted: "And they're not that substantial. They're a C-cup."

The moment the words were out, I wanted to crawl under the nearest tractor.

Ghost's eyebrows lifted slightly, amusement flickering in his eyes as he gave me a once-over. "More than a mouthful's a waste anyway," he murmured.

Heat shot through me, and I hated that my brain instantly filled in the blanks. "At least you treat your dogs really well," I muttered, trying to redirect the chaos.

His brow quirked. "Why wouldn't I?"

I tilted my head, my arms still crossed. "I've seen how you treat women firsthand."

That made him laugh again. "My dogs are loyal."

"A woman can be loyal."

He looked at me as if the idea itself was almost tragic. Another chuckle escaped him, and then, without a word, he turned on his heel and walked away, leaving me standing in the garage, dripping with disbelief and completely off-balance.

I stared after him, my chest tight with frustration. Had my loyalty just been mocked?

I had no idea. But one thing was clear: Ghost was a walking contradiction, and he was absolutely confusing as hell.

Chapter 8

The last time I was here, Ghost had been in a confusing, broody, sharp-edged mood. I wasn't sure I was ready to risk walking back into that.

But one of his guys had left a set of keys wedged in the gap of my windshield yesterday. Someone probably needed them. Unfortunately, that meant facing him again.

I pressed the gate button and braced myself for that familiar, gravel-edged voice to snarl through the speaker.

"Halston, hey! What are you doing here?"

That... wasn't Ghost. "I came to return some keys I found," I replied.

"Oh. Cool. Come on in."

The gate rumbled open, and I pulled into the same gravel spot as before. Grabbing the keys, I climbed out of the car. Blessedly, no dogs charged me this time.

As I turned the corner to the garage door, I spotted Henry standing there. "Henry."

"Thanks for bringing the keys back. Steve's been losing his mind trying to retrace his steps."

"Happy to save a man from his own forgetfulness."

Henry chuckled, taking the keys. Then he tilted his chin toward the next building over. "Ghost is in the gym, if you're looking for him."

I hesitated. Was I? I didn't even know. Our last exchange had all the emotional clarity of a hurricane. Still... curiosity got the better of me.

I ducked under the half-open roll-up door and scanned the space inside.

There were shelves stacked with barbells, a bench press to the side, and a thick sparring mat spread out across the far corner.

And there, at the back of the room, was Ghost.

He was shirtless, black running pants hanging low on his hips, exposing that obscene V-line that disappeared into the waistband like a promise I had no business thinking about.

Every punch he landed into the heavy bag sent shockwaves up the chain, the muscles in his chest and arms flexing with every move, ink stretching and rolling across his golden, sweat-slicked skin. He looked as if he had been carved out of trouble and violence.

Somewhere above us, hidden speakers played a slow, smoky blend of jazz and soul. It was music you'd expect to hear in a dark room with whiskey, not while watching a man demolish a punching bag.

He threw one more punch, then stopped. His chest heaved. His breathing deepened.

And then he turned and saw me. "Thought I wasn't gonna see you again, Tits."

I sighed loudly, already tired of his damn nickname for me. "One of your guys left his keys on my car last time I was here. I figured someone would want them back."

"Ah, yeah, that'd be Steve. Always leaving shit where it doesn't belong." He grabbed a towel from the bench and wiped his face and chest.

"Practicing for a fight?" I asked mostly to distract myself from staring at his hard body.

He shook his head, slinging the towel around his neck. "Nah. Just working out. Letting off steam."

I opened my mouth to respond, but he started singing along to the song that was playing.

"Before I hunt you down, grab your chin and kiss your lips..."

His eyes locked on mine, and I forgot how to breathe.

"You bring me back. I lay you down and grab your hips... and we lose all control..."

My entire body betrayed me, my pulse pounding. Mouth dry. Brain fried.

The deep rasp of his voice, the way he held my gaze, the lyrics dripping with seduction.

And then he winked.

That. Goddamn. Wink.

"You wanna give it a go?" he asked.

My mind short-circuited with all the wrong answers.

He raised an eyebrow. "Talking about the bag, sweetheart. Get your filthy mind out of the gutter."

Busted.

I laughed, caught red-handed. "Right. Of course."

Ghost walked over to a shelf, grabbed a pair of gloves, and brought them back to me. His fingers brushed mine as he helped me slip them on, the contact like static electricity across my skin.

"Take a swing," he said, stepping back.

I did. It landed with a soft thud.

He looked at me as if I'd insulted his entire bloodline. "You hit like a girl."

"Newsflash. I am a girl."

He smirked. "Yeah, but I expected more violence from you. You've got rage; I've seen it. You're just not putting your body into it."

I frowned. "What does that even mean?"

He stepped closer, adjusting my legs and stance with firm, confident hands. "Power doesn't come from your arms. It comes from your core. Rotate your hips, plant your feet–then throw the punch."

His hands slid down my arms, his fingers grazing my skin. Then they landed on my hips, firm and commanding. I tried to concentrate. I really did. But I was seriously losing to the little voice in my head that was begging me to be oh, so bad.

His scent was all around me now. He smelled of spice, soap, sweat, and sin. My brain turned to mush.

A soft sound escaped me. It was a half-sigh, half-moan I immediately regretted.

Ghost froze. His hands stilled on my hips. "Did I hurt you?" he asked, his voice suddenly lower, rougher.

"What? No!" I said quickly, flustered beyond salvation.

He watched me, his lips twitching. "You sure? You sound a little... breathless."

I rolled my eyes, ignoring the heat crawling up my body. "Let's focus on not getting knocked out, yeah?" I muttered.

"Fine," he said, grinning. "But just so you know, moaning during a workout sends mixed signals."

I said nothing.

He backed off, nodding at the bag. "Try again. Rotate. Exhale."

I took a breath and punched, this time with more force. The bag rocked a little.

"That's it," he said, nodding. "You're coachable. I like that."

"I bet you do." I threw a few more punches.

He grinned, clearly entertained. "You've got good instincts. You're a fast learner."

I smiled, pulling back, feeling oddly proud. "Thanks. I could feel the difference immediately."

"See?" he smiled. "It's all about technique."

I was caught off guard by this side of Ghost. "You're a good teacher."

His blue eyes gleamed. "Not even the thing I'm best at either, sweetheart," he boasted with a wink.

Oh, my God. Right back in the gutter.

"And here I thought you only trained dogs and emotionally stunted men."

Ghost laughed deep, brushing a knuckle under his jaw. "I don't train men, sweetheart. I break them."

That shut me right up.

Because I suddenly wasn't thinking about punching bags anymore. I was thinking about what he'd do if I let him break me.

Chapter 9

"What's that?" I paused, cocking my head.

Ghost looked up from unwrapping his hands. "What?"

"That sound. You don't hear it?"

He stopped, his brows pulling together as he listened. Then he shook his head. "Nope. I hear the wind and you overthinking things."

I rolled my eyes and wandered out of his gym, my boots crunching against gravel as I followed the faintest sound.

A soft meow.

I turned toward the black and gray shed near the gym that sat on cinder blocks.

Dropping to my knees in the dirt, I leaned down and peered under the shed. "Oh, my God." My voice softened. "It's so cute."

"What is?" Ghost's voice came from behind me, already laced with suspicion.

I turned to find him standing a few feet away. "There's a cat under your shed."

He tilted his head, unimpressed. "Don't tell my dogs."

I shot up immediately, eyes wide. "Where are they?"

"Inside." He smirked. "For now."

I let out a relieved sigh.

"You scared of my dogs?"

"Yes," I said, then added, "But right now I'm more scared they'll turn that cat into a chew toy."

Ghost chuckled, shaking his head. "That's fair. They've torn up worse."

I dropped back down, peering at the cat. The tabby was curled tight in a ball, its ribs visible. "It's starving."

Ghost shrugged as if he couldn't be less invested. "I don't feed strays."

"You have food. Just give it a little."

"No." He stepped closer, peering over my shoulder. "You feed it once. It keeps coming back."

"You fed me." I smirked without looking up.

He didn't miss a beat. "And now look at you. Following me around, trespassing, trying to move in stray animals. See how that works?"

I stood and turned to face him. "So you want it to die?"

Ghost lifted one brow, his tone completely flat. "If it's too weak to survive, it shouldn't be here. That's how nature works."

"Jesus, are you listening to yourself? It's a cat, not a defective machine part."

"Same rules apply."

"You're heartless."

"I'm realistic."

"You're something," I muttered, folding my arms.

He smirked again, cocking his head. "Something you keep coming back to."

"Because your idiot employee left his keys on my car."

"Excuses," he said. "You like being here."

"Only slightly more than a root canal."

He laughed, the sound deep and obnoxiously sexy. "Careful, sweetheart. You keep lying to yourself like that, you'll pull something."

I narrowed my eyes. "Fine. I'll go to the store and buy food for it."

Ghost's expression darkened. "No. You bring food here. That makes it my problem."

"Then I'll take it with me," I snapped. "Happy?"

"Ecstatic." He gestured toward the shed. "Grab it and go."

I turned back toward the cat, then hesitated. "It might have a family here."

Ghost let out a sharp, humorless laugh. "You're a happy-ending kind of girl, aren't you?"

"Something wrong with that?"

"Yeah. It's an illusion. A soft lie people tell themselves to sleep at night."

"So no fairy tales for you, huh?"

"I don't believe in fiction."

I gave him a hard look. "Are you going to throw me off your property?"

He looked mildly amused. "Why would I?"

"Just answer the question."

Ghost studied me for a long beat. "If you do something to really piss me off."

"Great," I said, smiling sweetly. "Let's see if I can manage that."

"What does that mean?" His jaw flexed. "Where the hell are you going?"

"I'll be back," I tossed over my shoulder.

Twenty minutes later...

Henry let me in without asking questions. I pulled into the same spot and popped my trunk, grabbing a bag of cat food, two bowls, and a few bottles of water.

Henry watched, arms crossed. "Does Ghost know you were coming back with all this?"

"Nope," I said, chipper as ever.

I knelt beside the shed, setting out the bowls and filling one with food, the other with water. Moments later, the cat peeked out. After a second of hesitation, it crept forward and began eating like it hadn't had a meal in days.

A grin spread across my face.

"There. You fed it. You happy now?"

I yelped and nearly toppled over. I turned to see Ghost looming behind me, his sweat-damp shirt now clinging to his chest. He was way too close.

"Yes," I beamed. "Very."

Ghost shook his head. "I'm not feeding it."

"Good thing I'm not relying on your generosity."

"You coming here every day to keep it alive now?"

"If I have to."

Ghost let out a heavy, suffering sigh. "You do if you don't want it to starve."

"Can it sleep in the shed?" I asked sweetly. "I'll get a cat door. You won't even know it's here."

His stare was long, sharp, and laced with silent curses. "You are way too invested in a five-pound rodent."

"It's not a rodent. It's a cutie."

He looked at Henry, who tried and failed to hide his laughter.

Ghost exhaled loudly, pinching the bridge of his nose. "Fine. But you're responsible for it. If it scratches up my gym mats or ends up in the ring with the dogs, I'm blaming you."

I bounced once on my heels. "Perfect! Because I bought it a bed."

Ghost groaned. "Of course you did."

Henry full-on laughed now as I trotted to the car to grab the bed, victory practically radiating off me.

As I walked, I couldn't help but grin.

He could act cold all he wanted. But Ghost didn't say yes because he had to. He said yes because somewhere beneath all the snark and barbed wire, the man actually cared.

And that made me think there was hope for him yet.

Chapter 10

I was feeding the cat when I saw Drew's truck pulling up the long gravel drive.

At first, I thought it was just him. But then I caught sight of Jen, Josh, and Niki in the truck with him.

Judging by the way Ghost strolled out of the house with a huge smile on his face, he was expecting them.

"Hey!" Drew said, grinning at me. "You made it here before us."

I was confused. He seemed to think I knew what they were doing here. "Came early to feed the cat."

"I didn't know you had a cat." Drew shot Ghost a look.

Ghost gave me a side-eye, his voice dry. "Yeah, the damn thing wandered onto the property. I wanted to shoot it, but Tits here is a bleeding heart."

I rolled my eyes. "You are so dramatic."

Jen tilted her head, stepping in close, her eyes narrowing slightly. "You're hanging out with Ghost now?"

There was something in her tone. Pure jealousy.

"I was just feeding the cat, not hanging out." I dusted my hands off. "I'm about to head out, actually."

Jen crossed her arms, clearly unconvinced. "How did you even get put in charge of feeding his cat?"

Her jealousy was ridiculous. It annoyed me. Ghost wasn't even hers to be jealous of, and her boyfriend was just feet away. Then it hit me hard... I was annoyed because she thought Ghost, like every other man in the world, belonged to her.

"You're not heading out, Tits." Ghost's voice cut through the conversation, drawing all attention back to him. "We're taking out the ATVs."

My stomach flipped. "Wait. What? We are?" I asked, eyebrows raised.

Ghost nodded toward the row of four-wheelers parked just beyond the barn. "Yeah. That was the plan."

It wasn't my plan. But apparently, it was now.

I watched as everyone picked an ATV, pairing up, hopping on like they'd done this a thousand times before.

That left two more ATVs sitting there, waiting.

I looked at Ghost. "I get one, and you can ride one."

Ghost arched a brow. "Have you ever ridden one before?"

I lifted my chin. "No. But how hard can it be? I drive a car."

Ghost laughed. "Jesus."

Then Drew chimed in from his ATV, shaking his head. "Yeah, I had a friend who lost a leg riding one."

My stomach lurched. "What?"

Ghost nodded. "ATVs aren't just oversized Tonka toys, sweetheart. They're powerful. Unstable." He stepped toward me, towering over me now. "There's a reason most accidents happen with beginners. It's not just about hitting the throttle and hoping for the best. It's about body positioning, control, and terrain adjustments."

Tits. Sweetheart. Really?

I sighed. "So dramatic."

"So stubborn," Ghost shot back. "Get on the back of mine."

I hesitated. I knew being pressed up against him for a long ride was a terrible fucking idea. Ghost was already under my skin. Already making me crazy with his relentless teasing, his inappropriate comments, his rough confidence that made me want him even when I knew I shouldn't.

Before I could decide, Jen shot off her mouth, "Let her stay if she's uncomfortable. She's not the adventurous type."

Drew nudged her behind him. "Stop."

"What?" she asked innocently. "I'm not saying anything she doesn't know already."

It wasn't just the jealousy radiating off her; it was the way she felt entitled to it, like she had some kind of unspoken claim over every man, like she had some inside knowledge about them I didn't. And maybe she did. She'd certainly slept with her fair share.

But Ghost wasn't hers to be jealous of.

My jaw flexed. Wanting to stay clear of Ghost's radar took a backseat to wanting to put her in her place. And the petty part of me? The part Ghost had been dragging out of me since day one? It decided I wasn't going to be quiet about this.

So, without hesitating, I turned to Ghost and did something Jen would have done.

My eyes flicked up to meet his, my lips curving into a sweet smile. "Ghost," I said softly, stepping in close on my tiptoes until our bodies were nearly touching.

His blue eyes sparked, watching me with amusement, one brow shooting up.

I traced a finger down his chest, slow and deliberate, feeling the heat of his body through his shirt. "If I ride with you..." I let my voice drop, let my lips hover just near his beard, since he was so much taller. I let my fingers drift lower, not touching anything inappropriate, but definitely flirting with the idea. "Are you gonna keep me safe?"

I heard him take a breath, and his hands clenched at his sides.

He gave a rough chuckle. "You got a death wish, Tits?"

"Just asking a question." I shrugged and lowered my voice so only he could hear. "Or do you want me riding something else?"

Ghost cursed under his breath, his fingers flexing like he was debating whether to grab me or throttle me. His lips formed a wicked smile. "Get on the back," he said, his voice rough. "I'll keep you real safe."

I bit my lip, satisfied, turning away to get on the ATV.

And when I glanced over at Jen, she looked ready to self-destruct.

Mission. Fucking. Accomplished.

I swung a leg over, climbing onto the back of his ATV.

"Atta girl," he said, and I rolled my eyes, trying to ignore the way his deep voice sent a little shiver up my spine.

The others pulled away on the ATVs, kicking up dust as they disappeared down the trail.

But Ghost didn't move. Didn't get on the ATV. He didn't even look at it.

Instead, his crystal-blue eyes burned into me. His mouth twisted into that signature Ghost smirk that made my stomach clench and my pulse spike.

I knew it was coming. I hoped he'd let it go, that he'd just get on the ATV and take off like nothing happened. But I was quickly finding

Ghost wasn't one to let shit slide. And apparently not when it involved me touching him.

"I realize you were trying to piss Jen off," he said, his voice low. "Because she was being her usual narcissist self."

I swallowed hard, looking up at him. "And?"

Ghost leaned in, closing the small gap between us, his presence overwhelming. "And it fucking worked."

I inhaled a sharp breath as his gaze dropped, sweeping down my body, then back up to my face, those damn eyes locking onto mine like a target. "But here's the problem, Tits."

My stomach tightened.

"You might've done it to piss her off..." He reached up, running his fingers slowly along my jaw, his touch barely there, like he was toying with me. "But all you did was turn me the fuck on."

A heat wave slammed through me, white-hot and unrelenting.

Ghost smirked. "Your hand on my chest, your blue eyes looking up at me like you were about to fucking beg for it..." He exhaled slowly, like just the memory of it was enough to make him lose focus. "You're lucky I had an audience, or I might've taken you right there."

Jesus fucking Christ. "Ghost—" It came out as a strangled whisper.

"Say the word," he cut me off, his hand still on my jaw, his thumb brushing against my bottom lip, teasing, pushing, destroying me.

I couldn't even breathe right. Because the look he was giving me told me if I said the word, Ghost would follow through. Right there. No matter who came riding back. And I wanted to. God, I wanted to. But instead, I pushed down the ache; the wildfire burning me from the inside out.

Ghost's eyes held my gaze, watching me, reading me too well. Then he leaned in, his lips brushing my ear, sending a shiver down my spine. "You can act like you don't want me all you want." His tone was pure sin, pure confidence, pure fucking Ghost. "But your body tells me a different story."

I clenched my jaw, digging my fingers into my thighs. "We should catch up," I said, somehow keeping my voice even.

Ghost smirked. "Whatever you say, sweetheart," he said, climbing on in front of me. Then he added, "Just know... sooner or later, I'm collecting."

That sent my stomach into knots.

Then he started the engine, and I had no choice but to wrap my arms around him as we took off.

Ghost was all muscle. Solid. Hard beneath my hands. My thighs were pressed tight against his. His scent was a perfect mix of leather and whatever cologne he wore. It was something dark, masculine, and completely addictive. And it was all I could smell as the wind rushed past us.

I bit my lip, fighting the heat creeping up my skin.

"Damn, you're really holding on tight back there, sweetheart."

I ignored him.

"No complaints, though. I kinda like having you all over me."

I ignored him harder.

Ghost grinned back at me, shifting slightly in the seat, and I swear, he did it on purpose, because suddenly, I was pressed tightly against his back, making me painfully aware of every part of my body that touched him.

"Tell me, Halston—" his voice dropped lower, nearly lost in the wind as we sped across the land. "Is this the closest you've ever been to a real man?"

I smacked his arm, heat burning through me.

He laughed.

Then, just as I was regaining control of my sanity, he braked hard, bringing us to a stop at the top of a small ridge.

Ghost turned his head slightly, his blue eyes gleaming with pure trouble as he looked back at me. "You feel that?"

I swallowed, confused. "Feel what?"

His lips curved. "How hard I am."

My stomach flipped. Oh. My. God.

I knew he was just messing with me, just being his usual vulgar, cocky, insufferable self. But that didn't stop the rush of heat that spread straight up the inside of my thighs.

"Might wanna hold on even tighter, sweetheart," he said as he revved the engine again, the vibration running through me. "We're just getting started."

Chapter 11

G host hit the throttle again, taking off before I even had time to recover from his last dirty comment.

We tore across the land, leaving the others far behind, since Ghost knew the terrain like the back of his hand.

I held on tight, pressing against him because I had to, not because I wanted to.

At least, that's what I told myself.

Ghost handled the ATV like it was an extension of himself, completely in control, while I was just trying to breathe like a normal human instead of focusing on his body beneath my hands, and the way his muscles flexed, the way his body heat burned into me even through our layers of clothing.

Ghost slowed the ATV to a halt near a small clearing. I couldn't even hear the other ATV engines.

"We're way ahead," I said, finally releasing my death grip on him.

"That's because you ride like a goddamn leech," he teased, grinning as he killed the engine.

I rolled my eyes. "Because you're a lunatic."

Ghost swung a leg off the ATV, then turned to me, offering a hand.

I didn't want to take it, not when I knew he'd use it as another opportunity to mess with me. But trying to get off by myself after clinging to him for the last fifteen minutes? Not happening.

With a sigh, I put my hand in his.

And just as I expected, he took full advantage of the moment, pulling me way too close as he helped me down. "You shakin', Tits?" he said with an amused smile.

"From the wind," I said, trying to back away.

But I had barely taken a step before my heel hit nothing but air.

Oh. Shit.

Ghost's hand shot out, yanking me forward just as I lost my balance, his powerful arms pinning me against him before I could tumble straight into the freezing-ass pond behind me.

"Jesus, Tits. Don't you pay attention?"

My heart pounded from the near miss. Or maybe from the way his body was pressed against mine, solid and warm, his hands gripping me tight.

I shoved at his chest, pushing away from him, but he didn't let go of my hips. "If you'd stop distracting me with your comments and insanely sexy body!"

Oh. Fucking. No. I snapped my mouth shut, my jaw immediately clenching.

Ghost's mouth stretched slowly into a devilish grin. "You were distracted by my body."

I glared. "I was distracted by your big, stupid mouth."

"So, you like my mouth," he said, his grip on my hips tightening.

What was it with this man and his hands on my hips? It was intensely intimate and distracting. "I do not."

His grin widened. "You like when I talk to you like that."

"I do not," I said adamantly, even as my entire body betrayed me, every nerve ending blazing to life just from the sound of his voice.

"Liar." He pulled me closer, spilling into my personal space, his voice dropping low. His breath, warm and minty, sent a shiver through me. "You want me."

I let out a breathless laugh. "You wish."

Ghost's smirk was dark, like he already knew it. "Yeah, sweetheart? Then why are your nipples hard?"

My face went up in flames.

Ghost let out a deep, sexy chuckle, his fingers trailing dangerously low toward my ass. "Tell me to stop," he whispered.

I didn't. I couldn't. Because the second I opened my mouth, I kissed him instead.

Ghost groaned, yanking me to him, his mouth opening against mine, devouring me like I was on today's menu.

My hands shot into his hair, gripping tightly, my body molding to his as he lifted me, my legs wrapping around his waist.

Ghost spun, pressing me against the nearest tree, his body pinning me in place, his tongue sliding into my mouth with slow, deliberate strokes that had me whimpering into him.

"Fuck, I knew you'd taste good," he whispered between kisses, his voice rough, his hands gripping tight at my thighs, my ass, keeping me close, grinding me against him in a way that made my brain completely shut down.

I moaned, heat pooling deep in my core, my fingers digging into his shoulders. My entire body was on fire.

Ghost tore his mouth from mine, his lips trailing lower, kissing, biting, marking his way down my neck. "You're so fucking responsive," he whispered against my skin. "Tell me how bad you want it, sweetheart."

"Oh, God," I whispered. I was so close to telling him exactly how badly I wanted it.

The distant roar of engines shot through our little lust bubble. The others were coming up fast.

Ghost broke the kiss, his breath choppy, his forehead pressing into mine as he reined himself in. "Fuck," he growled softly.

Then, as fast as he'd pulled me against him, he set me back on my feet.

I staggered slightly, my head still foggy, my body still aching for him, for more of what he'd offered.

And then, as the first ATV pulled into view, I felt resentment bubble up inside me. Ghost was a one-and-done man. He couldn't be seen kissing me. He couldn't have the good girl wrecking his reputation. I'd just let him own me against a tree, but the second other people were around, he dropped me like nothing had happened. It was infuriating.

But I didn't exactly want people seeing us kiss, either. I knew better than to want someone like Ghost with his reputation.

I took a slow, unsteady breath, trying to shake off the aftershocks of what had just happened.

Ghost stood just as still, his jaw tight, his hands at his sides. His eyes shot to mine, and he looked almost frustrated. Not his usual cocky, smug self.

The sound of engines rumbling closer yanked me out of my thoughts.

I took a shaky step back, still feeling the burn of his hands on my skin, the heat of his mouth on mine. I wanted to scream. Because fuck him. Fuck him for making me feel like that.

And fuck me for wanting it again.

I straightened, forcing a casual expression, just as the others pulled up beside us.

Josh was the first to cut his engine, grinning as he hopped off his ATV. "Damn, you two must have been haulin' ass," he said. "What'd we miss?"

I opened my mouth, ready to say something sarcastic.

But Ghost beat me to it. "Halston almost fell in the pond."

I whipped around to glare at him.

His blue eyes sparkled with amusement. The bastard was enjoying this.

"Jesus, Halston," Niki laughed. "What were you doing?"

I crossed my arms. "Trying to get away from him."

Ghost chuckled, stepping closer. Too close.

He leaned in, his breath warm on my ear as he whispered, just for me to hear. "You weren't trying that hard, sweetheart."

I shoved him away, my face burning, but his smirk only deepened.

Josh, completely oblivious to my inner turmoil, hit Ghost on the shoulder. "Alright, what's next?"

Ghost turned, flashing that dangerous grin of his. "We ride. We've got a lot more land to cover."

He climbed back onto his ATV, revving the engine, holding out a hand to me, like nothing had happened. Like he hadn't just turned me inside out with his hands, his mouth, his filthy goddamn words.

And that was exactly why I couldn't give in to Ghost. He would wreck me, and I might never recover.

Chapter 12

I closed the car door and headed toward the shed to feed the cat its dinner, zipping my jacket up to the top, shutting out the chill in the air.

Thankfully, working from home made it easy to stop by twice a day. And since Ghost's ranch was only thirty minutes away, the drive wasn't too bad. It gave me time to blast music and decompress before dealing with whatever mood Ghost was in.

I'd been feeding the cat for weeks now, and she was finally playing more, chasing bugs and swatting at flying insects. But she was still a little skittish.

I smiled as I approached the shed, my gaze catching on a brand-new cat door installed on the wooden wall. Someone had put it in. Ghost? Or one of his guys? I wasn't holding out much hope that he'd done it himself, but either way, it was thoughtful. Because no matter who installed the door, Ghost had to have given the okay. And that thought made me smile.

After filling the cat's bowl with food, I turned back toward my car.

The ranch was quiet. No one had come out to greet me when I arrived, and I hadn't seen Ghost all week. I wasn't sure if he was out or just busy, but I figured he'd find me if he wanted to. Plus, the sun was setting, and I didn't know my way around the ranch beyond the small area I usually saw, so I didn't bother looking for him.

I reached for my car door handle.

"Did you eat dinner yet?"

I jumped, startled, spinning. Ghost was standing just a few feet away, watching me like he'd been there for a while. "Uh. I..." I was completely caught off guard by his presence, yes, but also the question. "No."

"Do you want to stay for dinner?"

"Dinner?"

Ghost smirked. "I'm not asking you to prom, Tits. It's dinner."

It never ceased to amaze me how he could insult me and be considerate at the same time.

"Are you hungry?" he tried again.

I hesitated. "I could eat."

"Okay. Follow me."

I had never been inside Ghost's house before. The first thing I noticed was the wall of floor-to-ceiling windows, stretching to a thirty-foot peak overlooking the land. A huge, C-shaped sectional couch faced a roaring fireplace, filling the space with a warm glow.

It was stunning. "Wow," I said. "You have a beautiful home."

Ghost gave a small nod. "Thank you."

Then, a door creaked from the other side of the room. The dogs came bounding out, barking loudly.

I yelped and grabbed Ghost's arm, darting behind him for protection. I was plastered to his back and felt his body vibrate as he laughed. "Sitz!"

I peeked out from behind his arm. Both German Shepherds immediately stopped, sitting like statues.

I let out a shaky breath. "I'd be impressed if I weren't trying not to pee my pants right now."

Ghost laughed again, reaching back to grab my wrist. "Come on."

I tried not to think about his large, rough hand as it wrapped around my wrist, or how the heat from his skin was traveling up my arm, through my body. How just his damn hand was making me all hot and bothered. Good God. I was quickly finding out that everything about this man turned me on.

"I'm putting steaks on the grill. Do you want to work on the salad in the kitchen where it's warm?"

I cleared my throat. There it was again, that consideration. It was like a warm hug, but I wondered how long it would be before his mood shifted again. "Sure."

The kitchen was gorgeous, sharing a wall of glass with the living room.

Ghost laid out ingredients on the island, including a colander for rinsing the veggies. "Are you okay to find what you need if it's not out already?" he asked. "I have to go throw the steaks on."

"Absolutely."

I glanced toward the dogs, who were still sitting stiffly in the living room.

Ghost chuckled, following my gaze. "They'll sit there sweetly. I promise you."

I nodded, forcing myself to relax. "Okay."

I rinsed cucumbers and lettuce, stealing quick glances at the dogs every few minutes.

When Ghost walked back in from the back door, bringing the smell of the grill with him, my stomach rumbled. "You smell so good," I blurted. "I didn't realize how hungry I was until you came in here."

Ghost raised an eyebrow. "Really? For?"

Then he gave me that grin. The one that screamed pure trouble.

I rolled my eyes, smiling. "Food."

He clicked his tongue, smirking. "Shame."

I laughed, shaking my head.

We plated our food at the island, grabbing from a spread of salad, potatoes, grilled onions, and peppers to go with the steaks.

Ghost grabbed his steak, but when he stood in front of the grilled veggies, he looked over at me. "Any chance I'm hitting that tonight?"

I froze mid-reach, staring at him. "What?"

He shrugged, like he had just asked if I wanted extra dressing on my salad.

"No chance."

Ghost shrugged again, then proceeded to add onions and peppers to his plate.

My brows furrowed. Was that...? Was that thoughtful? Nobody wanted to make out with onion breath.

I stared at him, confused by my own reaction. "Did you just show consideration?"

He smirked. "I'm not a monster, sweetheart. I wouldn't wanna set your pretty pussy on fire."

Heat burned through me, spreading up my chest, neck, and face. "Oh, my God," I gasped. "The vulgar things that come out of that mouth."

Ghost's eyes gleamed with mischief. "You like."

"What?"

"The vulgar things that come out of my mouth, you like. Come on, admit it."

I gawked at him. "In no way do I like it."

"No one has ever spoken to you like that, have they?"

"Never," I assured him.

Ghost grinned, leaning slightly closer. "Trust me, you'll like the things that come out of my mouth. One in particular."

I stared at him, completely speechless.

"I'm just saying," he continued, his voice pure, wicked amusement. "A lot of shit rolls off this tongue because I know how to use it."

A fire shot through my body, hot, electric as I immediately pictured his tongue places I shouldn't be picturing.

Then he winked. Again. And just like that, my rationality went to war with my body. "The things that come out of your mouth—"

Ghost smirked. "Can easily go into you, sweetheart. If you'd let it."

I gasped. "You just have a gross answer for everything, don't you?"

He laughed, taking a bite of his steak. "If you hang around here long enough, you'll get used to it."

"I'm not sure I'll ever get used to your offensive come-ons."

"Kind of hot, though, right?"

I didn't say anything else, because as much as his unique brand of vulgarity caught me off guard, it also did seriously dirty things to my body.

"Yeah, I thought so," he said with a knowing smirk.

Chapter 13

We finished cleaning up the kitchen, the last clang of dishes echoing into a quiet that felt way too comfortable.

I folded the hand towel and glanced over. "Thanks for dinner. Everything was really good."

Ghost gave a nod. "Yeah. I know."

I rolled my eyes but smiled, sliding the final dish into the cabinet. When I looked back, I noticed he was wearing most of the meal. "You've got half the menu on your shirt."

He looked down at the splattered mess across his chest. Then he gave a slow shake of his head. "Damn waste of good food," he muttered.

He glanced back at me. "I'm gonna take the dogs out, change shirts, and start a fire out back. You in?"

I checked my phone. It wasn't even 7:30. Too early to go home. Especially when I was actually having... fun. "Sure, I—" I stopped mid-sentence.

Ghost was already grabbing the hem of his T-shirt and peeling it off like we weren't still standing in the kitchen.

And sweet merciful hell, the man was a walking anatomy lesson. Broad, tanned shoulders. Hard abs that flexed with every casual move. Tattoos sprawled across his chest and arms like they were inked by the gods themselves.

He was pure, carved, dangerous beauty. And I was staring like I had zero shame or survival instinct left.

Which at this point? Fair.

Get it together, I told myself as he disappeared outside with the dogs, like he hadn't just emotionally derailed me with his torso.

I followed, shaking off the heat spiraling inside me.

By the time I made it outside, Ghost had the fire pit going. The flames flickered against his silhouette, dancing shadows across the yard. He'd thrown on a clean shirt, a sleeveless black one that did nothing to hide his arms and everything to destroy my remaining self-control.

He dragged two chairs closer to the pit and dropped into one with that relaxed, lethal energy he always carried.

My eyes flicked to his shoulder, catching a scar I hadn't noticed before. "What happened there?" I asked, pointing at the rough mark near his collarbone.

He followed my gaze and grinned. "Some asshole stuck me with a jagged pipe."

My hand flew to my mouth. "Oh, my God."

He shrugged casually. "Occupational hazard."

I frowned. "What occupation involves being stabbed with a pipe?"

"Mine."

I shook my head at him. He smirked back.

My gaze drifted to another scar, barely visible above his eyebrow. "What about that one?"

Ghost huffed a laugh. "Honestly? No clue. I've busted that thing open so many times, it's just part of the landscape now."

"Don't you worry about messing up your face?" I asked only half-joking.

He leaned back. "Nope."

"Why not?"

"Because I'm not trying to win a beauty pageant."

"Could've fooled me," I muttered.

Ghost arched a brow, that slow, wicked grin spreading across his lips. "You think I'm pretty, sweetheart?"

I scoffed. "I think you know exactly what you are."

"Which is?"

"A cocky, arrogant, tattooed menace."

"You left out devastatingly charming."

"No. I didn't."

He laughed, tipping his head back slightly. "You trying to get under my skin?"

"Nope. Just trying to understand how someone who looks like you can be such a jackass."

"Balance," he said with a shrug. "Can't give the world everything."

I shook my head, smiling despite myself. He was infuriating. And maybe a little bit addictive.

Ghost reached down, grabbed a stick, and jabbed at the fire. "You want a beer or something?"

"Are you offering or hoping I say no?"

He looked over at me, his eyes glinting. "I'm offering. But let's not pretend I wouldn't enjoy watching you loosen up a little."

I rolled my eyes. "Trust me, Ghost. You don't want to see me drunk."

"Why not?" he grinned. "You bite?"

I smiled sweetly. "Only when provoked."

Ghost chuckled again, shaking his head as he stood. "Stay right there, sweetheart. I'll get us both a drink. I feel like this night's about to get more interesting."

And damn it, I wasn't sure if that excited or terrified me.

Maybe both.

Ghost returned with two beers. He handed me one without a word, then dropped back into the chair across from me, the firelight painting sharp shadows along his face.

"So," I said, taking a sip. "Do you ever actually relax? Or are you just permanently locked in fight-or-flirt mode?"

Ghost gave a slow grin. "Flirt mode is relaxing. Fight mode's just habit."

I smiled, but my eyes stayed on him. "You always like this? Closed-off one second, smartass the next?"

He didn't answer right away. Instead, he stared into the fire, his beer bottle loosely held in one hand.

"People don't usually get both," he said after a beat. "They get the surface. Sarcasm, charm, rough edges. Keeps things simple."

"And what about the people who want more than the surface?" I asked, softer now.

Ghost's eyes met mine across the flickering flames. "They don't stick around long enough to find it."

That answer hit deeper than I expected. "That's kind of a lonely way to live," I murmured.

He shrugged. "Better than letting the wrong person in."

I chewed on that for a second, then leaned forward, elbows on my knees, my beer dangling between my fingers. "You know, you talk like a man who's been through hell... but you wear it like armor instead of a warning."

His eyes narrowed slightly, and for a second, I thought I might've pushed too far.

Then he smirked. "You always talk like that? All deep and philosophical after dark?"

"Only when I'm talking to a guy who looks like he's built from trauma and testosterone."

Ghost chuckled again, leaning back in his chair, but there was something different in his expression now. A flicker of something softer. Vulnerability, maybe.

"You're a smart girl," he said. "But smart girls usually run when they realize what they're digging into."

"Is that what you want? For me to run?"

He didn't answer.

The fire popped, sending a shower of sparks skyward.

Finally, he said, "What I want and what I know better than to ask for... are two different things."

I took another sip of beer, then looked at him. "You're not as tough as you pretend to be."

Ghost's lips lifted into a slow, almost dangerous smile. "Careful, sweetheart. You keep peeling back layers, you might start to like what you find."

"Maybe I already do."

Chapter 14

I watched the flames dance, pretending I wasn't hyper-aware of the man sitting just feet away from me, so quiet, so still, like a storm biding its time.

Then I glanced at his rough, calloused hands, his knuckles scarred from years of use. Years of fighting.

Ghost must've caught me staring, because he glanced over and said, "Yeah, they're scarred pretty good. I've been fighting since middle school. One way or another."

I frowned. "I'm sorry."

He shrugged. "Don't be. Fighting comes in handy. Especially when people suck."

"I guess," I murmured, still watching him. There was something about the way he spoke matter-of-fact, like violence was just another tool in his belt. Like breathing.

Suddenly, he stood up, brushing off his hands. "Get up."

"What?" I said. "Why?"

"I'll show you something. It's good for a woman to know self-defense."

I raised an eyebrow. "Trying to call me weak without calling me weak?"

He smirked. "No. I'm trying to make sure you don't end up duct-taped in the back of someone's van."

I sighed, but stood. "Wow. Your motivational speeches are next level."

"I know," he said dryly. "Try not to swoon."

We stepped away from the fire, the cool night air brushing my arms as we found a flat spot in the grass. Ghost rolled his shoulders, all loose muscle and quiet control.

"Alright, throw a punch. Slow."

"You want me to hit you?"

"Sweetheart," he said, deadpan. "You couldn't hit me even if you were trying."

"Cocky much?"

He smirked. "Always."

I gave him a half-hearted swing. Ghost caught my wrist with one smooth, practiced movement. His right hand gripped the edge of my hand while his thumb pressed down against the back. He twisted my arm up toward my back, tight and controlled.

"Okay," I hissed. "That's extremely uncomfortable."

"Exactly." His voice was annoyingly pleased. "Pain is a great motivator. More pressure, more pain."

"Yeah," I said, wincing. "We're on the same page. Got it. Very motivating."

"Did I hurt you?" he asked, still holding me.

"Not yet. But I'd like to keep it that way."

He chuckled and let go. "Now do it to me."

"Ha! Yeah, right."

"What?"

"You're a damn tree, Ghost. I'm not even sure I can reach your wrist properly."

His grin widened. "That's just your fear talking. And maybe your height disadvantage."

"Oh, we're making short jokes now?"

"I'm just saying—dynamite comes in small packages, but you better learn how to detonate."

I groaned and then stepped forward. "Fine. Let's see if I can break a giant."

"That's the spirit."

I grabbed his wrist, mimicking the movement he'd shown me. I rotated my hips, twisted his arm back, and applied pressure.

Ghost didn't flinch. But he did smirk over his shoulder at me. "Look at you. Little badass in the making."

I smiled.

I let go, and he turned to face me, a grin spreading across his stupidly handsome face. "You really are a quick learner."

The praise hit me harder than I expected. "Thanks. I live for gold stars and alpha approval."

"You joke," he said, stepping closer, "but you like impressing me."

I grinned. "I like proving you wrong."

"Even better," he said with a wink. "Now, let's talk push kicks. You ever booted someone in the chest before?"

"Can't say that I have. I don't usually hang out with chest-kick-worthy people." I paused, then smirked. "Except maybe Jen."

Ghost barked out a laugh. "Yeah, I clocked that one from a mile away."

"Clocked what?"

"The fake smile. The compliments with a blade in 'em. Girls like that don't fool me. I've seen too many."

His answer hit something in me. "I like that you see through her."

He tilted his head slightly, watching me. "You wish Drew did too."

I nodded. "He's a great guy. But sometimes I think he's blind when it comes to her."

Ghost's eyes narrowed just a little, thoughtful. "He sees it. He's just gotta figure out when he's gonna stop pretending he doesn't."

That landed hard. "Damn," I muttered. "You ever been in therapy? You're kind of insightful for a guy who headbutts people for a living."

Ghost smirked, stepping in closer. "Nah. I hit shit instead of talk about it."

I laughed. "Fair enough."

He walked me through it–step, raise the knee, snap the foot out. Then we moved into palm strikes and, of course, the classic groin kick.

"If all else fails," he said, "aim low and hit hard. Nothing drops a guy faster than getting his manhood rearranged."

"Noted," I said. "Brutal and efficient. You'd make an excellent life coach."

Ghost laughed. "Only if you're into pain and profanity."

"Aren't you a walking Yelp review."

He flashed that slow grin again. "Five stars, sweetheart. If you survive the ride."

I shrugged, fighting my own smile. "I mean... I'm willingly hanging out with you, aren't I?"

His eyes swept over me, amused. "Yeah, and I'm still trying to figure out what that says about you."

"Probably nothing good," I muttered.

"Even better," he said with a grin.

I rolled my eyes, but my heart was pounding harder than it should've been. Maybe from the sparring. Maybe not.

I dropped back into my seat completely spent.

Self-defense with Ghost wasn't just physically exhausting. It was mentally exhausting. The man could wear you down with his mouth alone.

And not in the fun way. Well... not yet.

Out of nowhere, the cat bolted from the shadows like it'd been shot out of a cannon, leapt into the air like a furry lunatic, then dashed off sideways like it was drunk on Red Bull.

Ghost and I both broke into laughter, the kind that caught you off guard and kept going.

"Admit it," I said between chuckles, glancing over. "You like her."

He shrugged, looking off into the dark like the fire wasn't high-lighting the twitch of a smile on his face. "I admit nothing. You got no proof."

"Uh-huh." I tilted my head, still grinning. "You have a nice laugh."

That earned me a slow look, his blue eyes cutting to mine.

He cleared his throat. "Keep looking at me like that, Tits, and I might have to do something about it."

My pulse jumped like it'd just heard a gunshot. The way he was watching me, all confident and predatory, was unsettling and sexy at the same time.

And like an idiot, or maybe just a woman completely undone by the unexpected, electric chemistry charging the air between us, I leaned in and kissed him.

Ghost didn't hesitate.

His mouth slanted over mine. Full contact, no preamble. He tasted of beer. His hands found my waist, gripping tight as he dragged me into his lap.

I straddled him, my thighs pressing down on his, pressing against the very obvious bulge in his jeans. My hips rolled forward on instinct, grinding against his sizable erection, pulling a groan from his throat.

He kissed me harder. Hotter. Deeper.

Then he broke away with a muttered, "Shit. Sorry. It's fucking painful."

He shifted beneath me, adjusting himself with a grimace. I bit my lip to keep from moaning. He was hard for me. Me. The girl he called Tits, like it was a casual nickname and not something that made my entire body buzz with irritation and desire at the same time.

He wanted my body anyway, and I was good with that.

Ghost reached for me again, clearly ready for round two.

"Ghost!" a voice called from the distance.

We both froze.

My survival instincts kicked in. I scrambled off his lap like my life depended on it, my feet hitting the ground fast, my cheeks flushed, my pulse everywhere.

Ghost's jaw clenched. "Fuck." He turned toward the voice, already irritated. "Hold on, Tits," he muttered, stalking off toward the voice like a man who'd just had a dream rudely interrupted.

Reality came slamming back. Hard.

What the hell was I doing?

This wasn't some friends-with-benefits thing. He wasn't my boyfriend. Hell, he didn't even call me by my actual name. I was a thing to him. Temporary. Convenient. Something to ease the sexual tension for the night.

The man would have his fun and discard me like yesterday's garbage.

That realization shattered my bubble of lust. I'd almost done something really stupid. Well, something even stupider. I'd crossed the line.

Again. I needed to get out of here before I gave in to my newly acquired dark impulses.

The sharp edge of desire dulled, replaced with a wash of frustration. With him. With myself.

When he turned and started walking back toward me, I had already made up my mind.

"Have a good night," I said flatly, stepping back and drawing a clear line in the dirt.

He slowed, his eyes narrowing slightly. "Are you scared?" he asked, smirking, clearly amused.

"Of what?" I scoffed, already knowing where this was going, but not giving him the satisfaction.

"You know what."

"You don't scare me, Ghost." I stepped toward him, my eyes locked on his. "You just piss me off. Constantly."

That smug grin returned in full force. "Yeah, but you like it."

He could easily continue what we'd started with no consequences. I was the one who would pay. I decided not to play into his hand. "If I'm going to be coming around every day to feed your accidental pet, you could at least try learning my name."

He winked. "Sure thing, Tits."

I growled, turning on my heel. "You're insufferable."

"And you're still wet from that kiss."

It hit me hard, but I didn't stop walking.

Chapter 15

I stormed toward my car with Ghost's cocky laugh echoing behind me.

By the time I reached the car, my emotions were a full-blown riot. Anger. Frustration. Confusion.

And lust. So much godforsaken lust.

I had just been grinding against him like I was auditioning for a role in his fantasies. And that mouth. That toxic, vulgar mouth. I hated that I could already feel the ghost of his tongue, that my body remembered how easily he undid me. I hadn't wanted to stop kissing him; I wanted to keep going, keep feeling his hands on me, his mouth.

No. No, no, no. He was a cocky, emotionally unavailable wrecking ball who didn't even have the decency to use my name. And yet, I kissed him first. Again.

It was a moment of weakness. The way he had invited me inside his home, cooked for me, taught me self-defense.

I wanted him. That was the real problem. His vulgarity wasn't even scaring me off anymore. It was the fear of being used and cast aside.

I gripped the handle of my door, my knuckles white.

Before I could open it, I heard heavy footsteps behind me. A large, warm hand landed on my hip.

Yes, my hip. He couldn't tap me on the shoulder. He had to touch my hip.

I froze. My breath caught in my throat. My heart stumbled. His fingers pressed firm through my jeans, his palm hot, his touch familiar in a way that should not have felt that good.

No man ever grabbed me by my hips. It was so intimate. I fought the urge to turn and kiss him.

Then, like he knew exactly what he was doing, Ghost turned me slowly to face him.

His blue eyes locked on mine, no longer playful. They burned, intense, focused. His voice was lower than I'd ever heard it. "You leavin' mad?"

I lifted my chin, meeting him head-on even as my insides quaked. "Obviously," I breathed, trying to hide how wrecked I was.

He studied me like he was trying to read every reason behind the emotion.

Then came the head tilt and the loaded question. "You mad because I called you Tits... or because I stopped kissing you?"

I opened my mouth. Closed it. His thumb brushed over the denim at my hip, and my whole spine straightened.

His mouth curled at the corner, but there was something darker in his expression now. The teasing was still there, but it was laced with something deeper. Possessive. "You really want me to say your name, Halston?"

I shivered. Goddamn him.

"Say the word," he whispered, leaning closer, "and I'll make sure the next time you hear it from my mouth, you're not wearing a single damn thing."

A massive wave of heat hit me. Hard. I swallowed, my heart pounding so loud I could hear it in my ears.

He reached up, his knuckles brushing my jaw. "You felt good against me, Halston."

My breath caught in my throat. My skin ached where he'd touched me.

Then, like the devil he was, he leaned in and whispered, "Bet you'd feel even better under me."

I swear my knees almost gave out. I wanted to kiss him again. I wanted to do something reckless and stupid.

He saw it. He knew it.

And then the bastard had the nerve to smirk like he owned that power. "Go home," he said, backing away, his voice soft but commanding. "Before you do something you'll regret."

That snapped me back. Fury rose inside me like a storm cloud.

He turned me on. He made me want things I shouldn't. And then he had the audacity to shut it down like he was doing me a favor?

I stepped back, my jaw clenched, dragging my body out of his orbit with sheer force of will. "You're right," I said coldly. "I would regret it."

He smiled. That slow, smug, infuriating grin that made me want to slap it and kiss it all at once. "Good girl."

Oh, hell no.

The urge to kiss him again just to shut him up nearly overpowered me. But I didn't give in to that dark thought.

Instead, I turned, yanked my door open, and dropped into the driver's seat.

Ghost stood there, his arms crossed, watching me with the self-satisfied smirk of a man who knew he'd won.

I threw the car in reverse, spun gravel under my tires, and peeled out like I was escaping a crime scene.

Chapter 16

The next morning, I pulled up to Legacy Ranch.

The cool air carried a faint smoky scent from the fire pit last night—and just like that, I was back in it. The burn of his lips on mine, his hands gripping my hips. That voice, low and lethal, whispering that I felt good against him. That I'd feel even better under him.

Nope. Not going there.

I was here for the cat. Nothing else.

I pressed the gate button, expecting Henry or one of the guys to buzz me in.

"You back already, Tits?"

I sighed and pinched the bridge of my nose. Of course. "Open the gate, Ghost."

"Say please."

"Ghost..."

"Say it, and I might even learn your name today."

I clenched my jaw. He was the human embodiment of a smirk. "Not happening."

The gate stayed closed.

"Guess the cat starves, then," he said casually, like he wasn't actively holding a cat hostage.

"Oh my God," I ground out. "Please, Ghost."

The gate slid open.

I could hear him laughing through the speaker. "See? That wasn't so hard," he said, full smug mode activated.

I rolled my eyes and pulled through, parking in my usual spot with a bit more force than necessary.

When I stepped out of the car, Ghost was already outside, leaning against a post like he was posing for a goddamn Marlboro ad. Arms crossed, his eyes dancing with mischief.

He looked like a man who knew he lived rent-free in my head—and was charging me for utilities.

"Good morning," I said coolly, grabbing the new bag of cat food from the passenger seat.

"Mmm." He trailed after me with lazy steps. "You still mad at me after last night?"

I froze for half a second, but kept walking. "Nope."

"So, you're admitting you liked it."

I stopped, turned, and leveled him with a look. "What exactly do you think I liked?"

His smug grin widened. "Feeling me under you."

Heat shot all the way down to my toes.

My voice came out tight. "It was a mistake."

"Was it?" he asked, his voice low and coaxing.

Seriously? He even said it would be a mistake. Sometimes I was sure he was just toying with me to see what he could get away with.

I turned sharply, walking faster toward the shed. I needed space. Air. Maybe an exorcism.

As I crouched to pour food into the cat's bowl, I could feel Ghost behind me. His presence was impossible to ignore—warm, charged, annoyingly magnetic.

"I put in the cat door," he said.

I looked over my shoulder. "You?"

He shrugged, like he hadn't just cracked open my ribcage and softened the edges. "Figured it was getting cold at night. Might as well make it easier on the little thing."

"I thought one of the guys did it."

Another shrug. "No big deal."

I studied him, trying to pin him down. Ghost was a human paradox. Half temptation, half menace, and absolutely unreadable.

"Thank you," I said, my voice a little too soft.

His gaze held mine for a beat too long. "You're welcome, Tits."

Right. There it was.

I grabbed a handful of cat food and lobbed it at his chest. "Unbelievable!"

Ghost laughed and dodged easily. "Missed me."

"I hate you."

"You say that," he said, backing away with a smirk, "but here you are."

"You're the biggest pain in the ass I've ever met!"

He winked. "You like it. Admit it."

I shook my head, trying not to smile. I hated how much fun I was having. Again.

After he escaped my wrath, I stood there a while, watching the cat eat. Ghost was chaos, and yet somehow, this place... felt weirdly like peace.

When I finally turned back toward the car, Ghost was walking toward me. "You done throwin' cat food at me, or should I grab body armor?"

I narrowed my eyes. "Depends. Are you done calling me Tits?"

"Not a chance." He grinned.

I scooped a few kibbles off the ground and launched them at his head.

Ghost dodged again, not even flinching. "You gotta work on your aim."

"That's your department."

"Actually having aim?" he smirked.

I laughed. "You're the one who trained me."

"And now I'm regretting it. Just like a woman. No accountability."

"Unbelievable," I muttered with a shake of my head.

"You keep saying that," he said, rubbing a hand over his beard. "You know what is unbelievable?"

I sighed. "What, Ghost?"

He grinned. "That you still haven't asked me my real name."

That caught me off guard. My brows lifted. "You... never offered it."

"You never asked." His tone was almost teasing, but something in his eyes was serious.

I crossed my arms. "Fine. What is it?"

His grin grew, all teeth. "Wouldn't you like to know, Tits?"

I groaned. "I knew you were gonna do that."

He laughed full-throated, shameless.

I rolled my eyes and turned away, irritated.

"Kasper. With a K."

I turned back. "Kasper?"

He nodded once. "My real name."

"Kasper?" I repeated. "With a K? So... like Kasper the Friendly Ghost?"

He let out a quiet laugh, shaking his head.

"Considering everybody calls you Ghost, I guess it tracks."

He smirked. "Not exactly the friendly part, though."

I tilted my head, arms crossed. "Yeah, I can see that. You give off more likely to steal your panties than your heart vibes."

His grin turned wicked. "Only if they're lace."

He gave me that look—the one that stripped the air from the room and replaced it with heat.

I narrowed my eyes. "You'll never know."

Ghost chuckled, low and full of sin. "That sounds like a challenge, sweetheart."

I ignored the flutter in my chest. "Keep dreaming, Kasper."

His laughter followed me all the way to the car. "Oh, I do. Every damn night."

My pulse jumped, but I said nothing.

He grinned. "You gonna start calling me by my name now?"

I lifted a brow. "You gonna start calling me by mine?"

He paused and considered it for about a second. "Nah."

"You're an ass," I said, a smile tugging at my lips.

"And yet, you keep coming back."

"Keep saying that and maybe I won't come back. Then you'll be stuck feeding the cat."

He laughed again, leaning back against the wall.

I slid into my car, jammed the key into the ignition, and turned it. Click.

I frowned and turned it again.

Click. Click.

"You've gotta be kidding me."

I dropped my forehead against the steering wheel, muttering a string of curses into the leather.

Outside, Ghost was still watching me, one brow raised.

This day just kept getting better.

Chapter 17

G host offered to give me a ride.

Which on its own was already shockingly human of him.

But the part that really spun my head? He'd willingly told me his real name.

Kasper.

It still echoed in my head like a secret I wasn't supposed to know.

I stole a glance at him as he drove, the late-morning light cutting across his face. One hand on the wheel. His jaw was tight, clenched like he was biting back words, and his eyes hadn't left the road once.

I'd grown used to the versions of him that came with a warning label. Cold and cranky. Flirty and foul-mouthed. The kind of guy who couldn't go five minutes without calling me Tits and smirking while doing it.

But this quiet version? The one whose hands didn't touch me, whose voice wasn't baiting me every other second?

I didn't know what to do with him.

I let out a slow breath and turned my head toward the window as he followed the GPS to my place. The tension in the truck was starting to get under my skin, and not in the usual teasing, flirty way.

He rolled to a stop in front of my house and shifted into park, leaving the engine running.

I turned toward him. I was about to thank him for the ride. For trusting me with his name. For this... whatever the hell this was becoming.

But he beat me to it.

"I'll have your car looked at."

"What?"

He sighed like I was already being difficult, rubbing his jaw with that big, calloused hand. "I'll get Henry to take a look at it."

A warmth crept up into my chest so fast I almost didn't recognize it. Ghost. Kasper. He didn't do favors. He didn't even like people. Yet, he was going out of his way to help me. Again. It felt awkard, and kind of great at the same time.

"You really don't have to do that," I said, trying to play it cool.

He turned his head and cut me a look so dry it could've sucked the moisture out of the air. "I know I don't have to."

That was it. One sentence. But it said everything. He was doing it because he wanted to. And that did all sorts of things to me.

"Thank you," I said softly.

Ghost's blue eyes flicked to mine. And for once... they lingered. Not in that lazy, I'm-undressing-you-in-my-head way. But real. Like he wanted me to know he saw me.

Then, without a word, he gave a single slow nod.

I reached for the door handle, ready to step out and give myself a second to breathe.

"Halston."

My name stopped me cold. My heart stalled. I turned back. "Yeah?"

He was gripping the wheel tighter now, his thumb tapping the leather. And then, quietly, gruff and unpolished, he said, "Don't call me that around other people."

It took me a second.

And then I got it. Kasper.

The request could have easily pissed me off, like I was some dirty little secret. But this wasn't about shame. It was about trust. He didn't give that name to just anyone. But he gave it to me. At least, that was how I was choosing to see it.

I smiled, my fingers brushing the edge of the doorframe. "Okay."

His lips curled up, just barely, but it was there. A genuine smile. Quiet. Almost shy. And somehow sexier than any smirk he'd ever thrown at me.

"Thank you for the ride," I told him.

He gave another nod.

I stepped out, closed the door gently behind me, and started toward the house.

But I heard it. The low purr of the engine was still rumbling. He didn't drive off right away. He sat there. Just a few seconds longer.

And somehow, that meant more than any goodbye.

Chapter 18

The bar was loud, packed wall-to-wall with rowdy people drinking beer, two-stepping to the country music blasting from the speakers, and generally having the time of their lives.

I wasn't sure how the hell I'd ended up here, but when Niki suggested a night out, I agreed. So, she picked me up, and we headed to a strange bar I didn't know existed just outside of town.

After spending so much time at Ghost's ranch, I needed a girls' night. A night where I could breathe without having his voice in my head, whispering filthy things that made my thighs shake and my body twist in frustration.

But of course, he was here. Niki failed to tell me it wouldn't be just the two of us tonight.

Ghost had come with Josh and Drew. The cocky bastard was standing there, beer in hand, looking like the sexiest thing I'd ever seen. It was unnerving.

His pretty blue eyes locked onto me, that signature smirk playing on his lips like he already knew what was on my mind. Hell, he probably did. The man read me like a fucking book.

"Oh, hell yes!" Niki gasped, grabbing my arm. "We have to ride the bull!"

I followed her gaze. Sure enough, at the back of the bar, a giant mechanical bull sat in the center of a padded ring, surrounded by cheering drunk idiots. Great.

Drew chuckled, nudging Ghost. "Five bucks says she lasts less than three seconds."

Ghost just took a sip of his beer, his gaze snapping from me to the bull, then back again. "I don't know... She looks like she's got a little grit in her." His lips curved into a sinful smirk. "Still not sure she can handle something that powerful between her legs."

My body went up in flames.

That damn mouth. Those fucking innuendos. How was I supposed to stay objective when he was constantly luring me in with his insinuations?

Niki, of course, loved this. "Oh, she can handle it." She turned to me. "Right, Halston?"

I narrowed my eyes. "You're the worst friend ever," I said, making her laugh.

But I wasn't about to let Ghost win this round. So, I straightened my shoulders and walked toward the mechanical bull with something to prove.

The crowd parted as I stepped onto the mat.

The operator smiled as he helped me on. "You done this before, sweetheart?"

"Nope. But how hard can it be?" I realized it was the same thing I'd said about the ATVs. And look how that went.

A deep chuckle rumbled from where Ghost was standing, watching me with a look that made my stomach flip. "You hear that, boys?" he called out. "She thinks it's easy."

I shot him a glare. "Shut up."

He just grinned.

The second the bull started moving, I realized I was screwed. It jerked forward, nearly throwing me off immediately.

Ghost let out a sharp whistle. "Damn, Tits. You're barely holding on. That's a shame. I was really hoping to see some stamina tonight."

Laughter erupted around him.

"Fuck you, Ghost!" I shouted, gripping the handle tighter, trying to hold on, my thighs squeezing around the saddle as the bull bucked.

"That's the spirit, baby!" he called. "Just pretend it's me between your legs, and you might last a little longer."

That earned a round of loud hoots and whistles from the bar. A few guys banged on tables, one of them yelling, "Get it, Ghost!"

Even the operator was laughing as he tried to keep a straight face. "You two need a room or a ref?"

I was holding on with everything I had when Ghost cupped his hands around his mouth and shouted, "Don't forget to do that little whimper thing you always do right before you cum!"

The crowd lost it.

That was it. I lost my focus for half a second, and that was all it took. The bull lurched forward, and I went flying. I hit the padded mat with a graceless thud, lying there for a moment, staring at the ceiling, trying to regain my dignity.

Ghost's laugh was the first thing I heard. "Damn. And here I thought you were a rider."

I groaned, sitting up just as Niki and Drew pulled me to my feet, both of them dying laughing.

"You were so close!" Niki said.

"To what? Lasting four seconds instead of three?" I muttered.

I brushed the dust off my jeans and stormed toward the table where Ghost was already nursing a beer, looking way too pleased with himself. Drew and Josh were still laughing, and even a few strangers clapped me on the back as I passed, one of them shouting, "You gave it hell, girl!"

"Thanks," I muttered, grabbing the beer the waitress had just set down, and slid into the same booth Ghost was at.

Ghost's voice carried a telltale trace of a smile. "Hey, I'm proud of you, Tits. You gave it your best shot. But if you ever wanna practice riding something a little more... realistic, just let me know."

I gasped, my face going hot as hell, as Drew and Josh snickered.

Ghost grinned and took a swig of his beer, like he hadn't just ruined my night with one stupid, perfect line.

Niki was laughing so hard she had to hold on to Josh as all three of them headed to the bar to grab another round.

"I hate you," I muttered, when it was just the two of us.

"No, you don't," he teased, winking.

I didn't answer. Because he was absolutely right. But I was trying not to admit it to myself, so I sure as hell didn't want to admit it to him.

He leaned back in his chair, cocky and infuriating. "So," he drawled, "was it the bull or my commentary that made you fall off?"

I took a long drink before meeting his smug gaze. "It certainly wasn't your commentary."

"No?" His lips curved. "Thought maybe hearing me talk about you cumin' would've made you weak in the knees."

I smirked, leaning in slightly. "You wish you knew the noises I make before I cum."

His grin faltered for just half a second, just long enough for my pulse to spike with satisfaction, before he recovered.

"Oh, sweetheart," he said, his tone rough, "I plan to find out. And when I do? The entire ranch is going to hear the noises you make."

That promise stole my breath and made me ache involuntarily between my thighs. I faked a smile. "Keep dreaming, Ghost."

He raised his beer in a lazy toast. "Every night, Tits. Every. Damn. Night."

His words hit me like a body blow, shooting heat through me before I had a chance to guard against it. My thighs clenched instinctively under the table. God, I hated the way he could flip a switch inside me with just a few cocky words and that dangerous, half-lidded stare.

I wanted him. There was no use pretending otherwise. But I'd be damned if I let him be the one to toss me a smug smirk afterward while zipping up his jeans and calling me "Tits" on his way out.

He wasn't the relationship type. He wasn't even the callback type.

So I sat straighter, forced my face into the most unimpressed expression I could manage, and took another sip of my beer.

Ghost's eyes drifted lazily down to my lap and back up again, that maddening smirk spreading across his lips. "If you rode that bull half as good as I plan to make you ride me, I'm gonna need to start a line for tickets."

A dangerous flush crawled up my neck. Smug, hit-it-and-quit-it asshole.

"Fuck you," I said, standing abruptly.

His brows lifted, amused. "What, you going for another round on the bull? Gotta work on that stamina?"

"I'm going to ride that thing like I own it. Just so you and your fantasy can choke on your words."

"Can't wait," he murmured. "Better take notes, too. Practice makes perfect, sweetheart."

My blood boiled in frustration, humiliation, and God help me... arousal. Every nerve in my body was strung tight with it. The man and his comebacks. He was too quick-witted for my sanity.

But I just flipped my hair over my shoulder, tossed him a glare, and marched toward the mechanical bull with fire in my eyes and vengeance in my hips.

"Again," I told the operator.

He raised an eyebrow, but then shrugged. "Alright, sweetheart. Let's see what you got."

The second I got back on, the crowd stirred, people turning to watch again. Ghost's eyes were on me, a smile on his lips, like he hadn't expected me to get back up there.

The bull jerked forward, but this time, I was ready. I squeezed my thighs tighter, my grip firm, my balance steady as I moved with it, letting my body flow naturally instead of fighting it. I rolled my hips forward and tried not to think about the last time I'd done that, the night I'd kissed Ghost by the fire.

"Damn," Niki gasped. "She's actually doing it!"

Drew laughed. "Looks like someone took your advice, Ghost!"

Ghost's voice was thick with a smirk I could hear. "Yeah, she's got it now. But let's see if she can keep up that rhythm."

I lasted almost fifteen seconds before the speed kicked up again, and I was finally thrown. I landed much more gracefully this time, rolling to my feet with a triumphant grin.

The crowd cheered, and even the operator clapped. "That was impressive," he admitted.

I turned to Ghost, flipping my chestnut hair over my shoulder. "Well? Was that enough stamina for you?"

Ghost smirked, slow and cocky. "Solid performance. But I'd need a front-row seat to the encore to really judge."

I arched a brow. "You couldn't handle the encore."

His grin widened. "Sweetheart, I am the encore."

And with that, the cocky bastard gave me one last slow once-over before turning toward the bathrooms.

Chapter 19

My skin buzzed from the interaction. He was wearing me down. Every glance, every innuendo, every filthy word had me tied up and twisted inside.

I was catching my breath when a guy stepped up beside me. "That was impressive," he said, flashing a charming smile.

I turned, giving him a quick once-over. Tall. Good-looking. "Thanks," I said, still trying to shake off the way my body reacted to Ghost.

"Can I buy you a drink?"

I opened my mouth to decline.

"She's good," a deep, familiar voice said.

The guy's eyes widened slightly, his posture shifting as he took in the sight of Ghost standing right there, his presence as overbearing as ever.

"I was just—"

"Leaving," Ghost finished for him, his tone calm, but not friendly.

The guy hesitated, then gave me an awkward nod before walking away.

Ghost stepped closer, his blue eyes locking onto mine, his voice rough. "What the fuck are you doing, Tits?"

I took a step closer, my eyes challenging him. "Talking to someone who isn't an ass."

Ghost's lips curved. "Cute. But we both know that was bullshit."

"What part of it was bullshit?" I asked with an amused laugh. "You don't own me, Ghost."

His blue eyes darkened. "Then why do you let me get under your skin?"

Ghost's words hung between us, thick and suffocating like a challenge I wasn't sure I was ready to face. Because he was right. He did get under my skin. And I didn't want him to stop.

How fucked up was that?

I swallowed hard, trying to keep my composure, trying to keep the upper hand, like I hadn't just been caught practically melting at the sound of his voice. "Are you gonna make a habit of scaring off every guy who breathes in my direction?" I said, arching a brow.

Ghost smirked, stepping even closer. "Yep."

Heat shot up my spine, my heart hammering in my chest. "Wanna clue me in as to why?" My voice was steady, but my insides were an absolute mess.

Ghost chuckled low. "Because I already staked my claim."

My breath caught in my throat. I hated how my body reacted to that. I hated that he could turn me inside out with words, with a look, with a damn touch.

I tilted my head, stepping in just a little closer, close enough to feel his body heat, close enough that my lips grazed his beard. And I had heels on. "How about if I say no to that, sweetheart?"

Ghost chuckled. Then, his hand shot out, gripping my waist. "Then I guess we've got a problem," he said, walking me backward until my spine hit a support beam.

I let out a breath that felt more like a moan, my voice shaky but defiant. "Are you trying to intimidate me?"

Ghost tilted his head. "I'm trying to figure out if I should fuck the attitude out of you or let you keep talking until I cum in my jeans."

Jesus.

"You're... disgusting," I whispered, swallowing hard, picturing both scenarios.

"Right," he smirked. "And yet here you are. Breathless. Panties soaked."

He wasn't wrong. I was completely unraveling, and I hated how much I loved it.

"You like playing with fire, don't you?"

"I don't burn easily," I lied.

"Oh, sweetheart..." He leaned in, his lips barely grazing my ear. "You're already on fucking fire."

My knees wobbled, my restraint cracking.

"Say the word," he whispered, "and I'll take you out of here. Right now."

I took a breath, dragging it through my lungs like it could clear my head. It didn't. My body wanted him like he was oxygen, and I'd been holding my breath for months.

But I couldn't be one of his throwaway girls. I'd be damned if I gave myself to a man like him without making him earn it.

So I leaned up, letting my lips brush his, barely. "Nah," I whispered. "You don't get to have me just because your dick has a mouth."

His laugh was soft, sinful. "It's got great taste, too."

I smirked and then stepped back slowly. "Then savor the view, baby. 'Cause that's all you're getting tonight."

Then I turned and walked away, my hips swinging, my pulse pounding like a war drum, knowing damn well his eyes were still on me.

Ghost laughed. "Keep running, Tits." His voice was loud enough for me to hear over the music, cocky as ever. "I'll catch you eventually."

I knew if we kept this up, he would.

Chapter 20

I settled into one of the oversized leather chairs in Ghost's living room, my laptop on my thighs.

Ghost was outside, working with the ranch hands. He'd told me I could stay inside and wait for him, so that's exactly what I was doing, getting some work done while I waited for my ride home.

My car was still unreliable, still waiting for Henry to look at it, which wasn't a big deal. The man managed the entire ranch. So, I knew he would get to the car when he had time. Of course, it had been days of being stranded at Ghost's mercy. Not that I was complaining.

Well, maybe a little.

I opened my laptop, pulling up my latest project. It was a logo re-design for a boxing gym. The owner had asked for something bold, aggressive, something that would make people take notice. So I had been experimenting with gritty, urban fonts, shadowed figures mid-punch, and metallic textures that gave it a raw, industrial feel.

I was so locked into my work, my fingers flying over the trackpad, that I didn't hear the door open.

"What the fuck is this?"

I jumped, my laptop nearly sliding off my lap. "Jesus, Ghost!"

He stood just inside the doorway, sweaty, dirty, and looking like every woman's goddamn wet dream. His gray T-shirt clung to his chest, his jeans hung low on his hips, and his knuckles were streaked with grease and what looked suspiciously like blood.

His eyes shot down to my laptop. "What the hell are you doing?"

I scowled, trying to calm my racing heart. "Working. Unlike some people."

He grabbed a water bottle from the fridge, twisted off the cap, and took a long pull. His neck stretched back, his hard muscles shifting, and I was forced to look away before I made an idiot of myself.

Ghost dropped onto the couch, sprawling out. "Let me see," he said, nodding toward my screen.

I hesitated, then flipped the laptop toward him. "It's a logo redesign for a boxing gym."

His brows shot up. "You designing for a fight club now?"

"No," I said, zooming in on the details. "Just a gym looking for a refresh. They want something bold, something gritty."

Ghost rubbed his bearded jaw, studying the screen. "Not bad. But you should've used my face."

I snorted. "Oh, yeah? You think your face belongs on a gym logo?"

"Damn right." He smirked. "'Ghost's House of Pain.' Free black eye with every membership."

I laughed. "Yeah, I think that might send the wrong message."

He tilted his head, grinning. "Or the right one."

I rolled my eyes but couldn't stop my smile.

"Didn't know you had an eye for branding, Tits."

I sighed, still looking at the screen. "I'm a graphic designer, Ghost. It's literally my job."

Ghost let out a low whistle. "Damn. That's sexy."

I paused. Because of course that was his response. Not oh, that's cool. I'd love to see your work. He called my career sexy. Damn, the man knew how to twist everything to turn me on.

"You actually like doing this?" he asked.

I nodded. "Yeah. I like the freedom. I like making something out of nothing, creating things that help businesses stand out." I smirked. "And I love that I don't have to deal with people like you if I don't want to."

Ghost grinned. "So you're a hermit who gets paid to sit on her ass and drink coffee?"

I arched a brow. "Says the guy who gets paid to beat the shit out of people."

Ghost chuckled, then let his eyes drag over me slowly, deliberately. "Maybe I should hire you."

I snorted. "For what?"

"Personal branding," he said smoothly. "You could design me a nice logo. Maybe a banner. Something simple."

I rolled my eyes. "Let me guess. 'Ghost Will Fuck You Up'?"

He grinned, all slow and cocky. "See? You get me."

I laughed, shaking my head.

Ghost tapped his fingers against the armrest, watching me in a way that made my pulse quicken. "So you're smart," he mused, "creative, self-employed. And somehow still dumb enough to keep hanging around me."

I grinned, leaning back in my chair. "Well, nobody's perfect."

Then, he just got up and headed back out. He was almost at the door when he paused, just for a second. Then, without turning around, he glanced over his shoulder. "You need inspiration for those designs, I'll be in the barn. Shirtless. Sweaty. Looking real fuckin' good."

My mouth fell open, but before I could throw something at him, he walked out, chuckling.

Chapter 21

I had no idea why I agreed to this.

    Oh, wait, I did. Because Niki talked me into it, and I'd been so damn desperate to stop thinking about Ghost that I caved.

And now? I was sitting across from Mr. Preppy Politeness, listening to him talk about his love for Taylor Swift concerts like it was a personality trait.

I smiled, trying not to let my boredom show on my face.

"You know, I actually scored tickets to that new indie-pop band coming next month," he said, flashing me an eager smile. "I'd love to take you."

I forced a polite nod. "Oh, cool."

He grinned. "Yeah, I just love the atmosphere, you know? Plus, the last one was Ariana Grande. That woman is a goddess."

A red flag shot up like a firework.

Not because he liked concerts. But because every single one he mentioned was a girly concert.

I studied him carefully. Either he was a total pushover or he was saying this to impress me, which meant he thought I was that easy to manipulate.

Neither option sat well.

"I'm surprised you got tickets. Her shows usually sell out fast," I said.

"Oh, I know a guy who knows a guy," he said with a wink. "And let's be honest, I'd go again just to see her in those outfits. No shame."

I stared at him. Maybe it was all just an act.

"I even made a custom T-shirt that said 'Break Up With Your Boyfriend, I'm Bored,'" he added with a proud grin.

"You wore that... in public?"

"Oh yeah. Got a few looks, but it was worth it."

Okay, now I was more confused than ever.

Meanwhile, at the other table, I could feel Ghost's presence like a damn gravitational force pulling at me. He was sitting with Drew, Josh, Niki, and Jen, all of them not-so-discreetly watching my date unfold. Niki had set me up with this guy, and she had the audacity to invite everyone there so they could spy on me like I was their nightly entertainment.

Ghost, of course, was all too amused by the whole thing. He was sitting there with a perfect view of me and my date, that cocky smirk in place. The man was a menace to my entire existence.

I refused to look directly at him. Because every time I thought about him, I thought about the way he touched me, the way he talked to me, the way he ruined me for anyone else.

And Mr. Ariana Grande across from me did none of that.

I excused myself to go to the bathroom, needing a moment to breathe, to shake this off. I was ready for this date to be over, and it had only been twenty minutes.

But the second I stepped into the hallway, a wall of heat blocked my way.

Ghost stepped into my path. "Having fun?" he drawled.

I lifted my chin. "Actually, yes."

He smirked. "Really? 'Cause it sounds like your date's a total pussy."

I narrowed my eyes. He was right, and I blamed that on Niki. "Why? Because he likes concerts?"

His lips twitched. "Nah. Because he likes chick concerts."

I rolled my eyes. "So?"

Ghost's smirk turned devilish. He took a step closer, his body dominant, closing the already small distance between us. "Or," he said, his voice low and dangerous, "he's just saying that to get into your panties."

I swallowed hard. Why did I like him mentioning my panties? "I'm not stupid, Ghost. You think that didn't cross my mind?"

And now, with Ghost standing this close, I suddenly couldn't remember why I had even agreed to this date in the first place.

Ghost studied my face, reading every little shift in my expression like a damn human lie detector. "Tell me something, sweetheart." His voice was rough and full of heat. "Do you feel half of what you feel for me when you're close to him?"

My stomach clenched. "I—"

Ghost leaned in, his breath warm against my ear. "You think he's gonna kiss you the way I kiss you?" he whispered.

My knees nearly buckled. I swallowed hard.

He pulled back just enough to look into my eyes, his gaze daring me to lie.

I opened my mouth, but I had nothing to say.

He smirked. "That's what I thought."

Then, just to wreck me completely, he grabbed my face, tilted my chin up, and kissed me, good and hard, like he was branding me. His tongue slid against mine, slow and warm, his hand sliding into my hair, owning me, unraveling me, making me forget anything and anyone that wasn't him.

And just as I was on the verge of completely losing myself in it, he pulled away. Leaving me breathless and wanting him.

He licked his lips, watching me like he enjoyed every second of my unraveling. Then he whispered, "Enjoy your date, sweetheart."

He walked away.

I went back to the table, completely wrecked and turned on beyond reason. It was all I could do to concentrate on anything this guy was saying now.

His mouth moved and words were coming out, but I wasn't hearing a single one of them. Because all I could feel was Ghost's mouth on mine. All I could think about was the way he had kissed me just to prove a point, just to fuck with my head, just to remind me that no one could make me feel the way he did.

I shifted in my seat, clenching my thighs together under the table, trying and failing to shake the heat still burning through me.

I picked up my drink and downed half of it, pretending like I was fine, like I wasn't losing my goddamn mind over a kiss, like I wasn't one second away from dragging Ghost out of here and jumping him in the damn parking lot. Everything in me was pulling toward him. He turned me on like I'd never felt before. Just fucking torched me.

When I finally tuned back into the conversation, I realized my date was still rambling about his concert plans.

"So, yeah," he said, smiling like he was waiting for me to be impressed. "If you're free Friday night, I was thinking we could go see Taylor Swift."

I sighed. Not because of the concert. Taylor Swift didn't bother me. But I wasn't attracted to weak men. And I only knew that because of damn Ghost. His confidence was attractive. I loved how he owned everything he said and did. I loved how he owned all of my feelings right now.

"Exactly how often do you go to these kinds of concerts?" I asked, setting my drink down.

"I've been to, like, six in the last year. Love them. The whole experience, you know? The atmosphere, the music... it's just so fun."

I squinted at him, suspicion creeping in. There was something about the way he was talking, the way he was overselling it.

And maybe I was reading into it too much, but all I could think about was how Ghost never did that shit. Ghost didn't pander. He didn't try to curate himself to fit what he thought I wanted. Ghost was just Ghost. He was unapologetic, vulgar, rough around the edges, and masculine as hell.

And I liked that. Hell, I loved that. The only reason I hadn't let him in at first was because I didn't want to be used. Now, I had another reason to keep him at arm's length. I liked the dynamic we had. I enjoyed spending time at his place. I liked our sexy encounters, the flirting and the insane way his dirty words torched me.

This guy, though? He just wasn't for me.

I forced a tight smile, already mentally preparing my exit strategy. "That's... great. Really. But I don't think so. I hope you find someone who shares your interests, though."

I grabbed my bag and slid out of the booth, relieved to be done with this entire night. "It was nice meeting you."

But before I could make a clean getaway, he grabbed my hand and kissed me. His lips barely grazed mine before I pushed him away, stepping back.

He held up his hands. "Oh, uh, sorry. I thought I read that right. I thought I felt something there between us."

I sighed, choosing my words carefully, not wanting to hurt his feelings. "I appreciate the date, really, but there's just nothing here," I said, keeping my tone polite but firm. "I don't feel that way."

He looked genuinely confused. "Are you sure?"

Seriously? I forced another tight smile. "Very."

Before he could try anything else, I turned on my heel and headed straight for my friends.

Chapter 22

I slid into the booth, right next to Ghost, because that was the only damn seat left.

His thigh pressed against mine, solid, warm, and I was already unraveling from what happened in the hallway.

I didn't look at him or acknowledge the way his smug smirk was practically burning a hole in the side of my face. I ignored him and tried to pretend that my date hadn't just tried to kiss me out of nowhere, misreading every possible signal I wasn't giving.

Josh leaned forward, grinning. "So... how'd it go?"

Niki, ever the instigator, smirked. "Yeah, Halston. Tell us everything. Did you two hit it off?"

I waved the server down to order a glass of water. "I know you guys heard it. Stop pretending you didn't."

Drew laughed. "That was bad."

I sighed as the server set my ice water down. "I'm just glad it's over."

Josh looked disappointed. "Damn, I had high hopes for that one."

I shot him a look. "Did you?"

Niki snorted. "Please. You knew it was a disaster the second he walked in the door wearing a pink girl's shirt."

Josh grinned, shrugging. "I mean, yeah. We all did. But still. We were rooting for the guy."

Ghost finally spoke, his voice low and laced with amusement. "Yeah, sweetheart. What happened? I thought you two were hitting it off."

I snapped my head toward him, glaring.

The cocky bastard was smirking, looking completely pleased with himself, like he hadn't just wrecked me in the hallway and then left me to sit through the rest of my date in a daze.

I narrowed my eyes. "Oh, I don't know. Maybe it was the part where he spent the entire time trying to impress me with shit he thought I wanted to hear."

Ghost's lips lifted. "Yeah? Like what?"

I sighed, hating that he was enjoying this so much. "Like how he goes to every pop concert known to man. How he lives for chick flicks. Like how he's so in touch with his emotions and really values open communication."

Josh barked out a laugh. "Jesus. What a catch!"

Drew smiled. "You don't think he was just saying that to get in your pants?"

Before I could answer, Ghost spoke for me. "Oh, he definitely was."

I clenched my jaw. I hated how much he was enjoying this.

Niki grinned. "So, when's the second date?"

I groaned, covering my face with my hands. "Never. Not in this lifetime. Not even if the fate of the world depended on it."

Josh grinned. "So, you're saying there's a chance?"

I shot him a look that made him laugh.

I reached for my water, ready to drown myself in it, while Ghost let out a low chuckle, entirely too pleased with himself.

I shot him a glare.

But he just smirked, leaning in a little closer, his voice dropping just for me. "Didn't like his kiss, huh?" he whispered, his breath on my ear sending a shiver down my spine.

I swallowed hard. "Shut up."

His smirk deepened, his knee nudging mine under the table.

And just like that, my date didn't even matter anymore. Ghost had a habit of stealing all of my attention.

Ghost's knee pressed harder against mine under the table, his smug smirk still in place, his sexy blue eyes watching me too closely.

I knew I should have pulled away. I should have focused on literally anyone else at this table. But I didn't want to. Because I was still wrecked from that damn kiss in the hallway. His low voice and cocky confidence had already burned through me like wildfire. I could still taste him on my lips, still feel his hands on my damn waist, still hear the way he whispered dirty, possessive words in my ear.

God, I wanted him to do it again.

I shifted in my seat, forcing myself to take a sip of my water, ignoring the heat in my stomach.

Drew was talking. Josh was laughing at something Niki said. The conversation was still going, and I was trying to keep up.

But Ghost was still watching me. Still owning every damn thought running through my head.

He leaned in again, his voice low and private just for me. "So, was it a bad kiss, sweetheart? Or just the wrong kiss?"

I froze, my fingers tightening around my glass.

I felt him smirk before I even turned my head. The bastard looked like he had me exactly where he wanted me.

I swallowed, my throat suddenly too dry. "Ghost."

His lips curved. "Yeah, baby?"

Baby? Oh my God. My friggin' panties were soaked. "Drop it."

He tilted his head as if he was considering it, but we both knew the truth. Ghost never dropped anything. His gaze dipped to my lips, lingering, and suddenly I couldn't breathe.

His voice was full of heat. "You can tell me, sweetheart. Did it even compare?"

No, of course it didn't. But I wasn't about to give him the satisfaction of knowing that. The man's ego could afford to take a few hits.

I shot him a glare, forcing a smirk of my own. "Oh, I don't know, Ghost. Maybe I should go out with him again just to be sure."

His smirk vanished in an instant.

And just like that, the power shifted. His entire demeanor darkened, his cocky confidence morphing into something possessive and lethal all at once. His hand slid under the table, gripping my thigh just below the hem of my skirt.

I pulled in a sharp breath, my entire body tensing as his fingers flexed. His grip wasn't rough, just firm. "Try it," he said, his tone still low.

But his touch? Scorching. I swallowed hard, my pulse hammering in my ears.

He leaned in again, his lips brushing my ear. "Sweetheart," he whispered, his thumb dragging slowly over my thigh, "you go out with him again, and I'll remind you exactly who you belong to."

Oh, fuck. I swallowed hard, my entire body betraying me, heat flooding my veins, my thighs clenching before I could stop myself.

The smug bastard had the nerve to chuckle.

Josh's voice pulled me back, and I barely managed to pretend like I wasn't about to combust.

But Ghost didn't move his hand. He didn't let me forget exactly who had me in this state. And as the conversation continued around us, his thumb stroked my skin, just above my knee, his touch light, deliberate, setting me on fire.

I tried to ignore it. Tried to stay in control.

I wanted to ignore him because I didn't want anyone else to see how he was affecting me, but I couldn't. Not when he was this close, not when his voice was still lingering in my ear, full of deliberate, dangerous promises. And not when he was talking like I was his.

That thought completely wrecked me.

And judging by the way his grip tightened, the way his thumb brushed just a little higher, Ghost knew it too.

His possessiveness fucked with my head, made me think I could have more than a one-night stand with him.

I turned my head, forcing myself to meet his eyes, hoping to God he couldn't see just how wrecked I was inside. "Ghost," I whispered a warning, my voice dangerously shaky.

His lips tipped into a slow smirk, his fingers finally lifting away from my leg. But not before he said, "That's my girl."

My stomach flipped. I fucking hated him. Because I was trying to fight my attraction to him. And instead, I was sitting there, completely soaked, with my heart racing out of control, knowing damn well that if he pulled me outside right now and kissed me like he had earlier, I'd let him do it all over again. I'd let him do whatever he wanted. Because he owned all of my inner lust. And I thought about his hands on my body all day, every day. And because I seriously wanted to get my hands all over his beautiful body, too.

Chapter 23

The energy in the warehouse was electric.

The crowd was still buzzing from the fight. The air was thick with adrenaline.

Ghost had, as expected, fucking dominated. His opponent had barely lasted two rounds before hitting the mat like a sack of bricks. A knockout.

The crowd had finally started thinning, but people were still swarming him, stealing every second they could, taking pictures, asking for autographs, offering congratulations.

And he gave them what they wanted. That smirk. That effortless, cocky charm.

I stood off to the side with my beer, watching, pretending like I wasn't watching.

Niki nudged me. "You're staring."

"I'm observing."

"Mm-hmm," she said, smirking as she sipped her drink.

I rolled my eyes, taking a swig of my beer as I watched yet another woman drape herself over him like he was hers.

Whatever. I wasn't going to let any of it affect me. He wasn't mine.

But then, just as I was telling myself that, he looked at me across the crowd. Past the bodies pressing against him. He smirked, shooting me that damn wink. That stupid, knowing, torch-you-from-the-inside smirk and wink combination. The one that said I see you, sweetheart. And I know you see me too.

Fucking hell.

Heat shot through my body as I forced my expression into something bored and unaffected. But I knew he knew. That cocky bastard knew exactly what he was doing to me.

And he was loving every second of it.

"Hey, so…" Jen's voice cut in, drawing my attention. She stood beside Drew, both of them sipping beers. Her eyes flickered between me and Ghost before she gave me a pointed look. "What's going on with you two?"

I froze for half a second before masking it. "What? Who?" I asked, feigning confusion.

Jen scowled. "You and Ghost. That little show you put on when we took the ATVs out. You came on to him hard. Thought maybe you two had a thing."

Ahh. That. I had done it on purpose to piss her off. To stake a claim before she could. But she didn't know that.

I shrugged, keeping my expression neutral. "Nothing's going on. It was a joke."

Jen studied me, not looking convinced. "Are you sure about that?"

I took a drink of my beer, holding eye contact. "Positive." Not that it was any of her business.

She tilted her head like she was about to press, but before she could, Ghost broke away from the crowd and made his way toward us.

He was still slightly wet from his after-fight shower, his black shirt clinging to him, those sexy tattoos peeking out from under the sleeves. He was danger wrapped in muscle.

He grabbed a water bottle off the table, cracking it open as he dropped into the seat next to me. Too close. Close enough that I could feel the heat coming off his skin, and smell the faint trace of leather.

Josh clapped him on the shoulder and took a seat across from us. "Another one for the books, man."

Ghost smirked, taking a sip from his water bottle, his blue eyes flicking to mine for just a second before turning back to the group. "Barely broke a sweat."

Drew snorted. "I saw that last round. You almost ate that elbow."

Ghost smirked. "Almost. But didn't."

They launched into a full fight breakdown, but Ghost's attention kept sliding to me. Not obviously. Not enough for anyone else to notice. But I felt it like a touch I couldn't escape.

I tried to ignore him, focusing on my beer.

His thigh pressed against mine casually, like he wasn't trying to unravel me. Like he didn't just wink at me across the damn room knowing exactly what it would do to me.

He stretched his arm along the back of the booth, his fingers brushing the back of my neck just enough to send a spark down my spine.

I refused to look at him.

But he was watching me. Daring me to react.

Josh smiled at me over his beer. "So, Halston. How's the dating life treating you?"

I rolled my eyes. "Fantastic."

Drew chuckled. "That bad, huh?"

"I have a few guys I could set you up with," Jen said.

That wasn't happening. I'd seen the guys Jen hung out with, and I wouldn't touch them with a ten-foot pole. Except for Drew, of course. He was the only nice guy she hung around. But his connection to Jen meant he would never be a viable option for me. Girl code dictated you didn't touch a friend's boyfriend, husband, or ex.

"If he's anything like the last one, I'll pass," I told her.

Niki laughed, nudging me. "I work with a few guys who'd go for you. With your blue eyes, wavy chestnut hair, and killer body."

I flushed, shifting in my seat. "Niki–"

Jen immediately jumped in, her voice sweet with a razor edge. "You do have that cute, good-girl look down."

"Thanks?" I said, knowing full well it wasn't a compliment.

"But men prefer blondes," she added, stirring the ice in her drink, her eyes floating toward Ghost, like she was testing the waters, fishing for a reaction. And probably a compliment.

I clenched my jaw. Poor Drew. He really needed to cut her loose.

Ghost didn't even hesitate. He didn't even look at her. "Men prefer women who don't talk outta their ass," he said, tipping back his drink.

Josh choked on his beer.

Drew snorted.

I bit my lip, fighting a grin. I loved that he didn't subscribe to her bullshit. It made me like him even more. I seriously wanted to jump him then and there to reward him for putting her in her place.

Jen's face tightened, but she recovered quickly, flipping her hair like she didn't care.

Niki grinned, steering the conversation back. "Anyway. I know this really cute guy, Rick. He loves hiking, and he's really funny."

Drew smirked, nudging me. "You hear that, Halston? He's funny and likes to hike?"

Jen smacked his arm. "That's not a bad thing."

Josh shrugged, looking at me. "But he's not Halston's type."

Jen raised an eyebrow, her lips curving. "Oh? And what exactly is Halston's type?"

I hesitated for half a second.

And then, like a goddamn magnet, my eyes shifted to Ghost.

He caught it. And the bastard smiled. Like I'd just confirmed what I had been denying for weeks.

I swallowed, looking away, pretending I hadn't just walked into that one. "I don't know if I have a type," I finally said, forcing my voice to stay even.

Ghost hummed. "Bullshit."

I turned toward him, lifting an eyebrow. "Excuse me?"

He grinned, looking infuriatingly smug. "Sweetheart, you absolutely have a type."

I watched him. "Oh? And what's that?"

Ghost didn't miss a beat. "Men who wreck your life."

Josh snorted. "Jesus."

Drew laughed.

My brows furrowed. "So not true."

Ghost tilted his head. "Really? So tell me, sweetheart. What exactly made you sit through an entire date with Bradley the Soy Boy the other night?"

I groaned. "You're an ass."

Ghost chuckled. "Truth hurts."

"I stuck around for the date because I was being nice," I defended. "I absolutely did not like him."

He leaned in, his voice dropping to that low, teasing murmur that had been ruining my life since the day I met him. "But you do like men who piss you off. Get you all worked up. Make you think about 'em when you shouldn't."

My stomach clenched, my fingers tightening around my beer. I pretended he wasn't spot on. "Wow. That was a lot of words just to admit you're in love with yourself."

Ghost laughed. "Nah, sweetheart. That's just a bonus."

I bit my lip, fighting back my smile.

Josh leaned forward, watching our exchange with a little too much interest. "You two ever...?" he trailed off, wiggling his eyebrows.

I stiffened. "What? No."

Ghost just smirked, his eyes locked on mine.

Josh glanced between us, unconvinced. "Uh-huh."

Drew grinned. "Damn shame. The tension between you two is unbearable."

Niki rolled her eyes. "Not everything is about sex, you know."

Ghost chuckled, his gaze shooting toward her.

Then, just to be an asshole, he turned back to me and said, "Nah, but it'd be a hell of a lot more fun if it was."

My face lit up, my body reacting to his words, and the way his eyes settled on me. I was damn close to losing my goddamn mind. Because it sure as hell felt like everything was about sex when it came to Ghost. It was all I'd been able to think about since day one.

Chapter 24

J en was still sulking from Ghost shutting her down.

Niki was sipping her drink, thoroughly entertained by the conversation.

And me? I was trying really hard not to focus on the fact that Ghost had spent the last ten minutes making my life hell.

Or maybe making it better. I hadn't decided yet.

Josh, still amused, turned toward Ghost. "Alright, so if Halston has a type, what's yours?"

Ghost grinned, stretching out like he didn't care that he was even further in my space. "You really wanna know?"

Josh shrugged. "Yeah, man. Let's hear it."

Ghost's eyes darted to mine. Locked on and unrelenting. My stomach clenched.

That slow, cocky smile spread across his face. "Trouble."

I rolled my eyes. "Of course."

Niki smiled. "What does that even mean?"

Ghost lifted his beer, taking a slow pull. "It means I like a girl who keeps me on my toes. One who makes shit interesting."

Josh scoffed. "So, you like psychos?"

Ghost chuckled, shaking his head. "Nah. Just women who know what they want."

Jen made a noise in her throat. "That's convenient, considering you never stick around for them after."

Ghost arched a brow, amused. "Gotta make sure she wants the right thing."

My stomach flipped. That bastard. He said it like he was looking for the right girl, but his personal choices and offhand comments said differently.

Jen's nostrils flared, but she covered it with a sip of her drink. "Well, that's definitely not Halston, then," she said sweetly. "She has no idea what she wants."

Before I could snap something back, Ghost beat me to it.

His voice went low. Unapologetically sure. "That's where you're wrong."

Jen stared, caught off guard.

Ghost just smiled.

My chest tightened. It was a statement. A challenge. Yeah, she was wrong. He knew I knew exactly what I wanted, and the annoying ass was sitting pressed right up against me.

Josh, sensing the shift, cleared his throat. "Alright, well, this just got weird. So let's talk about something else before Ghost starts throwing punches."

Drew grinned. "What should we talk about, then? The weather?"

"Maybe we should all take bets on Halston's next date," Niki teased.

I groaned, dropping my head back against the booth. "Can we not?"

Josh laughed. "C'mon. It's fun."

Ghost leaned in a little, his voice dropping just for me. "Oh, I'm very interested in this conversation."

I turned my head. "Of course you are."

He smirked, tilting his head. "So? You gonna let them pick for you, sweetheart? See if they can find someone who actually keeps your attention?"

I narrowed my eyes. "Why? Are you volunteering?"

Ghost's smirk deepened. "If I was, we wouldn't be talkin' about dating."

My breath caught in my throat. I hated him. I really did. But I also really fucking didn't. I forced a scoff. "You're disgusting."

Ghost grinned and leaned into my ear, whispering. "Yeah, but I'm your kind of disgusting."

A shiver shot through me. Fuck. He was right. I seriously wanted him right now.

Drew cleared his throat, interrupting whatever the hell was happening between us. "Alright, so, new topic."

Josh snorted. "Good luck with that."

I tore my eyes away from Ghost and forced my attention back on my beer, gripping it like it could somehow save me from acting on all the dirty things I wanted to do to the jackass next to me.

But Ghost? He wasn't done.

His voice dropped again. "You're thinking about it now, aren't you?"

I swallowed hard. "Thinking about what?"

Ghost's lips curved, his eyes burning into me. "About how it'd feel to fuck me."

I nearly choked.

I snapped my head toward him, my pulse slamming in my chest, glaring at him.

He just smiled. "I thought so."

I pressed my thighs together and hated myself for it. I was losing my will to fight this man.

Drew started talking again, pulling my attention back to the group. But even as I tried to focus, even as I pretended like Ghost wasn't completely wrecking my sanity, I felt his fingers brushing against my thigh under the table.

I froze. My breath skipped. But I didn't move.

And neither did he.

His pinky nudged higher, trailing heat along my skin. My entire body went taut.

I glanced at him, my eyes slitting. "You're playing a dangerous game."

He didn't even look at me. Just smirked, keeping his attention on the conversation like he wasn't lighting me on fire under the damn table right there with our friends across the way. "Nah. I'm just trying to see how wet I can get you with no one noticing."

My jaw dropped. My thighs clenched tighter. "You're such an asshole," I muttered under my breath.

His fingers inched higher. "Yeah. But you haven't stopped me."

"I hate you," I whispered, trying not to squirm, running a hand through my hair like it would somehow cool me down.

"Liar," he said simply, finally turning his head and looking at me. "You love it."

I glared at him, but my body was giving me away.

His voice stayed low, just for me. "Tell me to stop any time, Halston."

My lips parted. But nothing came out.

I didn't want him to stop.

And he knew it.

His fingers stayed right there. His touch was slow, warm, maddening. I didn't breathe. Didn't blink. My skin burned where he touched me.

Two can play this game.

I slid my hand up his thigh, teasing the edge of his zipper. His body tensed.

Then I turned, my eyes wide and innocent. "You good, Ghost?" I asked sweetly.

His jaw flexed. "Peachy, sweetheart."

I smiled. Then, ever so slowly, I dragged my fingers just a few inches higher.

Ghost's nostrils flared. I could see the effort it took for him to keep his expression neutral while everyone else at the table kept talking.

"Something wrong?" I asked, my voice syrupy sweet. "You look a little... distracted."

His eyes sliced to mine, sharp and heated. "Keep this up, sweetheart, and I'll bend you over this table in front of our friends."

My breath caught in my throat at that image.

"Test me, Tits." Ghost let out a soft growl under his breath, his eyes burning into mine. "I want you to."

I pulled back my hand lightning fast, reclaiming my beer like I hadn't just poked the bear.

Ghost smirked. He knew he had won. He always did. He knew how to threaten me to keep me in check.

After the conversation died down, we headed out.

Ghost led me out of the bar with a possessive hand on my lower back. My car was still at his place, so he was giving me a ride back to my house.

But the second we reached his truck, and I moved to grab the passenger door, he didn't unlock it.

Instead, I was suddenly pressed flat against the door, his body crowding mine, caging me in. His hands braced on either side of my head, and I barely had room to breathe.

"Ghost—"

"You like teasing me, huh?" His voice was rough, barely above a growl. "Getting me worked up under the table like that?"

I swallowed hard, staring up at him. His face was so close, his breath warm, his blue eyes burning with something between amusement and unholy hunger.

"I was just returning the favor," I said, even though my voice wasn't as steady as I wanted.

He chuckled. "You think that was a favor?" His fingers brushed my hip, sliding to the bare skin above my waistband. "Sweetheart, that was a challenge."

Before I could smart-mouth him, his hand closed around my jaw and he kissed me hard, his mouth taking possession of mine with heat. His tongue swept in, stealing any sense I had left. His hips pressed against mine, and I felt how hard, hungry and completely out of patience he was.

I slid my hands up around his neck and grasped his hair, tugging. For a second, I lost myself. I wanted more. I needed more. My body was begging, even if my pride wouldn't let my mouth say it.

Then he pulled back.

I was dazed and breathless.

Ghost smirked, brushed his thumb over my swollen bottom lip, and casually opened the truck door like he hadn't just made my knees go on strike.

I stood there, still trying to blink the lust from my eyes and calm my racing heart.

And then he leaned close and whispered, "I can play that game way better than you, sweetheart. Remember that next time you try that shit under the table."

He held my stare as he added, "Or at least finish what you start."

My mouth dropped open.

He smirked.

And I got in the truck before I did something dangerous like climb him like a tree.

Chapter 25

Alex had just come in from the barn, sweat beading along his brow as he grabbed a cold bottle of water from the fridge. I was mid-text when I looked up and asked, "Hey, have you seen Ghost?"

"Yeah," he said, twisting the cap off and chugging half the bottle. "He's out checking a break in the fence."

I straightened. "Damn it. I needed to ask him something. I tried to call him, but he's not answering."

"I'll take you." He was already walking back out, not bothering to wait for my protest. "Come on."

I grabbed my water and jogged after him, slipping into the passenger seat of the UTV as Alex called Ghost.

"Yo," Alex said into the phone. "Got Halston here. She's lookin' for you."

There was a pause, and then Alex grinned and handed me the phone. "He wants to talk to you."

I took it, already bracing myself. "Yes?"

"You coming to see me, Tits?" Ghost's voice slid through the speaker like velvet dipped in sin.

I rolled my eyes. "I need to talk to you."

His laugh was low. "Yeah, you do. You miss me already? That preview by the truck last night got you wantin' more?"

I glanced at Alex. His smirk said he could hear every word. "Jesus, Ghost," I said, my face warming. "Focus. Where are you?"

"How bad you wanna know, sweetheart?"

"Ghost..." My voice held a warning, but my body didn't get the memo. I was melting down already. I could feel the wet heat between my thighs.

"Come on, just beg me a little. That sexy mouth of yours is good for more than sass, right?"

I flushed, nearly combusting on the spot from the images that popped into my head. With a sharp exhale, I shoved the phone back at Alex. "He's all yours."

Alex laughed, clearly enjoying himself. "So, where are you?" He hung up a second later. "Southern fence line."

I sat back, trying to cool the fire Ghost lit in me with his dirty words. Why the hell had I wanted to come out here again? The man was a menace. He was going to kill me with sexual frustration alone.

We rolled up ten minutes later, and my heart did a full flip.

There he was.

Ghost stood near the fence line, shirtless, the sun beating down on his beautiful body, every muscle in his back and arms flexing as he worked. His jeans sat low on his hips, covered with sweat and dirt, his hat tipped low to block the sun.

The thing about a man who worked with his hands was it showed he wasn't some soft, soy boy. It made you think things like he was the kind of man who could keep you safe, the kind of man who could handle any situation that came up.

It was one thing seeing him fight, sweat covering his abs in the ring. But seeing him like this on his land, grounded, dirty, working with his hands? Seeing him like this was something else entirely. It was intimate. Masculine. Dangerous to my sanity. Because I'd had those strong, rough, very capable hands on my body, and that memory was making me want it again.

My pulse kicked into overdrive.

He turned toward us, and even from a distance, I could see the smirk forming on his lips when he saw me.

"'Bout done," he said to Alex. "I'll give Halston a ride back."

Alex threw me a look as he hopped back into the UTV. "Try not to die from heatstroke."

Or horniness, I thought grimly, swallowing hard as Ghost reached for the tool bag.

Now it was just the two of us. And I had no chance in hell of keeping my composure.

"Enjoying the view?" he asked, wiping the sweat from his brow with the back of his forearm, his cocky grin tugging at the corners of his mouth.

I folded my arms. "Please. I've seen you shirtless before."

"Mm," he said, straightening to his full height, towering over me. "But you knew I was talking about me and not the land."

Shit. He had me there.

My eyes rolled so hard I almost lost my balance. "You're impossible."

He smirked, grabbing a water bottle from the back of the UTV parked nearby and twisting it open. "Easier than you think, sweetheart."

I laughed. I couldn't help it. He had offered himself up many times, and stupid me hadn't taken him up on it... yet.

He smirked, shooting me that sexy wink I was seriously growing to crave.

I cleared my throat. "I came to ask you something."

"That so?" He took a long drink, his eyes still locked on me over the rim of the bottle. "Or did you just miss me?"

My pulse spiked. "I didn't say that."

"You didn't have to. Your thighs were staring at me the second you stepped out of the UTV."

I gaped at him, then looked down at my denim cutoffs. "My thighs were what?"

"You heard me." He grinned, stepping closer, stopping just shy of my space. "They missed me. It's okay. I missed them too."

"Ghost—" I started, but my voice came out breathy and all wrong. I cleared my throat.

He leaned in slightly, his voice dropping. "You gonna keep staring at my sweat, or you gonna tell me what you came out here for, sweetheart?"

My cheeks burned. I wanted him to take the power out of my hands and just kiss me. But he wasn't accommodating. He was way too good at holding out.

He grinned wider. "Guess I have my answer."

I sucked in a breath, trying to gather what little composure I had left. "Do you ever shut up?"

"Sure," he said, lowering his voice to that sinfully low tone, "but then you'd miss hearing all the things I wanna do to you."

My brain damn near shut down. My mouth opened and then shut again. I had nothing.

His grin only grew. "Now," he said, "what do you need to ask me, Tits?"

I cleared my throat, trying to get my hormones under control. "The group's heading out tonight."

Ghost arched a brow. "Yeah?"

"There's a food truck festival over on Market Street. And then bowling after. Niki thought it'd be fun." I shrugged, trying to sound casual, like I hadn't spent all morning thinking about seeing him since Niki said she was leaving it to me to invite him. She knew I had a crush on him, even though I had never said as much. "I figured I'd see if you wanted to come."

His mouth curved as he turned back to his work. "You came all the way out here just to ask me that?"

I rolled my eyes. "Don't flatter yourself. I called you, but you didn't answer. And Alex was headed this way."

Ghost smirked. "Right. Totally believe that."

I ignored him. "But clearly, you've got work to do, so... no big deal."

He twisted the last piece of fencing into place, testing the tension before stepping back and brushing the dirt off his hands. "Nope. Just about finished here." He turned that lazy grin on me again. "We can head back to the house. I can shower and be ready in less than twenty minutes."

"That's... quick. It'd probably take me a lot longer."

He tilted his head, feigning thoughtfulness. "Yeah, women usually do take longer."

I raised an eyebrow. "Are we talking about getting ready, or...?"

He grinned, stepping closer. "Oh, we're definitely not talking about getting ready, sweetheart."

My jaw dropped as the implication sank in, heat shooting through me.

Ghost leaned in, his voice a low, dangerous whisper. "But if you ever wanna test that theory, I'm happy to let you try to outlast me."

My breath caught in my throat, threatening to choke me. "You're such a menace."

"Mm-hmm. And yet here you are, making a special trip just to invite me out tonight," he said, brushing past me to grab his tools and load them into the UTV.

I stared at his back, willing my pulse to calm down.

What the hell had I just signed up for?

The UTV bounced over the uneven pasture, kicking up dust as we headed back toward the house.

I sat beside Ghost, trying not to stare at the way his inked forearms flexed as he gripped the wheel. Like the man needed to flex any more than he already had by just existing shirtless.

The breeze cooled my flushed skin, but it wasn't doing anything to calm the fire burning underneath it.

"You're quiet," he said, his eyes on the terrain.

I shrugged, trying to play it cool, like I wasn't just objectifying him with my dirty mind. "Just wondering if I've lost my mind inviting you to hang out tonight."

He laughed.

We rolled to a stop near the porch, and Ghost hopped out first, then rounded the vehicle and offered me a hand. I eyed it.

"Not gonna jump out and hope I catch you?" he teased.

"Not in these boots."

He grinned. "Shame. I was lookin' forward to a handful of your ass."

I smacked his arm but took his hand anyway, hopping down onto the dirt.

Ghost didn't let go.

I looked up at him, my pulse suddenly too loud in my ears.

"You sure you wanna bring me tonight?" he asked, his voice lower now. "You never know when I'll open my mouth and say something completely inappropriate."

I tilted my head. "I'm kinda looking forward to it."

That slow, sexy smile pulled at his lips again. "Good. I'd hate to disappoint."

His thumb brushed across my hand before he finally released it and turned toward the steps. "I'll be ready in twenty minutes."

"Right," I said, trailing behind him. "Because men are always so fast."

Ghost's blue eyes gleamed with wicked humor as he glanced back at me. "That depends. You talking about getting dressed... or getting off?"

Heat torched my body. "Jesus, Ghost."

"Didn't realize you were praying, sweetheart," he said, opening the door. "But I do like when you moan my name."

I stood there on the porch for a full five seconds before I gained my wits and headed inside.

Chapter 26

The food truck festival was super crowded.

Lights twinkled overhead, music played from a stage at the far end, and people swarmed the gravel lot like they hadn't eaten in days.

Ghost stood beside me, freshly showered, his black T-shirt hugging his chest, his jeans slung low on his hips, and a backward cap that made him look too damn good for my own sanity. His eyes scanned the trucks like he was plotting a mission. "Alright," he said. "What's first? Fried Oreos or sliders?"

I grinned. "Both. Obviously."

We made our way through the crowd, grabbing a few things from the trucks.

Niki waved us down from a table she and the others had claimed, a half-eaten taco in one hand and a cocktail in the other. "Took you long enough!" she called out.

Ghost smirked, leaning in close enough for only me to hear. "Pretty sure she thinks we were late because I had you bent over the sink."

I elbowed him, heat devouring me. "We were literally five minutes late."

"Plenty of time," he added.

I shook my head, biting back a laugh as we reached the table. The gang had already made the rounds, trays stacked with tacos, sliders, skewers, and God knows what else.

"Grab whatever you want," Josh said, his mouth full. "Except the corn dog. That one's mine."

Ghost gave me a look. "He's got dibs on a corn dog. Adorable."

"You're not allowed to mock anyone," I warned as we took a seat across from the others. "You've had three sliders already, and we're only ten feet in."

Ghost grabbed another. "I'm bulking."

I rolled my eyes and stole a bite of his slider.

He didn't protest, just watched me with that look, like he was two seconds from dragging me behind a food truck.

We were mid-bite when Jen sauntered up, already half-buzzed. "Well, well. Ghost and you together in public."

"Don't push it," Ghost said, not even looking at her as he reached for his beer.

Jen narrowed her eyes at me but said nothing, probably because Ghost was watching.

Niki leaned over. "Bowling after this, right?"

"Yeah," Josh said. "Place a couple of blocks away. Cosmic lanes, black lights, bad music. Total vibe."

"Sounds like a disaster," Ghost muttered.

I grinned. "So you're in?"

He met my gaze. "If you're going, I'm going."

God help me. I was already ruined. We were seriously in sync tonight, and it was so dangerous for my resolve, because I wasn't even fighting it.

The bowling alley had black lights casting everything in a neon glow and early 2000s pop blaring through the speakers that somehow worked.

Ghost raised an eyebrow as he looked around. "This is what we're doing with our night?"

I nudged him with my hip. "Don't act like you're too cool for glow-in-the-dark pins."

He smirked. "I am too cool for glow-in-the-dark pins."

"Mm-hmm. We'll see."

Josh, Niki, Jen, and Drew had already grabbed a couple of lanes. Ghost and I went to join them.

I was halfway through lacing up my neon blue rental shoes when Ghost dropped beside me on the bench.

He leaned in close, his voice low and smug. "You ever straddled something that didn't end in horsepower or heartbreak?"

I snorted, shaking my head. "Are you looking for an answer or just trying out lines you read on the bathroom wall?"

His grin stretched wide. "I don't need lines, sweetheart. You're already blushing, and I haven't even said the filthy part yet."

I smiled, tugging the laces tighter. "Maybe I'm just embarrassed for you. That was weak."

He leaned in a little closer, his lips brushing just behind my ear. "Give me five minutes and a flat surface, and I'll give you something worth blushing over."

My breath stalled. Damn him.

I faked a smirk. "Haven't we already had the conversation about being embarrassed for offering a woman a few minutes of pleasure? You better bring your game up, Ghost."

He laughed, then gave my thigh a light squeeze before standing. "Oh, I will. But just remember you asked for it."

And with that, he strutted back toward the lane, leaving me hot, bothered, and trying not to watch the way his jeans hugged his ridiculously hard ass.

Niki handed me a ball, totally oblivious. "You're up!"

I stood, trying to get my head back in the game and out of Ghost's pants as I approached the lane.

Ghost leaned back on the bench, watching me walk away like I was the show. I tried not to let it go to my head, but I was very aware of my own ass in my faded cutoffs as I bent to throw the ball down the lane.

I took my shot. The ball rolled smoothly down the lane... and right into the gutter.

Groaning, I turned back to the group. "This is rigged."

Ghost was grinning like he'd just been handed his favorite weapon. "Don't worry, sweetheart. Not everyone knows how to handle balls."

I shot him a smirk. "Oh, I know how to handle balls just fine. I just prefer ones that aren't made of plastic and disappointment."

Ghost choked on a laugh, his eyes lighting up with that wicked amusement that always made my stomach flip. "Damn, sweetheart. You trying to kill me or turn me on?"

I grinned, grabbing my beer. "Little of both."

Jen cleared her throat, probably annoyed we were flirting in a place she couldn't make a scene without looking unhinged. She threw her ball straight down the middle for a strike.

Of course.

"Wow, Jen," Ghost said, still not looking at her. "That was impressive. Guess all that practice aiming for attention finally paid off."

Drew snorted into his drink.

I nearly choked on mine.

Jen's smile tightened, but she didn't say a word.

Ghost just sipped his beer, smirking like he hadn't just delivered a verbal slap with a cherry on top. "Your turn again, Tits."

I took the ball with a raised eyebrow. "If I win, you owe me."

He smirked. "What do you want?"

I leaned in close, letting my voice dip low, sweet and daring. "More than five minutes on a flat surface, that's for damn sure."

Ghost choked out a laugh. Like he hadn't expected that. Like I'd surprised him.

He stared at me for a second too long, then let out a low laugh. "Well, damn... Look who finally decided to play."

I smiled, smug. "Try to keep up."

He shook his head, still grinning. "Oh, I plan to. But if I win..."

"What?"

His grin went downright wicked. "You'll know when I collect."

My stomach flipped. My aim might've sucked, but damn if the night wasn't starting to feel like a win already.

I bent down to grab my ball and felt the burn of his eyes before I even stood up. "You gonna help me aim or just keep staring at my ass?" I asked, straightening and glancing over my shoulder.

Ghost leaned back in his chair, sipping his drink, his eyes glued to my legs and the frayed edge of my denim cut-offs. "Not my fault you wore those shorts, sweetheart," he drawled. "You bend over like that again and we're gonna find out how much weight that changing table in the bathroom can hold."

Heat shot through me so fast it made my breath hitch. I bit my lip, trying to tame the grin that spread across my face, but failed.

"Wow," I said with a laugh, glancing at him over my shoulder. "That's probably the filthiest pickup line I've ever heard in a bowling alley."

He just smirked, his eyes heavy on me like he was already imagining it. "You're welcome."

I turned back toward the lane, rolling the ball between my fingers. "Careful, Ghost. Keep talking like that, and I might just take you up on it."

He sat up straighter, that cocky look faltering just slightly, just enough for me to know I'd landed a hit.

I smiled. Sweet and smug. "Try to keep your head in the game, big guy," I said. "Unless you want me to embarrass you."

Josh overheard and howled with laughter. "Damn, Ghost. Halston's got you on the run."

"She's got me something," Ghost muttered under his breath, just loud enough for me to catch.

My cheeks flushed, but I didn't look at him.

I was staring at his ass when he stood for his turn. His fitted jeans, that broad back, and that cocky swagger... yeah, I looked every damn time. Couldn't help it.

When he got a strike on his next roll, he turned with a shit-eating grin. "Told you, just needed the right motivation."

"Oh, please," I rolled my eyes. "Beginner's luck."

"We'll see who wins, sweetheart." He stepped closer, lowering his voice just for me. "You remember the stakes?"

Oh, I remembered. Winner got to collect a favor of their choice.

I arched a brow, lifting my chin. "You sure you wanna lose to me?"

He grinned. "Sweetheart, if I lose to you, I'll go down smiling."

"That's crazy for someone so competitive."

"I'm seeing it as a win-win," he said, making me smile.

Chapter 27

I t all came down to the final frame.

Ghost stood at the line, bowling ball in hand, the weight of the game on his shoulders. Eight pins or more and he'd take the win. Anything less... and it was mine.

He looked back at me, his eyes narrowing playfully. "You nervous yet, sweetheart?"

I leaned back on the bench, letting one leg fall open, the edge of my denim cutoffs riding up higher on my thigh. My legs were practically spread for him.

His eyes flicked down, right where I wanted them.

I smirked. "Not even a little," I said sweetly. "You sure you're not nervous?"

His eyes darkened. "You're evil."

I winked, shooting him the sweetest smile. "Only when it counts."

He rolled his shoulders and turned back toward the lane, trying to shake it off, but I saw the hesitation. The distraction. The way his grip shifted on the ball. His head might've been in the game before, but now? It was in the gutter.

He stepped forward, swung back, and let it fly. The ball veered sharply to the side. Straight into the gutter.

I slapped a hand over my mouth, trying to hold back my laugh, but it burst out anyway.

"No!" Josh shouted from the next lane over, cracking up. "The champ has fallen!"

I doubled over, laughing so hard I could barely breathe. "You had one job, Ghost!"

He turned, his eyes narrowing, a smirk tugging at the corner of his lips as he made his way back. His gaze locked onto me, pure mischief in those crystal blue eyes.

He dropped beside me on the bench and leaned in close, his voice rough against my ear. "Spread your legs like that again, sweetheart, and I swear to God, next time it's not the game I'm finishing."

My breath hitched in my throat, threatening to choke me.

I cleared my throat, biting back a grin. "Sounds like a win-win to me."

He chuckled, his hand brushing over my bare thigh like a warning. "Keep talking like that and I'm collecting my favor early."

"Uh, I believe I won. That means it's my favor," I reminded him.

He smiled at me. "Bring it on, sweetheart."

The walk to Ghost's truck was quiet, the air thick with tension so sharp it felt like it could snap at any minute.

We said goodbye to everyone in the parking lot.

By the time we climbed into his truck, my skin was buzzing, my heart beating so hard I could feel it in my throat. I didn't say anything. Neither did he. But I felt him.

His hand brushed mine when I buckled in, and it was like striking a match.

He started the truck but didn't put it in drive. Instead, he turned in his seat, draping one arm over the backrest as his eyes dragged over me.

"So," he said, that gravel-low voice laced with trouble. "You won."

I raised a brow, trying to play it cool even as my thighs pressed tighter together. "I did."

"I won't mention how you cheated," he said with a smirk.

I laughed. "You say cheated, I say using your interest in my thighs to my advantage."

Ghost let out a full laugh that said he was amused. "Fair enough." He leaned in just a little, his voice a slow burn. "You figure out what you want yet?"

God, that question. It did something to me. Or maybe it was the way he said it.

I swallowed hard, forcing a smirk I wasn't sure I could back up. "I'm still deciding."

He cocked his head, his gaze dropping to my mouth before dragging back up. "Better be careful, sweetheart. Wait too long, and I'll assume you're giving it to me instead."

Fuck, he was gorgeous. I seriously wanted to climb in his lap. "I said I'm deciding. Not donating."

His grin stretched wide and filthy. "Keep talkin' like that, and I might just offer to help narrow it down for you."

I bit my lip, then turned my body to face him, matching the heat in his eyes. "Be my guest," I said. "If you were going to narrow it down for me... what would it be?"

His voice dipped lower, darker. "Right now?" He let his gaze crawl over me, slow and unashamed. "My guess is you want your legs over my shoulders and your mouth too wrecked to keep running."

My breath caught in my throat, my entire body lighting up like a fuse.

God help me. I wanted that to be my answer.

Chapter 28

The longer we drove, the more the silence twisted into something darker, something hotter. I couldn't stop thinking about it, about him. About his mouth on me, about finally doing the thing I'd been fantasizing about since the moment I saw him.

By the time we turned down my street, my nerves were shot. "You wanna pull into the driveway?" I asked. He usually dropped me at the curb if he had to drive me.

His hand tightened just slightly on the wheel. Then he glanced over, a slow, devilish grin curling at the corners of his mouth. He didn't say anything. He didn't have to. I knew he understood exactly what I meant.

My pulse was racing. I wasn't thinking about tomorrow. I wasn't thinking about consequences or complications.

I was just thinking about him. We'd been flirting, teasing each other all day. And I was ready for the payoff.

Ghost pulled into my driveway and killed the engine. The second I unbuckled, I turned to him, but he was already reaching for me, his powerful hands grabbing my hips as I slid over to straddle him in the driver's seat.

His mouth took possession of mine, hungry and demanding, his hands moving up my thighs, under my shirt, across my back. I moaned against his lips, grinding against him as the truck windows fogged over with our heat. His tongue stroked mine, his grip possessive, rough, perfect.

The way he kissed me was obscene. Addictive.

He cupped my breast through my bra and bit down gently on my bottom lip. I gasped.

"I love how you taste, sweetheart," he whispered, his voice thick with want. "You always taste like trouble."

I brushed my lips against his. "If you like trouble..." I whispered back, "...you're gonna love my prize for winning the game tonight."

His eyes sparked, his hands stilling on my body.

I leaned in, my lips grazing his ear. "That thing you suggested earlier? Legs over your shoulders?" I pulled back just enough to meet his eyes, every word rolling off my tongue like a dare. "That's what I want."

For the first time all night, Ghost actually froze.

His smirk faltered, replaced by something darker, hungrier. His eyes searched mine.

"Please tell me you're not fucking with me," he said, his voice low, raw. "Because if you're playing, Halston, I swear—."

"I'm not playing, Ghost. That's what I want you to do to me."

"Fuck," he muttered, almost to himself, before gripping my hips harder and pulling me up against him. "You just made my night, Tits."

Then he kissed me again, harder this time, like he was already picturing exactly how he was going to give me what I asked for.

I gently bit his lip in return, and he groaned, lifting his hips beneath me. I could feel how hard he was, and it lit something inside me, something hotter, wilder.

I was about to whisper, "Let's go inside," when his phone rang.

He ignored it.

I kissed him again, hoping it wasn't important, and that it would stop ringing.

Then it did.

He pulled back. "We should take this inside, yeah?"

I could see he was giving me the out, letting me make the call.

"We should," I said softly. And I immediately saw the amused disbelief in his eyes, like he couldn't believe he'd finally gotten me to say yes.

"I mean, you do owe me a favor. I think I'd be stupid not to collect."

He chuckled, rubbing his thumb over my bottom lip. "I always pay my debts."

That sent a shiver through me.

Then his phone rang again.

"Fuck," he muttered. He looked. "It's Henry."

I froze. My stomach dropped. "If you answer that, we both know this night is over," I said flatly. "It's going to be an emergency. Henry wouldn't be calling you otherwise."

He stared at the screen. "I can't ignore it."

I gave him a small, understanding smile. "I know."

He answered. I watched his face shift almost instantly. "Shit... Did you call the doc?" he asked. "Alright. I'll be there as fast as I can."

He hung up. "One of the mares went into labor. It's not going well."

Called it. This sucked.

Ghost stared at me, frustrated. "Fuck. I'm gonna have a serious case of blue balls."

I gave a soft laugh. "Sorry."

He leaned in and kissed me again, slow and soft this time, like an apology. "I'd say I could come back over after, but I don't know how long it'll take. Could be all night."

I nodded. I couldn't keep the disappointment from creeping into my voice. "Yeah. Probably. I hope she's okay."

"Me too." He exhaled, running a hand through his hair.

"I'll let you get out of here," I said, climbing off his lap and grabbing the handle to the passenger door.

"Probably better this way anyway, right?" he said behind me.

I paused as I was about to close the door. "What? Why?"

"You'd regret it tomorrow."

My heart clenched. "Are you saying you'd make me regret it?"

"I'm saying you might regret messing with me. You're a good girl." And that did it.

"Good night, Ghost," I said coldly as I slammed the door shut.

He rolled the window down. "Halston. Hey, come on. Don't be like that. I just—"

I flipped him off without looking back and stormed to my front door, slamming it shut behind me. I locked it and leaned against it, breathing hard.

Fuck him. And fuck Jen. I was so tired of the good-girl label, like it was some kind of weakness. Not to mention the way he kept flipping on me. He turned me on, then didn't have a problem pushing me away. Probably better this way? You couldn't promise a girl a prize for winning, then say something shitty like that. Asshole.

My phone buzzed. It was Ghost. I hit ignore.

Then, I opened my contacts and tapped Niki.

She answered on the first ring. "Hey, what's up?"

"Hey," I said, my voice still shaking. "You still want me to go on that date with that guy tomorrow? The athletic guy?"

There was a pause. "Yeah. I mean, if you're up for it."

"I'm up for it," I said firmly.

Chapter 29

I adjusted my harness, barely paying attention as Rick fastened his.

He was talking. He was saying something about proper foot placement and grip technique, but my focus was still on last night and how lousy the night ended. We were so close... Then he hit me with that bullshit where he turned me on, then shut me out. Wasn't it the woman who was supposed to be the tease?

Fuck him all to hell.

I spotted my so-called friends walking into the rock-climbing gym like it was their regular Saturday hang.

I froze. Seriously?

I excused myself and headed toward them, hands on my hips. "What are you guys doing here?"

Josh grinned. "Rock climbing sounded fun."

Drew smirked. "We thought we'd join in."

I rolled my eyes. "No. You wanted to spy. Why are my dates always a spectator sport?"

Of course, it was Ghost leading this disaster.

He gave me his signature cocky smirk, arms crossed over his broad chest. "We're just making sure the guy doesn't try anything inappropriate."

"Yes, exactly," Niki chirped, all fake innocence.

Jesus. I exhaled sharply, shooting them a glare before turning and heading back to Rick, who was watching the interaction with mild curiosity.

"Friends," I told him.

He nodded. "They can join us if they want. I can teach them too."

I snorted. "I doubt they want to learn."

"Speak for yourself, sweetheart." Ghost's voice slid over me smooth as silk as he joined us.

I shot him a look, but the bastard just winked at me.

"You can help me with mine," I said to Rick, mostly just to ignore Ghost.

Rick nodded, grabbing the harness and stepping close to help me into it.

He was adjusting the straps, his fingers brushing my hips, moving slowly.

Ghost's fingers suddenly wrapped around my wrist, tugging me away from Rick, his voice dropping to that low, dangerous rumble that always got me into trouble. "Do you remember what I said if you went on another date?"

My face flushed hot.

Ghost smirked. "I see you remember." His gaze flicked to my lips, then back to my eyes. "Do I need to show you who you belong to in front of everyone?"

My breath hitched. "You wouldn't dare."

His smirk deepened. "Wouldn't I?"

I clenched my jaw. "You don't date. You wouldn't want anyone to see us together."

"I will if I have to, Halston." He leaned in. "I think you know that. When it comes to winning or proving a point, I do whatever I have to."

And he was right. I knew he'd do it. He'd kiss me in front of the whole damn gym, in front of Rick, in front of our friends, just to prove a fucking point.

I swallowed hard. "Hey, it's yourself you'd be outing."

Ghost chuckled, dark and low. "I'll take you down with me."

I exhaled sharply. "Why? What did I do?"

His eyes locked onto mine, his voice dipping even lower. "You let him touch you, sweetheart."

His gaze was scorching, making it impossible to breathe properly. "We're not together, Ghost." I barely got the words out. "You sleep with random women. What do you even want with me?"

His expression didn't change, but the tension in his jaw tightened. "You don't know?"

My pulse skyrocketed. "No."

His voice was a rough whisper. "I'm waiting for you to give in to me, Tits. I'm waiting for you to break, for you to want me so bad you can't stand it. For you to beg me for it."

Torched. My panties were drenched, my entire body on fire.

"You had that last night, Ghost. I practically threw myself at you."

"I had an emergency. I had to go," he insisted. "She made it through after twelve intense hours, by the way. I didn't get to bed till nine this morning, so I'm running off like three hours' sleep."

"I'm glad she's okay," I said sincerely. "And I'm sorry you didn't get any sleep."

"You wanna make it up to me? You could ditch this guy and come back to my place with me." His hot breath grazed my ear as he leaned in. "I'll wear you out so good you won't remember why you were mad."

I ignored the shiver that shot down my spine because I was still pissed. "Except for the fact that I'd regret it, according to you, right? If you don't want a good girl, then why do you keep messing with me?" I whispered, my breath shaky, my chest rising and falling too fast.

His eyes burned into mine. "That's not what I said, Halston." His voice was gravel and heat. "I love that you're a good girl."

I stood there with my arms crossed.

He leaned in even closer, his mouth barely grazing mine, his breath hot against my lips. Then he gave me a filthy smirk, like he already had me on my knees in his mind. "Because the best part about a good girl is how fucking sweet she sounds when she finally breaks and begs to be wrecked."

I gasped, and my legs nearly gave out, my hand shooting to his shoulder for support.

The bastard shot me that wink-smile combo, then turned around and walked away like he hadn't just wrecked my entire damn existence.

Rick stepped up beside me. "You ready?"

I blinked, shaking off my lust. "What?"

"To climb."

I swallowed, glancing at Ghost, who had rejoined our group, arms crossed, watching with sharp amusement.

No way in hell was I letting Rick touch me again.

"No," I said, pulling back when he reached for my gear. "I can do it."

I didn't miss the nod of approval Ghost shot me. Then the bastard laughed. He knew exactly how to control me into doing what he wanted.

Rick's eyebrows dipped, clearly not liking that answer. But he stepped back. "That guy your boyfriend?" he asked, tilting his head toward Ghost.

I sighed. "No. Ghost doesn't date."

But I could tell by the way Rick's jaw tightened, by the way his eyes flicked back toward Ghost, that he didn't quite believe me.

He threw an up nod toward Ghost. "Wanna race?"

I stiffened. Oh, shit.

Ghost's smirk was pure menace. "Sure," he said smoothly.

Then, without hesitation, he grabbed a harness and strapped it onto himself, fast as hell, like he'd done it a thousand times before.

I exhaled sharply. This can't be good.

Niki nudged me, grinning like a kid at Christmas. "Rick is fighting for your attention."

I scowled. "What he's doing is asking for trouble."

Josh snorted. "He's obviously jealous of Ghost."

I crossed my arms. "He doesn't even know me well enough to be jealous."

Drew rubbed his hands together, grinning. "This is getting good."

I turned my attention back to the guys. They locked themselves in, ready.

The entire gym was watching now.

Rick had talked a big game about being an expert climber. But I already knew. I already fucking knew Ghost was going to win. I just knew it. Because I knew Ghost.

The second the instructor blew the whistle, they were off.

Rick moved fast, faster than I expected, his form solid, his confidence clear. He had done this before. That much was obvious.

But what he hadn't accounted for?

Ghost.

Ghost didn't just climb. He moved fluid, calculated, like every muscle in his body was built for this exact moment. He didn't hesitate. Didn't fumble. He didn't second-guess his steps.

While Rick was focused on form, Ghost was focused on speed.

And it was over before it even began.

Ghost hit the top first, tapping the buzzer with a lazy smirk before turning and looking down at Rick, who was still scrambling to catch up.

The entire gym erupted, some cheering, some laughing, all of them watching as Rick finally tapped the buzzer several seconds later, breathing hard.

Josh whistled. "Damn. That wasn't even close."

Niki grinned, nudging me. "Your date's ego is gonna take a hit."

I exhaled sharply, watching as Rick stared at Ghost, clearly not expecting to lose, especially not by that much.

He climbed back down first, his expression clearly irritated as he unhooked himself from the harness.

Ghost took his time. Because of course he did. Egomaniac.

He climbed back down like he had all the time in the world, unhooking himself and stretching his arms out like he wasn't even slightly out of breath. Then, just to be a smug bastard, he turned toward me, flashing that damn smirk, running a hand through his messy hair.

I scowled. He was so fucking pleased with himself.

Josh chuckled. "That was painful to watch."

Drew smirked. "Painful for Rick."

I looked toward Rick, who was still shaking out his hands, clearly frustrated.

He turned to me, forcing a small smile. "Guess your friend is a natural."

My friend. I swallowed. "Yeah."

Rick exhaled, rubbing his jaw. "Didn't see that coming."

Neither did I. I mean, I thought he was going to win. I knew he was ridiculously competitive. I knew he was strong as hell. But watching him win so effortlessly? I kind of felt bad for Rick.

Rick glanced at Ghost, then back at me. "You wanna grab something to eat?"

I hesitated. Because honestly? I was done with this date. I had already known Rick wasn't my type, but now I had Ghost in my head, smirking like he owned every single thought running through my mind. And I guess he did.

But before I could answer, Ghost spoke for me. "She's not hungry."

My head snapped toward him. "Excuse me?"

Ghost shrugged. "She's got plans."

I crossed my arms. "Oh, do I?"

He grinned. "Yeah. With me."

Rick looked between us, his eyes narrowing slightly. "Oh. So, you two are a thing?"

I opened my mouth... I had no idea what to say.

Ghost beat me to it. "Something like that."

My stomach dropped, my breath caught, my entire body reacting to those three little words.

Rick gave me a look, like he was trying to figure me out, and then finally nodded. "Got it."

And just like that, he turned and walked away.

I exhaled sharply, running a hand through my hair. Jesus.

Ghost just looked pleased as hell.

I turned to him, my eyes blazing. "What the hell was that?"

His smirk didn't fade. "What?"

I narrowed my eyes. "Something like that? Are you serious?"

He tilted his head, feigning innocence. "Would you have preferred I say nothing?"

I clenched my jaw. "Yes."

Ghost chuckled, stepping closer, his voice low and teasing. "Liar."

I sucked in a sharp breath. He was too close. Too damn smug. Too... him. "I am not lying," I bit out.

Ghost just smirked. "Sweetheart, I know you." His voice dropped, turning rough, dangerous. "I know exactly how wet you are right now just thinking about how much you liked hearing me say that."

Oh. My. God. Heat flushed through me, a pulse of arousal hitting me so fast, so hard, it was actually infuriating.

I let out a sharp, humorless laugh. "Wow. That ego must have its own zip code."

He didn't flinch, just kept looking at me like he was two seconds from backing me against the wall and picking up where we left off last night.

But I was still pissed.

"You're seriously delusional if you think I have plans with you," I said simply. "I might never have plans with you again."

His smirk faded just enough for me to see the flicker of something else behind it.

"Because I'm not in the habit of getting strung along by a guy who spent months riling me up, teasing me, making promises he couldn't even keep. You remember that promise, right?" I stepped in closer, my voice sugary sweet. "Legs over your shoulders, remember? Or was that just another one of your lines?"

He said nothing. His jaw tightened. His eyes flashed.

But I wasn't finished. "So yes, Ghost. I am hungry. But I sure as hell won't be ordering from a menu that forgot how to deliver."

Then I turned and walked away, leaving him standing there with that unreadable expression and the fire I hoped was burning in his gut.

Because I knew damn well the humiliation of last night was still burning in mine.

Chapter 30

The taco bar was packed, the neon lights buzzing faintly overhead as we slid into our booth.

Plates piled high with tacos, chips, and salsa covered the table, along with a pitcher of margaritas that Niki insisted we needed.

Josh smirked as he took a sip of his drink. "So, Halston, how was your date? Think Rick is the one?"

Drew snorted. "Yeah, the one who got his ass handed to him by Ghost."

I rolled my eyes, grabbing a chip. "It was fine."

Niki raised an eyebrow. "That bad, huh?"

I sighed, dunking the chip into the salsa. "He was nice."

Ghost chuckled, leaning back in his seat. "Sweetheart, that's code for 'never gonna happen.'"

I ignored him and turned back to Niki. "He was just... not for me."

Drew grinned. "Not your type?"

I hesitated for a second too long.

And of course, Ghost caught it.

His eyes held a spark of satisfaction as he reached for a taco. "Maybe she just prefers a man who knows how to win."

Josh barked out a laugh. "Damn."

I exhaled sharply, shaking my head. "I knew you were going to win."

Ghost stilled, his taco halfway to his mouth, clearly not expecting that answer. "Yeah?"

I shrugged. "You're too damn stubborn to lose."

Ghost grinned, his deep chuckle rolling through the space between us. "That might be the best compliment I've ever gotten."

Drew smirked. "Kinda romantic, actually."

Josh snickered. "Nothing says romance like 'too damn stubborn to lose.'"

Ghost just smirked at me, tapping his fingers against the table like he was filing that information away.

Niki sighed dramatically. "Well, that's a shame. Rick was kind of cute."

Drew grinned. "Not after that climb."

Josh nodded. "Man looked like he saw his whole life flash before his eyes when Ghost beat him."

"He should've trained harder," Ghost said, completely unfazed, and took a bite of his taco.

I rolled my eyes, taking a sip of my drink. "You really are insufferable."

Ghost leaned in slightly, his voice low enough for only me to hear. "And yet, you can't stop thinking about me."

My stomach flipped, heat shooting up my neck. He was right. I shoved a taco into my mouth just so I wouldn't have to answer.

Ghost chuckled, reaching for his drink, looking way too satisfied with himself.

I set my taco down and leaned in just enough that our shoulders brushed. "You should be careful looking so smug," I said, my voice low but clear. "It's easy to act like you're on top when no one at the table knows you bailed when it counted."

His smile faltered. His eyes flicked to mine, sharper now. More focused. "Is that right?" he murmured.

I tilted my head, my smile sugary sweet. "I mean, anyone can talk a big game. Doesn't mean they know how to finish."

His nostrils flared just slightly, and I knew I'd hit the mark.

Josh laughed at something Drew said across the table, oblivious to the quiet tension suddenly crackling between us.

Ghost leaned in, so close I could feel the heat off his body. "You wanna test that theory, sweetheart?"

I met his gaze head-on. "Nah. I already did."

Then I popped the rest of my taco in my mouth and looked away, smiling as he sat there, for once, with nothing to say.

He didn't react immediately. Just sat there, sipping his drink like he hadn't just been called out.

But then he leaned in, his shoulder brushing mine. The hair on the back of my neck stood up before he even opened his mouth.

His fingers tapped the side of his glass, that familiar rhythm he always fell into when he was holding something back.

He tilted his head, his lips near my ear now so close I could feel the warmth of his breath. "You think you're punishing me by walking away?"

My stomach clenched.

A cocky smile curved on his lips, cutting deeper than it had any right to. "You're just proving how badly you wanted me between your thighs in the first place."

Right there, in the middle of a goddamn taco bar with laughter all around me, I forgot how to breathe.

Because I did want him. And he knew it. Worse? He was right. It was the reason I was so pissed about it.

And the smug, satisfied look on his face told me he'd felt the exact moment I realized it.

That bastard.

The conversation kept rolling, mostly at my expense. I should have expected nothing less.

Niki leaned forward, still not over it. "So, Halston, did Rick at least try to make a comeback after getting wrecked?"

Drew snorted. "Doubt it. He probably went home to rethink his life choices."

Josh shook his head, grinning. "I mean, the dude challenged Ghost. Who the hell thought that was a good idea?"

I sighed, picking at my plate. "He wasn't a bad guy."

Ghost smirked, sipping his drink. "Just not me."

I shot him a look. "Jesus Christ."

Josh chuckled. "He's not wrong, though."

Drew grinned, leaning back. "Yeah, let's be real. You weren't into the guy."

I sighed dramatically. "Would you all like me to fill out an official form stating my lack of attraction? Maybe send out a press release?"

Niki grinned. "We just like watching you get flustered."

I let out a loud breath, sipping my margarita. "Well, congrats. You're all thriving."

Ghost chuckled, his eyes locked on mine, a slow, knowing smirk stretching across his face. "Some of us more than others."

My stomach tightened. I refused to give him the satisfaction of reacting.

Jen, who had been quiet for most of the conversation, spoke up, her voice carefully neutral. "So, Halston, if you're so picky, what exactly are you looking for?"

I blinked at her. "What?"

She shrugged, holding her drink. "What's your ideal guy?"

I hesitated. I couldn't say Ghost. And I had nothing else, because he was all I thought about.

Josh grinned. "Yeah, Halston. Spill."

Niki smirked, clearly enjoying this. "I mean, we know it's not the hiking dude."

Drew nodded. "Or the soy boy."

Ghost just sat there, watching me, waiting, his blue eyes damn near daring me to say what we both already knew.

I forced a casual shrug. "I don't know. Someone who's confident, funny, doesn't play games."

Ghost smirked. "Sounds a lot like me, sweetheart."

I narrowed my eyes. "It also sounds a lot like a psychopath." As soon as the words were out, I cringed. I'd basically just insulted myself by listing off traits I wanted in a man, then called them psychopathic. The man drove me insane.

Josh snorted. "So, you're saying you like a little bit of chaos?"

"Eloquently put," I said with a laugh. "I'm saying I'd like to eat my damn tacos in peace."

Drew grinned, looking at Ghost. "She's dodging the question."

Ghost smirked, his eyes locked onto mine. "She's dodging a lot of things."

My body burned. I focused hard on my plate.

Ghost let the conversation drift, watching me like he could see straight through me.

Then, out of nowhere, he dropped it. "I want you to rebrand the ranch."

I froze, my chip halfway to my mouth. My eyes shot to his, slowly lowering it back onto my plate. "Are you serious?"

Ghost leaned back, nodding. "Completely."

I studied him, looking for the catch. "This isn't just to mess with me some more?"

He grinned. "We can do both."

I let out a sharp exhale, shaking my head. This man was going to be the death of me.

Chapter 31

The kitchen at the ranch was warm, filled with the smell of fresh coffee.

Henry sat across from me, flipping through the rough sketches I had laid out on the table. He studied them with a serious expression, his lips pressed into a firm line.

"We need somethin' clean," he finally said, his voice deep and thoughtful. "Classic, bold. None of that overly fancy shit. People should see it and immediately know what we do here."

I nodded, tapping my pencil against my notepad. "Right off the bat, I was thinking something rustic but sleek. Maybe a branding-iron-style emblem. Strong, traditional, something that'd look good on whiskey bottles and horse trailers alike."

Henry hummed, nodding slowly as he considered it. "Yeah, that's good. I like that. But you should run whatever you come up with by Ghost. He's the one who gets the final say."

I bit back a sigh, knowing this was coming. Ghost might let Henry run the day-to-day at the ranch, but this was his land, his business. If

I were designing something to represent it, I'd have to deal with him sooner or later.

Yes, I was still pissed at him for bailing on me Friday night. Not because he had to rush home and help the horse, but because of the copout shit he'd said to me.

Henry stood, stretching, before grabbing his hat off the counter. "He's out back. I'll let him know you're workin' on it."

I nodded. "Sounds good."

He tipped his hat slightly, then walked out, leaving me alone in the kitchen with my laptop and sketchpad.

I rolled my shoulders, tugged my hair into a messy bun, and got to work.

I was deep in concentration, adjusting the lines of the branding iron design, when the scent of leather and pure, infuriating arrogance filled the space.

I didn't look up. I didn't need to.

Ghost leaned against the counter, watching me. "Well, well. Look at you, all serious and hardworking."

I ignored him. Pretended like the sound of his voice didn't send a slow, unwelcome heat shooting through me.

"Henry says you're working hard on the design for my ranch," Ghost mused, his voice full of that deep smugness that always made me want to slap him... or climb him.

He pushed off the counter and strolled over, moving with that easy, confident swagger that made it impossible not to look at him.

I refused to. I kept my focus on my screen.

"You working on a design just for me?"

I rolled my eyes, clicking away on my laptop. "For the ranch."

"Which is mine," he pointed out.

I sighed. "Yes, Ghost. For your ranch."

He exhaled dramatically. "So, what? You're not even gonna ask for my professional input? I am, after all, a man of refined taste."

I snorted. "Your idea of branding is a bottle of whiskey and a middle finger."

He laughed.

I arched a brow, still refusing to look at him. "So, you came in here to give me your professional design opinion?"

Ghost chuckled low, and then he was right behind me. "Nah. I came in here to fuck with you."

I exhaled, keeping my focus on the screen, but my pulse was already kicking up.

He wasn't touching me. Not quite. But he was close enough that I could feel his body heating my back. The smell of Ghost and sweat and pure temptation clouded my thoughts.

His voice came out all smug, and too close to ignore. "You still mad at me about running out on you the other night?"

I kept my eyes on the screen, my fingers poised over the keyboard. "Nope."

"I'm not buying it, sweetheart," he murmured, and I could feel the grin in his voice.

I clicked twice. Deliberate, focused. "I'm not mad. I learned a valuable lesson."

Ghost's voice dropped, smooth and cocky. "And what lesson would that be, sweetheart?"

I finally turned and met his eyes over my shoulder. "That I should stop confusing your mouth with your intentions. That I should learn to deal with the disappointment."

His smirk twitched, faltered just enough for me to see it.

I turned back to my laptop, letting the words hang between us.

There was a pause. One beat. Two.

Then his voice dropped again, rough. "You keep calling it disappointment, Halston... but every time I get close, you let me."

My breath caught.

"I touch you, and your body forgets every reason you're mad. I whisper in your ear, and you come undone." He leaned in, his mouth near my neck, his voice a sinful whisper. "Tell me I'm wrong."

I didn't move. Didn't breathe. Because I couldn't. I couldn't tell him he was wrong.

And he fucking knew it.

So, I did the only thing I could do. I got back to work, turning my attention back to my screen.

I stiffened as he leaned in further, his breath warm against my neck. "That serious little face," he whispered, his voice like pure heat. "Bet I could get it to fall apart real fast."

I swallowed hard and kept typing. I didn't react or turn my head.

His voice dropped. "That serious little face. Makes me wonder if you'd look the same way ridin' me."

My fingers fumbled on the trackpad.

Shit.

Ghost smirked. "That a little twitch, baby?"

I clenched my jaw. "No."

"Pretty sure it was."

I ignored him and kept working. I didn't want him to see how much he was getting to me.

But Ghost was relentless.

He leaned over, watching my screen, his breath just barely brushing the side of my neck. "Y'know," he mused, his voice smooth as silk, "I like watching you work. So damn focused. Wonder if you'd make those same little faces—"

"Ghost," I warned.

"—if I had you bent over this table."

I fucking choked. On my own spit, trying to inhale.

Ghost grinned, pleased with himself.

I cleared my throat, refusing to look at him. "Not interested," I lied, clicking my mouse aggressively.

Ghost chuckled, stepping back. "Sure, sweetheart. You're not interested. That's why your ears are pink. And I guess you wouldn't be interested in getting fucked senseless in my bed?"

I groaned, rubbing my hands over my face. "I hate you."

"Nah," he said with that damn smirk still in his voice. "You just hate how much you like me."

I wanted to yell at him to take me to his bed and fuck me senseless, just to call his bluff, just to see if he'd find a reason to back out again.

"You're real bad at hiding it, you know," he said.

My eyes were glued to my screen, pretending I wasn't hanging on every syllable. "Hiding what?"

Ghost chuckled, the sound dangerously satisfied. "How bad you wanna turn around right now."

I swallowed.

His hand brushed my shoulder, teasing. "But you won't," he breathed, his voice hot against my ear. "Because you think you have self-control."

I clenched my jaw, fighting back the shiver trying to crawl up my spine. "I do have self-control."

His fingers trailed slowly down my arm before retreating. "You sure about that?"

I clenched my hands into fists.

He laughed, stepping back, and I turned to glare at him.

Big mistake. Because he looked smug as hell, his blue eyes taunting, his arms crossed over his chest, his body one hundred percent relaxed while I sat there on fire.

Ghost tilted his head, taking me in. "There it is."

I narrowed my eyes. "There what is?"

"That shitty poker face."

I groaned. "I do not have a shitty poker face."

He smirked. "You do, baby. You so do. I can read you like a damn book."

I loved when he called me baby. I kept that to myself. "God, you're annoying."

He exhaled dramatically. "And yet, you love it."

"Nope. Not even a little."

Ghost let out another low chuckle. "Keep lying to yourself."

I straightened my shoulders, giving him my best unimpressed look. "Do you ever shut up?"

He grinned. "Not when I'm enjoying myself."

I rolled my eyes. "Well, enjoy it somewhere else."

Ghost chuckled. "Mm. Think I'll stay right here."

I shook my head, trying to focus on the design, but Ghost wasn't going anywhere. Neither was the way he made me feel. He just stood there, arms crossed, muscles flexed just enough to be a problem.

My eyes swept over him. I had been in his lap. I'd felt those muscles wrap around me, had felt the way he moved, the way he—

Nope. Not thinking about that.

His eyes darkened, his smirk lazy and knowing. "Oh, sweetheart. You just keep proving my point."

"Which one? There are so many."

He laughed. "You know you still want me."

I swallowed, my stomach doing an embarrassing little flip. I seriously did have a shitty poker face. "I'll never be a one-off woman," I shot back.

His eyes shifted. "Is that why you keep resisting me?" He laughed, a deep resounding laugh, like he had just figured out the solution to world hunger. "I thought maybe you were playing hard to get. Oh, Tits," he said, his voice low, gravelly. "I got your number now."

Fuck. The man and his strategizing. I tried daily, hell hourly, to keep from acting on the dirty thoughts this man provoked. I knew eventually he was going to break me. And, damn it, I think I just handed over the blueprint.

He was smirking at me, letting me know he had me all figured out. Then he turned away and headed for the back door. "Don't work too hard, Tits."

I rolled my eyes, but my lips betrayed me, twitching into a smile. Even though it was dangerous as hell. I was dying to see what he was going to do next.

Chapter 32

T he barn smelled of fresh hay and the deep, earthy scent of horses.

Warm light filtered through the wooden slats, casting golden streaks over the row of massive, muscular animals watching us curiously from their stalls.

I wanted to check out the stables and the horses to get a feel for the heart of the ranch before I got too far on the design.

Ghost walked ahead of me, his broad shoulders stretching the fabric of his shirt, his confident stride making it clear this was his domain. But honestly, what wasn't? The man seemed comfortable in any situation.

He reached out to pat the dark bay stallion in the first stall, whispering something low that I couldn't hear over the pounding of my own heart. He looked too damn good here. Like he belonged in a western magazine spread, all rugged and effortlessly in control.

"You actually taking an interest in ranch life, Tits?" he teased, casting me a knowing smirk over his shoulder.

I rolled my eyes, pretending my face wasn't already heating up. "It's research for the rebrand. And I like animals."

Ghost's lips curved into something wicked. "Good to know."

"Why is that good to know?"

His smirk deepened. "Because if you're into big, strong beasts, I should be right up your alley."

He chuckled, clearly pleased with himself.

I didn't even blink. "Only if they come with a warning label and a leash."

"Oh, sweetheart," he drawled, his eyes gleaming with mischief. "Careful. Say things like that and I'll start thinking you want to be handled."

I gave him a slow, unimpressed once-over. "Please. If I wanted to be handled, I'd order something off Amazon. Comes quicker and doesn't talk back."

He barked out a laugh, shaking his head as he tapped on the stall door.

As we walked, Ghost pointed out different horses, telling me which ones were bred here, which ones were trained for competition, and which ones were retired champions. His voice was smooth, confident, and full of pride.

Then he stopped in front of a stall, gripping the wooden beam casually, and gestured to a gorgeous black stallion with a gleaming coat and sharp eyes. "This guy right here? Triple Crown winner. Fast as hell. His sperm is worth a fortune."

I raised my eyebrows, impressed. "Wow."

Ghost shot me a lazy smirk. "Almost as valuable as mine."

My eyes went wide, and he just stood there grinning, looking like a damn devil in faded jeans.

"Oh my God," I shook my head, smiling.

He laughed, tilting his head with that dangerous glint in his eyes. "What? I'm just saying if I ever decide to put a price tag on it, I could make a killing."

I smacked his arm, but he just caught my wrist, holding it easily as his smirk widened. "Admit it," he said, his voice low and teasing, "you thought about it for a second."

"I did not," I lied, trying to yank my arm back.

Ghost chuckled, finally letting me go, but not before trailing his fingers down the inside of my wrist, leaving a tingling path of heat in their wake.

"Relax, Tits," he said, turning back toward the stall. "Just trying to educate you on how valuable a good stud is."

I groaned, shaking my head hard, but I couldn't stop smiling. This man was killing my self-control.

"I'm ready for the rest of my tour," I said, trying to avert my attention from Ghost.

"Absolutely. Right after we ride."

I froze. "Ride?"

"The horse, Tits... Unless that's an invitation?"

The image of me riding him popped into my head.

"You're thinking about it now, aren't you?"

"Yes," I said with a snarky tone. "Right along with whatever else you dreamed last night."

He laughed.

I eyed the massive horse in front of me like it might decide to swallow me whole at any second.

Ghost stood beside me, his arms crossed over his broad chest, watching me with an amused smirk that only grew the longer I hesitated. "Something wrong, Tits?"

I shot him a look. "Do you see the size of this thing?"

He gave the horse a pat on the side, his calloused fingers stroking over its dark, shiny coat. "He's a horse, not a damn dinosaur."

I crossed my arms. "Easy for you to say. You probably learned to ride before you could walk."

Ghost shrugged. "Pretty much."

"And you're a giant compared to me."

He laughed. "You are pretty short."

I sighed, still staring at the towering stallion. "I've never done this before."

Ghost let out a low chuckle. "No shit. I could tell the second you walked in here with those wide eyes, like you thought we were about to sacrifice you to the ranch gods."

I glared at him. "I don't think that."

He smirked. "Then why do you look like you're about to bolt?"

I bit my lip, shifting on my feet. "Because this thing is huge, and I enjoy my spine being intact."

Ghost stepped closer, his voice dropping into that low, taunting drawl that always made my toes curl. "Don't worry, sweetheart. I'll be right behind you the whole time... makin' sure you don't fall."

I sucked in a breath, my stomach flipping violently at the way he said it, like he was talking about something else entirely. Because I was starting to see sex in everything, just the way he did.

The man was making me feral.

Chapter 33

With Ghost's hands on my waist, he hoisted me up onto the saddle, his grip firm, effortless, sending a rush of heat straight through me.

I let out a squeak, gripping the saddle like my life depended on it.

Ghost stepped back, his smirk in full force. "Damn, Tits. Didn't know you could make that noise."

I shot him a glare. "Ghost."

"What?" he grinned. "It was cute. Do it again."

I laughed despite myself.

Ghost chuckled, stepping up beside me to adjust the reins in my hands.

I pressed my lips together, trying to ignore how close he was, how his hands brushed over mine, how his thumbs grazed my wrists as he adjusted my grip.

He leaned in. "Relax, sweetheart. You're stiffer than a damn fence post."

"You try relaxing when you're sitting on a moving mountain."

Ghost chuckled again but didn't back away. "That's why I'm here. Just follow my lead."

Then, without warning, he swung himself onto the horse behind me, his solid, muscled body pressing into my back, one arm slipping around my waist to hold the reins with me.

I froze. Oh. Oh, no. This was worse.

I wasn't worried about falling off anymore. I was worried about the way his body felt against mine, the way his breath brushed my temple, and the way his grip on my waist made my entire body tingle.

Ghost leaned down, his lips dangerously close to my ear. "Still nervous?"

I swallowed hard. Very nervous. But I wasn't about to admit that. So, instead, I cleared my throat and said, "Nope. Totally fine."

Ghost chuckled, and I felt it. Everywhere.

"Sure, you are, Tits," he said.

With a light nudge of the horse, we started moving.

The gentle sway of the horse beneath us should have been calming. It should have made me feel in control, like I could actually do this without making a fool of myself. But with Ghost's body pressed against my back, his arm casually resting around my waist, and his warm breath fanning against my ear, calm was the last thing I felt.

I was tense, my grip on the reins too tight, my breath coming too fast.

Ghost chuckled behind me, low and knowing. "Relax, Tits. You're ridin' a horse, not holdin' on for dear life on a rollercoaster."

I forced my grip to loosen. "You're not the one in the front, responsible for steering."

Ghost made a noise in the back of his throat. "Yeah, but I'm the one responsible for keepin' you in the saddle if you panic and decide to launch yourself off."

I twisted slightly to look at him. "That's not going to happen. You see how far it is to the ground?"

He laughed. "Don't look down. If that helps."

"It doesn't."

Ghost chuckled, his breath hot against my ear, making my pulse trip over itself. "I'm just sayin'," he continued, his voice thick with a smirk I could hear. "I've seen people panic and do some real dumb shit."

"I'm not people."

"No?" He shifted slightly, his arms tightening around me, making me hyper-aware of just how close he was. "So you're tellin' me that if this big boy starts movin' a little faster, you won't scream and grab onto me like I'm your last hope?"

"I wouldn't scream."

Ghost made a sound. "Oh, sweetheart, I think we both know that's not true."

I froze, my whole body flushing at his words, at the way he said them, with that low, cocky promise. "You're such an ass," I replied, staring straight ahead.

He laughed again, his fingers brushing my hip, teasing. "Yeah, kinda."

I opened my mouth to call him a name, but then he squeezed my waist, guiding me into a gentle turn as we moved farther into the open pasture.

And just like that, all the fight in me evaporated. Because, damn him, I liked this, liked being here, liked the warmth of him at my back, the solid weight of his body against mine, the thrill of riding a horse for the first time while he was the one in control.

The sky overhead was softening to gold, streaks of orange and pink melting together as the sun lowered toward the horizon. The cool breeze carried the scent of fresh grass, damp earth, and horses, but I was far more aware of his scent. He smelled of something masculine, like leather, sweat, and that delicious Ghost smell that did bad things to my thoughts.

I exhaled slowly, trying to keep my voice steady. "So, do I get a grade for my first lesson?"

Ghost made a thoughtful sound. "Hmm... I dunno. You did squeak when I put you in the saddle."

"That should not count against me."

"Eh, depends. Was it out of excitement? Or pure, unfiltered terror?"

I rolled my eyes. "A mix."

He laughed. "Alright, then you get a solid B."

I turned my head, raising a brow. "Not even an A-minus?"

"Nah." He leaned in closer, his lips almost grazing my ear, sending a shiver down my spine. "But you might be able to earn some extra credit."

Heat flared in my stomach, my fingers tightening around the reins. "You and your mouth," I muttered under my breath.

Ghost laughed again, his grip on my waist tightening just slightly, just enough to make my pulse kick up. "You love my mouth, sweetheart."

I clenched my jaw, refusing to respond. He wasn't wrong.

He steered us toward the small wooden bridge that led across the creek, with the sound of water bubbling gently beneath us. The rhythmic clip-clop of the horse's hooves against the planks filled the air, and for a second, the world felt peaceful. Just the two of us. Just this moment.

Then he opened his damn mouth.

"Y'know," Ghost said casually, his voice a low rumble against my back, "you sittin' in front of me like this, ridin' together, feelin' all that body heat between us... I gotta say, sweetheart—"

"Don't," I warned.

Ghost ignored me completely, leaning in closer, his lips barely brushing my ear, his tone wicked. "This is probably the closest you'll ever get to ridin' me."

My entire body went up in flames. "Ghost!"

He just threw his head back and laughed, the sound deep, cocky, and completely unrepentant. "Oh, come on, Tits," he drawled, his tone pure sin, "you were thinkin' it."

"I was not."

"Liar."

I groaned, my entire existence reduced to a puddle of embarrassment and unwanted arousal.

Okay, it wasn't exactly unwanted.

But as we rode, his words looped in my head on repeat, an annoying little echo I couldn't shake. 'This is probably the closest you'll ever get to ridin' me.'

What the hell did that mean? Was it just another one of his cocky little comments, meant to get under my skin, make me blush, make me fumble for words? Or was he actually saying I'd never get to ride him?

Because if that was the case... I hated it. I hated how much it bothered me. And I hated even more that my brain wouldn't let it go. I should have fired something back at him. Something snarky... anything to wipe that smug look off his ridiculously good-looking face.

Chapter 34

I didn't let it drop. I couldn't.

So, I twisted slightly, just enough to glance back at him, my expression deceptively calm despite the absolute riot of emotions happening inside me. "What do you mean, the closest I'll ever get to riding you?" I shot out before I thought better of it. "Like you don't want me to?"

He let out a low chuckle. "Still thinking about that, are you, Tits?"

His words infuriated me even further. He didn't answer my question. "Oh, I get it now," I mused, tapping a finger to my chin like I was deep in thought. "You're the type that talks a big game but doesn't actually deliver. Classic overcompensation. Gotcha."

Ghost's grin faltered for half a second.

Then he laughed, his arms tightening slightly where they rested around me. "That so, sweetheart?" His voice had an edge now, like I'd just stepped into dangerous territory.

I shrugged, pretending to be unimpressed. "I don't know, Ghost. It's just kind of funny. You keep talking about me riding you, but it's starting to sound like wishful thinking."

That got him.

His grip on the reins tightened, his thighs flexing against mine, and then his mouth was right back at my ear, his breath hot, his voice a velvet-covered threat. "You really wanna test that theory, Tits?"

Oh, shit. He called my bluff.

I swallowed, keeping my face neutral even as my pulse hammered out of control. "Just calling it like I see it."

Ghost exhaled a sharp laugh, shaking his head. "Careful, sweetheart."

"Or what?" I challenged.

He leaned in, his nose grazing my jaw, his voice full of promise. "Or I'll make damn sure you don't just ride me. You'll be fucking ruined by me."

My breath caught in my throat, my brain short-circuiting. I couldn't even form a response.

Ghost kicked the horse into motion again, leaving me completely wrecked and stewing in my own dirty thoughts.

Then he shifted in the saddle, adjusting me slightly, pulling me back onto his thighs. Just enough that...

Holy. Hell. I felt him. All of him. Hard. Thick. Nestled perfectly beneath me, right where I wanted him to be, just without all the damn clothing in the way.

My entire body locked up as heat flared through my core. I swallowed hard, trying desperately to focus on something, anything other than the fact that I was sitting directly on top of Ghost's very obvious, very sizable erection.

And, worse, he wasn't moving away. No. He let it sit there, let me feel all of him, let the moment stretch long enough to make me acutely aware of the fact that he was well aware of it, too.

Oh God. I needed to get my head out of the gutter, needed to focus on literally anything else: the trees, the horses, the fucking clouds in the sky. I needed to redirect away from the heat radiating off him, the way his breath felt against my neck, or the fact I was painfully, shamefully turned on right now.

But it was all I could feel. His warmth was against my back, his thighs under mine as I practically sat in his lap. His fingers were still resting lazily on my hips, like he had all the damn time in the world. And his cock, thick and unforgiving, was cradled against my most intimate spot, like it fucking belonged there. And at that moment, I wanted it to belong there. I wanted to strip away our clothes and feel his warm skin against mine. I wanted his hands on my hips, helping me, guiding me as I rode his...

Shit. Redirect.

I let out a slow breath, steadying myself, willing myself not to react. Pretending I didn't want to roll my hips just a little and chase the friction I knew would feel so good.

Ghost chuckled behind me. Low, deep, and dark.

He knew. Of course, he fucking knew. Because Ghost read me like an open book. Because my body was betraying me. It always did when he was around.

"Somethin' wrong, Tits?"

His voice was rough and amused, and it made my entire body shiver. I clenched my jaw, forcing my voice to come out even. "Nope. All good."

Ghost hummed, dragging his fingers slowly along my waist, just enough to make my skin prickle. Those hands on my waist. I seriously wished I were facing the other direction right now, straddling his thick thighs.

"Really?" he murmured. "Because you feel real tense all of a sudden."

I swallowed. Dying. Absolutely dying. "Just, uh... adjusting to the movement of the horse," I said.

Ghost made a thoughtful sound, his fingers tightening slightly on my hips. "You sure about that?"

I nodded quickly. "Yep. Totally sure."

He laughed, his body shifting again, his hips pressing forward just slightly.

I took a sharp breath. God help me.

"Mmm," he said, his lips way too close to my ear. "Coulda sworn you were sittin' real pretty in my lap just now, squeezin' your thighs together like you're tryin' real hard not to do somethin' about it."

I shivered, heat spiking through my entire body, my mind racing to think of something, anything to say that wouldn't immediately make me ignite. And that sexy drawl he had that always thickened when we were at the ranch. Between that, his damn voice, the way we were pressed together, and the filthy things he was saying to provoke me, I was fighting the urge to turn around and take advantage of him.

And Ghost was just getting started.

"You know, sweetheart," he said, his fingers brushing up my ribs, barely skimming the underside of my breasts, "if ridin' a horse with me gets you this worked up, I can't imagine what ridin' me would do."

My breath caught, a strangled, mortified sound leaving my throat.

Ghost just grinned, shifting his grip on the reins, pulling the horse to a stop.

I wasn't sure whether I was relieved or disappointed. But one thing was painfully clear. I was in so much trouble with this man because I didn't know how much longer I could fight my lust for him.

I exhaled sharply, trying to get my damn heartbeat under control.

"You survived," he said, his voice filled with mock pride as he leaned back slightly, his hands still resting lightly on my hips.

I rolled my eyes. "Barely."

He chuckled, his breath teasing the back of my neck. "Now, was that so bad?"

I resisted the urge to groan. The riding part? Not bad, because I knew he would keep me safe. The part where Ghost was pressing up against me, wrecking my ability to think straight, making me question every last shred of my self-control? Yeah, that was beyond bad.

I cleared my throat, reaching for the saddle horn to dismount. "Okay, lesson over. Let me down."

Ghost didn't move. His fingers tightened slightly on my waist. "Lesson's over when I say it's over, sweetheart."

A shiver ran through me. I needed to distance myself from him. Now. "Ghost," I warned.

He sighed. "Fine. You wanna get off? I'll help you."

Before I could protest, Ghost slid an arm around my waist and lifted me clean off the saddle and set me on the ground with him, my body pressed against his for a brief, breath-stealing moment.

I barely had time to steady myself before his hands settled on my damn hips again, his grip firm, possessive. "See?" he said, that lazy, cocky smirk curving his lips. "Didn't even let you fall."

Oh, I was falling all right. Just not in the way I wanted to admit.

I stepped back quickly, putting space between us before I did something insanely stupid, like drag him down into the hay and make bad choices. "I think I'll stick to ATVs," I said, dusting myself off, trying to dust the lust off with it.

Ghost laughed, shaking his head. "Yeah, 'cause those don't put you in nearly as much danger."

I shot him a pointed glare. "It's not the danger I'm worried about."

His grin widened. "No?"

I walked right into that. See? Mush. My brain was still back there with my thighs on his. Feeling his hard...

I spun on my heel, heading for the barn doors. "I need water."

"Need somethin' wet, huh?" Ghost called after me, his voice dripping with heat and laughter. "You sure you're not already wet, sweetheart?"

I groaned. "You and your damn mouth!"

His laughter followed me, and as much as I wanted to be annoyed... I wasn't. Because I was wet, and he knew it. I was intensely turned on.

And I was already wondering when he was going to use that mouth on me next.

Chapter 35

I grabbed the handle of the front door, taking a deep breath before pushing it open.

Ghost texted me earlier, saying he wanted to see the finished logo and go over any possible changes.

I didn't expect to walk in and see her sitting at his kitchen island. A gorgeous redhead. Effortlessly pretty.

Jealousy hit me like a lightning bolt.

I wasn't the jealous type, had never been. But seeing her sitting there, close to Ghost, laughing at something he'd said, had me clenching my jaw so hard I thought it might snap.

Ghost looked up. "Halston, this is Candace. She's my social media manager. She manages my online presence for the fights and the ranch."

I forced a smile, shifting my attention to her. "Well, that explains a lot. No wonder his socials are full of thirst trap posts."

Candace grinned. "Got to get the ladies to the fights somehow."

I gave a small laugh, keeping my tone light. "No, I completely agree. If I were managing it, I'd do the exact same thing."

"Well, it's nice to meet you, Halston." Candace smiled warmly. "I've heard a lot about you."

That made me pause. My gaze flicked to Ghost, but he was already watching me, a small smirk playing at his lips. "All bad, I'm sure," I said, shooting him a glare.

Candace laughed. "Sounds like she knows you pretty well."

That shouldn't have made my entire body go rigid. But it did. The idea of her knowing Ghost, really knowing him, did something ugly to my insides. But I didn't let it show.

I slid between them, setting my laptop on the counter, needing something to focus on. "Alright, here's the logo."

The screen lit up, displaying the gold 3D emblem. It was a bold, rustic design featuring a stylized horse's head within a circle. Above it, in striking letters, was the name Legacy Ranch.

Beneath the logo, in a smaller, elegant but strong typeface, was the tagline: Gold Blood. Elite Breeding.

Candace's eyes widened. "This is incredible."

Ghost leaned in, his eyes scanning the design, his jaw tightening slightly before he gave a slow nod. "Gold Blood—like blue blood, but superior?"

"Exactly."

Ghost exhaled, shaking his head. "That's fucking brilliant. I love the wordplay."

A small flicker of pride warmed my chest. "I'm glad you like it."

"Elite breeding," he said. "Damn, Halston, you've outdone yourself."

Hearing him say that in that voice, all gravelly and low, mixed with the high praise, did things to me. I took a breath. "Your invoice will reflect my expertise," I said, making him laugh.

Candace laughed too, then clapped her hands together. "I can't wait to get to work on your next post. This is so great. I can do so much with this."

"Yeah, it's damn good." Ghost turned to me. "Send that to her so she can get started."

I pulled out my phone. A second later, his text came through, sending me Candace's contact information. I forwarded the logo over, then set my phone down. "There, I sent it."

Candace checked her phone and smiled. "Perfect. Thank you, Halston."

"You're welcome."

They immediately started talking business again, discussing strategies, post ideas, things I should not have been irrationally annoyed about. But the more they spoke, the more irritated I became.

I couldn't watch it anymore.

I pushed away from the counter, grabbing my laptop. "I'll let you get back to it."

Ghost's eyes snapped to mine. "We're almost finished. Stay. We'll get that payment taken care of."

I didn't want to stay. But I did. Clenching my jaw, I sat down, waiting while they wrapped things up.

Candace finally stood and grabbed her bag. "It was nice to meet you, Halston."

"Yeah, you too."

Candace seemed nice. She really did. And it wasn't her fault if she'd fallen into Ghost's trap and slept with him. He was irresistible with his stupid good looks, that lethal body, and that vulgar mouth that turned me into sexual mush. Candace got a pass. It was Ghost I was pissed at.

The second she walked out the door, Ghost turned to me. "Let me Cash App you the money. I really do love what you came up with."

"Great, Ghost. I'm glad you love it." The words came out sharper than I had intended.

Ghost's brows lifted. "Whoa. I said I loved the logo."

"And?" I snapped.

"Then why the hell are you pissed?"

I crossed my arms. "When am I not pissed? I swear it's my default around you."

He tilted his head slightly, studying me. "No. This is something specific. You weren't pissed when you walked in."

Damn him. Why was he so intuitive when it came to me? He paid attention to everything I said, every move I made. It had to be how he was so good at fighting. He studied his opponents like a poker player studies his opponents for tells.

His eyes narrowed slightly, and then he grinned. "That's it," he said slowly. "It's about Candace."

I clenched my jaw. Shit.

Ghost's smirk deepened. "You're wondering if I fucked her."

"Ghost, I don't give a shit who you fuck."

His grin stretched wider. "Oh, sweetheart, it's so obvious that you do."

"You fucking wish."

He laughed, shaking his head. "I love that your mouth is getting more and more vulgar the more time you spend with me."

I scowled. "You bring it out in me."

"Am I off base, though?" He stepped closer, closing the distance between us. "Because every muscle in your body is tense as hell right now."

I clenched my jaw harder, willing my body to relax.

Ghost leaned in, his lips hovering right next to my ear. "Careful, sweetheart," he whispered. "You're gonna crack that pretty little jaw."

I swallowed hard.

He pulled back just enough to look me in the eye, still dangerously close, his lips inches from mine. "It's eating you up inside," he mused, his voice smooth. "Wondering if I fucked her."

"It is not," I ground out, hating how easily he read me.

Ghost smiled. That smug, knowing, infuriating smile. "Don't worry, sweetheart. I haven't fucked her," he said. "I don't mix business with pleasure. Business is business."

"Good for you," I said, relieved, though I refused to show it. "Although that's not exactly true now, is it?"

He tilted his head, waiting.

"You've been trying to screw me for months," I said coolly. "And yet, here we are. You just hired me to do your rebrand. Business and pleasure, all tangled up in one smart-ass package."

Ghost smirked and took a slow step closer, his eyes steady on mine. When he spoke, it was serious in a way I didn't expect. "Maybe I just wanted a reason to keep you around without giving you one more excuse to run."

That shut me up.

I felt the words hit somewhere I didn't want to acknowledge, like he'd reached past my sass and found the part of me I kept locked up when it came to him.

He watched me for another second, letting the silence settle between us.

Then, as casually as if he hadn't just knocked the wind out of me, he added with another smirk, "Also, your ass looks real good on my property."

I scoffed, trying to shake off the punch his words landed. "So, hiring me was just your way of... what? Keeping me on a leash?"

His smirk deepened, but this time it wasn't mocking. "No leash, sweetheart," he said, stepping in until the air between us practically snapped with tension. "If I wanted you tied up, you'd know."

My breath caught.

His voice dipped lower, rougher. "You're not mad anymore, are you?"

I opened my mouth, then closed it. Because I wasn't.

I swallowed hard.

His eyes flicked to my chest, his smirk growing. "Your breathing's all fucked up, sweetheart."

I scowled, hating that he noticed.

He leaned in even closer, his breath warming my lips. "Are you ready to stop fighting me now? We both know you want me, that you've wanted me ever since I wrapped my arms around you at the range."

"You're fucking delusional," I said, but my voice lacked heat.

Ghost's gaze dropped to my lips.

I tried not to look at his. I failed.

He ran his tongue across his lower lip, wetting it slowly, and I took a sharp breath.

His smirk deepened. He leaned in... and the bastard wet my lips for me with a slow, torturous swipe of his tongue, pulling a soft moan from my throat.

Then he kissed me slow, deep, his tongue teasing, coaxing, owning me.

When he pulled back, he studied my face. "I'm gonna make this real easy for you, sweetheart." His voice was low, edged with pure dominance. "You can walk away right now. Go home. And we'll do this little tease dance again later."

I didn't move.

He watched me like a predator who already knew he'd won, his blue eyes dark, wicked. His fingers slid down my arm, teasing just enough to send a shiver rolling through me.

His lips curved into a knowing smirk. "You're still standing here." His voice was rough. "Should've walked out that door five seconds ago, sweetheart."

I lifted my chin, desperate to hold on to some control. "Maybe I'm just waiting to see what you'll say next."

Ghost made a noise deep in his throat, a dark chuckle that I felt between my legs.

His fingers traced back up my arm, his touch so damn light it was infuriating. "Nah, sweetheart," he said, tilting his head. "You're waiting for me to touch you. You're standing here, breathless as hell, hoping I'll take control, pin you against that wall, and make you beg for my cock."

A sharp gasp left my lips, heat slamming through me so hard I felt dizzy.

Ghost just grinned, confident and filthy. "You want me to take the decision out of your hands."

My eyes darted away, then back to him. How did he always know what I was thinking?

Then he leaned in, right at my ear, his breath hot. "Tell me you want me."

My stomach clenched. I couldn't breathe.

His hand slid up my waist, caressing my skin beneath my shirt. I swear to God my knees almost gave out.

I swallowed hard. "You said you already know I do."

Ghost pulled back, watching me, his smirk downright devastating now. "Say it anyway."

I opened my mouth to argue, to hold on to a shred of pride. But I couldn't. Because I did want him. So fucking bad.

I lifted my eyes to his, my pulse hammering. "I want you."

Ghost dragged his thumb across my lower lip, watching me, owning every breath I took. "That's my girl." His voice was low, dark, so fucking smug.

And I lost it. I grabbed his shirt and yanked him closer, sealing my mouth against his.

Ghost groaned deep. He'd been waiting for this, waiting for me to give in. His hands gripped my hips hard, dragging me against him, pressing me into his body, all heat, all muscle.

I couldn't think. I didn't want to think. I was so tired of thinking when it came to fighting my feelings for him. All I knew was I was desperate, starving, and he was the only thing that would satisfy the ache clawing inside me.

"Fuck, Halston." Ghost's voice was raw against my lips, his hands already moving, making me melt.

One second my feet were on the ground. The next he was lifting me, my legs wrapping around his waist, my back hitting the wall as his mouth devoured me. It was rough, messy, fucking desperate. Exactly how I was feeling.

And when he pulled back just enough to grin down at me, his eyes burning, his breath heavy, his cock hard as hell against my core, he smirked. "Knew you wanted me."

Chapter 36

"You smell good," he said against my throat. "Sweet. Like sin."

I let out a shaky breath. "I think you have that backwards."

He chuckled low. "No, sweetheart. I'm corrupting you, not the other way around."

And God help me, I wanted to be corrupted. I spent so much time wanting this ever since I first saw him, ever since he started teasing me with his filthy, sexy, vulgar mouth.

Ghost set me down in his bedroom. My feet hit the floor, the back of my thighs brushing against the end of the mattress.

He pulled back, his movements controlled but urgent as he pulled my shirt up over my head and tossed it behind him. He reached behind me with his right hand and unhooked my bra with a flick of his fingers.

His mouth was on me before the lace hit the floor, his tongue flicking over my nipple as he sucked it into his mouth.

I gasped, my head falling back, pleasure shooting through me.

"Fuck," he murmured, biting down gently before rubbing it with his tongue. "Your tits are fucking perfect."

Heat shot through me, sharp and insistent. He was relentless. Kissing, biting, licking his way down my stomach before dropping to his knees in front of me. "Kasper."

"I like my name on your lips," he whispered, hooking his fingers into the waistband of my leggings.

He dragged them down along with my panties, and grabbed my hips, helping me to lie back on the edge of the bed, my ass barely hanging off.

Before I could even catch my breath, he spread my legs wide. I pushed against his chest, blush and heat shooting from my head to my toes.

But he left no more time for modesty. "Let me wreck you," he said as he sealed me with his mouth, hot and demanding.

I nearly lost my damn mind.

"You're soaked," he whispered, licking up my center before sucking my clit between his lips. "So fucking wet for me."

"Yes," I gasped, my fingers tangling in his hair as his tongue flicked and swirled, driving me insane.

He wasn't lying when he said he knew how to use his tongue. He ate me like a man starved, groaning against me like this was his favorite thing to do.

I whimpered. It was too much. And not enough.

He sucked harder, his fingers digging into my thighs as he held me in place.

"Kasper," I gasped, already on the edge.

He hummed against me, driving me higher, the vibrations making my toes curl, causing me to cry out.

Then, just when I thought I'd fall apart, he stopped. I made a sound of protest, but before I could form words, he was standing again, pulling me up off the bed, against his body.

His mouth covered mine. I tasted myself on his tongue and moaned, my fingers fumbling for the snap on his jeans.

"Needy little thing," he muttered, amused.

I blushed, and he chuckled, his cocky grin making my knees weak. Then he unfastened his jeans and pushed them down, revealing a big bulge in his black boxer briefs.

My pulse kicked into high gear, and I could feel it in my ears.

He discarded his boxer briefs and dropped them on the floor. My mouth went dry. He was bigger, thicker than I'd ever seen, and hard. Fucking perfect.

"Like what you see?" he asked, smug.

I rolled my eyes, even as my pulse pounded between my legs.

He smirked. "Yeah, you do."

Then he was lifting me off the floor, laying me further back on the bed this time.

He leaned down to grab something from the floor, and I pulled up to see where he'd gone. Then I saw him grab a condom from his wallet.

He quickly tore into it and rolled it down the length of his cock, then crawled onto the bed and pried my thighs apart. No hesitation. No patience.

He pushed into me, stretching me, sliding in until he could go no further, filling me. "Fuck," he growled. "You're so goddamn tight."

His body pressed down, and he slammed inside me. I cried out, arching against him. He didn't build up to it. He fucked me hard from the first stroke, his hips snapping forward.

"This what you wanted?" he said, his teeth grazing my jaw. "This what you've been thinking about?"

I moaned, my nails digging into his shoulders. It was exactly what I'd been consumed with. Thoughts of him. Us.

"You feel that?" he growled, his thrusts deep and ruthless. "You're all fucking mine."

He kept up the pace, his hips rolling forward, his body rubbing into me, teasing my clit.

I shattered around him, pleasure exploding through me so fast, so violently, I didn't even have time to brace for it. But the pleasure didn't stop. The ripples kept coming as he continued to drive into me.

And I couldn't stop telling him how good it felt, the words just spilling out of me like secrets I couldn't keep any longer, practically screaming. "Oh, Kasper! Oh. My. God!"

He groaned, slamming into me harder, dragging it out until I was begging him to never stop.

His jaw clenched. His thrusts became erratic, desperate. Then he cursed, his body tightening, and I felt it, the hot rush of his release as he groaned into my neck, gripping me tightly, stroke after stroke, until he slowed to a stop.

Ghost dropped beside me, his chest rising and falling with steady breaths.

I didn't get up right away.

I just lay there, trying to catch my breath, feeling the way my body hummed. My pulse was still pounding, the aftermath of him settling deep in my bones. He had shattered my expectations, wrecked me, just like he promised. I'd had orgasms before with my vibrator, but this had been so much better, more intense.

Ghost was beside me. One arm was stretched above his head, the other resting low on his stomach. His eyes were fixed on the ceiling, with a faint grin playing at the corner of his mouth. "Fuck," he said, breaking the silence with a breathy chuckle. "You went so fast."

I groaned and threw a hand over my face. "I couldn't help it."

He turned his head toward me, his voice smug but low, coated in that signature Ghost-brand teasing. "You didn't even let me try to ruin you. I barely got warmed up."

I peeked through my fingers and gave him a look. "Ghost."

"I didn't even break a sweat," he added with a cocky grin, his voice full of fake offense.

I smacked his chest lightly, making him laugh harder, the kind of laugh that vibrated beneath my hand and made my heart twist just a little.

This wasn't just sex. It was something else, something more intense than I ever expected. The kind of thing that left an imprint and made me almost forget who we were and what this was supposed to be.

But I knew who he was. Kasper. Ghost. One and done. And I refused to be the girl who stayed when she shouldn't.

I took a slow breath, forcing myself to move, slipping out from under the sheets as quietly as possible, my feet dangling over the side of the bed.

Ghost didn't stop me. Didn't reach for me. Didn't say a damn word.

But I felt him. I felt his eyes on me as I sat up, as I reached for my clothes. I didn't dare look at him. Because if I did, I might see something in his expression that made me hesitate. And hesitation? That was dangerous.

The bed shifted as he moved, sitting up, rubbing a hand down his face, down his beard. Then he said, "Gonna get a shower," and stood, heading for the bathroom.

He didn't tell me to stay. Didn't so much as glance back. And I wasn't expecting him to. Hoping? Yes.

But the way he left the bed first, the way he said it so simply, like this was just another night, like I was just another fuck, sat wrong in my chest.

I forced myself not to think about it. Not to feel it. Instead, I pulled on my clothes, grabbed my phone and laptop, and let myself out before I could do something stupid.

Like wonder if he expected me to be gone...

Chapter 37

I almost turned down a day out with my friends.

I took a rideshare to the go-kart track, the same as I had the day before when I left Ghost's house in shame after leaving his bed.

I hadn't wanted to face him because I didn't want to deal with the awkwardness of sneaking out of his house like a one-night stand, even though that's exactly what I was to him. I'd known it before I ever let him touch me, before I let him ruin me in the best possible way.

So, I did what I always do. I played it cool. I told myself it was fine. That I could compartmentalize. That I could show up today with our friends, act normal, and pretend like I wasn't still feeling the sting of reality slapping me in the face.

Ghost was a one-and-done guy. I knew that. And yet, I still felt like an idiot for how much it bothered me. And I wasn't even sure if it was because I genuinely enjoyed hanging out with him all the time, or if it was because I still wanted to keep fucking him.

Maybe a little of both.

So, as I walked up to meet everyone at the track, I plastered on a neutral expression, refusing to let anyone, especially him, see a damn thing.

Ghost was already there near the starting line, looking like he had no business being that attractive in just a T-shirt and light blue jeans.

His sharp blue eyes locked on me the second I got close, flicking down my body like he was cataloging every detail, like he could still feel me under him.

My breath caught in my throat, remembering everything we did, how good it'd felt.

I pushed it aside.

I greeted everyone, made jokes, pretended like I wasn't shaken, hurt, pissed off, completely at war with myself over the way things ended yesterday.

And Ghost, he acted completely normal. Which only made me want to hit him.

"About time you showed up, Tits," Ghost said, crossing his arms over his chest, his signature smirk firmly in place. "Glad your rideshare driver didn't steal you away. Hate to see you get snatched up before I have the chance to beat your ass on the track."

I rolled my eyes. "Charming as always."

Jen's voice cut in. "You took a rideshare here?"

She sounded entirely too interested in that little fact. Or maybe it was the fact that Ghost knew I'd taken a rideshare that she was so interested in.

I shrugged. "My car is at Ghost's house. It's having issues."

Jen's eyes flicked between me and Ghost, her brows pulling together just slightly. She was putting pieces together, but I wasn't about to help her finish the puzzle.

I wasn't in the damn mood.

Ghost looked entirely too entertained by the whole thing.

He definitely noticed that I wasn't looking at him. I wasn't engaging in our usual back-and-forth. Which only made him push harder. "You didn't have to rideshare, sweetheart," Ghost mused, his voice smooth as sin. "I would've picked you up. Hell, you could've just stayed at my place and saved yourself the trouble."

I finally met his gaze, and his grin deepened, like he could see right through me. I fed the cat today and then left immediately without saying anything to him, without seeking him out. He knew I was off, and if I knew Ghost, he knew exactly why.

I forced a carefree smile, my voice dripping with fake sweetness. "That's cute, Ghost. Really. But we both know that wouldn't have been necessary."

His brows ticked up. "That so?"

"Yep."

He watched me, his expression unreadable.

And then he just grinned again, shoving his hands into his pockets like I hadn't just tried to dismiss him. "Whatever you say, sweetheart."

Why did something so little make me feel bad about being a bitch? I didn't want to be mean to him. I knew what I was getting into with him. Everyone told me exactly who he was. It wasn't like I hadn't expected exactly what happened.

"Alright, enough flirting," Drew said.

"Who's flirting?" I snapped.

Ghost smirked. "You are."

I shot him a glare.

He winked.

I narrowed my eyes at him, but he just found that hilarious. And his damn smile almost pulled a smile from my lips. I had to fight hard to keep it down.

When it was time to gear up, Ghost sidled up next to me, watching as I strapped on my helmet.

His voice was low. "Hope you're ready to lose."

I huffed, adjusting the strap beneath my chin. "We'll see about that."

His eyes flicked to my lips, then back to my eyes. "We will."

And then he was walking away, climbing into his go-kart like he hadn't just set my whole damn body on fire. He knew exactly how to twist me to his will. My stupid, traitorous body was a total pushover for this man.

The race was fast, reckless, and filled with way too much shit-talking.

Drew almost spun out on a sharp turn, Jen got stuck behind Josh, and Ghost was in the lead the whole damn time. Until I caught up.

I could see the moment he realized I was about to pass him. His head turned, his lips curling into a wide smile.

Then? He cut me off.

I was about to yell something that probably would have gotten me kicked out of the facility when we crossed the finish line with Ghost in first place, me right behind him.

Smug asshole.

I pulled off my helmet, fully prepared to tear into him.

Ghost was already out of his kart, waiting for me, grinning.

"That was dirty."

He put a hand to his chest, mock offended. "Dirty? That was strategy."

I scowled. "That was being a dick."

His grin deepened, his eyes sliding down my body. And then, just to piss me off even more, he said, "Sore loser is a good look on you, sweetheart. Almost as good as the one you had yesterday under me."

I gasped, and he laughed.

The absolute menace.

After the race, everyone was still hyped up on adrenaline, talking about going to grab food.

I should have been focused on that. But I could feel Ghost watching me.

And then, just like that, he grabbed my wrist, tugging me aside and out of earshot of everyone else.

He turned me to face him, his voice lower, serious. "I didn't plan on saying anything about it," he admitted.

My stomach tightened. "But?" I asked, my voice steady despite the war inside me.

He exhaled, rubbing the back of his neck. "But I was disappointed as fuck when I got out of the shower and you were already gone." His eyes pinned me in place. "I was planning on a second round. Thought you'd join me in the shower."

God help me. Heat shot down my spine.

That should have made me happy. Hell, it did make me happy. But I couldn't stop myself from being snarky. "You should have known better."

He smirked. "Should I?"

I rolled my eyes. "Yes."

He leaned in, his voice smooth like fucking whiskey. "Then explain why you're so pissed, sweetheart."

I refused to answer that, to give him the satisfaction. He was right. I only left to beat him to the punch before he could discard me. I was actually pissed off for no reason. He was telling me it was a simple miscommunication. But I couldn't make myself downshift.

So, I just glared.

And Ghost just grinned.

I should have walked away. I should have left Ghost standing there, his cocky grin etched into my nerves, and gone back to the group like nothing had happened.

But I didn't. Because I couldn't.

Instead, I was still standing way too close to him, my pulse still racing, my body still buzzing from his words.

Ghost smirked, reading everything I wasn't saying. "You're quiet all of a sudden, Tits. What's wrong?"

I crossed my arms. "Nothing."

His smirk deepened. "Liar."

"What do you want me to say, Ghost? That I should have stuck around yesterday? That I should have waited in your room like a good little hookup ready for round two?"

His eyes flicked down my body, darkening. "Would've been nice."

I clenched my jaw, anger sparking through me.

Of course, he was completely unaffected, standing there with his arms crossed like I wasn't on the verge of losing my damn mind. I was furious at the way my body still wanted him, even knowing better.

I stepped closer, so close I could feel the heat radiating off him.

And then, with the calmest voice I could manage, I tilted my head and whispered, "That's too bad, Ghost. Because I don't do repeats."

His smirk dropped.

For the first time since I'd known him, Ghost actually looked thrown.

I turned before I could see him recover, walking back toward the group, feeling his eyes burning holes in my back the entire way.

Chapter 38

B y the time we all left the go-kart track and headed across the street for food, I could still feel the tension between us.

Ghost was watching me like he was trying to decide what to do next. I didn't give him a chance.

At the restaurant, I sat between Drew and Niki, across from Ghost, ignoring the way he looked at me the entire time. I laughed with everyone, talked shit about the race, and acted normal.

And Ghost let me.

I knew this wasn't over. Because Ghost didn't like being told no. And I had just walked away from him. I couldn't wait to see how this was going to play out.

He was watching me like he was waiting for me to slip up, waiting for me to acknowledge him. Too bad. I wasn't playing. I kept my focus on the food, the conversation and the group. Anything that wasn't him.

Which is exactly why I noticed it before he did.

Jen slid her chair just a little closer to Ghost. Twisting her hair around her finger, giving him a look like she was three seconds away from crawling into his lap.

I clenched my jaw. She'd obviously noticed the tension between the two of us and had taken it as an opportunity to slide in there and try for his attention again.

Jen never cared that Drew was right there when she flirted with other guys. She had zero shame in it. She leaned in, placing a hand on Ghost's arm. "So, Ghost..." She smiled, lowering her voice slightly. "How come you really don't have a girlfriend?"

I could have choked on my drink. Jen was shameless.

Ghost glanced at her, one brow lifted. "Who says I don't?"

Jen pouted, tilting her head. "You're too much of a player for that."

Ghost didn't deny it. He just smirked, taking a sip of his water.

"Maybe you just haven't found the right girl," she said then.

The heat in my stomach changed into something dark and annoyed as hell. Because any woman hitting on Ghost would bother me, but Jen bothered me the most. She was supposed to be my friend, and it had to be obvious to everyone in the group by now that I was interested in him. Even if I did have to keep playing like I was repulsed by his personality.

Jen grinned, biting her lip.

My grip tightened on my fork. My eyes shifted to Drew, who was deep in conversation with Josh and hadn't noticed the way his girl-friend was shamelessly flirting right across the table.

Ghost shook his head, but he didn't outright reject her. Which pissed me off. Even though I had no right to be mad, even though I had no claim on him, my jealousy when it came to him was a raging, uncontrollable thing. And he knew it from my encounter with Candace.

When he finally looked back at me, his smirk deepened.

The smug bastard knew exactly what he was doing.

Dinner carried on, conversation floating around the table, but I barely processed any of it. Not when Ghost was doing everything he could to drive me insane, all the while keeping it completely subtle to everyone else at the table.

He stretched his arms back, his shirt lifting just enough to expose the sharp cut of his abs, drawing my eyes. Then he rolled his neck, letting out a deep, satisfied sigh that made my thighs clench. He licked his lips. Slowly. Deliberately. He kept brushing his fingers along his glass, dragging them up and down, his touch slow and lazy, and way too damn suggestive.

I wanted to throw my fork at his face... or straddle him in that chair. At this point, it was a toss-up.

He was enjoying every second of my suffering. But I wasn't going to break. Not when we were sitting here, surrounded by people, playing a game no one else knew about.

So I ignored him. At least, I tried to. Until Niki got up to go to the bathroom.

Ghost leaned over toward me, resting his elbows on the table, dropping his voice just enough so that only I could hear. "You can keep pretending, sweetheart. But I know."

My pulse quickened. I swallowed. "Know what?"

His eyes washed over me, dark and knowing. "That you want me. Again."

The heat that surged through me was humiliating. I tightened my grip on my napkin. "You're so full of yourself."

Ghost just smirked and leaned back in his chair, dragging his tongue across his lower lip before saying casually and louder so everyone at the table could hear. "Sure. I'll give you a ride home."

I froze.

Jen perked up instantly, her expression souring as she looked from Ghost to me. "I thought you took a rideshare, Halston?"

I shrugged. "I did."

Ghost watched me closely, waiting for my answer.

A second stretched. Then another.

Then I nodded. "Okay."

I wanted to put Jen in her place, and I couldn't make myself say no to him. I wanted to see what he had to say next. So, I let him drive me home.

Ghost had one hand on the wheel, the other resting on the gearshift, his fingers drumming lazily. But I wasn't fooled. He was waiting for me to say something, for me to invite him in, for me to admit that I wanted him.

But I wouldn't. I'd already given in once. I wasn't going to let him have that satisfaction again.

So when he pulled up in front of my place, I unbuckled my seatbelt and reached for the door handle without hesitation. "Thanks for the ride," I said smoothly, stepping out onto the curb like I was totally unaffected. Like I wasn't burning up inside just from sitting in a truck with him. I wanted to invite him in and let him own me all over again. Because apparently I was brain damaged.

Ghost leaned his arm against the window, watching me with those sharp blue eyes, with an unreadable smirk playing at his lips.

I refused to look at his mouth. Refused to think about what it felt like against mine.

"I'll see you tomorrow," I added.

He lifted an eyebrow. "I'll pick you up."

I paused, my fingers tightening around my keys. "I can get a rideshare," I said too quickly.

Ghost's smirk widened. "Sweetheart, I'm picking you up."

"I can—"

"I'm picking you up," he said again, slow, deliberate, final.

I exhaled sharply through my nose, glaring at him. "You're annoying."

"Yeah?" His grin turned downright wicked. "Then why do you want me so bad?"

"Hell if I know," I said, before I could stop myself, the truth spilling out.

The air crackled between us, hot and dangerous.

His grin turned wicked, entirely too satisfied.

I narrowed my eyes. "You're a jackass."

"You're obsessed."

"Goodnight, Ghost."

"Sweet dreams, Halston."

I spun on my heel and slammed my door behind me before I could do something stupid.

I was in trouble. Because Ghost knew exactly how to get under my skin.

Chapter 39

I was sipping my coffee when I heard the deep rumble of Ghost's truck outside.

Right on time.

I grabbed the second to-go cup from the counter and headed outside. The air was crisp. The sun was barely up. I decided upon waking up this morning that I was done being mad. I was putting it behind me because I was sick of being upset, and I still had to feed the cat every day.

I could be civil, sweet even.

Ghost was leaning against his truck, watching me with those unreadable blue eyes. He was dressed in a black hoodie with dark jeans and a sexy smile on that sharp, too-handsome face. He looked like trouble. He always did, but there was something about him in the hoodie that cried deviant.

"Morning," he said.

I handed him the cup. "Morning."

He took it, lifting an eyebrow. "What's this?"

"Coffee."

He smirked. "Yeah, I got that. Why?"

I shrugged. "Because I have an espresso machine and a conical grinder, and I make damn good coffee."

Ghost took a slow sip, his eyes on me the whole time. Then he gave a small nod. "Not bad."

I smiled. "Not bad? That's it?"

"Alright, it's good." He took another sip. "Real good."

I laughed. "That's more like it."

Ghost pulled open the passenger door, gesturing for me to get in. No teasing, no snarky comments, just casual Ghost.

I hopped in. "Thank you."

When we pulled up to the house, I had barely gotten out of the truck before Lulu came trotting over from the shed, weaving between my feet like I'd been gone for days.

"She heard your truck and came running. She must've missed me." I crouched down, scratching under her chin. She purred loudly, pressing against my legs.

Ghost grabbed something from the back of his truck before walking toward the house. "Feed your damn cat before she starves."

"She's not my cat," I said, scooping food into her bowl.

"Right." His voice was dripping with sarcasm. "And I'm a virgin."

I rolled my eyes, smiling.

The cat ate happily while Ghost leaned against the porch railing, sipping his coffee. "Henry looked at your car this morning."

"Oh?"

"It needs a part. He ordered it, but it won't be here for at least a week."

"So, that means it's running?"

Ghost shrugged. "It started once, not saying it'll start again. It's unreliable. If it does start, I wouldn't drive it too far."

I sighed. "Great."

He smiled.

"Well, just tell me how much the part is and I'll Cash App it to you."

"I already paid for it."

I nodded at him in a no-kidding sort of way. "And I want to pay you back for it."

He shrugged. "It's not necessary. I'm not hurting for money."

"I'm not either," I shot back.

"I bet I have more than you do."

I rolled my eyes at him. "I didn't think it was a contest."

"If it was, I'd win."

He was infuriating, but I laughed. "Probably."

He shot me a smirk and a wink.

Something in my chest clenched. Damn him. "Thank you. That was very considerate."

Ghost nodded, lifting his coffee. "Don't mention it, Tits."

I forced myself to look away.

The cat was waiting by the shed, its striped tail flicking as it sat expectantly by the food bowl, meowing. I laughed. "I fed you."

"I see you've got her trained already."

Ghost was wearing jeans and a fitted grey T-shirt that hugged his muscular frame, his hoodie gone now, his black Doc Martens finishing the look. The man was a fucking Viking god. So damn distracting.

"Or maybe she's got me trained," I said, bending down to pet her.

"That's usually how it works with women."

I shot him a look. "Is that so?"

He smirked. "Mmm. Not sure about you yet. I still haven't figured out if I've got you trained or if you just keep showing up because you like looking at me."

I let out a breath, shaking my head. "Jesus, your ego. Don't listen to all those thirsty Instagram messages. They'll say anything to get laid."

Ghost laughed. "Maybe. But you are looking at me."

Damn it. I had been looking. He always knew it. It was like he watched my every move. And that was so unsettling... and insanely hot. The man strategized everything and everyone.

I turned away, refusing to engage further. It was irritating the way he kept baiting me, toying with me. And, damn it, I hated how he saw right through me... Or maybe I liked it. I couldn't decide.

Ghost chuckled, clearly enjoying himself. "What's wrong, Tits? You don't wanna admit it?"

Hell, no. I wasn't admitting it, even if he knew it already. "You don't need help stroking your ego, Ghost."

He shrugged at me. "I can stroke it myself, but it just feels better when you do it."

A wave of heat shot through me at that image.

He was just watching my reaction as he grinned at me.

I was speechless. I literally had no comeback for that. Nothing.

I stood up, dusting my hands off as I turned toward my car.

Ghost laughed and followed, his hands in his pockets, strolling like he had all the time in the world. "You heading out?"

"I have work to do."

He raised an eyebrow. "From home?"

"Yes, Ghost. I do have an actual job, remember?" Bitchy, I know. But he had me between lust and anger, constantly teetering between both. And it was exhausting. I needed release, and I couldn't rely on the one-use only man to give it to me again. Messing with him was too dangerous. I guess my vibrator was going to have to do.

"And yet, here you are. Every damn morning."

I sighed. "Are you gonna let me leave or are we gonna have a whole debate about my life choices?"

"Oh, you can leave, sweetheart." He smirked. "Assuming that car of yours actually starts."

I froze, dread clenching in my stomach. I knew he'd just jinxed it. Before I even put the key in the ignition, before I even turned it, I knew it wouldn't start.

Sure enough. The engine sputtered and died.

I groaned, resting my forehead against the steering wheel. "Of course."

Ghost grinned. "Hate to say I told you so."

"Do you, though?"

"Nope."

I sighed, rubbing my temples.

Then Ghost's phone rang.

He pulled it from his pocket, glanced at the screen, and his entire body went still. The cocky smirk vanished. "It's my mom."

His voice had lost its usual teasing tone.

I watched as he answered, his tone clipped. "Yeah?" His jaw clenched. "Shit."

"What is it?" I asked when he hung up.

Ghost ran a hand through his hair, exhaling sharply. "It's my grandmother. I have to go to the hospital. I'll drop you off on the way."

I straightened. "I can ask Henry to take me home."

"Henry has work to do. I'll drop you off."

I shook my head. "No. You need to get up there now. That's more important than me getting home right now. I'll just go with you."

"Are you sure?"

"I'll just sit in the waiting room."

"It might take hours."

I met his gaze. "I'm not worried about it."

Ghost studied me for a beat. Then he nodded. "Alright. Let's go."

Chapter 40

I stayed by the doorway, not wanting to intrude as Ghost walked into the hospital room.

His family was already there. His mom, dad, and two brothers were all gathered around the frail, elderly woman in the hospital bed.

I watched as his grandmother smiled at them, lifting a shaky hand. "My boys," she whispered.

Then, her eyes flicked toward me. Her expression turned playful. "Which one of your girlfriends is she?"

One of Ghost's brothers, the taller one with dark hair like their mother, grinned. "Kasper's girlfriend."

Ghost immediately shook his head. "She's not my girlfriend."

His mom shot him a disapproving look. "That's rude, Kasper."

His grandmother chimed in at the same time. "Kasper!"

Ghost laughed. "I'm sorry, Gran. But she isn't my girlfriend. I'm just stuck with her for the day."

I shook my head.

His grandmother motioned me over to her bedside.

When I was beside her, she leaned in and whispered. "Don't worry about him. He may seem like a grizzly, but once you get to know him, once he lets you into his heart, he's the most loyal and docile baby kitten."

I laughed softly, despite myself. That seemed very unlikely.

"How did you two meet?" his mom asked.

"I showed up at one of his fights."

She tilted her head. "How long have you been together?"

I shook my head. "We really aren't dating."

His grandmother sighed dramatically. "That's a shame. She's so beautiful," she told Ghost. "What's wrong with you?"

I smirked at him, enjoying the moment.

Ghost exhaled. "She rescued a cat that wandered onto the ranch. Now I can't get rid of the cat or her."

His brothers burst into laughter.

I just rolled my eyes and ignored him.

"Kasper!" his mom scolded.

His grandmother reached for my hand, giving it a weak squeeze. I covered her hand with both of mine, feeling how cold it was.

She looked up at me, her eyes glassy with age and exhaustion. "My David died when I was fifty-five," she whispered. "How will he ever recognize me when I see him?"

My throat tightened. I squeezed her hand gently. "He will."

She blinked, her eyes focused solely on me.

I smiled down at her. "Soulmates are drawn to each other. He'll recognize you."

A slow, peaceful smile spread across her lips. "I never thought of it that way," she murmured. "I believe you're right."

The entire room turned quiet.

Then... The machines started beeping.

The smile fell from my face as doctors rushed in, ushering everyone out of the room.

In the hall, I stood back from the family, giving them space.

Minutes later, a doctor stepped out, speaking in hushed tones. "Would you like some time?"

Ghost's mother nodded through fresh tears. "Yes. Thank you, doctor."

I stayed in the doorway as his family said their final goodbyes.

I watched as Ghost leaned down, whispering something I couldn't hear, then kissed his grandmother's forehead.

I had to get out of there.

I had to breathe, had to get myself under control. I didn't want him to see me all raw, emotional, and vulnerable. Ghost didn't like weakness. He was strong, unshakable, and if he saw someone's soft spot, he would exploit it. I refused to let him see mine.

I hurried down to wait by his truck, wrapping my arms around myself against the cool night air, willing the tears to stay back.

Chapter 41

The drive back was silent. It was dark, late, almost eleven.

Ghost's jaw was tight, his hands gripping the steering wheel, his mind obviously somewhere else. On his grandmother.

I hesitated, then reached out, placing my hand gently over his on the gearshift. For a second, he didn't move, letting me comfort him.

Then he pulled away.

I tried not to let it bother me, but I felt the tears welling up in my eyes. Everything was pushing down on me. The way his grandmother looked up at me with such loving, sweet eyes. The heartbreak the family was going through, that I knew Ghost must be going through. And the way he was always pulling me in with his teasing, then pushing me away.

As soon as we pulled up, I jumped out of his truck without saying goodbye, since I didn't trust myself to speak without bursting into tears.

I went straight inside.

But before I could shut the door, Ghost pushed it open. "Why the hell are you running away from me?" he demanded. "I'm not gonna hurt you."

I wiped at my stupid tears, turning to him angrily. "You might be an asshole to me sometimes, but I know you're not going to hurt me."

"Then why are you running?"

I swallowed, my chest tightening. "I didn't want you to see me cry."

Ghost's expression darkened. "Why the hell not?"

I exhaled a shaky breath. "Because you'll see it as a weakness and use it against me."

His brows furrowed, and for the first time, I saw genuine confusion cross his face. "I only do that to my opponents."

I let out a bitter laugh. "Aren't I your opponent? Haven't you fought me every step of the way? Haven't you been looking for my weaknesses just to expose them?"

Ghost didn't answer. He knew I was right. Everyone was an opponent of sorts.

His lips parted slightly, but no words came. Instead, he lifted both hands to my face and wiped my tears away with the pads of his thumbs.

His touch was gentle, completely at odds with the ruthless fighter. "Shit. I'm sorry." His voice was rough. "I didn't even think about how all that with my grandmother would affect you."

His words hit something deep inside me. There was a softness in his eyes I had never seen before. Something raw and unguarded. Something that unraveled me. And suddenly, all my reservations, all my sensibility... Gone.

I leaned into him, my lips finding his, my hands sliding up around his neck as I opened my mouth over his, letting my tongue slide against his, tasting him.

Ghost didn't hesitate. His arms wrapped around me, pulling me into his body, his grip possessive, greedy.

I rose onto my toes, pressing closer, trying to get up to his mouth comfortably since he was so much taller. And as if he had the same thought, he lifted me, my legs wrapping around his waist, my body molding against his.

He walked us deeper into the house, one hand gripping my thigh, the other sliding into my hair.

The heat between us was instant, uncontrolled, borderline reckless.

He pressed me against the wall. His mouth was hot and urgent, claiming mine with the kind of kiss that left no room for doubt. No hesitation. His tongue swept into my mouth, tasting, teasing, taking.

I felt the hard lines of his body pressing into mine, the heat of his skin, the delicious scrape of his beard against me as his lips trailed down my neck.

He pulled away from the wall. "Bedroom?"

I pointed down the hall, my pulse hammering.

Ghost didn't hesitate. He carried me down the hallway, his mouth finding mine again, kissing me like he was starving.

By the time we reached my room, I was already unraveling, breathless, dizzy with need.

He turned the knob, kicking the door shut behind him. Then he was lowering me onto the bed, his body settling between my thighs, and oh, God, yes. I barely had time to process before his hands were everywhere, gripping my hips, pushing up my shirt, dragging his rough fingers along my bare skin.

His mouth followed, hot, demanding, sucking, biting, licking down my throat until I was whimpering, writhing beneath him.

"Jesus, sweetheart," he groaned against my collarbone. "I've been wanting this for days."

I was stunned for a split second, because he never admitted stuff like that. But he always made me admit it.

My fingers tugged at his shirt, desperate to feel his skin against mine.

Ghost let out a low chuckle. "Fuck, I love how eager you are," he said, sitting up just long enough to rip his shirt over his head, tossing it to the floor.

Then he was back on me, pressing me into the mattress, his weight solid, intoxicating.

"Missed me, huh?" he teased, dragging his tongue across my bottom lip, not quite kissing me, making my nipples ache.

I refused to give him the satisfaction of an answer.

So instead, I arched up, pressing my body against his, letting him feel exactly how much I'd missed him.

His sharp inhale was the only warning I got before he flipped us, rolling onto his back so I was straddling him, his hands gripping my waist, holding me exactly where he wanted me.

I could feel him straining against his jeans beneath me, so hard.

And God help me, I wanted more. I wanted everything he was offering.

Chapter 42

"Knew you couldn't stay away," he said, dragging his hands up my thighs, his thumbs brushing just under the hem of my shirt.

"Shut up, Kasper," I whispered against his mouth.

His smirk was pure sin.

Then, in one swift move, he sat up, pulling my shirt over my head, his lips already moving over the skin of my throat as he unhooked my bra and helped me out of it.

His hands slid down my back, his mouth trailing lower, lower, until he was sucking one of my nipples into his mouth, groaning as I gasped, my nails digging into his shoulders.

"That's it, sweetheart," he whispered, switching to the other one, his tongue flicking, teasing, driving me insane.

My head fell back, my hands cupping his face, my body already aching for him.

"Tell me," he said, nipping at my skin, his fingers slipping beneath the waistband of my jeans, pulling the snap open.

"Tell you what?" I breathed.

"How bad you need me," he rasped, pushing my jeans and panties down in one move, leaving me bare against him.

I clenched my jaw, not responding.

Instead, I reached between us, unfastening his belt, popping the button of his jeans.

His body tensed beneath me, his breath hitching as I slipped my hand inside. "Fuck, Halston," he groaned. "Keep that up and I'm not gonna last much longer."

I smirked, dragging my palm over his cock.

He flipped me back onto the mattress, causing me to yelp, his hand gripping my jaw, his blue eyes burning into mine. He gave me a soft kiss.

Then he got off the bed, and I quickly sat up. "Hey!"

He laughed as he grabbed the condom from his wallet and held it up so I could see it, to let me know he wasn't going anywhere.

After discarding the rest of his clothes, he rolled the condom on and settled between my thighs on the bed.

The moment he thrust inside me, I arched, my breath catching, my fingers digging into his back, holding onto him.

"Fuck," he groaned, his head dropping into the crook of my neck. "Tight as hell, sweetheart."

I whimpered, my nails raking across his skin, my legs tightening around his waist.

He pulled back, just enough to look down at me, his eyes heated.

I didn't have words. Didn't have the ability to speak. But he read me anyway. He always did.

Ghost smirked sinfully, then pulled back, almost out, before slamming into me deep and hard.

A sharp cry left my throat, my head falling back against the pillows.

"That's it," he said, his voice gravelly, his rough hands gripping my thighs, keeping me wide open for him as he fucked me.

I gasped, clenching around him, trying to breathe, trying to keep up, but Ghost wasn't letting me adjust. He wasn't giving me space. He was taking. Consuming.

And my body fucking loved it.

"Yeah, you like that, don't you?" he whispered, watching me, reading every reaction, every moan, every desperate arch of my body.

I swallowed hard, my hands clenching the sheets, the heat between my legs pulsing.

His smirk deepened. "Can't even answer me, huh?"

I shook my head, breathless, wrecked, already close to the edge.

Ghost chuckled, low and deep. "Poor thing," he said, gripping my jaw, forcing me to meet his gaze. "Can't even handle me."

I whimpered, my nails digging into his forearms, my body tightening, my thighs trembling.

Ghost's smirk faded into something darker. "Fuck," he gritted out, thrusting deep, harder, making my toes curl. "You're squeezing me so goddamn tight."

I barely had time to process before his hand slid between us, his thumb rubbing slow, delicious circles against my clit. A sharp gasp left my lips. I was gone. Completely, utterly gone.

"That's it, sweetheart," he said, his pace picking up, his movements deliberate, controlled.

I cried out. The pleasure was too much, too fast, every muscle tensing, tightening. I was seconds away from shattering completely. My breath was coming out in short and shallow gasps.

"You gonna cum for me?" he whispered, his lips trailing fire down my throat, his body demanding everything from me as he slammed into me, rolling his hips.

I barely managed to nod, my body coming apart, fucking shaking as I let out little whimpers.

"Yeah, you are," he groaned. "Gonna cum all over my cock like a good girl."

That was it. That was fucking it. I fell apart, my orgasm ripping through me, my entire body clenching around him as I screamed his name.

Ghost cursed, his movements turning erratic. Then, with a low, wrecked groan, he followed me over the edge, thrusting over and over, tensing, shuddering.

His body slowed to a stop. We stayed there tangled, breathless.

Then, after a few moments, Ghost rolled over, dropping onto his back. "Fuck, Halston. That was..."

I gave a soft laugh. I couldn't help it. The tension was completely gone, and my body was buzzing something serious. "I know. You don't have to say it." Then I rolled to face him, propping my chin on his chest. "But if you did want to say it again... you know, for my ego... Oh, wait. You're the one with the ego," I said, breathless, smiling.

Ghost laughed, deep and unfiltered, the kind that rumbled through his chest beneath my hand. "Sweetheart," he said, brushing a knuckle under my chin. "My ego's only this big 'cause you keep feeding it."

I grinned. "Oh, so this is my fault now?"

He smirked, his eyes gleaming. "Damn right it is. You keep making all those pretty noises, looking at me like I hung the moon. What do you expect?"

I tilted my head and gave him an innocent look. "What do I expect? Have you seen the size of your cock? You ruined me."

He threw his head back and laughed again. "Shit, say stuff like that in public and I'll be dragging you to the nearest bathroom stall, baby."

I burst out laughing, playfully shoved his shoulder and dropped back onto the mattress.

My thoughts dipped to the inevitable. I didn't want a repeat of last time. I didn't want to feel like a fool. Again.

I finally let out a slow breath, breaking the silence. "I would get up and leave, but this is my house."

Ghost smirked, his blue eyes half-lidded with exhaustion. "Right. You want me to leave."

I turned my head slightly to look at him. "That's what you want, right?"

There was a pause. Then, unexpectedly, he sighed. "Normally, yes."

I turned onto my side, watching him. "But?"

Ghost rubbed a hand over his bare chest, exhaling heavily. "But it's late, and after the day we've had... I'm friggin' exhausted."

I didn't know what to say to that. So, I said nothing. It had been a long day, and he'd lost his grandmother, so I understood what he was saying. But him wanting to stay had nothing to do with me. And yeah, it sucked a little.

His eyes met mine, the teasing gone for once. "I'll make you a deal. Let me catch a couple hours of sleep, and I'll head out before you even wake up."

I let out a soft laugh, shaking my head, trying to act unaffected by his choice to stay. "It's not my rule, Ghost. You're the one that hits it and quits it."

His lips curled slightly, and just before his eyes closed, he let out a small, lazy chuckle.

I should have turned away. Should have closed my eyes and gone to sleep. But I didn't. Instead, I watched him. I studied the peaceful way all his features relaxed as sleep took him over.

My last thought was how he would treat me tomorrow in the daylight after what we'd done.

Chapter 43

I woke up wrapped in his arms.

The weight of him, the warmth of his body pressed against mine, the slow and steady rhythm of his breathing against the back of my neck. It was all so unexpected, so unfamiliar, so perfect.

Ghost's arm was draped over my waist, his hold solid, unyielding.

I had a clock with a projector, so the time was right on the ceiling above me in neon blue. It was almost eight already. But I wasn't in a hurry to move. I let my eyes flutter closed again, savoring the rare moment of peace, of warmth.

Ghost stirred.

A sharp breath left his lips, his body shifting behind me. Then, his head lifted slightly. "Shit." He jerked upright. The sudden movement pulled his warmth away from me, his voice gruff and half-awake. "I can't believe it's almost eight."

I turned, still blinking away sleep, watching him scrub a hand over his face and down his beard.

"It was a really long day yesterday," I said, stretching my arms over my head. "Your body obviously needed the sleep."

Ghost exhaled. "I gotta get moving. I need to get home and feed the dogs."

I nodded, swallowing the disappointment that settled in my stomach.

Back to reality.

"Yeah, I'm sure they're starving," I said, hoping I was keeping my voice light and unreadable. "I'll be there shortly to feed the cat."

Ghost swung his legs off the bed, running a hand through his messy hair.

I got out of bed and immediately pulled on a shirt. For the first time in my life, I'd fallen asleep naked. And it hadn't felt awkward until now.

"Mind if I take a quick shower before I leave?"

"Be my guest," I told him.

He went into the bathroom, and I heard the water turn on. I headed to my dresser to get a pair of underwear.

Then he came back from the bathroom, his eyes sweeping over me, darkening. "You wanna join me?"

My breath caught in my throat. I wasn't expecting that. I wasn't expecting him to want anything to do with me after last night. He'd already broken his rule in sleeping with me twice.

"So there's no confusion this time," he said with a sly smile.

I met his gaze, and for once, it wasn't distant or unreadable. It was the same look he had given me last night when he was inside me.

And God, I liked it so much. Too much.

I didn't answer. Didn't hesitate. Didn't overthink. Instead, I reached for the hem of my tank top, pulled it over my head, and dropped it onto the bed.

Ghost's eyes followed the movement, his lips parting slightly.

I quickly pulled the dresser drawer open and pulled out the box of condoms that had been there since Niki had given them to me for my birthday as a push to get back on the horse. Tearing it open, I pulled out the row, ripping one apart at the perforated edge.

Because if last night was a mistake. I wanted to make it again and again.

Then, without another word, he took hold of my wrist and pulled me with him.

The second we stepped into the bathroom, he pulled me against him, his hands hot on my skin, his mouth covering mine.

The water was running, steam rising.

Ghost pressed my back against the cool tiles, his mouth dragging down my neck, over my collarbone, lower, lower.

My fingers tangled in his wet hair, my body already aching, already wanting more.

He was hard and beautiful.

Grabbing the condom wrapper, he tore it open, then rolled it down the length of his rock-hard cock. He lifted me, his hands gripping my thighs, pinning me against the wall as I clenched him with my thighs.

His lips found mine again, the water cascading down his broad shoulders, dripping over the muscles in his back.

"Kasper!" I gasped as he slid into me, filling me.

His hands tightened on my hips, his movements slow but deliberate, like he was savoring every second of this.

I clung to him, my head tilting back as he drove deeper, harder, his name slipping from my lips again.

He growled against my skin, his fingers digging into my flesh, his body pressing me tighter against the wall as the water poured over us.

His lips brushed my ear, his voice raspy, wrecked. "You feel so good, Halston."

A breathless laugh escaped me, but it was swallowed by a moan as he thrust deeper, sending me spiraling.

Then, slowing again, he pressed into me until he couldn't go any further and ground his hips against me, causing a swirl of pleasure to shoot through me, making me cry out.

"You like that, sweetheart?" he whispered.

I nodded, gasping as he did it again, continuing to watch my expressions as he teased me with his slow hip rolls.

"Kasper," I cried out.

"What, sweetheart?"

"You're...Oh, God," I bit out through the intense pleasure. "You're torturing me."

His smile turned wicked, his voice rough as he leaned in, his lips brushing my ear. "That's not torture, sweetheart..." he whispered, dragging his hips slower, deeper. "That's called foreplay. Torture starts when I stop."

Then he did it again, just to prove his point, and I broke with a cry.

He continued to press into me, his hips grinding upward, his body rubbing against my clit, my toes curling tightly.

Then, he picked up the pace, and my breathing kicked up.

His thrusts became faster, harder, hitting that already way too sensitive spot.

My body clenched, coiled. "Kasper!"

The tension snapped, and I came undone, crying out against his shoulder, my body shuddering around him.

Ghost groaned, his rhythm faltering, his jaw clenching as he gave in to his release, his body tensing. Stroke after stroke, he finally came to a stop inside me.

His head dropped down on my shoulder, his breathing ragged, his grip still firm on my thighs.

After the shower, we made our way back to my bedroom.

Ghost pulled on his jeans, buttoning them, then glanced at me, smirking. "Have you ever done that before?"

I tugged my shirt over my head. "What?"

"With a guy. Before me?"

"Showered?" I asked, my tone dripping with sarcasm. "No. Never."

He laughed. "That's not what I mean."

I rolled my eyes. "I know. I wasn't a virgin, Ghost."

He smiled, lifting an eyebrow. "You're pretty tight."

My face heated, and I turned away, focusing way too hard on finding my socks.

Before I could escape further, his fingers caught my chin, turning my face back to him. "What?"

I shook my head, feeling stupid for even thinking about it. "I don't want to say."

Ghost's eyes stayed on mine, searching, waiting. "I'm not gonna judge you."

I exhaled, dropping my gaze to his chest, avoiding his eyes. "I've had sex..."

Ghost's brow furrowed slightly, his hand falling from my chin. "Why are you ashamed of that?"

I shook my head quickly. "I'm not. I'm just..."

His lips curved slightly, his eyes studying me like he could see right through the bullshit. "Your face is betraying your words."

I sighed, pulling away and tugging on my jeans, avoiding his stare. "It's just that I'm not experienced like..." I stopped myself, clamping my mouth shut before I said something stupid.

But Ghost had already figured it out. His lips twitched. "Like Jen?"

My stomach twisted. That was exactly who I had been thinking of. Her words had been on a loop in my head ever since the night she threw them in my face. That Ghost needed someone like her, not me.

I hesitated, then nodded.

Ghost laughed, shaking his head. "Thank the fucking Lord!"

I was surprised and then relieved. Just like that, he put me at ease. Like it was nothing. Like it didn't matter. And maybe it really didn't.

Ghost finished dressing, pulling his shirt over his head, then reached for his phone. He glanced at me, his expression shifting back into something neutral, unreadable. "This didn't mean anything."

There it was.

I rolled my eyes, letting out a dry laugh. "I didn't think that it did."

"I just mean... I don't date."

"You made that clear."

He nodded, seemingly satisfied with my answer.

"Just because you made my toes curl doesn't mean I'm going to start doodling your name in my notebook."

He laughed low. "Good. But if you did doodle my name, I'd expect flames around it. Maybe a warning label." His voice dropped, cocky and full of heat. "You know... hazardous when wet."

That made me think of sex in the shower again, heat shooting through me. I shook my head at him. "You are a walking warning label."

"You say the sweetest things, Tits," Ghost said with a laugh, heading for the bedroom door. But before he left, he paused, turning back, his blue eyes locking onto mine. "I'll text you the gate code so you can feed the cat."

Then, he was gone.

I stood there for a moment, staring at the empty doorway, processing what had just happened. Because Ghost or one of his guys always let me in the gate. But he was giving me the code.

I smiled to myself. It wasn't much. But it was something. Even if it was only about the cat.

Chapter 44

When I showed up at Legacy Ranch in a rideshare, Ghost was already outside.

"I completely forgot I was your ride."

I laughed. "Me too, at least until after you'd already left."

He nodded toward my parked car, sitting near the garage. "The part came in. Henry fixed it."

I glanced toward the car, then back at him. "Thank you. It was generous of you. I'll have to thank Henry."

Ghost shrugged. "Well, you were starting to look like you lived here."

I rolled my eyes. "Can't have that."

He laughed and gave a shrug that said he agreed.

I sighed. "Well, thank you. I appreciate it."

His blue eyes held mine for a beat. Then he nodded once, like that was the only acknowledgement I was gonna get.

I made my way toward the shed, expecting to see the cat waiting for me like usual, but she was already eating food in her bowl.

I stopped mid-step, watching her eat the last few pieces. "Did you actually feed her?"

Ghost crouched down next to the cat as she finished the last bit of food. "She earned it."

I raised an eyebrow. "So, you like the cat now?"

"Hell yeah." He rubbed her under the chin, and she purred loudly. "She came running over to me when I got home with a big fat rat in her mouth."

I wrinkled my nose. "That's disgusting."

Ghost laughed, clearly unfazed. "Well, if she keeps earning her keep like that, she's welcome to stay as long as she wants. Right, Killer?"

I scowled. "Killer?"

Ghost grinned, scratching behind her ears. "Yeah, you should've seen the way she batted that rat around like her little bitch."

"Gross."

"What? It was impressive."

I shook my head. "You can't name her Killer. She's a girl."

Ghost raised a brow. "Haven't you ever heard of a girl with a guy's name?"

I laughed, crossing my arms. "I don't think that applies to the name Killer."

Ghost rubbed his knuckles under the cat's chin, his voice low and playful. "How about Lucifer?"

I gasped dramatically. "That's the devil!"

Ghost smirked. "If you had seen her this morning, you'd be agreeing with that name right now."

I scrunched my nose, the image of her with the rat flooding my mind, making him laugh again.

"How about if we shorten it to Lu?" he suggested.

"How about Lulu?" I smiled, petting her head. "I like Lulu."

Ghost let out a dramatic sigh, shaking his head. "That's such a girly name."

"She is a girl."

"Yeah, but she hunts like a demon."

I laughed. "I like Lulu."

Ghost sighed again, rubbing his hand over his beard. "I guess it's only fair since you rescued her."

I beamed in victory. "Lulu it is. What do you think about that, girl?" The cat purred even louder, rubbing against my hand.

Ghost shook his head. "Damn cats already spoiled."

I smiled, but then the thought hit me. "I guess there's no reason for me to come over every day now." My voice came out casual, but the words felt... wrong. Like I didn't want them to be true.

The space between us grew quiet.

Then he said, "No."

I looked up. "No?"

Ghost leaned against the shed. "You still have to come over."

I raised an eyebrow. "Why?"

He gave a quick shrug. "I'm sure she'll piss me off again."

I laughed, and for some insane reason, it made me happy.

Ghost shifted, rubbing the back of his neck. "Listen, I wanted to talk about you running out on me at the hospital."

I exhaled. "I thought we talked about that already." Then the thought of us in my hallway, my bed, my shower flooded my brain, torching my brain cells.

I pushed it aside.

"You talked about it. I didn't get to say what I wanted to say last night."

"Oh. Okay."

Ghost's expression was unreadable. "I appreciate what you did for my grandmother. She talked about seeing my grandfather again ever since he died."

I swallowed, remembering the way his grandmother had smiled at me, how she had asked if her David would recognize her. "You could tell how much she loved him." My voice was soft. "They must have had some kind of love."

Ghost's jaw tensed slightly, like he wasn't used to talking about this stuff. "From what I hear, they did." He let out a breath, running a hand through his hair. "Anyway. Thank you for putting her at peace. I hadn't seen her that happy in a while."

I stared at him. Ghost, the man who had spent months annoying the hell out of me, teasing me, pushing my buttons, just thanked me.

I smiled softly. "I'm happy I got the chance to meet her."

Ghost nodded.

I tilted my head, trying to lighten his obvious discomfort. "And who'd have guessed you had a family?"

His lips curled slightly in a smile. "Everybody comes from somewhere."

I smirked. "Yeah, but I just assumed hell opened up, and you crawled out."

Ghost let out a deep laugh, shaking his head. "That's funny," he said, as if it was the first time I'd ever been funny.

I grinned, sticking my tongue out playfully.

Then Ghost pulled out his phone and glanced at the notification he'd just received. He pushed the button on his phone to open the gate, then looked back at me. "It's my mom."

The crunch of tires on the gravel driveway caused us both to turn.

A black SUV pulled up, the driver's side door opened, and Ghost's mom stepped out.

She walked toward us, her expression warm, with a smile curving on her lips.

"Hi, Mom," Ghost said.

"I just wanted to stop by and let you know Christmas dinner is at seven sharp," she told Ghost as she closed the distance between us. "Come as early as you want, though."

Before he could respond, her eyes landed on me, and she smiled warmly. "You can be as casual or as dressy as you'd like."

I blinked a few times. "Me?"

She nodded as if it was obvious. "Of course. I'd love for you to join us."

"I'm sure she has plans, Mom," Ghost told her.

I hesitated for half a second, then shook my head. "I actually don't. That's very kind of you."

Ghost's mom smiled, pleased. "Everyone should spend the holidays with family. You can be part of ours this year."

I just stared at her, speechless. It was the kindest thing anyone had said to me in a long time.

Ghost let out a mock sigh, rubbing his temples. "Thanks, Mom. Now I'll really never get rid of her."

"Kasper!" his mom snapped.

I laughed, shaking my head.

"Aren't you insulted?" she asked me.

I shrugged, still smiling. "I'm getting used to his gruff behavior and insults."

His mom shook her head, clearly exasperated. "You're lucky you found a woman who puts up with you."

Ghost just smiled at his mom.

After his mom left, we stood there for a moment, watching as the SUV disappeared down the long gravel drive.

I tilted my head. "Will it be awkward for you?"

Ghost turned toward me, arching a brow. "Why? Because I've seen you naked?"

My face heated, my breath catching in my throat at the way he was looking at me, his clear blue eyes searing into me. "I was gonna say to have me at your parents' house."

Ghost's lips curved into a slow, devious smile. "Sweetheart, the only awkward thing about having you at my parents' house is knowing I can't bend you over the nearest surface and fuck you stupid whenever I want."

My entire body went up in flames. "Jesus, Ghost."

He grinned completely unrepentant, leaning in, his voice dropping to a sinful tone. "Tell me you weren't thinking about it."

I scowled, refusing to give him the satisfaction. "I wasn't."

Ghost's grin deepened. "Sure you weren't."

I crossed my arms, narrowing my eyes. "So what, you're saying you have no self-control?"

"Oh, I have self-control," he insisted, his gaze dropping to my mouth, his tongue sliding across his lower lip. "But I also have a damn good imagination. And right now? It's working overtime picturing you on my bed, naked, legs spread—"

"Ghost." My voice came out strangled, and he gave a cocky laugh, enjoying my torment.

"You asked, sweetheart," he drawled, standing up straight, his expression smug as hell. "Now, be a good girl and try not to think about me fucking you on my childhood bed while we're at my parents' house."

My entire body locked up, my mouth falling open in pure, mortified frustration.

Ghost winked. "Good luck with that."

Chapter 45

C hristmas at the Aureus house was something I never expected
to be a part of.

I didn't even remember it was Christmas until Ghost's mom
stopped by. I hadn't actually done anything for Christmas since losing
my parents.

And yet, here I was, carrying a bag with a carefully wrapped chocolate pecan pie into their house, my nerves barely in check.

I hadn't told Ghost I'd made his favorite dessert, mostly because I
didn't want to hear his smart-ass comments about it. That's why I put
it in a small bag, so he wouldn't see it and ask me about it, since I parked
my car at his house and had driven with him.

I texted his mom the day before, asking what I could bring, and
when she mentioned that Ghost rarely ate dessert but loved chocolate
pecan pie, I made one.

Now, as I stepped inside, the warmth of the fireplace and the scent
of home-cooked food surrounded me, making me feel both at ease and
completely out of place at the same time.

The house was already bustling with energy, filled with the sounds of laughter and conversation.

His entire family introduced themselves to me.

Ghost's mom, Eleanor, greeted me warmly, pulling me into a hug. "I'm so glad you could make it, Halston."

I smiled. "Thank you for inviting me."

Ghost's dad, Joseph, was tall, broad-shouldered, with graying dark hair and sharp blue eyes. The same intense stare Ghost had. "Welcome, sweetheart," he said with a deep chuckle. "It's good to meet you properly this time."

Ghost's two brothers introduced themselves next.

Nathan, the eldest, looked a little like their dad. He was dark-haired and serious, with an air of responsibility about him.

Jackson, the youngest, was the complete opposite. He was blonde, wild-eyed, and wearing an easy grin that screamed trouble.

The entire family had the same beautiful blue eyes as Ghost.

"So you're the girl who got past Kasper's bullshit," Jackson teased, shaking my hand.

I laughed. "I wouldn't say that."

Nathan smirked. "You're standing here, so I'd say you have."

Ghost rolled his eyes, grabbing a beer from the counter. "Are we done?"

His dad and brothers laughed, and Ghost shook his head, leading them outside for drinks.

I stayed inside with Eleanor, bringing the dessert into the kitchen.

I set the pie down on the counter. "Chocolate pecan pie."

Her eyes sparkled with laughter. "And you didn't tell him you were making it, did you?"

I shook my head. "Nope. I figured I'd let it be a surprise."

Eleanor beamed. "You're sneaky. I like you."

I grinned, pushing up my sleeves. "Need help with anything?"

"If you're offering, I won't say no."

We worked side by side, preparing the final touches for dinner.

The house smelled amazing with the aroma of seasoned turkey, roasted vegetables, and fresh bread Eleanor made from scratch.

"You're good in the kitchen," Eleanor noted as I helped season the potatoes.

I shrugged. "I grew up learning a little bit of everything."

She nodded. "Smart girl." Then she changed gears completely. "So, tell me about you and my son."

I gave a small laugh, focusing on the potatoes. "We're just friends."

She raised an eyebrow. "Friends?"

I smiled. "I know. Hard to believe, right?"

"Very."

I laughed. "I think I caught him off guard. He's used to a certain type of woman, and I'm... not that."

Eleanor watched me closely, something knowing in her expression. "I wanted him to meet a nice girl like you."

I smiled, a little caught off guard by the sincerity in her voice. It was a sweet thought. I let out a small, amused sigh. "He's not interested in nice girls. We really are just friends."

Eleanor shook her head, clearly exasperated with her son. "You know," she said, "you're the first girl he's brought home since high school."

I froze, staring at her. "Really?"

"Really."

"You invited me, though. He couldn't exactly tell me not to come."

"Mmm. Couldn't he?" she mused, giving me a knowing look. "Kasper has never been one to shy away from speaking his mind."

I thought about it. She had a point. Ghost wasn't the type to bite his tongue or do something he didn't want to do. If he really didn't want me here, he would have made sure I knew it. But he didn't. And I wasn't sure what to do with that realization.

Dinner at the Aureus family table was nothing short of amazing.

Everything was delicious. The turkey was perfectly seasoned; the vegetables roasted just right, and the warm, buttery bread was soft and perfect.

For a moment, I let myself forget the fact that I hadn't spent Christmas with anyone in six years. I let myself relax into the warmth of his family, feeling like I belonged in a way I hadn't felt in a long time.

After dinner, dessert was served, and as soon as Ghost took his first bite of the chocolate pecan pie, he groaned. "Mom, you have outdone yourself. This is your best pie yet."

Eleanor barely glanced up from her plate. "Halston made that."

Ghost's fork paused mid-air.

He turned to me, then leaned in close, lowering his voice so only I could hear. "Two things you do well."

I raised an eyebrow, curious. "What's the other one?"

His eyes darkened, a knowing, intimate smile playing on his lips. "The way you roll your hips to meet mine..." He let the compliment hang there unfinished.

Heat rushed to my face, my stomach tightening into knots. I didn't know what to say. Ghost ran hot and cold, never giving me solid footing. And when he said something sweet, it completely threw me off balance, caught between loving it and hating that he'd confuse me again before I could blink.

I just stared at him, my blush deepening.

Ghost winked, satisfied with my speechlessness, and went back to his pie like he hadn't just wrecked my ability to think properly.

After dessert, the guys headed outside to play a game of football, leaving Eleanor and me to clean up the kitchen.

"They do this every year?" I asked, rinsing off a plate.

Eleanor chuckled. "Every year. It gets competitive, so don't be surprised if you hear some yelling."

I laughed. "I feel like competition is Ghost's love language."

Eleanor smiled, shaking her head. "You're not wrong."

I glanced out the large window above the sink, my hands slowing as I took in the scene outside. Ghost was standing in the yard, a football tucked under one arm, his grin wide and unguarded as he talked with his brothers and dad. The fire pit from earlier was still smoldering, casting a faint glow across the open field, the cold winter air visible in their breath as they talked and laughed.

I wasn't sure why I kept staring. Maybe because I was seeing another piece of him, another glimpse of Kasper instead of Ghost.

I wasn't sure which one I liked more.

"He's different around you," Eleanor said.

Her voice brought me out of my thoughts. I glanced at her, surprised. "How do you mean?"

She dried a plate, giving me a knowing smile. "You're figuring it out."

I wasn't sure if that was true. I wasn't sure if there was any figuring Ghost out.

Chapter 46

As the boys huddled back into the house, Eleanor ushered them into the living room.

"Your father and I are about to sit down and watch a Christmas movie. You all should join us."

Jackson immediately groaned. "Not one of those Hallmark ones, right?"

Eleanor smirked, crossing her arms. "What if it is?"

Jackson sighed dramatically. Then he took a seat on the floor. "Fine. Just don't expect me to get emotional."

Nathan chuckled, grabbing another beer, before taking a seat on the floor too. "I'll sit in too."

Ghost's parents settled into their recliners, which were on either side of the couch, but were at least a foot closer to the television than the couch was.

Ghost stood near the hallway, shaking his head. "Count me out."

I frowned, half-smirking. "You don't like Christmas movies?"

His blue eyes were flat. "They're all the same. They all end with the same happily ever after sappy ending."

I tilted my head, curious. "What's wrong with that?"

He exhaled, shaking his head. "Happily ever after doesn't really exist."

I let out a small laugh, but the way he said it made something tighten in my chest. "Every relationship has its ups and downs," I pointed out.

Ghost rolled his eyes.

I studied him, realizing this wasn't just about movies. "You have a pretty great family. You should be really thankful for it."

Ghost's jaw tightened slightly. "I am grateful for my family. But 'happily ever after' love is still bullshit."

I shook my head. "Love can be amazing. And if you're together long enough, you learn how to compromise in a way that the great days can outweigh the bad days. Just ask your parents."

Eleanor smiled from her spot on her recliner. "That's right." Then she looked at me, her expression kind and curious. "You obviously know that from experience. How long have your parents been together?"

I hesitated for a brief second. I considered brushing it off, making a joke. But Eleanor had been so kind to me, and I didn't want to lie to her. I swallowed. "They were together for twenty-five years. But they passed away six years ago. Car accident."

The entire room went silent.

I cleared my throat, forcing a small smile. "Sorry. I didn't mean to spoil your night. That's why I don't talk about it. It's a mood killer."

Eleanor immediately shook her head, her voice gentle but firm. "No, honey. You absolutely didn't spoil anything. But we are very sorry for your loss."

Joseph nodded, his deep voice warm and sincere. "You're always welcome here, Halston."

I blinked rapidly, my throat tightening. "Thank you." I barely knew this family, and yet they treated me like I belonged here.

I turned to Ghost, who was watching me. I lifted a brow, tilting my head toward the couch. "Watch the movie with us?"

Ghost didn't respond right away. His gaze searched mine, his jaw flexing slightly, like he was debating whether to give in. He finally gave a nod.

The warmth of the thick blanket wrapped around me as I sank into the couch, cozy and comfortable, my attention drifting in and out of the Christmas movie on the screen as it started. I wasn't sure how I ended up on Ghost's couch, surrounded by his family, but somehow, it felt less strange than it should have.

"Can I get up under there?"

I turned to look at Ghost beside me. He'd gone to throw his beer bottle in the trash, and now he was back and looking down at me. "You... want under the blanket?"

He shrugged. "Yeah."

I hesitated, then lifted the edge. "Sure."

Ghost slid in beside me, his body pressing tight against mine, his warmth sinking through my thin pajamas.

His closeness threw me off. There was plenty of room. We were the only ones on the couch. His brothers were lying on the floor in front of us, and his parents were in their spinning recliners just ahead, on both sides of the couch.

So why was he so... close?

I ignored it, shifting my focus back to the movie.

Then, his hand landed on my thigh.

I stilled, glancing at him. He wasn't looking at me. Maybe he didn't realize where his hand was.

His fingers moved. Slowly. Deliberately. His hand snaked its way up my thigh to the waistband of my pajama pants.

I sucked in a sharp breath, my stomach clenching with anticipation and panic all at once. He knew exactly what he was doing. And I didn't know what to do. There was a room full of people just in front of us, and Ghost was playing with fire.

I pressed my hand over his, stopping him before he could go any further. "What are you doing?" I whispered, my voice an uneasy warning. But something darker, more dangerous in my head, was asking why I was stopping him, something begging me to let him touch me.

His lips curved slightly, his eyes never leaving the screen. "Entertaining myself."

I cut my eyes, barely suppressing a gasp of disbelief over that callous response. "I'm not your entertainment."

Ghost gave a small laugh, then leaned in, his breath hot against my ear. "Let me in."

My breath stalled. His warm lips barely grazed my ear, then he flicked his tongue against my earlobe.

My pulse shot up, my entire body tightening.

"Let me in, sweetheart," he whispered again.

"Are you insane?" I whispered back, breathless.

"Sometimes."

He threw me a wink and that smile I wish I didn't find so sexy. Knots threaded through my stomach.

I let him in.

He moved past my waistband, his hand slipping into my lace underwear, past the small patch of trimmed hair, sliding two fingers inside me. It sent a fire through me, my body trembling, my breasts tingling.

I let out a small whimper. His long fingers felt too damn good.

"You're so wet," he whispered.

I said nothing. If I opened my mouth, I knew I was going to cry out from the pleasure, or let loose a string of obscenities. Instead, I leaned into his arm and pressed my mouth against the back of it, moaning. My right hand had a death grip on his arm as he continued to pleasure me with his strong fingers.

My left hand accidentally grazed his lap in an attempt to gain some control over my lost senses. I realized he was as turned on as I was when I felt his rock-hard cock, which only turned me on more. I stroked him over his sweatpants and felt a rumble of a deep groan vibrate his body.

As I palmed his erection, his long fingers rubbed at the sensitive nub along the wall, his thumb circling into my clit each time he went in and out.

And oh, my... I wanted to yell out how good it felt.

I could feel sweat beading on my forehead, my legs shaking as my orgasm took hold, and I had to stop from arching my back so I wouldn't call attention to us. I bit down on the back of his arm as the pleasure crashed over me in waves.

His fingers slowed, and my body spasmed as his fingers brushed my way too sensitive clit.

I let up my bite on his arm, my breathing ragged as I held onto his shoulder for support.

I dragged my eyes up to meet his.

"You're sexy when you're cumin' all over my fingers," he whispered.

His words sent a blush through me.

Then he pulled his fingers from my panties...

And the bastard stuck them in his mouth, his eyes holding mine, sucking them like a lollipop, undoing me all over again.

Chapter 47

After the movie ended, everyone was still lounging around.

Eleanor stood and stretched. "If anyone gets cold, there are extra blankets in the hall closet."

I smiled at her. "Thank you," I told her as she followed her husband across the house to their room.

Jackson smirked. "Not that it matters. There are no extra rooms."

I eyed him. "What?" No extra rooms? I didn't want to be disrespectful to his parents and sleep in Ghost's room. Then again, he might not even want me in his room.

Nathan jumped up from his spot on the floor. "Four-bedroom house."

Jackson grinned. "Ghost doesn't do sleepovers, though."

Ghost, who was still beside me on the couch, said, "Damn right."

Jackson turned to me, grinning like the devil. "You can share my room. I don't have any rules."

I laughed. His brothers knew him well.

But before I could respond further, Ghost's hand wrapped around my wrist. "That's not fucking happening."

Without another word, he pulled me up and led me out of the room. I barely had time to glance over my shoulder, catching the knowing smirks on his brother's faces before Ghost tugged me down the hall, his grip firm.

Ghost's old bedroom was exactly what I expected. It was minimal, dark, and a little rough around the edges, like him. The walls were bare, aside from a few old fight posters, and the furniture was simple and worn-in. A queen-size bed dominated the space. The sheets were dark gray, and the room smelled faintly of cedarwood.

I was sitting up, leaning against the headboard, while Ghost lay stretched out beside me, wearing nothing but black boxer briefs, his arms folded behind his head, his tattooed biceps flexing slightly. The sheets barely covered his lower half, leaving way too much bare skin on display, and I had a perfect view as I looked down at his body.

We'd been talking for a while, the conversation drifting to high school, old stories, things I never imagined he'd share with me. Not that it was anything too personal, but it was still stuff I didn't know about him, like where he hung out when he cut class.

Then my eyes drifted lower, taking in the scars littering his chest, mixed in with tattoos. Some were small, barely noticeable. Others were thicker, deeper, reminders of just how much he'd been through.

I reached out instinctively, brushing a faint line along his ribs. "How'd you get this one?"

Ghost exhaled through his nose. "That? Broken rib. Punctured my lung."

I yanked my hand back. "Oh, my God!"

Ghost laughed, shaking his head. "Relax, I survived."

I made a face, shaking off the wave of disgust rolling through me. "What you do is dangerous."

He stretched, the movement making his abs tighten; the scars shifting slightly. "The fighting?"

"Yes!" I threw up a hand, exasperated.

Ghost smirked, rolling onto his side, his head propped up on one arm.

That's when I made the mistake of really looking at him. The man was all muscle. His biceps, his chest, his solid thighs, his ridiculously defined abs. I'd seen his ass, and even that was rock hard.

I narrowed my eyes, tilting my head. "Do you even have an ounce of body fat on you?"

Ghost's smirk widened. "Of course."

I raised a brow. "Where? Because I'm not seeing it from where I'm sitting."

Ghost chuckled, rubbing a hand over his chest lazily. "I keep a little. Can't be all muscle."

"Well, I don't have all that muscle. I eat pretty decent, but I don't have six-pack abs or anything."

Ghost's expression shifted, amusement flickering across his face. "That's good."

"It is?"

His beautiful blue eyes locked onto mine. "Yeah. I like women who are soft." His voice dropped slightly. "Inside and out."

Heat spread through me, my stomach tightening involuntarily.

Damn him. He was turning me on again.

Chapter 48

I could still feel the warmth of his words lingering in the air between us, but I needed to change the subject before I lost myself completely.

I didn't know what to expect. What we had between us was far from anything I'd ever done. And then there were his rules. I didn't know how many there were, but even his brothers knew he had rules.

"Why don't you date?" I asked, tilting my head.

Ghost shrugged. "Because I don't want to."

I raised a brow. "That's not an answer."

"It sure as hell is," he said, a playful smile on his lips.

That was fine. If he didn't want to talk about it, I wouldn't push it.

So instead, we talked about other things, about our teenage years, how different our lives had been growing up.

At some point, the conversation drifted back to relationships. And to the inevitable question of body count.

"I've been with..." I hesitated, almost saying a lot of guys, but that would be a lie. I didn't lie, no matter how embarrassing it was. So I told him the truth. "I've been with one guy. Or... two now, I guess."

Ghost's eyebrows lifted slightly. "That explains so much."

"Like?" I asked, my defenses spiking. If he mentioned I was inexperienced... I swear I was leaving this room.

His eyes held mine. "Like why you're so fucking tight."

Blush heated my body, and I covered my face with my hand. His body flashed in my head. The things we did, the things he said. His vulgar, but somehow sexy words that torched me every time. It was the only time I'd ever lied to him. I did like when he talked dirty. I liked it way too much.

He chuckled and gently removed my hand from my face. "I like it, Tits. Matter of fact, thinking about it is making me hard."

I pulled my hand from his. "Don't say things like that. I'm trying really hard not to think about that right now."

He laughed. "Fair enough. Tell me about this one guy. How has there only been one?"

I exhaled, my fingers brushing over the sheets. "I was in bed with him when I got the call from the hospital about my parents."

Ghost stilled, his playful expression fading into something more serious. "I'm sorry. That had to be hard."

I nodded, swallowing past the tightness in my throat. "It was. I closed everyone out for a long time." After a moment, I shook off the sadness, forcing a small smile. "Anyway, how many girlfriends have you had total?"

Ghost smirked. "Do you mean actual relationships or just the ones who thought they were my girlfriend? Should it include all the bathroom, car, and outside sex as well?"

"Jesus," I said, earning a laugh from him. I rolled my eyes, ignoring the sting of disappointment in my chest. I knew he'd been with his fair share, but hearing it was another thing. "Actual relationships, Ghost. I don't even want to know how many you've slept with."

He smiled. "One."

Shock ran through me. "One?"

He stretched, his muscles flexing as he yawned. "It started in high school. Lasted a few years. It was... disappointing. Never saw the point afterwards."

"So, what? Now you just hook up with women and move on?"

Ghost shrugged. "Pretty much."

I sighed, choosing not to react. Instead, I turned the question back on myself. "Well, I've had four boyfriends."

He raised a brow. "And you never slept with any other than the one?"

"No."

Ghost looked genuinely surprised. "Why not?"

I smiled wryly. "My first boyfriend was when I was twelve. That lasted about a week."

Ghost grinned. "That doesn't count."

I laughed. "Fair enough. The next two were in junior high and high school. The first one lasted a month, and the other was three months. But I wasn't ready to have sex, and I wasn't going to let anyone push me into it until I was ready."

Ghost nodded. "I can respect that. And the last one?"

I sighed. "My senior year. We were together for about six months before we slept together."

"That had to be... How many years ago?"

"Six."

Ghost's eyes widened. "Damn. That's a long time to go without sex."

"It didn't bother me."

Ghost tilted his head, watching me closely. "So, you're a serial monogamist."

I shrugged. "If you want to call it that. When I like someone, I'm with them and only them."

Ghost chuckled, shaking his head. "That's cute."

I cut my eyes at him. "What's that supposed to mean?"

He sat up, leaning closer. "I am not the monogamous type. I hope you don't expect that from me."

I exhaled, feeling something sharp twist in my chest. I already knew that, but hearing him say it so bluntly still stung. Especially since we'd had sex. I guess I was like all women out there who hoped she'd be the one to change the man. Not that I expected two nights of my inexperienced hands and body to be anything special to a man like Ghost.

The man fucked me so good; I was confusing myself. This was whatever it was. I knew it wasn't going anywhere. I wasn't delusional.

I pushed the confusion aside. "I don't expect anything from you, Ghost."

His blue eyes darkened, his smirk growing. "Perfect."

Then, before I even saw it coming, he grabbed me by the hips and dragged me down the bed until I was beside him, causing my pulse to quicken.

I loved how he took what he wanted, so powerful. It was intoxicating.

Then, his mouth was on mine, his lips firm, demanding. Everything inside me screamed that this was a bad idea. But it felt so damn good that I kissed him back.

He pulled away just slightly, his lips brushing against mine.

"What is this?" I whispered.

Ghost smirked. "You got off. I can't?"

I laughed, rolling my eyes. He continually caught me off guard with that mouth. "I guess it's only fair."

His smirk widened, his fingers trailing along my jaw, down my neck. "This means nothing," he whispered.

He felt the need to keep pointing that out, telling me not to get attached to him. I held his gaze, my stomach twisting in knots. I could play his game... or die trying. "Less than nothing," I agreed.

His eyes flickered, something devilish flashing across them. Then he smiled and leaned into me.

And just like that, I was in deeper.

Chapter 49

Before I knew it, Ghost was helping me out of my pajamas. Then he quickly discarded his own.

It started slowly, his hands roaming over my bare skin, rough palms, teasing fingertips.

His mouth was hot, insistent, as he kissed a slow, torturous path down my throat.

I shivered, a mix of nerves and need, my fingers gripping his broad shoulders. His weight pressed down on me, solid and unrelenting, his lips trailing lower, grazing my breast before capturing my nipple between his lips.

I gasped, arching into him.

He groaned. "Fuck, I love the sounds you make."

I swallowed hard, my breathing ragged.

His teeth scraped ever so slightly, followed by the soft stroke of his tongue, a delicious contrast that made me whimper.

He lifted his head, grinning down at me, his blue eyes searching mine. "You're still shy, aren't you?"

I scowled. "No, I–"

His thumb brushed over my other nipple, and my words died in my throat, a breathless moan escaping.

"Yeah," he said, smirking. "That's what I thought."

Ghost didn't let me hide. He was trying to coax the shyness out of me with every touch. I could tell he loved this, seeing me like this. And God help me, I loved the way he looked at me like he was starving and I was the only thing that could satisfy his hunger.

"Tell me what you want," he whispered, his hands already slipping lower, his thumbs brushing over the sensitive skin of my hips.

I bit my lip, my body on fire, but my voice refused to cooperate.

He chuckled, shaking his head. "Not gonna tell me?"

I shook my head, defiant.

"That's okay," he whispered, sliding lower, pressing a kiss to my stomach. "I already know."

Before I could brace myself, he pushed my thighs open, and his mouth was on me.

I cried out, my fingers grabbing fistfuls of the sheets as his tongue flicked, teased, stroked deep.

"Fuck, you taste so sweet," he groaned, holding me down as my hips arched off the bed. "You're soaking for me."

I whimpered. He sucked, and I stifled a cry, trying to stay quiet.

"Still not gonna admit it?" he teased, his tongue circling slowly, wickedly.

"Kasper," I gasped, desperate. He hummed against me, the vibration sending pleasure rocketing through me, making me cry out.

"You don't have to say it, sweetheart," he murmured, his voice thick with lust. "Your body tells me everything I need to know."

I felt the pressure building. It was too much, too intense. I was right on the edge. So close I could taste it.

And then he stopped.

I whined, glaring down at him as he crawled back up my body, grinning like a devil. "You're a fucking tease," I accused breathlessly.

He laughed, nudging my thighs apart again with his knee. "Nah. Just making sure you're ready for me."

Rolling on a condom, he pushed inside me in one deep stroke, filling me completely in a way that shot pleasure through my body.

My head fell back, a broken moan slipping free.

"Jesus, fuck," he groaned, gripping my hips, holding still. "You're so goddamn tight."

I could barely breathe. The pressure was overwhelming.

Then he pulled back slowly, before driving into me harder, making me cry out.

"Yeah," he said, his voice rough. "That's what I wanna hear."

I quickly covered my mouth, trying desperately not to let the rest of the house hear the intense pleasure he was causing.

His pace was merciless, each stroke deep and demanding, his body owning mine.

"You feel that?" he said, his lips brushing my ear. "That's me ruining you for any other man."

I shuddered, my body burning up.

He chuckled, pressing a kiss to my throat. "You like it when I talk dirty, don't you?"

I shook my head, but the way my body clenched around him gave me away.

He laughed, shifting his angle, hitting a spot that sent white-hot pleasure searing through me, making me cry out again.

"Fuck, Halston," he groaned, gripping my thigh and hooking my leg over his hip. "You're gonna make me cum if you keep squeezing me like that."

"Don't stop," I gasped.

His eyes blazed, his pace increased, his thrusts hard and deep, rubbing against every nerve ending.

My entire body tightened, pleasure swelling, peaking, spiraling out of control. Then I threw my head back, my orgasm crashing over me, stealing my breath.

Ghost's release followed seconds later, his body shaking against mine. His mouth was on my neck as he drove inside me again and again with his release, my skin muffling the groan that escaped his mouth.

It took a few moments, and Ghost pulled up with a chuckle.

"What?" I asked.

"You love the way I talk to you in bed," he said with a smirk.

I scowled, rolling my eyes. "I do not."

His grin widened. "Liar."

I opened my mouth, ready to argue. But he kissed me, stealing the words right off my tongue.

Chapter 50

I woke up before Ghost did, squinting against the soft morning light.

For a second, I just lay there, processing everything that had happened the night before.

We both agreed it meant less than nothing. It was how it had to be. I had to stay unaffected by the man if I wanted to keep getting fucked by him... and escape with my sanity.

I shifted under the blanket, suddenly aware of his warmth beside me.

Ghost was still asleep, sprawled out over the bed, his bare chest rising and falling steadily, the blankets pushed low on his waist, revealing those delicious sharp V-lines.

His arms were relaxed, but even in sleep, he looked powerful and sexy as hell.

I needed to get up before I let my mind wander too far into dangerous territory.

Slowly, I sat up, slipping out from under the blanket. But before my feet even touched the floor, a strong arm shot out and grabbed me by the waist.

I yelped as Ghost pulled me back to him, my back pressing against his solid chest.

His voice was low and groggy, his lips close to my ear. "Where do you think you're going?"

I swallowed, ignoring the bumps racing down my arms. "To the bathroom."

His grip loosened slightly, but he didn't let go. "Hmm."

I turned my head slightly. "Were you awake this whole time?"

Ghost cracked one sleepy eye open, smiling. "Maybe."

His hands slid lower, his fingers slipping under the hem of my shirt as his lips brushed my ear. "I'm so hard right now," he whispered, his voice shooting heat through me.

I moaned, immediately picturing him.

His voice was rough from behind me. "Are you picturing my cock right now, Halston?"

I pushed my body back against him and nodded, then quickly shook my head.

He laughed. "Am I confusing you?" he asked, gently biting my ear.

I moaned again. "You know you are."

He chuckled.

"I smell bacon," I said then.

"And?"

"That means your parents are awake."

"I'll be real quiet," he whispered, his hot breath sending a shiver down my spine.

His teeth grazed my shoulder, and his hand cupped my breast, his thumb stroking my nipple through the thin fabric.

I dropped my head against his shoulder as my body arched into his touch.

His other hand trailed down, slipping beneath the waistband of my panties, his fingers teasing me before slipping inside.

I gasped, my thighs instinctively parting, and his grip tightened. "Damn, you're already soaked." His voice had a cocky undertone that sent a wave of desire through me.

I whimpered, my hands gripping his wrist.

"Quiet now," he whispered, his fingers stroking slow circles over my clit. "Unless you want my mom and dad walking in on me making you cum."

I bit down on my lip, struggling to stay silent, my breath coming in short, shallow gasps.

Ghost smirked against my neck, his lips pressing to my pulse, his teeth scraping just enough to make me shudder. "Fuck, you love this, don't you?"

I shook my head, still desperately clinging to denial. But I did. I loved everything he did to me. The man knew how to work me, how to push every button, how to soak me with his vulgar mouth.

His fingers slipped lower, teasing, dipping just inside before retreating, torturing me with his slow, calculated movements.

"You gonna tell me no again?"

I didn't say a damn thing.

Ghost growled, his patience snapping. "That's it. Lay back for me, Halston."

He flipped me onto my back, covering my body with his, his weight pinning me down.

Then, his mouth was on mine, hungry, consuming, his kiss stealing every ounce of air from my lungs. His hand slipped between us, and when he slid two fingers deep inside me again, I gasped into his mouth.

"That's right," he whispered against my lips. "Just like that. Let me hear you, baby."

My hips rolled against him, begging for the pleasure that was building fast.

"Fuck," he groaned, watching my face, watching me fall apart beneath him. "You think about this at night, don't you? You touch yourself thinking about me?"

I blushed, my hand shooting up to cover my face, horrified to let him see the truth.

He grinned. "That's so fucking hot, sweetheart," he said, thrusting his fingers deeper, harder, his thumb rubbing circles over my clit.

I was seconds from breaking, my body trembling, shaking. I reached out, my hands gripping tightly to his back.

Ghost's mouth brushed my ear, his voice rough, demanding. "Cum for me."

And I did. Hard.

A silent scream ripped through me, my entire body locking up as I shattered.

"Fuck," he said, watching me, his blue eyes dark with hunger.

Then he pulled my panties off completely, shoving his boxer briefs down and off.

"You still worried about the bacon?" he teased, as he got up to grab a condom from his dresser.

Rolling the condom over his cock, he positioned himself between my legs. I opened my thighs wide for him, welcoming, breathless. "I don't give a damn about the bacon."

Ghost grinned and grabbed my wrists, pinning them above my head. And then he buried himself inside me until he could go no further.

I cried out. It was too damn good.

"Fuck," he growled, holding still for a second, letting me adjust. "You're so goddamn perfect."

He started moving, each thrust deep. He was all over me, inside me, his mouth on my throat, my jaw, my lips. His hands dropped to grip my hips, my thighs, my ass, owning me.

And I let him own me. Because, God, I wanted him to. I wanted to belong to this man in every way.

I lifted my hips to meet his thrusts as he drove into me, fighting desperately to hold back the scream threatening to break free.

I was already teetering on the edge again.

Ghost felt it, saw it, his movements turning harder, rougher, faster. "You gonna cum again for me?"

I whimpered.

"Yeah, you are," he whispered. "Cum all over my cock, Halston."

His dirty words sent me spiraling over the edge, my body clenching around him, holding him so fucking tight, my orgasm crashing over me.

Ghost groaned, his own release following fast, his body tensing, his hands gripping me tightly.

By the time I had taken a shower and made my way to the kitchen, the whole house was awake.

Eleanor was at the stove, flipping pancakes, while Joseph sipped coffee at the counter.

Nathan and Jackson were seated at the island, already eating.

"Morning," I greeted everyone, trying to act normal, act like I hadn't just been fucked senseless by Ghost while they were just feet away in the kitchen.

Jackson grinned. "Damn, you look well-rested. Sleep good?"

I ignored him, pouring myself coffee. He had Ghost's sense of humor. The ladies were in for a real treat when he got older.

Eleanor turned and smiled. "Good morning, sweetheart. Hope Kasper didn't keep you up with his snoring."

I almost choked on my coffee. "I didn't hear him snore."

Nathan smirked. "So you did sleep in his room."

I narrowed my eyes. "There were no extra rooms. Was I supposed to sleep outside?"

Jackson grinned. "I mean, I did offer..."

"Shut up, Jackson," Ghost's voice came from behind me.

I turned to see him walking into the kitchen, looking sexy as hell with damp hair, no shirt, his sweatpants hanging low on his hips.

My body reacted to the sight of him. A breath escaped me, and I bit my lip. What was wrong with me? He'd just completely wrecked me, and I already wanted him to do it all over again.

He stretched, his muscles flexing before dropping into the seat beside Nathan.

I quickly turned back to my coffee, willing myself not to look at him again.

"Here, Halston," Eleanor said, placing a plate of pancakes and eggs in front of me.

"Thank you," I said sincerely, grabbing my fork.

"You wanna help me at the ranch today?" Ghost asked casually, spearing his scrambled eggs.

I hesitated, surprised by the question. "Do you want me to?"

Ghost shrugged, not looking up. "You'll be there to feed the cat."

Jackson snickered. "Look at you, getting attached."

Ghost shot him a glare, and Jackson grinned even wider. Yep. Just like his brother.

"If you stay, be prepared to work."

I shrugged. "I can handle it."

Ghost leaned back in his chair, watching me closely. "That right?"

I met his gaze, lifting my chin. "That's right."

His lips curved slightly, like he was enjoying this. "We'll see about that, Tits."

I sighed. "You were doing so well, Ghost. Almost made it a full morning without calling me that."

He winked. "Can't let you get used to it."

Eleanor shook her head. "I don't know how you put up with him, Halston."

I sighed, exaggerating my exhaustion. "I don't either, honestly."

Jackson laughed. "She likes him. That's why."

I picked up my fork and threw a pancake at Jackson's face.

Nathan and Joseph burst out laughing, while Eleanor muttered, "I swear, you boys never grew up."

Chapter 51

The drive back to Ghost's ranch was quiet.

After spending Christmas with his family, we headed back to feed the dogs and Lulu, the weight of the holidays still hanging in the air.

I hadn't told him about the sign. And I wasn't sure how he was going to react. Henry had sweetly offered to take care of it while we were away.

The moment we pulled up, I knew he saw it. How could he not? We were staring at it while he punched the gate code in.

There was a brand new black metal sign hanging over the entrance of the ranch. It bore the logo I'd created for him with the gold 3D horse's head inside a circle in the center of the sign. Legacy Ranch was in big, bold letters above that and Gold Blood. Elite Breeding, smaller, just under the logo on the sign.

I held my breath as Ghost's eyes landed on it. "Merry Christmas," I told him.

His jaw clenched immediately.

Shit.

He drove through the gate. Pulling into his parking spot, he put the truck in park. He killed the engine but didn't get out.

Instead, he turned to me, his voice tight. "You're responsible for that?"

I swallowed, nervous. "Yes."

His grip was still on the steering wheel. "That was expensive. I know because I paid for the first one, and yours is more elaborate."

I hesitated. "I thought you'd like it."

His lips pressed together. "I didn't get you anything."

"I didn't expect anything," I said honestly. Because I actually didn't expect anything in return. I hadn't been thinking about what he might do for me when I ordered the sign. My only thought was wanting to replace the old broken one and hoping he'd like it. "I didn't do it for a return gift."

He let out a sharp breath, his voice turning colder. "I didn't know we were in a relationship."

I stared at him, stunned. "Wow. That's where your head went?"

Ghost turned away, gripping the steering wheel tighter.

I shook my head, my voice perfectly calm. "I didn't ask you for anything, Ghost. I don't want anything. And who said we need to be in a relationship for me to give you a gift?"

Nothing. No response. Just that damn jaw clench again.

I sighed, my frustration trying to break through. "I just wanted to do something nice for you. You paid for my car repairs. You've been hauling me back and forth."

Ghost exhaled sharply. "When it's something like that, don't you think you should run it by me first?"

I threw up my hands. "That negates the surprise."

Silence.

"I'm confused. Why are you really angry with me? I feel like your anger has something behind it I'm not seeing."

He just continued to look at me with that damn scowl, like he was debating how to handle me.

"Jesus, Ghost. I'm not planning a wedding and a white picket fence in my head, if that's what's worrying you."

Ghost didn't answer. Instead, he shoved the door open, stepped out, and slammed it behind him.

I sat there fuming, trying to decide if I should go after him or just go home.

I'm apparently a glutton for punishment, so I went after him.

I rounded the truck, but before I made it two steps, he came back out of the house, walking straight toward me.

That's when the dogs came running, barking, charging straight at me.

I barely had time to react before Ghost said, "Freund!"

The dogs skidded to a halt, sniffing me before immediately sitting.

My breath stuck in my throat. I looked up at him, my heart racing.

"Merry Christmas," he said, his voice calm, softer than before. "You won't have to go through the daily drill anymore."

I was speechless. I knew what this meant. Ghost told the dogs I was a friend. I had earned his respect. And in turn, I had earned theirs.

All the frustration I had been feeling moments before vanished. "Thank you."

Ghost shrugged, shifting on his feet. "It's not expensive, like your gift."

I shook my head, my chest tightening. "It was the best gift you could have ever given me."

Before I could stop myself, I stepped forward, reaching up and grabbing the back of his neck, kissing him.

Ghost exhaled sharply against my lips, his hands gripping my waist, pulling me against him, kissing me back.

After he released me, he headed inside to feed the dogs, and I wandered over to feed Lulu.

I crouched near the shed, refilling Lulu's bowl. She purred, rubbing against my leg before settling in to eat.

As I stood, I caught sight of Henry walking toward the barn.

I headed over. "Hey, Henry."

He turned, giving me a nod and a friendly smile. "Hey, Halston."

I shoved my hands into my jacket pockets, rocking on my heels. "Just wanted to say thank you for fixing my car."

Henry smiled. "It was my pleasure. You sticking around for a while?"

I laughed softly. "Seems like it."

His gaze flicked toward the new sign at the entrance of the ranch. "That was a nice thing you did for Ghost."

I glanced at the sign. "Didn't seem like he thought so at first."

Henry chuckled, shaking his head. "That man doesn't know how to accept kindness."

"Why was he so upset about it? I could tell it wasn't just about the money."

Henry exhaled, crossing his arms. "Because the last person to touch that sign did it to hurt him."

Something cold ran through me. "What do you mean?"

Henry hesitated, then sighed. "Ghost's ex is the one who broke the sign."

I was taken aback at the mention of her. "What?"

"Drove her car straight into one of the wood posts that holds it up."

A sharp silence settled between us.

I waited for more information, but Henry didn't elaborate. He just stood there, his expression closed off now, like he'd already said too much.

I swallowed. "Why?"

Henry's lips pressed into a thin line. "That's Ghost's business if he wants to let you in on it."

I exhaled, my mind turning over possibilities, but Henry's tone made it clear that the conversation was over.

I waved goodbye to him and walked back toward the house.

Whatever had happened between Ghost and his ex; it was something he wasn't ready to talk about. I was guessing that was his one relationship, and it obviously wrecked him seriously for him not to want to even try another relationship. I wasn't sure I wanted to know the story there.

Ghost's voice broke the silence. "You ever notice that cat follows you everywhere?"

I glanced down. Sure enough, Lulu was trotting right behind me, her tiny paws crunching softly against the dirt. I smiled, my chest warming. "She follows you too."

"Nope."

I raised an eyebrow. "She doesn't?"

"Nope."

I frowned, glancing back down at Lulu, who was staring up at me, her big green eyes wide. "Maybe she's just afraid of the dogs. You always have them with you."

Ghost gave me a pointed look. "Even when I tell them to stay, she still doesn't follow me."

I slowed my steps as I watched Lulu weave between my feet.

Ghost chuckled. "She's imprinted on you."

I looked back down at Lulu. She bumped her head against my leg, then hopped up onto a rock, staring at me like she was waiting for my next move.

A feeling settled in my chest, warm and unexpected. She had chosen me to be her family.

I grinned, scratching under Lulu's chin, her purring growing even louder.

Ghost watched me, his lips tugging into a half-smile. "Looks like you're stuck with her."

I glanced over my shoulder, smirking. "Like you're stuck with me?"

His blue eyes sparkled as he gave a slow nod. "Exactly like that."

Chapter 52

The sun was already warming my skin when Ghost pulled the utility task vehicle up to the house.

I'd gone home to change into my cut-off denim shorts, a black racerback tank top, my black hiking boots, and a faded ball cap to block the Texas sun with my thick ponytail hanging out the back.

It was Christmas, but it might as well have been spring with the seventy-degree weather.

Ghost eyed me as I climbed into the passenger seat, his gaze dragging slowly down my legs. "You trying to kill me?" he asked.

I grinned. "It's hot. I'm dressed for the weather."

His eyes lingered a second longer than necessary. "You're not wrong."

He had on jeans and a white tee, his jeans snug on his thick thighs, a black Stetson on his head. He looked like every ranch girl's fantasy. The man didn't even have to try.

We bumped along in the UTV, checking the fence for any signs of damage, tossing tools and posts into the back as we went.

At one stop, I bent down to check the bottom line of wire, and when I glanced back, Ghost was just standing there, watching me. "What?" I asked.

He shook his head, that cocky grin spreading slowly. "Nothin'. Just thinkin' you look real damn good covered in dirt."

I laughed, wiping sweat from my neck. "Maybe I should apply for a job. Think you could handle having me around all day?"

He leaned against a post. "Bad idea."

"Why?"

His eyes dropped to my ass. "Wouldn't get a damn thing done."

I laughed. That did serious things to my ego. "I guess I'll take mercy on you and keep my job, then."

He grinned. "Awful considerate, sweetheart."

We kept cruising for a while with the rumble of the engine beneath us, and country music playing low from the Bluetooth speaker.

The fence ran along a tree-dotted pasture, and Ghost slowed to a crawl when we came up on a spot where the wire had slipped off the post.

He parked, hopping out. "Looks like we've got a loose line."

I stayed in my seat until he called back over his shoulder, "You gonna help or just stare at my ass?"

I laughed, climbing out. "If I'm helping, I expect hazard pay."

"You already get paid in attention and breakfast tacos."

I smiled, stepping in close as he worked on the wire, meeting his smug grin with one of my own. "I want something I really want."

That caught his attention. His brows lifted, and his gaze sharpened as it slid over me slowly, like he was trying to read between every syllable. "And what's that, sweetheart?"

I let the silence linger, watching him tighten the fence wire before answering. "I want something from you. And whenever I want it, you have to give it to me."

His eyes darkened immediately. The smile that tugged at his mouth was all heat and trouble. "Something of a sexual nature?"

I gave him a teasing shrug. "Could be."

"Oh, hell," he said, licking his lips. "Now we're talking."

I tilted my head. "So, deal?"

He stood up to his full height, tossed the tool into the UTV bed, and stepped closer, invading my space. "Let me get this straight... You can claim it... whatever it is, any time you want?"

"That's the deal."

His voice dropped low and thick with want. "You're gonna be the goddamn death of me, Halston."

I smiled sweetly. "You say that like it's a bad thing."

He let out a deep laugh. "Bad? No. Just gonna need to keep my jeans extra roomy from now on."

I laughed, walking back to the UTV, feeling his eyes glued to me the whole time.

"You know," he called from behind me, "if this is how fence checks are gonna go, I might let more of 'em break on purpose."

I laughed again. I liked working with him on the ranch, just the two of us. Being at his place was the only time we got to be alone.

By mid-afternoon, we were filthy. My hands were covered in sweat and dust, my tank clinging to my skin. Ghost had long since shed his shirt and tossed it in the back of the UTV. His chest and abs glistened with sweat. His tattoo-covered body was on full display, his biceps flexing every time he used the post driver.

I was trying to focus. Really. But I was only human.

He handed me a pair of gloves and pointed to the toolbox. "Grab me the pliers and one of those tensioners."

I passed him the tools, standing just close enough to get a good view as he crouched down, his muscles flexing in his back and shoulders. I was trying to keep my focus on the job, but the man looked good in the sun. His skin was tan, and his hair dark from being damp. His forearms were roped with muscle.

"You stare any harder, you're gonna set me on fire," he said without looking up.

I jumped. "I wasn't staring."

He looked over his shoulder, grinning. "Sweetheart. You were gawking."

"I was helping."

"You were perving."

I laughed. "I was doing both."

He smirked and tugged the line tight with one smooth pull. "Fair enough."

When he finally stood up, stretching tall, he looked over at me with that familiar look in his eyes. "Damn," he said, his eyes scanning me. "You really do make dirty look good."

"You checking fences or checking me out?" I teased, glancing sideways at him.

He didn't even pretend to be ashamed. "Multitasking, sweetheart. I'm damn good at it."

I laughed, shaking my head.

We drove a little farther as the sun started its descent in the sky, painting everything in a soft, warm orange. I understood what he loved about this place. Something about it was grounding, peaceful.

"There," he said, pointing ahead.

A section of the fence looked warped, probably where a steer had pushed through or something had leaned too hard against it. He stopped the UTV, hopped out again, and grabbed a few tools from the back.

I got out too, trailing after him. "What do you need?"

He shot me a look over his shoulder. "Just you. Stand there and look pretty while I work."

I rolled my eyes, picked up the spool of wire and tossed it toward him. "Try again. I'm earning my hazard pay."

He laughed. "Fine. Hold that post steady while I clamp this."

I held the fence while he crouched low, his muscles flexing.

Ghost glanced up at me, his eyes catching mine for a beat longer than necessary. "You know..." he said, tightening the clamp with a grunt, "I take back what I said."

My brow furrowed. "About what?"

He leaned back on his heels, wiping the sweat from his brow with the back of his wrist. "That first day—when I called you high-maintenance."

I blinked, surprised by the sudden admission. "Seriously?"

He nodded, his voice quieter now, more thoughtful. "You've been out here in the heat. Getting your hands dirty. No complaints. No whining. Just jumping in and doing the work."

I smirked. "If I knew all it took to impress you was wrangling fence posts, I would've skipped the eyeliner and sarcasm weeks ago."

He chuckled under his breath. "Wouldn't want you to skip the sarcasm. That's half the entertainment."

My lips quirked, but I didn't say anything else. Not because I didn't want to—but because he had just admitted he was wrong.

And that was rarer than a day without attitude on this ranch.

"Still thinking about what you're going to claim?" he asked, not even looking up.

"Maybe."

"You know you're driving me crazy, right?"

I grinned. "That's the goal."

He stood, brushing off his hands, sweat glistening on his chest. "You're pushing me hard, sweetheart."

I raised a brow. "Is that a compliment?"

"Hell yeah, it is," he said. "You've had way too much of my attention today. That's not easy to do."

My heart stuttered at the heat in his voice. I loved that my body had that effect on him. It was empowering and addictive. Especially since he had the same effect on me.

When I walked back to the UTV after helping him tighten a section of wire, I heard him groan behind me.

"Damn," he said. "That ass is distracting."

I turned, laughing. "Ghost."

He stalked forward, wrapped an arm around my waist, and threw me over his shoulder, ass up like I weighed nothing.

I squealed. "What are you doing?"

He smacked my ass, making me yelp. "I've been watching you in those shorts all damn day. You really thought I was gonna make it back to the house without having you first?"

I was breathless, laughing, and turned on all at the same time. "Ghost!"

"Shhh," he said, his voice thick and low. "I'm so fucking hard, I can't think straight."

He carried me into the equipment shed, slammed the door shut behind us, and turned the lock.

Sunlight filtered through the dusty windows, streaking across old tractors, tools, and a workbench that had absolutely no idea it was about to become very multipurpose.

"Ghost," I laughed breathlessly, squirming on his shoulder. "You're out of your mind."

"Damn right I am," he said, setting me down but not letting me go. His hands slid up from my hips, tugging me forward until I was pressed against him. "You've been driving me insane all day. In those shorts. That little tank. That smart-ass mouth..."

"Yeah?" I said, my eyes holding his stare.

"You've got five seconds to tell me to stop," he said, his voice rough as his hands skimmed my thighs.

I smirked. "Go."

Chapter 53

"Damn, Halston," he said, a slow, cocky grin tugging at his mouth. "You keep coming out of that shell like this, and I'm never letting you go back in." His hand slid up my side, his thumb brushing just under my tank top. "I fucking love watching you turn bold on me."

He tossed his hat aside. His mouth was on mine before I could fire back, hot and hungry. He kissed like he fought, with full-commitment, no hesitation. His hands were already under my shirt, his rough palms sliding up my sides.

"You're dangerous," he growled, dipping his head to kiss the curve of my neck. "You and that good-girl smile, sayin' shit like 'hazard pay' and then lookin at me like you wanna ruin me."

"Maybe I do," I whispered, my hands already tugging at the snap of his jeans. "You ever think of that?"

His mouth curved into a devilish smile against my skin. "You're well on your way, sweetheart."

I didn't care about dirt or grease or the fact that we were in an old equipment shed.

I wanted him. Right here. Right now.

He kissed me hard, hot, urgent. My fingers went up around his neck as he backed me into the nearest workbench, sweeping aside a rag and some tools without ever breaking the kiss.

"You're too damn tempting," he whispered against my lips, his hands slipping under my shirt, dragging up my ribs. "Walking around in those tiny-ass shorts, flaunting those legs. Hell, your tits in that tank. What were you trying to do to me?"

"Nothing," I whispered, lying through my teeth. "Just trying to help with some fence work."

"Bullshit," he growled, lifting me onto the edge of the bench, spreading my legs so he could step between them. "You wanted to break me."

He yanked my shirt over my head, my hat coming off with it, and tossed it aside, his gaze dropping to my bra, his hand grazing over the lace.

"I'm not broken yet, sweetheart," he murmured, nipping at my jaw, "but you're getting close."

I laughed, breathless, as his mouth found the spot behind my ear that turned my spine to liquid. "You think I'm doing all this on purpose?"

"Oh, I know you are," he said. "And now I'm gonna show you what happens when you tease me all damn day."

His fingers slid up my thighs, making good on every look he'd given me since this morning.

And this wasn't slow and sweet. This was a man completely wrecked from wanting me all day. And damn if I didn't love it.

His hands were everywhere, roaming my bare skin, teasing the edge of my shorts. His mouth was on my neck, kissing and biting down just enough to make me gasp, to make me want more.

"You know how many times I've thought about doing this?" he growled against my skin, dragging his lips across my collarbone. "Lifting you up, tearing these tiny-ass shorts off, and fucking you right here?"

I shivered, my fingers digging into his shoulders. "What stopped you?"

He leaned back just enough to look at me, his eyes burning with need. "Nothing now."

I lifted for him, and he pulled my shorts and panties down my legs, letting them fall to the ground.

And just like that, he dropped to his knees between my thighs, his hands gripping my hips, his mouth finding me with a groan that vibrated straight through me.

"Fuck, Halston," he whispered, his lips brushing against me. "You taste like sin. You sure you're still a good girl?"

I moaned, dropping my head back.

He ate me slowly and skillfully, like he was savoring every second, every gasp, every roll of my hips, every breathless moan that escaped me. My hands gripped the edge of the bench, my knuckles white, my body taut as he pushed me right to the edge.

And then he pulled back, just before I could fall apart. I whimpered in frustration. "Kasper..."

He looked up, his mouth wet, and his eyes dark with something feral. "I'm not going anywhere, sweetheart. We're just getting started."

I nodded, barely able to breathe.

He stood, grabbing a condom from his wallet, because of course he was always ready. He shoved his jeans and boxer briefs down just far enough, rolling the condom on. My eyes dropped, and I swear I lost the ability to think. He was so fucking beautiful and hard.

"Tell me, sweetheart," he said, his voice thick with lust, brushing the head of his cock along my wet opening. "You want it?"

"Yes," I whispered, desperate. "Please."

That's all he needed.

He drove into me in one powerful thrust, making me cry out, making the tools on the bench rattle from the force. I opened my legs wider, my fingers clawing into his neck, grounding myself as he pulled back and thrust again, harder this time.

"Jesus, you feel like heaven," he growled, slamming into me again and again, setting a brutal rhythm that had me unraveling fast.

He wrapped one hand around the back of my neck and kissed me hard, swallowing my moans as his hips pounded into mine. Every thrust was pure fire. Every sound he made, every groan, every curse, sent me closer to the edge.

"Been thinking about this all day," he whispered against my mouth. "You. Me. Just like this."

"It's all I ever think about since I met you," I said, breathless.

Ghost froze for half a second, just long enough for me to feel the full weight of what I'd said.

Then his eyes locked on mine, wild and blown with heat, his voice rough as sin. "Fuck, Halston... you can't say shit like that to me unless you want me to lose my goddamn mind."

He drove into me again, burying himself.

And the truth just kept coming. "All I think about is you. Every damn day. Every time I touch myself, every time I can't sleep... it's you."

He kissed me hard and hungry. Then he pulled back. "Jesus, sweetheart. You keep that shit up... I'm gonna end up giving you everything you never knew you wanted."

Then he slowed up, grinding his hips into me, and my head immediately dropped back, a rough moan escaping my lips.

"There you go, baby. I know you like that."

My eyes were rolling back in my head as he rolled his hips against me, gripping my ass to his body as he tortured me. "So damn much," I cried out.

"Had to reward that little mouth of yours. See what happens when you tell me the truth?"

"Yes, Kasper!"

Ghost clenched his jaw and picked up the pace, squeezing my ass as he drove into me.

And when I finally shattered, my body convulsing around him, he let loose a curse and buried himself inside me again and again with a low, guttural growl as he came hard, his hips practically vibrating against me.

He pulled back just far enough to look at me and said, "You look so damn good like this. Completely ruined. All mine."

"All yours," I agreed, my eyes burning into his.

He smiled, satisfied with my answer, and kissed me.

I couldn't even argue. Every part of me still throbbed with the echo of him. And I couldn't deny that I loved hearing him say I was all his.

Even though it was dangerous to want. I wanted to be his.

Chapter 54

It had been forever since I'd had a proper girls' night, just me and Niki.

Between work, Lulu, and spending almost every free moment at the ranch with Ghost, my social life had become nonexistent. The only time I saw Niki these days was at the underground fights, which didn't exactly count as quality best-friend time. So when she suggested a night out, I agreed without hesitation.

I needed a break. I needed a distraction from Ghost, from the way he got under my skin, from the way he made me feel too much for a man I wasn't allowed to get attached to. When we had sex in the shed, the way he'd said I was all his was still running through my head, and I couldn't shake it. He made me feel like I was special to him when he said stuff like that, but how long was that going to last before he said otherwise?

We both took a rideshare so we could drink as much as we wanted to, and hit up a local bar, one of those places that wasn't too crowded but still had good music, cold drinks, and a couple of pool tables tucked in the back.

Niki and I grabbed a high-top table, ordered drinks, and made our way to the pool tables, cue sticks in hand.

"I'm gonna kick your ass," Niki teased, chalking the tip of her stick as she lined up the break shot.

I smirked. "Big words for someone who scratched on the break last time."

She rolled her eyes. "That was one time."

I laughed, taking a pull on my beer just as a group of guys approached us.

They were confident, bordering on cocky, the kind of guys who probably thought they were smooth but had nothing on Ghost's effortless arrogance.

One of them, a tall, dark-haired guy with a perfectly practiced smirk, leaned against the pool table, his eyes trailing over me like he was already undressing me in his mind.

"Ladies," he said, flashing a charming grin. "Need some company?"

Niki rolled her eyes, unimpressed.

I smiled politely, shaking my head. "We're good, thanks."

Another guy, who was blonde, muscular, and a little too clean-cut, stepped up beside Niki. "How about a round of doubles? Losers buy the next round?"

The thought of Ghost finding out some random guy bought me a drink or played pool with me sent mixed messages to my brain. On the one hand, I wondered if he'd even be jealous if he knew. On the other hand, it felt wrong to even entertain any other man. Because I had Ghost. Or at least, I had his body. And as much as I hated to admit it, he had so much more of me than that. I was having crazy, filthy, carnal sex with him, and I wasn't allowed to want more.

"We have boyfriends," I told them.

The dark-haired guy raised an eyebrow, clearly not buying it. "You sure about that?"

"Positive," I said, flashing a sweet, unapologetic smile. "But thanks for the offer."

The guy smirked, tipping his beer toward me. "Well, if you change your mind..."

I wouldn't. Not for him. Not for anyone.

Niki and I watched them walk away, then she turned to me, arms crossed. "Boyfriends?"

I sighed. "Don't start."

Niki arched a brow. "Halston. You literally just told some guy that you had a boyfriend."

"It was just an excuse. I didn't come here to get hit on. I came out to hang with you."

Niki smiled. "Awww. Still, I can't believe you blew off some hot guys to hang with me. I would have understood."

"It's me and you tonight."

She nodded. "This is Jen's favorite spot to play, and if she was here, she wouldn't have turned them down."

I laughed and took a swig of my beer. "Well, she has issues she needs to work on," I said, causing Niki to laugh.

I just wanted to go out, drink, dance, and have fun. But of course, the universe had other plans.

We had just ordered another round of drinks when Niki stiffened beside me.

I followed her gaze. And my stomach dropped.

Across the bar, Jen was sitting in a booth... with a guy who wasn't Drew.

She was laughing, her fingers brushing his arm, her body angled toward him like he was the only person in the room.

I stared, my hands squeezing into fists at my sides. "Tell me I'm hallucinating."

Niki exhaled, shaking her head. "You're not."

I didn't hesitate. I marched straight toward Jen, my pulse pounding, my anger boiling over before I even reached the table.

She looked up just as I stopped in front of her booth, her eyes widening for half a second before she covered it with a smile. "Halston! Niki! Girls' night too?"

I ignored her fake enthusiasm, crossing my arms. "I know Drew doesn't know about this."

Jen's smile faltered. She glanced at the guy beside her, then back at me, lowering her voice slightly. "No. And don't you dare tell him."

I tilted my head, my voice calm but sharp. "I will if you don't."

Jen's eyes flashed with irritation. "You're supposed to be my girl."

I let out a short, humorless laugh. "And you're supposed to be a good friend and girlfriend. You're not being either. Cheating and putting us in this position."

"Niki has my back."

Niki shook her head, taking a step back. "Uh-uh. You're on your own on this one. Drew doesn't deserve what you're doing."

Jen's jaw clenched, her eyes darting between us. "Have some loyalty."

I stared at her, disgusted. "Loyalty?" I shook my head. "I'm done here."

I turned to leave, Niki following close behind, but Jen's voice rang out behind us. "Fuck you both."

I stopped, glancing over my shoulder, my tone sarcastic. "Enjoy your night." I nodded toward her date, then smirked. "And that guy looks like a douche."

I didn't wait for a response. I just walked away, leaving Jen and her terrible decisions behind.

Chapter 55

After girls' night, I went home feeling drunk and content.

Niki and I ended up at another bar after leaving Jen behind. We got a little tipsy and bad-mouthed Jen the rest of the night. Then we called another rideshare to drop us at home.

The night had been fun, a much-needed distraction, but it hadn't been enough. Ghost was still in my head. Like always. And I wanted him to be here right now.

I showered, letting the hot water wash away the lingering smell of the bar, then threw on pajama shorts and a black t-shirt before climbing into bed.

I wasn't toasted anymore, but still feeling pretty good, and the thought to text Ghost crossed my mind. But I knew drunk texting him might just lead to me acting like an idiot, and maybe ruining what we had. Whatever that was.

I was just about to turn off my light when my phone vibrated on my nightstand.

It was a text from Ghost. ***How was your night?***

I smiled at the screen. He never asked about my night. I loved knowing he was thinking about me.

I could have texted back, but I hated long conversations over text, and I wasn't about to type out a novel.

So, instead, I hit call.

He answered on the first ring. "You hate texting that much?" His voice was low and smooth.

"Yes," I smirked. "Plus, I wanted to hear your voice."

His chuckle sent a slow, delicious shiver down my spine. "Careful, Tits. You keep saying things like that. I'm gonna start thinkin' you actually like me."

I smiled, settling deeper under the covers. "How was the rest of your day?"

"Same as always. Worked on the ranch."

"Sounds fulfilling."

"Very. I actually got something done today without you there."

I laughed. "But it wasn't as much fun without me, was it?"

"Definitely less entertaining."

I didn't like that response. "You can do better than that," I said softly.

He chuckled, that low, lazy sound I loved way too much. "You get all needy when you're tipsy, sweetheart."

I smiled. "Do not."

"You do," he said, still laughing. "You want compliments? Fine. You make everything more fun. Even fixing fences and shoveling shit."

I laughed. "See? Was that so hard?"

"Not hard yet," he whispered.

"Ghost." My tone was a weak warning.

"What?" he asked innocently. "I'm just saying, your drunk voice is doing things to me."

"Well, you're turning me on too."

"Yeah?" He waited a beat, then asked, "Is that why you called instead of texting? To torture me?"

I swallowed, my body vibrating. "I wanted to hear your voice."

"Yeah?" His tone was softer now. "Well, I wanted to hear yours, too."

My chest squeezed. I closed my eyes, smiling. "You did?"

"Course I did," he said. "How was your night out?"

"It was fun. Niki and I played pool and had a couple of drinks. Some guys tried to hit on us, but we weren't interested. Then we ended up at another bar before heading home. Oh, we also ran into—"

"They hit on you?" he asked, cutting me off.

It took me a minute to circle back to the part of the conversation he was talking about. "That's what guys do at bars, Ghost."

"And you told them to fuck off, right?"

I laughed, biting my lip, loving the edge in his tone. "Of course. I didn't go there to get hit on. I went to have fun with Niki."

There was silence again. "Good girl."

I swallowed. Why did I love his approval so much?

"Did you?"

"Did I what?"

"Did you have fun with Niki?"

I nodded. "Yeah, sure."

"Did you think about me? While you were out?"

I felt my cheeks flush hot and my body catch fire. I didn't know if it was just his voice or the way his words came out dripping with sexual innuendo. Because yes. Yes, I had. "What kind of question is that?" I deflected.

He chuckled. "A yes or no one."

I stayed quiet.

"Come on, Halston. Tell me the truth. Remember what happens when you tell me the truth?"

A moan slipped out.

"I knew you'd remember," he said with another chuckle. "Were you sitting at that bar, drinking with Niki, thinking about the way I spread your legs and fuck you so hard you scream my name?"

Jesus Christ. I swallowed hard, clenching my thighs together under the blankets. "Yes."

"That's my girl," he said. "You're blushing right now, aren't you?"

"Shut up."

He laughed, and my stomach fluttered. "You know what I want?"

I licked my lips, my pulse picking up speed. "What?"

His voice dropped an octave lower, the way it always did when he was about to say something that would ruin me. "I want you to touch yourself."

My breath hitched. "Ghost." It was meant as a warning, but came out more like a plea.

"I wanna hear you. Just like you sounded in the shed. Put the phone to your left ear. Use your right hand."

My skin prickled, heat pooling between my legs. I knew I shouldn't. But I wanted to. I wanted to do exactly what he told me to do. He brought out a darker side of me, and I liked it.

Silently, I shifted under the covers, bringing the phone to my left ear as my right hand slid down under my waistband. "Okay."

"Is your hand in those sexy lace panties?"

"Yes."

"Good girl," Ghost whispered. "Now, touch that pretty pussy for me. I want to hear what I do to you."

I moaned. His dirty words were going to be the death of me.

"Stick those fingers inside now, baby."

I gasped as my fingers found my slick heat, my body already ready for him, just from his voice, his words, his commands.

"That's it. Get yourself nice and wet."

My breath was ragged, my body vibrating with pleasure and anticipation.

Ghost groaned. "Fuck, I wish I was there. Wish I could feel you. You know how wet you get for me? You know how crazy that drives me?"

I bit my lip, stifling a moan.

"Don't hold back, Halston. Let me hear you."

I let out a soft whimper, my fingers circling that sensitive spot, my body arching slightly off the bed.

"That's my girl." His voice was pure sin, dark and rich, dripping with desire. "Do you wish it was my fingers instead? Do you wish I was there, making you cum with my tongue instead of your hand?"

A shaky breath left me. "Yes."

He groaned. "I bet you taste so fucking good right now."

"Kasper." I was so close, my body tensing, my hips rocking against my own hand.

"Cum for me, Halston. I wanna hear you when you fall apart."

I shattered, moaning his name, my body trembling as I came undone, my breath harsh with uneven gasps.

"Fuck, Halston. That was the hottest thing I've ever heard."

I smiled lazily, my body warm. "You're such a bad influence," I told him, grinning into the phone.

He chuckled. "You love it."

I really did. I couldn't keep denying it either. I was past that point.

Chapter 56

After hanging up with Ghost, I couldn't sleep. Not even close.

I tossed and turned for half an hour, staring at the ceiling and arguing with myself until I finally gave in to the stupid, impulsive idea clawing at the inside of my skull. I wanted him. Plain and simple. And if he wasn't going to come to me, I was going to him.

I called a rideshare, pulled on my pajama pants and a hoodie, grabbed my phone, and slipped out.

As I punched the code into Ghost's front door, I hoped the gate and front door notifications didn't wake him up. I was collecting my payment, and I wanted it to be a surprise.

His bedroom door was open.

It was dark, but the soft glow from the baseboard lights lining the hallway cast just enough light to see him sleeping peacefully on his back, his chest bare. The comforter was kicked halfway off the bed; the sheets resting low across his hips. His sculpted torso made my mouth go dry.

God, he was beautiful.

I slipped out of my clothes, dropping them to the floor one by one, then climbed into his bed and straddled him, pressing my bare body against his as I leaned down and kissed his neck.

His voice rumbled, low and sleep-rough. "Are you actually on top of me naked right now, or am I just having the best fucking dream?"

I laughed softly. "I'm here for my hazard pay."

He let out a breathy laugh, his eyes still closed. "You're fucking dangerous, you know that?"

I kissed my way down his chest.

Then he opened one eye and squinted at me. "Tell me you didn't drive here drunk."

"Of course not," I said, biting at his nipple. "I took a rideshare."

"Drunk?" he asked, his voice going gravelly again. "That might be just as dangerous. People take advantage of sweet, sexy drunk women."

I smiled against his skin. "I'm not drunk, Ghost. I'm barely buzzed."

His jaw clenched as my tongue flicked over his nipple. "That orgasm didn't satisfy you, sweetheart?"

I shook my head, grinding my hips down against his hard cock beneath me. "I need you."

He groaned low, tortured. His hands flew to my hips, gripping tight. "Jesus, Halston," he growled. "You showing up here like this... crawling into my bed naked, tasting me like that..."

I kissed my way higher, flicking my tongue against his earlobe. "Told you. I'm here to collect."

His hands came up to cradle my face, forcing me to look down at him. His blue eyes were heavy with heat. "You know you're playing with fire, right?" he said, his thumbs brushing my cheeks. "You do shit like this, and I'm not gonna let you leave this bed."

I rolled my hips slowly, feeling the way his cock flexed beneath the thin fabric separating us. I smirked. "Is that the payment?"

"No," he growled. "That's just interest."

I leaned down, pressing my lips to his. "Then give me what I came for, Ghost."

He flipped us before I could blink.

One second I was on top, in control, and the next, I was beneath him. Ghost's hard body pinned me down, his mouth sealing mine, his hand sliding between my thighs like he knew exactly what I needed.

Spoiler alert. He did.

"I pictured you in your bed, hand down your panties," he whispered against my lips, his breath hot. "I was wishing you were here. In these sheets. Moaning my name."

I couldn't believe he'd just confessed that to me. I swallowed hard, breathless. "I'm here now."

"Yeah, you are," he said, dragging his mouth down the column of my throat, licking the skin just above my clavicle.

His hand cupped my breast, his thumb brushing over my nipple. I arched into his touch.

"I don't even think you realize what you do to me," he whispered, his voice raw, dark. "Every time you laugh. Every time you sass me. Every time you bite that goddamn lip..."

I shuddered beneath him, my hands gripping his shoulders. "Then show me."

He kissed me again, deep, consuming, like he wanted to brand me from the inside out. His fingers teased and stroked until I was gasping, writhing beneath him, begging without words.

He pulled back just enough to look down at me. "You want your payment?" he asked, his voice low, dangerous.

I nodded, my breath ragged.

"Then keep your hands on me, sweetheart," he growled. "Because I'm not stopping until you're wrecked."

Then he parted my thighs, pushing them wide open, and his tongue was on me, his fingers gripping my thighs, holding me.

He slid his tongue up, circling my clit a few times before sucking it, then did it again.

I choked out a cry, my legs spasming.

"You're shaking, baby," he said, his voice smugness and heat.

I whimpered, my body on fire, my control slipping fast.

He hummed against me, the vibrations shooting through me.

I was on the edge, sweat beading on my body.

And then his mouth left me.

"Kasper."

"Yeah, baby?" His voice was a whisper as he discarded his boxers and rolled on the condom.

I let out a strangled noise as he moved up my body, licking, teasing. His mouth brushed against my lips in a slow kiss.

I whimpered, lifting my hips against him, feeling just how hard he was, how ready he was. "Please," I whispered. "I can't wait."

He groaned, gripping his cock, running it through my wetness, teasing me. His eyes locked on mine, watching every response.

I gasped as he buried himself inside me, filling me.

"Fuck yes." His voice was ragged, wrecked, his forehead dropping to mine. "So goddamn good."

I clung to him, my body arching. And then he moved. Slow at first, just enough to make me feel every inch, every drag, every delicious bit of friction.

My eyes widened when he pulled my hips up off the mattress, pushing deep until he could go no further. He held my hips like that, pumping slowly, grinding against me in small circles.

I cried out as he held that slow pace. "Oh... Yes... Kasper."

"I know what you like, sweetheart," he said, his voice thick with restraint.

"God yes, you do."

He smiled, our eyes still locked. "How's that hazard pay, baby?"

"Too good," I bit out.

My nails dug into his back as he moved, dragging over every sensitive nerve ending.

And the way he watched me, his eyes dark, full of heat, full of want, only made it worse.

Better. Hotter.

"I love watching your face when I'm inside you," he whispered. "Every twitch, every gasp. Every damn time I make you fall apart."

I whimpered, already unraveling.

Then he sped up. Hard. Unforgiving. His hips slammed into mine, his hands gripping my wrists, pinning them above my head as his mouth opened over mine, devouring my moans.

He continued to drive into me, torturing me as my body climbed higher, begging for release.

I cried out, "Don't stop, Kasper!"

My body spasmed as I screamed out, my orgasm overtaking me.

He was breathing hard, his lips brushing the side of my neck when he gave in to his own release, finishing with fast pumps and a groan he buried in my neck.

Ghost slowed inside me, letting the last waves of pleasure dissipate.

Then he dropped back on the bed.

I collapsed beside him, still shaking, my body humming from the aftershocks. My breath caught on a laugh. "That was... incredible."

Ghost let out a deep, satisfied exhale. "Fuck yeah, it was."

I turned my head, grinning despite how wrecked I felt. "Consider the hazard pay... paid in full."

He chuckled, low and wicked. "Sweetheart, that was a bonus round. You're gonna need a whole new contract at this rate."

I laughed, letting my eyes drift shut, still trying to catch my breath. "Send it to my inbox."

"You sure you're ready for the fine print?"

My lips curled. "Bring it on."

He reached over with a laugh, giving my thigh a firm squeeze.

After letting myself enjoy a few moments of aftermath, I sat up, scooting toward the edge of the bed. "I should get going."

His arm shot around my waist, pulling me back against his bare chest. "Stay."

I turned my head, surprised. "You don't do sleepovers."

"It's late," he said simply. "You don't need to be calling a rideshare at this hour."

"I'm a big girl," I said, pulling away again.

He gripped my hips, dragging me back to him. "Don't start that shit. We both know that has nothing to do with you being safe at night."

I exhaled. "Fine. But I'll be okay."

I moved, and once again, he dragged me back with a frustrated growl. "I said stay the night."

I laughed, breathless. "You're seriously turning me on right now."

He grinned at me as I smirked at him over my shoulder. "You like being thrown around? That get you off?"

"Just when you do it," I whispered sweetly.

He groaned low, his hands already moving around me, pulling me further into him. "Stop eyefucking me, sweetheart, or I'm gonna throw you down and ruin you all over again."

I bit my lip, trying to fight the rush that rocketed through me.

He saw it. Felt it.

He growled. "Fuck me, sweetheart. You are a sweet fucking surprise."

I smiled, but my body was already lit like a fuse. "I don't know how the hell you do that," I whispered.

His brow arched. "Do what?"

"Completely wreck me... and somehow still have me turned on," I said. "Like, I should be ruined. Out of commission. But here I am, lying here thinking about round two."

Ghost's smile turned molten as he pulled me down on the bed and pinned me with his thigh. "That's because your body already knows what your mouth is still too proud to say."

"Is that right?" I asked with a smirk.

He leaned over, brushing his lips against mine, smug and soft all at once. "That's right. I can read that body like a book, sweetheart."

"If you're such an expert reader, maybe you should study the sequel. I think you'll find the plot gets even dirtier."

Ghost's grin turned feral as he rolled back over me, his body pinning mine with effortless heat. "Oh, sweetheart," he whispered against my mouth, "I was hoping there'd be a sequel."

His lips dragged down my neck, his voice thick and rough. "And trust me, I'm the kind of bastard who reads the dirtiest chapters twice."

Chapter 57

The smell of fresh coffee and sizzling bacon filled the kitchen as I worked at the stove, humming softly to myself.

Ghost was still asleep. After the second round, the man had earned his sleep.

I figured I'd let him sleep in and make him breakfast.

I slid the bacon onto a plate, grabbed the eggs, and cracked them into the hot pan, the butter sizzling on impact.

Then Ghost's voice, still heavy with sleep, came from right behind me. "You trying to fatten me up, Tits?"

I jumped, startled, the spatula flying out of my hand like it had been shot from a cannon.

He chuckled, low and smug and way too satisfied with himself.

I turned to shoot him a glare, but it died in my throat the second I saw him. He was barefoot, his hair a mess, and he was wearing nothing but a pair of low-hanging boxer briefs.

And Jesus fucking Christ. I forgot how to breathe. How to function. How to do anything but stare at him like a damn idiot.

His abs. His biceps. The sexy ink covering his chest and arms. The sharp V-line. The man was carved out of sin, pure muscle, rough edges, and raw sex appeal. And my already sex-worn body had the audacity to tighten with need again.

Then I dropped the pan right onto the floor, eggs splattering everywhere.

Ghost raised a brow, his lips tugging into a cocky smirk. "Did you just drop breakfast because of me?"

"Yes. You distracted me."

He laughed, stepping closer, slow and deliberate, his eyes dragging down my body like he could read every filthy thought in my head. "You mean my nearly naked body distracted you?"

I bent to grab the pan, but Ghost was faster. He caught my wrist, pulling me back up. His other hand landed on my hip, firm and possessive.

His voice dropped to that low, teasing drawl that always made my knees weak. "You've seen me naked before, sweetheart. You had me inside you not even six hours ago."

I bit my lip, my pulse kicking up as I swayed closer to him.

He noticed. Oh, he noticed.

His eyes glowed with heat and laughter before he leaned in, his lips brushing my ear, his breath hot against my sensitive skin. "You want me again already, don't you?"

I clenched my thighs and growled under my breath. "It's so frustrating. How do you do that to me? It's kind of embarrassing."

Ghost pulled back to look at me, smirking like the cocky bastard he was. "I'm just built different, baby."

I let out a laugh, swatting at his chest–like that would do anything to stop the pull between us.

He kissed me then. His lips played with mine, his tongue sweeping in just enough to make me shiver, just enough to make me want. His hands slid around my waist, pulling me closer, until there was nothing between us but skin and heat.

I sighed against his mouth.

"Come on," he said, brushing his lips against mine. "Let's take a shower."

"Together?" I asked, hopeful.

"That was the idea," he said with a laugh, nudging me toward the hallway.

"I have to clean up this mess first."

"I'll clean it up. You go get started," he said, smacking my ass as I turned. "You take longer. And I've got a fight in a few hours."

I nodded, biting my lip to hide my grin as I headed toward his bedroom.

Chapter 58

We pulled up to the property just after sunset. The entire place was lit up like a damn underground fortress. Armed guards in all black stood at the gate, checking everyone in with hard stares and even harder grips on their rifles.

This was no joke.

Ghost rolled the window down, one arm casually draped over the steering wheel like he wasn't even phased.

One of the guards stepped up to the truck. Blonde, tall, built like a damn linebacker. He looked in at us and said, "This is a private event. Your name has to be on the list to get in."

Ghost gave his name.

The guy raised a brow. "No shit? Let me see your license."

Without a word, Ghost reached into his wallet and handed it over.

The guard glanced down, squinting at the ID. "This says Kasper."

Ghost smirked. "Yeah. That's my real name." He said it cocky, but not in a dickish way—like a man who knew exactly who he was and didn't need to prove it.

The guard flipped through the clipboard, double-checking. Then his eyes widened. "Oh, shit. That is your real name."

He handed the license back with a new level of respect in his voice. "It's nice to meet you, sir. I've heard plenty about you."

Ghost gave him a half-smile. "Glad my reputation precedes me."

"Yes, sir."

"Just call me Ghost."

"Yes, sir—uh, Ghost." The guy nodded, clearly trying not to fangirl. "I already laid down a hundred on you. I can't wait to see you in action."

Ghost chuckled. "I'll try not to disappoint."

I laughed as we pulled through the gate, and he glanced over at me with a raised brow. "What?"

"You're like a celebrity. That guy was star-struck."

He just shook his head, but I could see the amused twitch at the corner of his mouth.

"I'm sleeping with a fight god." I teased, throwing it out there with full dramatic flair.

He laughed. "You're cute, sweetheart."

There was a space reserved right up front, marked with a sign that said Ghost in bold black letters.

Ghost pulled into the space. He killed the engine and rounded the truck to open my door like a gentleman.

"Thank you," I said, but instead of stepping out, I reached for his shirt, pulling him in until he was wedged between my thighs.

I kissed him. My tongue slid past his lips to taste him, my hands going around his neck. I didn't care that we were in the open or that someone might see. I kissed him until my head spun, until I was seriously considering dragging him into the backseat and making him miss the damn fight.

When I finally pulled back, breathless and needing more, I whispered against his lips, "I had to get in one last kiss, since I'm not allowed to touch you in there. I have to stand with our friends and act normal. Keep my hands to myself."

He smirked, brushing his thumb across my bottom lip. "Don't worry, sweetheart," he said, his voice dipping low. "I'll be mentally ripping your clothes off the whole time."

That sent a shiver down my spine and all sorts of dirty pictures through my head.

The venue was an outdoor setup, and the crowd was massive. Booths lined the perimeter, selling everything from overpriced burgers to craft beer in plastic cups. Somewhere in the distance, music was playing, thumping low beneath the hum of voices and shouts.

Ghost and I had just gotten through the main entrance when he turned to me. "I gotta go check in. I'll see you after the fight."

I nodded, trying to keep my tone casual, even though I already felt a little on edge. "Be careful out there."

He smirked. "Always, sweetheart."

Then he hit me with that devastating smile-wink combo, the one that turned my brain to mush and made my thighs clench without warning.

And just like that, he was gone, swallowed by the crowd.

I exhaled slowly and made my way through the bodies, scanning for familiar faces near the front of the massive platform stage that had been set up for the fights.

I spotted Josh first, tall and easy to find. Drew was beside him, and Nikki waved me over when she saw me. It was just the three of them. No Jen.

Interesting.

As I got close, Nikki handed me a cold beer with a grin. "Here you go, babe."

"Thank you, sweetie," I said, taking it gratefully, twisting the top off.

"Ghost here yet?" Drew asked, looking around.

"He's back there getting ready."

"Cool. I heard he's got three fights today."

"Three?" I blinked, the beer suddenly not as appetizing. One was hard enough to sit through without chewing my nails off, but three?

"Don't worry," Josh said, slinging an arm across my shoulders. "Ghost hasn't lost one yet."

I nodded, trying to swallow the worry rising in my throat.

I knew he was good. He was terrifyingly good. But this was the first time I'd been at one of his fights since we started sleeping together.

I didn't want to see that pretty face marred. I didn't want to see him hurt.

But I had to act nonchalant. Chill. Just another spectator in the crowd.

No one here knew about us, not even Nikki, and I told her everything. But with Ghost, it felt like if I said it out loud, it would break whatever was happening between us. He wasn't a relationship guy. He didn't do labels or long talks. He slept with women and never saw them again.

So I wasn't really sure what we were doing. All I knew was I felt lucky he hadn't kicked me to the curb yet, and I was going to enjoy whatever this was for as long as he let me.

The crowd started to shift and tighten, voices rising.

And my pulse kicked up.

Because somewhere behind that stage... Ghost was getting ready to fight.

Chapter 59

The crowd was wild, pressed in tight around the makeshift arena under the open sky.

The first fight had already started, fists flying and blood spraying, but I barely watched.

My beer sat untouched in my hand, my eyes fixed on the entrance at the back of the platform. I couldn't focus, couldn't breathe properly, not with the adrenaline humming low in my chest like a warning.

The first two fighters tore into each other like animals, with pure brutality. No strategy. Just fists, rage, and the desire to break something.

It wasn't like that when Ghost fought. Ghost studied. He watched. He learned how to dismantle his opponents from the way they moved, the way they breathed. Every hit he threw had purpose behind it. His fighting was strength, yes, but also strategy, skill, and knowledge.

That was the first thing I noticed about him the first time I watched him fight. He didn't just fight to win. He fought as if he already knew he'd win.

The match ended in a mess of blood and cheers with one man slumped on the mat while the other threw his hands in the air, victorious and panting like a rabid dog.

The announcer's voice boomed through the speakers, barely audible over the roar of the crowd. "And next up—undefeated in every match he's entered—give it up for... Ghost!"

I shot up straight, yelling his name along with the rest of the crowd as he stepped into the light.

That cocky smirk was painted across his face like a promise. God, he looked dangerous.

We all cheered, the energy vibrating through the space like a live wire.

He was one of the crowd favorites, and not just because he was undefeated, but because people loved to watch him fight. He moved like no one else in that ring. MMA style. Fast as hell, ducking, weaving, slipping out of reach like he was two steps ahead of every punch. It's why, despite the chaos of each match, he always walked away without much damage to his face.

The other fighter stepped into the ring, pacing, flexing, trying to rile the crowd.

Ghost didn't even flinch.

He tilted his head, gave the guy a once-over, then said loud enough for the front row to hear: "Hope you brought a pillow. You'll be sleeping this one off."

Laughter broke out.

I grinned.

The guy snarled, cracking his neck. "I'm gonna pummel that pretty face, Ghost."

But Ghost just smirked like he'd already mapped it all out in his head.

The bell rang.

And damn, he was beautiful in motion. Every strike was precise, every dodge fluid. He wasn't just fighting; he was dismantling, letting the guy wear himself out with wild punches, absorbing only what he had to, and always moving. The hits he did land were brutal. Sharp. Smart.

The fight didn't last long. None of his ever did.

And when his opponent finally went down, crumpling like a broken marionette, the crowd exploded.

Ghost stood over him, breathing hard but grinning like the cocky bastard he was, his chest rising and falling, wrapped knuckles stained red.

Still undefeated.

I screamed, clapping and yelling his name, but quickly reined it in, like I didn't want to throw him down and kiss the blood off his mouth the moment I could get close enough.

Because damn, that was my fight god.

The crowd was still buzzing from his win when Ghost made his way over to us, weaving through bodies like he hadn't just beaten a man half to death ten minutes ago.

His shirt was off, abs slick with sweat and streaked faintly with someone else's blood, his hands still wrapped. He looked like sin in motion, grinning, smug, and riding that post-fight high.

I handed him a cold beer the second he reached us. "For the champ," I said casually.

He took it with a cocky grin. "Thanks, sweetheart. You always take such good care of me."

"Yeah, well, don't get used to it," I replied, rolling my eyes like I wasn't imagining all the ways I wanted to climb him later.

He cracked the beer and took a long pull, still watching me like he could see straight through the mask I wore for the others.

"You see that fight?" he asked, licking a bit of foam from his bottom lip. "Made that motherfucker tap faster than women do when I've got my mouth between their—"

"Jesus, Ghost," I cut him off, swatting his shoulder with the back of my hand. "Can you not talk like that in public? So vulgar."

He just smirked, completely unfazed. "Just making conversation."

"Disgusting conversation. No one wants to hear about your slutty conquests."

"No?" he asked, his eyes sparkling mischievously. "You're telling me you're not going to fantasize about me when you're alone in the shower later?"

Josh snorted on the other side of me, shaking his head. "You two never quit, huh?"

"Not my fault she's obsessed," Ghost said, tipping his beer toward me with a wink.

I rolled my eyes, playing my part as always. "Please. Listen to you. You're the one obsessed with who I'll be thinking about later. Trust me, you're the only one thinking about you."

Everyone laughed.

Ghost leaned in slightly, his voice low enough that only I could hear it. "You didn't say that when you were begging for my cock last night."

I hoped my face stayed neutral on the outside, because inside my heart felt like it stopped in my chest. "Jesus, Ghost. You know I have a shitty poker face," I whispered through a tight smile.

He chuckled, taking another sip of beer. "You're lucky I've got another fight to burn off this energy, or I'd take you behind that food truck and make you scream."

"Charming," I said, lifting my beer to my lips, smirking just enough to let him know he was getting to me.

Josh glanced between us. "I swear, one of these days she's gonna cave and actually let you take her out."

Ghost tilted his head, that shit-eating grin back in full force. "One of these days, huh?"

I shrugged. "Don't hold your breath."

"I doubt it," Drew said. "Halston is too much of a good girl for Ghost here."

Ghost grinned at that, his eyes shooting to me. "I do love to ruin good girls."

My breath caught in my throat. Holy hell. The man was killing me.

We stood around talking and laughing about the last fight, the ridiculous guy selling glow-in-the-dark cotton candy, and the dude in the crowd who kept yelling "Finish him!" like we were in a damn video game.

Ghost leaned against the railing beside me, relaxed, loose from the win.

Drew was mid-story, something about a bachelor party gone wrong in Tijuana, when a woman approached us.

She was tall and blonde. Every inch of her was engineered for male attention.

"Hi," she said, smiling directly at Ghost, completely ignoring the rest of us. "Can I get a picture with you?"

Ghost didn't hesitate. "No problem."

She handed her phone to me, then all but threw herself at him, her arms wrapping around his neck, pressing those massive fake tits right into his chest. She leaned in close, giggling like she'd just won the lottery.

I gave a tight smile. "Sure. I'll take that for ya."

I took a few pictures, then handed her the phone back.

Then she slipped a card, or maybe it was a napkin, who the hell knew, into Ghost's hand. "Call me," she purred. "I'll entertain you some night when you're bored."

Ghost just smiled with smooth confidence and put the number in his pocket like it was nothing, like I wasn't standing right there. And maybe it was nothing to him. But it felt like a knife to my heart. A sharp little twist that made my stomach clench. I hated the jealous streak I had when it came to Ghost. It was a shitty feeling I didn't enjoy.

I didn't say a word. I didn't even flinch. Because we were with our friends. Because we weren't anything. He'd said it more times than I could count. Don't get attached. I don't do relationships. This means nothing. And I'd agreed that it was just sex. That was the deal.

So, I swallowed the lump in my throat, forced the burn in my chest down where it belonged, and looked away. "I'm gonna grab another beer. Anyone else want one?" I asked, hoping my voice was casual.

The guys said yes, and Nikki nodded, handing me her empty. "You're a saint."

"Only on weekends," I said with a smile I didn't feel. And then I walked off with the sound of Ghost laughing behind me, chasing me through the crowd.

I was just pulling a few bills from my pocket when a warm body pressed up behind me, his arm reaching past mine to hand the vendor his card. "I got it," Ghost said, his voice low by my ear.

His chest brushed against my back. I could feel all of his heat, muscle and smug energy. I shivered, betrayed by my own damn body. "You didn't have to do that," I said, trying to sound unaffected.

"I wanted to," he said simply.

I glanced up at him, my walls still halfway up. "Thanks."

He nodded.

I grabbed my beer, still trying to keep my emotions locked down.

Ghost gathered the four bottles and cradled them effortlessly in one arm. I gave him a weak smile, one that said I appreciated the gesture.

He tried to make small talk on the walk back, something about the next matchup, some guy he'd trained with, but I just gave a nod and a tight-lipped smile. Not cold. Just... distant.

Out of the corner of my eye, I saw him adjust his grip, transferring all the bottles to his left arm, pressing them against his chest.

Then, he dipped his right hand into his pocket. Without a word, as we passed a trash can, he pulled out the woman's number and tossed it away like it was nothing, like she meant nothing.

I couldn't lie. My heart did a quiet little backflip, and relief washed over me.

Then his palm landed on my ass, making me yelp and laugh in surprise. "Asshole!"

He just shot me that devastating smile-wink combo that was cocky and playful and so damn hot, I felt my thighs tighten. "Careful with that," I warned, eyeing him, "if you don't want me attacking you in public."

His grin turned wicked. "Save that for the drive home, sweetheart."

Chapter 60

I pulled up to Legacy Ranch, my mind still buzzing from her early morning call.

Jen had begged me not to tell Drew. She told me she was drunk and wasn't in her right mind, and that she promised it wouldn't happen again.

I didn't believe a word of it, but I told her I'd think about it.

I hated disloyalty, hated being put in a position where I had to choose between keeping a secret and doing the right thing.

So I did the only thing I knew how to do when I was frustrated. I drove to Ghost's ranch.

Maybe he'd piss me off enough to distract me from everything else, or fuck me so good I could forget for a while.

After feeding Lulu, I found Ghost in his gym, shirtless, his body slick with sweat as he landed a sharp series of punches against the hanging bag.

I leaned against the doorway, watching for a moment. "Hey."

He barely glanced at me, his fists still flying, muscles rippling with every movement. "You look like you've got something on your mind."

I sighed, stepping inside. "You could say that."

Ghost threw one final punch, then grabbed a towel, wiping his face. "What happened?"

I shook my head. "Jen pissed me off. I don't want to talk about it."

He eyed me for a moment, then nodded. "Fine. You wanna work some of that frustration out?"

"How?"

He smirked. "By letting me kick your ass."

I rolled my eyes. "Oh, great. That sounds fun."

Ghost chuckled, tossing me a pair of fingerless gloves. "Come on, smartass. Let's see what you remember from last time."

I sighed but slipped the gloves on. This was better than sitting around overthinking everything.

We moved to the sparring mat, Ghost rolling his shoulders as he faced me. "Alright. Let's see if you remember the wrist lock I showed you."

I nodded, stepping forward, reaching for his wrist like he had taught me before. But this time, the second I grabbed him, he twisted out of my hold effortlessly and swept my legs out from under me. I hit the mat with a soft thud, looking up at him.

He grinned. "No hesitation, Halston. If you're gonna go for it, commit."

I groaned, getting up. "You could've warned me."

"An attacker wouldn't warn you."

I sighed, rolling my shoulders. "Fine. Again."

We repeated the move, and this time, I managed to lock his wrist, but before I could finish, he reversed it, twisting my arm behind my back and pinning me.

His chest pressed against my back, his breath hot against my ear. "Too slow," he said.

I gritted my teeth. "You're cheating."

"I'm winning."

I elbowed him in the ribs, and he let go, laughing as I spun to face him again.

"Better," he admitted.

We kept sparring, moving through different techniques, his hands correcting my form, his body brushing against mine in ways that were far too distracting. It kept bringing me back to everything Ghost did to me. I loved the way he spoke to me—so vulgar and insanely hot. The way he made me cum. How he made me scream from insane pleasure.

We were close. Too close to concentrate on technique.

Ghost had my wrist in his grip, guiding me through another self-defense move. His voice was low and patient; his body pressed just enough against mine to steal my attention.

I loved the banter and the way he taught me with total focus, like I actually mattered to him. Maybe I didn't. Maybe this was just something to pass the time for him. But in that moment, in every moment like this with him, I didn't care.

So when he grabbed me again, I moved on him, leaning into him, kissing him.

Ghost froze for half a second, his grip tightening on my arm like he hadn't expected it, like I had caught him off guard.

Then his hands shifted, sliding from my wrist to my waist, pulling me to him. His mouth slanted over mine, the hesitation gone, shifting to hunger. The controlled fighter vanished, replaced by something raw and untamed.

I moaned against his lips, my hands going up behind his neck, pulling him closer as his tongue slid against mine, teasing, tasting, owning every bit of my response.

Ghost moved us toward the wall, his hands hot and possessive, gripping my hips, pinning me between him and the mat on the wall behind me.

"Is this what you wanted?" he said against my lips, his voice dark, already knowing the answer.

I arched into him, my breath catching as his fingers slid under my shirt, exploring my skin. "Yes," I said proudly.

He did this so easily, so effortlessly. Wrecking me with a single touch.

I hooked a hand into the waistband of his sweats, pulling him closer, needing to feel more, and he let out a low, satisfied groan as he pressed against me. God, he was all muscle. I ran my hands down his chest, over every hard ridge, my breathing ragged, my body vibrating with anticipation.

His lips found my throat, his tongue sliding up my skin, his hands gripping my thighs and lifting me, forcing my legs around his waist.

I moaned as his hard erection pressed against me, my body already aching for him. I pulled my shirt up over my head.

Ghost's blue eyes darkened, his gaze dropping to my bare skin as he removed my bra, his hands immediately gripping my waist, pulling me closer, tighter, deeper into this thing I shouldn't be doing but couldn't seem to stop.

His breath was hot against my throat, making my entire body shiver. "You sure?" he whispered against my skin, his voice rough, full of restraint he was barely holding onto.

It was like he had to keep checking, making sure I knew what I was getting into. No strings. No commitment. Just sex.

My lips brushed against his jaw as I whispered, "Less than nothing, remember?" Even as I said the words, I knew I was in too deep already. I craved what he had to offer, and I was willing to risk getting burned to have it, again and again.

Ghost let out a deep, guttural sound, somewhere between a laugh and a groan, before his mouth took possession of mine, taking everything I was offering and then some.

I moaned into him, heat spreading through me like wildfire.

He took us down, and my back hit the mats beneath us as he stripped off my jeans and panties until I was naked beneath him.

He left me there for a minute, my breathing ragged as I watched him in anticipation while he went over to his wallet on the bench and grabbed a condom.

After discarding his sweats and boxer briefs, he settled between my thighs, his weight solid and warm.

His hands were everywhere, exploring, claiming. His lips dragged down my neck, hot and unrelenting, his teeth scraping gently, making my entire body jolt with need. "You get me hard as fuck, you know that?" he whispered against my skin. "You like hearing that?"

I shivered, my thighs tightening around his waist, my hands gripping his broad shoulders. "Yes," I whispered as his mouth continued its path, his tongue flicking over my nipple, his teeth tugging, his lips sucking until I was restless beneath him.

"Fuck, Halston, I swear I could spend all day sucking on these tits."

I let out a breathless moan, arching into him.

"You sound so fucking sexy when you moan for me."

I grabbed his face, bringing his eyes to meet mine. "You're killing me with your damn teasing."

Ghost chuckled, that deep, delicious sound that made my stomach flutter, then dropped his head and bit down on my nipple just enough to make me gasp. Then he rubbed it with his tongue and whispered. "You love it, sweetheart. Every filthy word, every dirty thing I whisper in your ear. You fucking love it."

I did.

I felt the evidence of it between my legs, the wet heat that had me squirming, desperate, aching for him to just give me what I needed. But he was taking his time, dragging his mouth lower, his teeth scraping my stomach, his tongue following his hands as he parted my thighs wider until I was completely open for him.

"Fuck, look at you. So goddamn perfect. So goddamn wet. You've been thinking about me all day, haven't you?"

My pulse sped up, my hips lifting on instinct, searching for relief. "Kasper."

"That's right. Say my name."

His tongue found me, his mouth claiming me, his fingers digging into my thighs, holding me right where he wanted me.

I choked on a curse, my body shaking, my fingers clawing at the mats beneath us, useless against the pleasure he was causing.

He was a goddamn menace, working me like he owned every inch of me.

"Fuck, I could do this all night. Could make you cum on my tongue over and over and over again. Would you like that? Would you let me?"

I moaned, my body on fire, my control slipping fast. "Yes! Fuck yes."

He laughed against me; the vibrations sending me spiraling closer. "You taste so fucking sweet. Addictive."

I was on the edge, dangling, needing.

And then he pulled away.

I let out a strangled noise, part frustration, part desperation, my eyes flying open just as he moved up my body, pressing his chest to my breasts, his mouth brushing against my lips in a slow, teasing kiss. "Kasper."

"Not yet. I want to feel you cum around my cock," he said, rolling on the condom.

I whimpered, lifting my hips against him, feeling just how hard he was, how ready he was, how fucking thick and solid and perfect he was against me. "Please," I whispered. "I need you."

He groaned, gripping his cock, running it through my wetness, teasing me. His eyes locked on mine, watching every response.

I gasped as he buried himself inside me, filling me.

"Fuck yes." His voice was ragged, wrecked, his forehead dropping to mine. "So tight. You feel so goddamn good."

I clung to him, my body arching. And then he moved. Slow at first, just enough to make me feel every inch, every drag, every delicious bit of friction.

Then he sped up. Hard. Unforgiving. His hips slammed into mine, his hands gripping my wrists, pinning them above my head as his mouth opened over mine, devouring my moans.

He continued to drive into me, torturing me as my body climbed higher, begging for release.

My hips raised over and over again to meet his. And when I climaxed, the pleasure crashed through me like a tidal wave as I screamed his name.

His groan was rough and deep, his hips rolling, his hands gripping my thighs, keeping me close, holding me as he let go completely until he was empty.

We lay there, breathing hard, his body heavy and perfectly warm against mine.

Then he laughed, dropping a kiss to my lips. "Goddamn, Halston. That was... Fuck."

I grinned, still trying to catch my breath. "So damn good," I said, my fingers brushing lightly along his bearded jaw. "I really needed that."

He smirked, his eyes skimming over my face. "Yeah?"

I let out a slow, steady breath. "So much."

"Lucky for you, sweetheart..." He leaned in, his lips brushing my ear. "I'm available for all your emergency needs. No appointment necessary."

I raised an eyebrow. "You offering 24/7 service now?"

He winked. "For you, absolutely."

"You might be sorry you said that," I told him, making him laugh.

Chapter 61

Ghost and I were in a group text with Drew, Jen, Niki, and Josh. Drew started it, asking if anyone wanted to go out and grab a drink tonight. It was less than an hour later that we all agreed to meet up at Max's bar downtown.

Ghost texted and asked if I wanted a ride, and we ended up driving together.

I wondered what he would tell people if they caught us getting out of the same truck. He'd blow it off, of course. He'd probably tell them my car was still broken down or something. Whatever. I was happy just to be around him tonight. Any night, honestly.

Everyone was already sitting around the table, drinks in hand, when Ghost and I walked in.

Jen zeroed in on us immediately. "Does this mean you two are dating?" she asked, her voice dripping with fake curiosity, but her eyes reflected jealousy.

I rolled my eyes.

But Ghost didn't even hesitate. "Because we walked in the door together?" A smug grin spread across his lips. "Fuck. I better watch who I walk next to."

The guys laughed.

I laughed. I saw that smart-ass answer coming, but somehow it didn't bother me. More than anything; I was just happy to keep fucking him as long as he was going to let me. Because so far, he hadn't walked away.

I expected her to push, to dig further, but instead, her focus shifted, her attention returning to Drew, who had his arm wrapped around her like he had no idea what kind of person he was holding onto.

I tensed, my stomach twisting with frustration. She hadn't told him, and neither had I. It made me feel like a fraud of a friend to Drew.

Ghost spoke to me, drawing my attention back to him. And just like that, the night moved forward.

I felt completely comfortable around him, like there was no weight, no tension, just easy conversation. And it felt dangerous. Because I liked it way too much. I was flirting with that line between like and love and leaning awfully hard toward the latter.

At some point, Ghost excused himself to go to the bathroom, and not even two seconds later, Jen did the same.

I frowned, my suspicion immediately flaring. I didn't trust that girl for a second not to try something out of jealousy. So I excused myself too. I had to see if my suspicion was right.

When I stepped out into the hallway near the restrooms, I froze, then quickly darted back around the corner so they couldn't see me.

Jen was already there with Ghost. She had him pushed against the wall, her hands to his chest. Then she leaned in, her lips pressing against his.

My stomach dropped.

I had suspected as much. This was exactly the kind of shit Jen pulled whenever she felt like attention wasn't on her. She couldn't stand it. She couldn't live with the fact that Ghost had been around me all night, talking to me, laughing with me, that he had been hanging around me for months.

I was used to her bullshit, but seeing her kiss Ghost?

A flash of anger shot through me so fast I saw red. My stomach knotted. I wanted to rip every perfect, bleached-blonde strand of hair out of her head.

But it was Ghost's reaction I was most interested in. And I didn't have to wait long.

Ghost immediately pushed her off him. "What the fuck are you doing?" His voice was sharp, cold.

Jen smiled, all fake innocence. "You know what I'm doing."

Ghost's expression darkened. "No, I really don't." He took a step back, his hands brushing off his shirt like she'd tainted him just by touching him.

Jen rolled her eyes. "Come on, Ghost. You and me? It makes sense. We make sense. And you know it."

Ghost let out a short, humorless laugh, shaking his head. "That's funny. 'Cause I was just thinking how fucking delusional you are."

Her smile dropped, replaced by something ugly.

"I would never betray Drew like that," Ghost added, his voice flat.

Jen waved a dismissive hand. "Drew understands that I have needs, and he doesn't fulfill all of them."

Ghost's eyes flashed. "The fuck did you just say?"

Jen stepped closer, her voice dipped in seduction, her fingers lifting to trace his collar. "I'm saying... you could be the one to fill in the gaps."

My stomach clenched.

Ghost's head tilted, his expression unamused. "You're serious?"

Jen leaned in. "You didn't say you don't want me."

Ghost's entire face shut down. His eyes went cold. His smile turned razor sharp. "You're right. I didn't." He took a slow step forward, crowding her space, his voice dropping to something low and almost seductive... until it wasn't. "I also didn't say I wouldn't fuck a hole in the ground if I was desperate enough."

Jen's face twisted with shock and offense. "Seriously? You're gonna pretend you're not into me? Come on, Ghost. You're running around with Halston like she's some kind of prize? Be real. I'm ten times the woman she is. I'm hotter, sexier, way more your type."

Ghost's smirk grew, but his tone was flat. "If I wanted fake and plastic, I'd fuck a blow-up doll."

Jen's mouth fell open, and Ghost turned and walked straight into the men's restroom, leaving her standing there, stunned, pissed, and humiliated.

I exhaled sharply from my spot around the corner.

And just like that? Ghost put an end to Jen's bullshit with one brutal fucking sentence.

I hurried back to the table. My heart was pounding and my mind spinning. She'd kissed him, and he hadn't betrayed me. Not that he was mine, but it made me happy just the same.

I sat back down, my breath uneven, my hands clenching in my lap. I didn't know what to say, what to think. Ghost had just shut Jen down completely. Just for Drew? I didn't know. He didn't mention me at all.

My stomach flipped, my chest tightened, my brain scrambled to make sense of it. Of course, he was just being loyal to Drew. That was all. It meant nothing. But still... I felt a warmth creeping through me. And not because, for once, someone chose me over her. It was because it was Ghost.

I barely had time to settle my thoughts before Jen struck again. "Ghost hit on me when I went to the bathroom." The words came out so smoothly, so casually, like they were the undeniable truth.

Drew looked at her. "What?"

Jen flipped her hair, smirking. "I told you. I'm everyone's type."

I shot out of my chair so fast it scraped against the floor, my pulse spiking with rage. "Why are you lying?" I demanded, my voice sharp and disbelieving.

Jen rolled her eyes. "Oh, come on. You're so naive, Halston."

I stepped closer, my hands curling into fists at my sides. "Do you just need attention that badly? He did not hit on you."

Ghost walked up. His blue eyes sliding between us, his brow furrowing. "What are you talking about?"

I turned to face him, my breath uneven, my anger boiling over. "I'm talking about her constant need to stir up shit." I glared at Jen. "About her pathological need to be the center of attention."

Ghost's jaw tightened, his gaze locking onto Jen.

I took a step closer to her, my voice steady, sharp, unwavering. "I was over there by the bathrooms. You hit on him. You kissed him. He pushed you away and told you he would never betray Drew."

Jen's face twisted with irritation. "Why are you being such a bitch tonight?" she snapped.

I let out a short, humorless laugh. "Why? Because you're lying about a really good guy."

Jen scoffed, folding her arms. "What do you care? You think you're even a blip on his radar?"

The words hit something inside me, but I refused to let it show. Instead, I met her gaze head-on. "Probably not."

Then I turned to Drew. "Niki and I saw her out with another guy a few nights ago. I don't imagine she told you."

Drew's expression darkened as he turned to her. "No," he said coldly. "She didn't."

Jen's head snapped toward me, her eyes burning with hatred. "You bitch!"

I smirked. "Takes one to spot one."

Her lips parted, looking like she was caught between anger and disbelief. She narrowed her eyes. "Why are we even friends?"

I smiled, letting out a long breath. "Good question." I stepped back from the table. "I wondered the same thing. Luckily, that's something I can remedy."

I glanced around the table at the rest of my friends. "I'll catch up with the rest of you later."

And with that, I walked out, leaving Jen and all her bullshit behind.

Chapter 62

I had barely made it outside, my heart still pounding, my hands shaking with leftover frustration, when I heard footsteps behind me.

"Hey! Are you leaving? We did drive here together."

I turned. Ghost was standing a few feet away, his eyes locked onto mine.

I let out a slow breath. "Sorry. I just needed air. I had to get out of there before I kicked her ass."

Ghost's lips lifted into a smirk, his amusement undeniable. "I would've paid to see that."

I rolled my eyes, but still ended up smiling.

He took a step closer. "She's never been a very nice person."

I exhaled. "No. And I let it go on for way too long."

Ghost nodded. "You ruined your friendship by sticking up for me."

I shook my head. "She ruined our friendship. And you didn't deserve to have your name smeared for something you didn't do."

Something changed in his expression. His smirk faded, replaced by something heavier. "I've never had any woman do that for me."

I hesitated. There was a compliment in there somewhere, and it pulled at my heart. "That's a shame." I exhaled, shaking my head. "Because you're a pretty great guy... when you're not being a total dick, of course."

Ghost laughed, a deep, genuine sound that sent a warm pulse straight through me.

Damn. I really, really liked his laugh. My eyes raked over his lips. I leaned up on tiptoes and kissed him.

His hands wrapped around my waist, and his mouth pressed back into mine, his grip tightening. The kiss was slow, deep, unhurried, like we had all the time in the world.

And damn. He was good at it.

We'd barely made it to the truck before I grabbed him again, dragging him back down to me. My lips seeking his mouth, hot and hungry.

A low growl rumbled in his chest. His hands locked onto my hips, lifting me, pinning me right up against the truck, my back hitting the cool metal as I wrapped my legs around him.

"Fuck, sweetheart. You're gonna get me arrested, shoving your tongue down my throat in public."

I laughed breathlessly against his mouth, my body grinding against him in all the right places. "I'll bail you out."

"You planning on bribing the cops with those perfect fucking tits? 'Cause I'd let you off with a warning. Maybe just a slap on the ass."

I gasped as he palmed my ass, giving it a firm squeeze, his grin all teeth and heat as he shoved open the back passenger door and tossed me inside, closing the door behind us.

He was on me before I could even catch my breath, climbing over me, covering me, pressing me into the leather seats.

I moaned, feeling his muscles ripple beneath my fingertips, feeling him, every inch of him, hot and hard, pressed right against the heat between my thighs.

His hand gripped my jaw, angling my face, his mouth devouring mine.

His voice was a rough whisper against my lips. "You like getting fucked in my truck? Huh? You like fogging up my goddamn windows like some horny little thing who can't keep her hands off me?"

I let out a ragged breath, my thighs tightening around him, my fingers gripping his beard. "I—"

I didn't even get the words out before he flipped me onto my stomach, dragging my hips up, pressing his body against my back, his teeth grazing my shoulder. "I know you do. You fucking love it. Love how I make you cum so hard you can't even think straight."

I bit my lip, my whole body vibrating beneath his touch, my hands gripping onto the armrest.

He shoved my skirt up around my waist and pulled my panties down to my knees. After rolling a condom on, he pushed inside me.

I moaned as he slid out slowly, teasing me. Then he slammed into me. Hard and deep.

A sharp cry ripped from my throat, my nails digging into the armrest, my entire body bowing beneath the force of it.

"Fuck, Halston."

The truck rocked with every punishing thrust; the windows fogging up, the sound of his gritted curses, of my ragged moans filling the small space.

"You feel that? Feel how fucking deep I am? This little pussy was made for me."

I was losing my mind, lost in the overwhelming pleasure, lost in him, his filthy fucking words.

Ghost's fingers dug into my hips. His pace was relentless, his voice rough and dark and delicious against my ear. "I can feel how close you are. You gonna cum for me, sweetheart? Gonna cum all over my cock like a good girl?"

I whimpered, my whole body trembling, my legs shaking, the pleasure cresting so fast, so hard as I tightened around him. "Kasper!"

His thrusts were erratic; his grip bruising. Then, with a few final thrusts, he groaned, his body shuddering, his mouth hot on my neck as he let go.

The windows were completely fogged, and the inside of the truck was hot from the heat we had created.

I let out a slow, shaky breath as I turned in the seat, staring up at him, my body still buzzing, still trembling.

Ghost settled on top of me, his skin hot against mine, his breath uneven as his blue eyes met mine.

I let out a soft laugh. "Don't worry. I know this doesn't mean anything."

Ghost lifted up, putting a hand to his chest in mock offense. "That hurts, Halston." His voice was half amused, half sarcastic. "I'm not a piece of meat."

I laughed, tilting my head toward him. "Fuck you, Ghost," I threw back playfully.

He laughed, his chest still rising and falling fast, his slick body pressing against me.

I stared at him for a moment, my heart still pounding, my stomach twisting into something complicated. Because the truth was, he had the potential to be a one-woman man.

And I really wanted him to be.

Chapter 63

The underground fight was tucked beneath an old bar on the outskirts of town.

The entrance was hidden through a narrow, graffiti-tagged alley, down a set of stairs so steep it felt like descending straight into hell. The air inside was thick with sweat and whiskey, the space crammed with rowdy spectators pressed shoulder to shoulder, their shouts echoing off exposed pipes and low concrete ceilings.

Josh, Drew, and Niki were already there, standing near the ring that sat on a raised platform, a drink in each of their hands. The dim, flickering bulbs overhead gave the whole place a seedy, desperate kind of energy, the kind that made it feel like anything could happen at any moment.

I pushed through the crowd, my stomach twisting as I caught sight of Ghost in the ring, shirtless, his scarred knuckles wrapped, flexing at his sides. He looked calm, lethal, completely in control.

Josh leaned in toward me. "You hear about the high roller?"

My eyes were still locked on Ghost. "What high roller?"

Drew gestured toward a man in an expensive suit standing near the edge of the crowd with a whiskey glass in one hand, a cigar in the other. He looked out of place here, too polished and composed, but the deadly gleam in his eye said he belonged just fine.

"He put out a bounty," Drew said, his voice low. "Ten grand to whoever can beat Ghost tonight. And ten grand to Ghost if he beats them."

I felt my stomach drop. "Are you serious?"

Josh nodded grimly. "Yeah. Word got out fast. Every fighter in this place suddenly thinks they've got a shot at taking him down."

My hands clenched into fists. Ghost was already a target every time he stepped into a fight, but this? This made him a marked man. "Does he know?" I asked.

"Oh, he knows," Niki said. "And you know what that cocky bastard said?"

I glanced at Ghost again, already knowing it was something I wasn't going to like before she even said it.

"He said, 'Make it twenty and I'll take two of them at once.'"

I exhaled sharply. Of course, he did.

The announcer stepped into the ring, lifting a mic. "Ladies and gentlemen, we have a special treat tonight! A fighter's bounty has been placed. Ten. Thousand. Dollars to the man who can take down Ghost!"

The crowd erupted, a mix of boos, cheers, and drunken shouts.

I forced myself to breathe, watching as Ghost cracked his neck, rolling his shoulders back like he was undaunted, just loosening up for a normal fight.

Then the announcer grinned. "Who wants a shot?"

A man stepped forward. Then another.

I swallowed hard. Two of them.

Ghost tilted his head, then smirked at the high roller. "Hope you have the cash to back it up."

I gritted my teeth. Cocky son of a bitch.

The fight was brutal. Fast, unrelenting, violent in a way that sent adrenaline straight through my veins. Ghost was dodging and countering like a man who had done this a thousand times over, but the two fighters weren't making it easy. They were coming at him hard, swinging with wild, desperate force, knowing that if they took him down, they were walking away with ten grand.

And then, as the ropes rattled from the impact of a body slamming into them, I felt it as the high roller slithered up beside me.

He was calm, composed, watching the fight with detached amusement, the kind of casual cruelty that made my skin crawl. He took a slow sip of his whiskey in a crystal glass, exhaling as he tilted his head toward me.

"He fights like a man with nothing to lose."

I stiffened. My gut immediately told me not to engage.

"I wonder how he'll fight when he actually has something to lose."

My blood ran cold. I turned my head slowly, locking eyes with him. His expression didn't change. He wore a small smirk. There was a knowing look in his eyes.

"Excuse me?" My voice was steady, but my pulse was pounding.

He swirled the whiskey in his glass, watching Ghost take another brutal punch before retaliating with a savage knee to the gut.

"Men like him?" he said, shaking his head. "They thrive in chaos. But take away that edge? Give them something fragile? Something that makes them hesitate?" He smiled at me, and my stomach twisted. "They fall apart."

"If you're waiting for Ghost to fall apart," I told him, my eyes hard. "You'll be waiting a long fucking time."

The man chuckled. "Oh, honey, I knew I'd like you."

"You say that like you know me."

"I've been watching Ghost. And the people around him."

My body locked up with tension.

I turned my attention back to the ring, trying to brush off the creepy feeling the guy gave me.

Then, one of the fighters grabbed Ghost from behind, locking his arms while the second one came barreling toward him.

A dirty fucking move.

I gasped, my stomach twisting as the guy's fist flew forward. And then, in the blink of an eye, Ghost ducked. Fucking ducked. The guy's punch landed square in his own teammate's face.

The crowd went insane.

Ghost didn't hesitate. He ripped out of the guy's grasp and spun, landing a brutal spinning elbow to his jaw that sent him sprawling onto the mat.

The second guy barely had time to react before Ghost was on him, grabbing his arm and twisting it behind his back in a move so fluid, so fast, it looked effortless.

Crack. The man screamed. His arm was definitely broken.

The ref jumped in, waving his hands wildly, signaling the fight was over.

The crowd erupted.

Ghost fucking won.

My entire body was humming, my heart still hammering from the fight, from the high roller's words, from the sheer dominance Ghost had just displayed.

Ghost straightened, rolling his shoulders like he hadn't just destroyed two men at once.

The high roller let out a low, impressed whistle. "Now that," he said, "is the real deal."

By the time Ghost made it out of the ring, the high roller was waiting for him.

He didn't even hesitate, stepping right up to Ghost, offering him a nod of approval. "You didn't disappoint."

Ghost was still catching his breath as he wiped blood from his lip with the back of his wrapped hand. "Good to know."

The man smirked. "Had to make it harder for you. Had to see if you were really as good as they say."

Ghost narrowed his eyes. "And?"

"And I was right to put my money on you." The man extended a hand. "I want you to fight for me. Exclusively."

Ghost didn't shake his hand. Just lifted a brow. "That so?"

The high roller smiled. "We'll talk soon," he said, then nodded to one of his men, who then handed Ghost two fat stacks of cash with a band on each. Forty thousand dollars.

And just like that, he walked away.

Chapter 64

I leaned against the wall just outside the locker room, my foot tapping with leftover adrenaline. Somewhere behind that door, Ghost was showering, rinsing away blood and sweat from going full beast mode on two men at once.

The sounds of the underground fights were still echoing through the stairwell, muffled by concrete and distance.

It wasn't long before the door pushed open again, and Ghost emerged freshly showered, his hair damp, a black T-shirt clinging to his still-wet skin, his gym bag slung over his shoulder.

Even after a fight, he looked like sin on two legs.

He spotted me and gave that signature half-smile, the one that made me want to both roll my eyes and pull him into that locker room.

"Great fight," I said, pushing off the wall as we started toward the parking lot. "Two guys was stupid, though."

He smirked, cocky as ever. "Aww, Tits. Were you worried about me?"

I rolled my eyes hard. "Of course I was. Am I not supposed to be? Am I just supposed to keep fucking you and not care that you put yourself in that kind of situation?"

We reached the truck, and he threw his bag into the backseat with a careless swing of his arm.

"Am I not allowed to worry about you?"

He didn't answer with words. Instead, he turned, took my face in his hands, and kissed me slowly. The kiss dulled my anger but amped up the burn low in my stomach.

I pulled back just enough to meet his eyes. "You think you can kiss me to keep from answering personal questions?"

He smiled, then kissed me again.

I guess so. Absolute menace.

When he pulled back, his breath was warm against my skin.

I looked up at him, still riding the high. "Can I say I don't like the high roller? Am I allowed to voice my opinion on that?"

His expression sobered slightly. "Of course."

"Because he admitted to checking you out and the people you surround yourself with. He knew who I was when he came up to talk to me. He knew I knew you."

Ghost nodded, his jaw flexing. "Okay. I see your concern. I'll handle him. Make sure he leaves you alone."

"You're missing my point," I said, my voice calm. "I don't trust him, and I don't think you should trust him either."

He stilled for a second, then looked straight at me. "Look at me, sweetheart. Do you trust me?"

"Yeah. I do."

"Then let me handle the high roller. You just stand there and look pretty."

I rolled my eyes again, more out of habit than anything, and it made him laugh.

He leaned in and kissed my lips, then gently bit my bottom lip, pulling it between his teeth before letting go. A shiver raced straight down my spine. "You make me wanna do bad things I know I shouldn't wanna do."

His smirk turned devious, his eyes hooded with that dark heat, the only emotion he never bothered to hide from me. "Sweetheart, I count on you wanting shit you shouldn't," he whispered, his thumb brushing over my lip like he wanted to start all over again. "'Cause the second you stop wanting the wrong things... I'm gonna lose all my fucking motivation."

I tried to breathe. Failed.

"So what? I'm your sinful little muse now?"

He stepped in, his fingers gripping my hip with that wicked look in his eyes. "You're my walking, talking bad decision. And, fuck me, I've never had a better one."

I let out a shaky laugh, even as my body leaned into his. Because there was a compliment in there with the insult. "We should go," I said, but it came out breathless.

His laugh came out rough. "Yeah. Before I bend you over the hood and give these security cameras a hell of a show."

I swallowed hard, my pulse pounding in my throat. "You can't say stuff like that, then just make me walk back to my car."

Ghost took my wrist and rounded the front of the truck. He pulled the door open smoothly, with that lazy, satisfied smirk still playing on his lips. "Come on," he said, his voice low. "I'll give you a ride to your car."

"That's very sweet of you," I said, climbing up.

The second my foot hit the step, and I started pulling myself inside, his hand landed on my ass with a firm smack, making me yelp and shoot him a smile over my shoulder. "Hey! Stop touching me unless you want me turned on more than I already am."

He grinned like the complete menace he was. "Can't help it. It's right there. Begging for attention."

The air between us still buzzed with sexual energy, tension curling tight under my skin like a lit fuse. Ghost drummed his fingers on the steering wheel, glancing over at me now and then, his smirk returning every time he caught me sneaking a look at him.

When we pulled into the lot where I'd parked earlier, he threw the truck into park, and I reached for the handle. "Thanks for the ride," I said, half turned toward him. "I appreciate it."

His hand caught my wrist before I could open the door. "Or," he said, his voice lower now, "you could follow me back to my place."

I was surprised by the invitation. "Yeah?" I asked, lifting a brow, playing it casual, even though my stomach flipped. It never ceased to amaze me when he gave a little on anything. "You want me back in your bed tonight?"

He leaned back, draping one arm over the wheel, the other resting across the seat behind me. "Sweetheart, I want you in every position tonight." His grin curved wider. "But bed's a good place to start."

I bit my lip, trying not to smile, but failed. "Okay," I said, finally opening the door. "I'll follow you."

"Knew you couldn't say no to a night with me."

"Please," I said with a smirk. "I just want to make sure you don't cry alone about that punch to the ribs later."

His laughter followed me out of the truck. "Bring that mouth to my place, Halston. I've got a few ideas on how to keep it busy."

I shut the door and turned toward my car, a wide grin on my lips, my pulse already racing.

Because, yeah... I was definitely following him home.

Chapter 65

G host invited all of us to a hockey game.

The moment we stepped into the packed arena, the energy hit me like a body check against the boards. The sound of skates cutting into the ice mixed with the thunderous cheers of the crowd surrounded us.

I'd never been to a hockey game before, but I had to admit, it was electric.

Ghost, stoic as ever, led us through the crowded concourse, his sharp blue eyes flicking toward the ice now and then, already reading the game.

The puck dropped, and the action was fast and aggressive. The players moved like they had rockets strapped to their skates, slamming each other into the boards, battling for control in the corners.

I flinched as one player took a hard slapshot from the blue line; the puck flew past the goalie's glove side and straight into the net. The horn blared, the crowd erupted, and I turned to Niki, who was practically bouncing in her seat.

"God, hockey players are so hot," she swooned.

I laughed. "Some of them. But they're notorious for missing teeth."

She grinned. "You just gotta find one that still has all of them."

I rolled my eyes. "Why are you always throwing me under the bus?"

"Because you're the single one here."

"Ghost is single."

She laughed. "Yeah, but that's his choice. He prefers meaningless sex with random women."

"I can have meaningless sex with random guys, too."

Ghost, who had been watching the game with zero reaction, spun his head sharply toward me. "Oh, hockey players are your thing?" His voice was dangerously smooth, his smirk just a little too smug. "I can introduce you to one."

I shook my head vehemently. "I don't want—"

Before I could even finish the sentence, Niki gasped. "Wait, seriously? You know them?"

Ghost's smirk widened. "Yeah. A few of them."

And just like that, I was being dragged down near the locker room entrance after the first period ended.

Ghost stood there, throwing chin nods at a few players coming off the ice. Sure enough, he knew them, and he introduced us.

And of course, this would happen; one of them immediately started flirting with me. "So what are you doing later?" he asked, wearing that easy grin that most guys with athletic talent and a roster full of admirers had mastered.

I didn't even think about it. The words were out of my mouth lightning fast. "Sorry. I'm seeing someone."

Obviously, I wasn't. But I wasn't interested in the hockey player, and I was just trying to be nice about it. Because all I wanted was Ghost. All I craved was the moment we could be alone together again.

Before I could process what I had just said, Niki practically squealed beside me. "You are? I didn't know that!"

I nodded, playing it cool. "Yep."

By the time we made it back to our seats, Ghost was distant, borderline rude.

His jaw was locked, his fingers drumming impatiently against the armrest as the next period started. He barely reacted when one of the players got sent to the penalty box for roughing, or when the goalie made a miraculous glove save on a breakaway.

I was done with it.

I leaned over, nudging his arm. "Come with me to grab some beer."

He barely glanced at me. "Not thirsty."

I rolled my eyes, my tone taking on a hard edge. "I don't care. Come with me."

Ghost let out a sharp sigh, standing reluctantly.

I led him toward the concession area. The second we were out of earshot of our friends, I turned on him. "What the hell did I do now?"

Ghost folded his arms, leaning back against the wall, his broad shoulders blocking part of the hallway. "What are you talking about?"

"You know damn well what I'm talking about. You've been a jerk since you introduced us to the players. If it was gonna piss you off to do it, then why did you do it?"

Ghost didn't respond. Instead, he grabbed my wrist and pulled me out of the crowd, stopping me near the hallway that led to the public bathrooms. "Since when are we dating?"

I stared at him, stunned at the sharpness of his tone. "Why are you trying to pick a fight?"

His blue eyes burned into mine, his fingers still wrapped around my wrist. "I'm not. I'm just saying that we're not dating, and I don't want you telling people that we are."

"Bullshit." I glared at him, not backing down. "That was jealousy. Plain and simple."

"Don't get this twisted, Tits. I don't get jealous," he said, deadpan.

That one hurt, like a punch to the gut I wasn't prepared for. I mean, I knew what this was. But I think I still wanted to know he felt something for me besides lust.

I swallowed, my chest tightening, my voice flat, unaffected, because if I let myself feel it, it would hurt more. "I said I was seeing someone to be left alone. I didn't want to be introduced to the players in the first place. Niki did. And I wasn't interested in that guy who hit on me. I tried to be nice and spare his feelings, so I said I had a boyfriend. Nothing more. Nothing less."

I pulled my wrist out of his grip, stepping back. "I'm not telling anyone that we're anything. But I am getting damn tired of your bipolar mood swings."

Ghost let out a bitter laugh, shaking his head. "That's your fault. You're the idiot that keeps coming around my place, around me."

My stomach dropped.

Then he said the one thing I never expected to hear from him.

"You know what? You're tired of me? Fucking leave. I don't want you here."

The words hit like a slap, stealing my breath. I should have expected it. Ghost was hot and cold, push and pull, always on the edge of pushing me away completely. But that didn't mean it didn't hurt like hell.

I let out a slow breath, swallowing the lump in my throat. "Keep pushing me away, Ghost." I turned, shaking my head. "Eventually, I'll get the hint."

And I meant it. I wasn't going to fight him. If he didn't want me around, if he wanted me to walk away, I would.

But before I could take another step, Ghost grabbed my arm, yanking me back into him, his hands gripping my waist, his mouth taking control of mine.

I gasped against his lips, my body betraying me completely, my hands clutching his arms for balance. I wanted to fight him, wanted to tell him he was an ass, that he didn't get to kiss me after saying that shit to me.

But he held me so tight, his lips molding against mine, and suddenly, I couldn't think straight anymore. My knees went weak, my resolve shattered, my heart pounding as he deepened the kiss, his fingers digging into my hips like he couldn't stand the idea of letting me go.

This man. This infuriating, impossible man. He didn't want me to leave.

But he refused to ask me to stay.

Chapter 66

Ghost's hands were firm, guiding me backward as his mouth devoured mine, his kiss hot, demanding, impossible to resist.

I barely registered where we were until my back hit a door, and I pulled away, breathless. "Ghost. This is the men's room."

He gave me that cocky, knowing smile, his eyes dark. "And?"

I swallowed, my pulse pounding in my ears, my skin on fire from his touch.

Before I could argue, he gripped my waist, turned me, and led me into one of the stalls, locking the door behind us.

The click of the lock sent a shiver down my spine, my heart slamming into my ribs. This was reckless. This was insane.

Ghost spun me, pressing my back against the cool metal of the stall, his body pressed against mine, his breath hot against my ear. "Tell me to stop, sweetheart."

That sent a hot bolt straight between my legs. He was giving me an out if this place was too much for me. My hands slid up over his hard chest, my eyes meeting his. I shook my head.

His hands were everywhere, his mouth devouring mine. His kiss was rough and consuming, making me lose myself.

I moaned against him, my body already aching for him.

His hand slid down between our bodies to work the snap of my jeans, his touch sending heat rushing straight through me, his name slipping from my lips like a breathless confession.

I felt him grin against my mouth, his hands skimming lower as he helped to push my jeans down. I quickly kicked my jeans and underwear off and onto the floor.

Ghost undid his jeans and pushed his boxer briefs down just enough to release his cock, already hard with need. Pulling the condom from his wallet, he rolled it on.

Gripping my thighs, he lifted me. Right there against the stall door, with no restraint, no room for anything but him.

And then he pushed into me in Ghost fashion, one hard push till he filled me up, making me cry out.

I gasped, clinging to his shoulders. "Kasper!"

"Say my name again, sweetheart," he whispered against my ear, his breath hot.

He started to move. A slow, grinding rhythm that made my toes curl.

"Kasper," I gritted out through the pleasure.

"Fuck yes, baby. You feel that?" he murmured, thrusting again. "That's me ruining you for anyone else."

He didn't rush. He dragged it out—every roll of his hips made me breathless.

"Fuck," I whimpered.

"Oh yeah," he growled, picking up the pace. "That's the sound I wanna hear."

His hands gripped my ass, snapping his hips harder and faster.

"You gonna cum for me?" he asked, his voice rough. "Gonna soak my cock while I fuck you against the goddamn door?"

I whimpered. "Kasper. Please."

His eyes held mine. "You get all wet and needy when I tell you how I'm gonna fuck you senseless, huh, baby?"

"Yes," I said, breathless.

"That's my girl."

His thrusts turned punishing, desperate, unrelenting as my back pounded against the stall door.

His hands gripped my hips, controlling every movement, his lips hot against my throat, his breathing ragged as he drove me closer and closer to the edge.

I bit down on his shoulder, stifling a cry, my body tightening around him, my nails digging into his back as I came undone in his arms.

He gave in to his release, his groan muffled against my skin, his body tensing, holding me so tightly I could barely breathe.

Ghost's hands were still gripping my thighs.

I ran a hand through his hair and kissed him, my tongue darting inside to rub against his.

We heard the door open, and I broke the kiss.

There were footsteps.

Ghost stilled.

My heart jumped into my throat. Shit.

There was the sound of a zipper, and a steady stream hitting the toilet bowl in the stall beside us.

I slapped a hand over Ghost's mouth, my eyes wide. I didn't trust him to keep quiet. I just knew he'd try to embarrass me or something.

He gave a muffled laugh, his whole body shaking against mine.

I shot him a glare. Don't. You. Dare.

But then, that bastard started licking my palm.

Licking. My. Damn. Hand.

It was a slow, deliberate drag of his tongue. I sucked in a sharp breath, my body reacting in a way it absolutely should not be reacting at this moment.

His teeth grazed the soft skin of my palm. Then he gave a small, playful bite.

My eyes widened further, my silent warning now desperate. Stop it.

But he just grinned against my hand like a cocky devil, laughing silently.

The man in the next stall flushed the toilet.

Ghost pressed his lips against my palm, slowly kissing the center, causing me to shiver and bite my lip.

Then finally, there were footsteps again, heading away, toward the door. And the sound of the door as it swung open and shut.

Ghost lost it. A deep, rumbling laugh shook his chest as he pulled my hand away from his mouth, his grin infuriatingly smug.

I smacked his arm. "You absolute menace."

He chuckled. "You're the one who covered my mouth, Tits."

I scowled. "Because you were going to make a sound."

He shrugged, unapologetic. "Not my fault you've got a hand that tastes like fucking heaven."

I gaped at him. "Did you... did you just compliment how my hand tastes?"

Ghost smirked. "You have no idea the things I could say about how the rest of you tastes."

Heat flared through me. "I hate you sometimes."

He leaned in, his lips grazing my ear, sending a fresh wave of electricity through my body. "No, you don't."

I shivered.

"You love when I get my mouth on you."

I moaned at his words. "Not in a disgusting public restroom."

He pulled back, arching a brow, his cocky smirk never fading. "Then why are you still wrapped around me, sweetheart?"

Damn him. Damn him for making me want him again already.

I pushed at his chest, my face hot. "Put me down, you animal."

Ghost laughed, finally setting me on my feet.

But before I could turn away, he gripped my chin, tilting my head up so our eyes locked. He kissed me again. Slower this time. Deep. Deliberate. Like he wasn't quite ready to step back into reality.

And neither was I, because this was the Ghost I kept getting addicted to. The one who didn't push me away. The one who held onto me like he wanted me to stay.

Chapter 67

G host had another fight tonight.

As I was getting ready, my phone buzzed with a message from him. *Need a ride?*

I mean, I have a car. I sent back.

I don't mind picking you up

I smiled at my screen and typed. *I'd like that.*

Ghost pulled up to my place, his truck idling in the driveway.

When I slid into the passenger seat, he glanced over, his eyes flicking over my body briefly. I had on hip-hugging blue jeans and a black fitted v-neck T-shirt that I'd tucked in just at the front behind the button. Very casual.

"You look nice."

Coming from him, the compliment felt bigger than it should have.

I smirked. "You clean up okay yourself."

He chuckled, shaking his head as he pulled onto the road. "You ready for tonight?"

I nodded, though there was a tiny pit in my stomach.

The out of the way warehouse was packed. It was high-energy, tense, and borderline chaotic.

Niki, Drew, and Josh had already saved seats, and I slid in beside them, scanning the crowd. Ghost hadn't come out yet, but I could feel the anticipation in the air, the way people were talking about him, waiting for him to step into the ring.

I'd watched Ghost fight many times, but lately, it had been getting harder and harder to watch.

I was falling for him. And that made every punch, every hit feel like a personal attack on my heart.

When he finally stepped into the ring, the crowd erupted, the sound deafening, but I barely heard it. My focus was entirely on him, and the way his muscles flexed, the way his eyes darkened with intensity. He moved like a predator. He was calculating, focused, and completely in his element.

Ghost took a few hard hits, but he gave them back twice as hard.

I clenched my fists, my heart pounding against my ribs, my breath catching every time he took a punch. It wasn't like I thought he'd lose. Ghost was too damn good for that, too damn stubborn. But that didn't mean I wasn't worried.

Then, just as his opponent made a misstep, Ghost landed a devastating roundhouse kick, sending the guy crashing to the mat.

The crowd exploded.

The ref counted, but the guy didn't get back up.

I exhaled, finally releasing the breath I hadn't realized I was holding.

As he raised his fists in victory, his eyes swept the crowd, finding me instantly. He shot me a smile and that damn wink that set me on fire. I couldn't help but smile back.

A lot of people had already cleared out of the enormous warehouse, but we stood around, drinking and talking.

I took a sip of my beer, laughing at something Josh said, when out of nowhere, Ghost grabbed my bottle, took a drink from it, then handed it back like it was nothing.

I froze for a second, watching him as he walked away to get his own beer at the window, completely unaware. He'd just broken character in front of everyone and didn't even realize it.

Everyone was staring at me.

"What was that?" Niki asked, her eyebrows raised.

"What?"

She nodded toward the beer still in my hand. "Ghost just drank from your beer."

I nodded, acting unconcerned. "Yeah? And?"

Niki smirked, glancing at Drew and Josh. "Is that who you're seeing?"

Drew's head snapped toward me, his brows furrowing. "Are you two together?"

Before I could answer, Ghost reappeared with a beer, his voice calm and unaffected. "No. I don't do relationships, you know that."

"Please," I said with exaggerated disgust. "I am not dating Ghost."

He shot me an oh, really look.

I tried really hard not to smile.

"There's way too much tension between them. No way they're sleeping together," Josh said.

"Maybe you can bring this new guy around sometime. I know it's a new thing, but I think we'd all like to meet him." Niki said.

"Absolutely," Josh agreed.

Ghost nudged me. "Yeah, Tits. Who is this mystery man? We'd love to meet him."

I shot him a raised brow. He was enjoying egging it on. And he told me so with a smirk.

"Nobody you know," I said, then took a long swallow of my beer, leaning my head back.

"Does he fuck you good in bed?" Ghost asked.

I spit my beer out, spraying Ghost, coughing.

Everyone laughed.

Ghost chuckled, completely nonchalant as I wiped beer from my chin, glaring daggers at him.

Niki was still laughing, shaking her head. "Don't embarrass Halston."

Ghost smirked, turning to her. "Oh, sweetheart, she's not embarrassed. That was pure panic."

I crossed my arms, playing the part. "It was shock, asshole. Normal people don't ask their friend if the guy they're sleeping with fucks them good."

His grin widened. "Good thing I'm not normal."

"That's for damn sure," I told him, but he just shot me his signature grin and wink, trying to undo me, making me groan.

Drew chuckled, shaking his head. "Jesus, man."

Josh leaned in. "I mean, now I kind of wanna know."

I smacked his arm. "Josh!"

Ghost clapped a hand over his chest, feigning offense. "Wow. So I ask, and I get beer spit on me. But Josh asks, and you just politely say his name?"

I laughed. "Because Josh isn't a menace to society."

Ghost smirked. "Disagree. He wore white socks with black slides the other day. That's some straight-up serial killer shit."

Josh laughed, flipping him off.

Niki grinned. "But really, Halston. We wanna meet this mystery man."

Ghost leaned in, elbowing me with a smirk. "Yeah, Tits. Why are you keeping him all to yourself?"

I narrowed my eyes. He was enjoying this way too much.

I sipped my beer, shrugging. "He's private."

"Oh?" Ghost quirked a brow. "What's he got to hide? Small dick?"

I almost choked again.

Josh and Drew cracked up, and Niki was covering her mouth, trying not to spit out her drink.

"Ghost!" I snapped.

His lips twitched, and his eyes lit with amusement. "What? I'm just trying to get a feel for the competition."

"There is no competition."

"That right?" He took a step closer, tilting his head, his voice dropping into that dangerous, cocky drawl. "Because I could swear, last time you were under me, you were moaning like I was the best thing that ever happened to you."

Heat flared through me, and I gasped, my eyes snapping wide.

Drew and Josh stopped laughing.

I pointed a warning finger at Ghost, trying to play it off. "You're such an asshole."

He just grinned, leaning down. "Not what you were saying when you were screaming my name."

I was going to murder him.

For a split second, everything froze.

The laughter died. Niki's eyes went huge, and Drew and Josh exchanged glances, clearly catching on.

I was stuck, my brain flatlining, because what the actual fuck did he just do? Ghost didn't do relationships. Didn't do attachment. Didn't want anyone to know about us. I was the one trying to play it off, and here he was, outing us.

I turned to him, my stomach flipping, but his face was casual, unreadable, like he hadn't just dropped a nuclear bomb on everyone's night.

And then he winked.

Ghost was playing it off like a joke. Just enough to stir the pot, but not enough to out us. He went too far just to fuck with me.

Unbelievable.

I turned to him, rolling my eyes. "Yeah, okay, Ghost. In your dreams."

His smirk deepened. He took another long sip of his beer, watching me over the rim. He knew exactly what he was doing.

Drew let out a low whistle, shaking his head. "Damn, dude. That was some confidence right there."

Josh chuckled. "Gotta respect the commitment to the bit."

Niki narrowed her eyes at me. "So... you're really not seeing anyone?"

I didn't let it show that my heart was still pounding a little too hard. Instead, I shook my head, taking another sip of beer. "No, I'm not seeing anyone. And if I was, it definitely wouldn't be this asshole."

Ghost hummed, clearly amused by my answer. He leaned in slightly, teasing. "So I'm still in the running, then?"

I laughed, nudging him with my elbow. "Not a chance."

Ghost made a mockingly wounded face, placing a hand over his chest. "Damn, Tits. You're breaking my heart."

Everyone laughed.

And just like that, disaster was averted.

Chapter 68

"Jen is here," Niki said suddenly.

We all turned in the direction she pointed.

"Great," Drew said with a shake of his head. "Sometimes I wonder why I went for Jen instead of you."

I let out a dry laugh, shooting him a look. "Probably because she crashed our date, pulled you into the bathroom, and screwed your brains out."

Drew chuckled, rubbing a hand over his face. "Oh. Yeah."

"After that, I really didn't stand a chance."

Drew sighed. "Yeah. She always has to win, doesn't she?"

"Always."

He exhaled, shaking his head. "I'm sorry for that. I should have apologized a long time ago."

I shrugged. "Don't worry about it. We're better off as friends."

Ghost tilted his head slightly. "You two dated?"

I shook my head. "No. Jen crashed the first ten minutes of our first date, so technically, we never dated."

Ghost let out a low chuckle, shaking his head. "She's a special kind of person. I'm surprised it took you this long to oust her."

"She's probably here to beg you to take her back," Josh told Drew.

"Stay strong," Ghost told him.

But she surprised everyone when she looked at me. "I want to speak to you," she said, her tone no nonsense.

I sighed, but I didn't argue.

Ghost took my beer for me, and I thanked him before following her out of the warehouse. We headed through the huge roll-up doors, and across the grass, away from the group, my patience already wearing thin.

As soon as we stopped, she spun around, her eyes sharp, her tone accusing. "You ruined my relationship with Drew."

I let out a laugh, crossing my arms. "You ruined your relationship with Drew by cheating on him. Take responsibility for your actions."

Jen shifted her weight, blurting out, "I do."

I shook my head. "No, you don't. You never have."

She opened her mouth to speak, but I wasn't done yet.

"You've never been a good friend. You're always putting me down. And Niki, Drew, and Josh. You're a horrible person. I tolerated your bullshit for too long, and honestly? I don't even know why."

Jen's lips formed a smirk, her confidence as misplaced as ever. "Because my hotness elevated your status."

That pissed me off. "You're so fucking full of yourself. Why are you even here tonight?"

"You blocked my calls. And you turned everyone against me."

"Because you treated Drew like shit." I shook my head. "And I didn't turn anyone against you. You did that yourself by cheating on Drew. Not to mention, you kissed Ghost and then lied about it. You couldn't stand seeing me laughing with him, could you? You couldn't stand that it wasn't you."

Jen's smirk wavered for a second. "You wouldn't know what to do with someone like Ghost. You're a goody-goody. He's never going to go for someone like you, Halston. So, you can stop drooling over him, because it's never gonna happen. He needs someone like me. Someone who knows their way around the bedroom."

I arched a brow. "You mean a slut?"

Her eyes flashed with anger. "You're just jealous."

I laughed, shaking my head. "Of what?"

Jen lifted her chin. "Because I'm not afraid to show my sexuality. And you're... you."

I laughed. If she only knew how many times I'd had Ghost. She'd probably die of shock... or jealousy. But I wasn't going to reveal that to her just to win.

"Have you actually gotten him to sleep with you?" she asked, with a laugh of her own, like the idea was ridiculous.

"Worry about your own life, Jen, because it's spiraling fast."

"I knew it!" she spat. "He hasn't even given you the time of day. You can flirt with him all you want, but once he sleeps with you, he'll dump you. You can't keep someone like Ghost."

"Ghost is none of your business," I told her. "You know nothing about him."

"I know he'd get bored of your inexperience and move on to some-one more confident, like me."

"There's a difference between sexual confidence and being a whore," I spat, sick of her shit.

That did it. Her hand swung up, aiming for my face.

Instinct took over, and I caught the side of her wrist with my right hand, my thumb pressing against the back of her hand. I swung around, twisting her wrist, bending her hand up, forcing her fingers toward her back, locking her wrist.

Jen let out a pained gasp. "You're hurting me!" she cried.

"Are you done swinging on me?" I asked.

"Yes!"

I let go and shoved her back slightly, creating space between us.

Jen stumbled but quickly recovered, her face twisted in rage. "Our friendship is over!" she screamed.

"Too late," I growled. "I called it a week ago."

She let out a sharp, humorless laugh, her expression turning wicked. "Now I'm gonna take him from you."

I tilted my head and laughed. "Good luck."

Jen could charm her way into any man's bed. But Ghost wasn't the kind of guy to screw a friend's ex. And more importantly? He had already proven he didn't want her.

I took comfort in that.

I walked back to the group, my pulse still pounding from the adrenaline of what had just gone down.

Niki's eyes immediately scanned me, her brow furrowed in concern. "Are you okay?"

Before I could answer, Josh smirked. "Did you see her? She's fine." He turned to me, grinning. "Where'd you learn that?"

I shrugged, feeling a small burst of pride. "From Ghost."

Josh's eyebrows shot up. "You taught her that?" he asked, looking at Ghost.

Ghost simply nodded. "I did."

Josh laughed. "Nice! You might have to teach the rest of us some moves."

He smiled. "You know where I live."

Drew sighed and ran a hand over his face, shaking his head. "I'm so sorry Jen took our problems out on you."

I waved it off. "It's not your fault. She's used to getting what she wants."

Ghost let out a low chuckle, shaking his head. "This is a seriously rude awakening for her."

Drew let out a slow breath, looking down at his beer. "She was always one foot in, one foot out, but I loved her. I should have cut her off a long time ago."

Ghost scoffed. "I've been telling you that for how long?"

Drew sighed. "I know. I had to come around in my own time, I guess."

Ghost arched a brow, his lips curving slightly. "Are your eyes open now?"

Drew looked up, exhaling. "They are."

Ghost smirked, tilting his beer toward him. "Welcome to the club, man."

Drew laughed, shaking his head.

I stood there, debating whether to tell Ghost that Jen planned on going after him to spite me.

I decided against it.

Ghost turned to me with a proud smirk. "You executed that wrist-lock perfectly."

I smiled, feeling a warm rush of pride. "Thank you."

Ghost's smirk widened slightly. "I was seriously impressed."

My cheeks heated at the unexpected compliment, and I hoped no one would notice the blush creeping up my face.

Ghost, of course, noticed. And because he was Ghost, he couldn't let it slide.

"You're sexy when you blush," he whispered.

"Yeah?"

He nodded. "You're something else, Tits."

I smiled. Even his compliments turned me inside out.

Chapter 69

G host pulled into my driveway, the engine idling softly as he shifted into park.

I turned to him, my heart still racing from the events of the night, from the way he flirted with me right in front of everyone, to the way he'd praised me for executing the wristlock on Jen.

"You wanna come in?" I was holding my breath, hoping he wouldn't turn me down.

Ghost looked at me, his blue eyes calculating, before giving a small nod. "Yeah."

I smiled and released that breath, stepping out of the truck.

Ghost followed me inside, the door shutting with a soft click behind him. The house was quiet, dimly lit, and warm.

I kicked off my shoes by the door and glanced over my shoulder. "You did good tonight."

He shrugged, taking a seat on the couch. "Guy had a heavy right hook, but nothing I couldn't handle. Though you looked like you were gonna leap into the ring and throw hands yourself."

I laughed, moving to the fridge to get two beers. "I was just invested."

Ghost smirked, taking the bottle I handed him. "I could tell. You go feral when I bleed."

"You're not wrong," I said with an unapologetic shrug, cracking open my cap. "Also, thanks for holding my beer like it was some kind of trophy."

He grinned. "It was a trophy. You should've seen Jen's face when I took it from you like it was mine. She damn near imploded."

I snorted. "Yeah, she seriously can't handle the idea of you and me."

"When she swung on you," he said, narrowing his eyes. "You handled that shit like a pro. That wristlock was damn flawless."

I gave him a mock bow with prayer hands. Well, the best I could with my beer in my right hand. "Thank you, sensei."

He rolled his eyes with a laugh. "But seriously—I'm proud of you, Halston."

I set my beer on the counter and slipped my hands behind my back under my shirt, unhooking my bra, but still listening intently.

"You didn't even flinch. You stood your ground, looked her in the eye, and—"

I tugged one strap down under my shirt, then the other, pulling the whole thing out through my sleeve and tossing it on the counter.

"—and you..." Ghost's voice faltered.

"So much better," I sighed, stretching my arms above my head with a relieved groan. "That thing was stabbing me all night."

Ghost blinked. "Right. Uh... stabbing."

I picked up my beer and turned to see why he'd gone silent. I couldn't help the smile that tugged at my lips when I saw the look on his face. Ghost was frozen, his beer halfway to his lips. "Did you just do the Flashdance bra move?"

I broke out in laughter. "I guess I did."

His eyes darkened, his smirk widening. "That was so fucking hot."

I sipped my beer, cocking a brow, a grin spreading across my lips. "You gonna survive, tough guy?"

Without answering, Ghost tipped back his bottle and drained the rest in one long pull, like he was trying to douse the fire I'd just lit under his skin.

"You planning on pulling anything else out from under your clothes tonight?" he asked, his voice lower now, rougher.

I laughed, shaking my head as I headed to the fridge. "You're parched, huh?"

"You have no idea."

The way he was looking at me had my stomach twisting with heat, my body humming with awareness. "Do you want another beer?"

"Yes, please." Ghost set his empty bottle down and leaned back on the couch, still watching me like I was the most interesting thing in the room. "Now, all I can think about is the first time I saw you."

I smiled, grabbing him a beer from the fridge. "When you bumped into me and spilled beer all over me?"

He grinned. "You had a white shirt with a white bra. So fucking sexy."

I handed him the beer, rolling my eyes. "You were obnoxious."

He took a sip, smirking. "I'm good at that."

I smiled back. "And then some."

Ghost chuckled. "I don't know why, but I like that my obnoxious behavior didn't scare you off."

I raised a brow, heat flooding my body. He'd actually just admitted something to me. "Are you saying you like me?"

"Whoa. I wouldn't go that far."

I laughed, shaking my head. "But you like my ability to learn fighting moves quickly."

He nodded, taking another swig of his beer. "I do."

"And my Flashdance bra move?"

His grin widened. "Definitely."

"How about my tits when they were doused in beer?" I teased.

Ghost exhaled sharply, his grip tightening around his beer bottle. "Too fucking much."

My stomach flipped. Every reaction, every sound he made, fueled my fire. I liked the way he was looking at me, like he wanted to devour me where I stood.

I took a long pull of my beer, then set it down on the side table, my pulse pounding in my ears. Ghost was always the tease, the aggressor.

This time, I was taking control.

I took his beer from him and set it on the side table with mine.

Grabbing the hem of my shirt, I pulled it over my head, dropping it onto the floor.

Ghost's jaw clenched, his eyes raking over my bare skin, his body stiffening.

"How about no top?" I asked as I knelt on the couch and straddled his lap.

He groaned, his fingers gripping my hips, his eyes flashing with pure, unfiltered hunger. "Fuck yes."

A thrill ran through me. I had never felt so in control, so wanted.

Ghost's brows lifted slightly, his lips curving into a slow, wicked grin. "Oh, shit," he said, amused. "Are you about to seduce me, Tits?"

My stomach tightened at the heat in his gaze.

He leaned in, his voice dropping to a low rasp, his breath brushing against my ear. "Gotta say... I like this role reversal. You takin' what you want. It's sexy as fuck."

A shiver shot through me.

His eyes shot down to my lips, then back up. "So tell me, Halston. What exactly are you about to do with me?"

His challenge hung thick in the air between us, his smirk downright filthy.

"Whatever I want," I said and leaned in, pressing my lips to his bearded jaw. I ran my tongue up his neck, tasting the salt on his skin, inhaling his masculine scent.

Ghost let out a low groan. His grip on my hips tightened, his body rock-hard beneath me. A low chuckle vibrated in his chest. "Jesus Christ, Tits."

I smiled against his neck, kissing a slow trail up to his jaw, teasing him.

His hands slid up my sides, his thumbs sweeping across my nipples. He was taunting me back, testing how far I was willing to take this game.

I leaned into his touch, silently daring him.

He let out a dark, wicked laugh, his breath ragged. "Fuck, look at you. Little good girl finally realizing she likes to be bad."

I smiled at him. "Just for you," I admitted. "I wanna be bad for you."

He groaned. "I like when you admit it. But will you fall apart screaming beneath me first?"

I shivered, heat torching me at the way his gravelly voice dripped with filthy promises. His thumbs swept over my bare nipples again, and I gasped, my body jerking against him.

Ghost growled, his lips brushing my ear. "That a yes?"

I couldn't speak. His touch was torturing me, trying to take my control.

He chuckled again and rolled his hips up into me, his aroused cock pressing against me through our jeans.

I let out a low, tortured moan, my fingers sliding up to his shoulders.

"No?" he mocked, his voice low, sinful. "So if I slide my hand down these jeans, I won't find you soaking wet for me?"

I shook my head and clenched my thighs around him, but that only made him smirk.

Ghost dipped his head, biting lightly at my bottom lip before sucking it into his mouth. When he pulled back, his eyes burned with hunger. "Lying little thing."

I let out a shaky breath, my body betraying me.

Ghost grinned, his hands sliding lower, his fingers popping open the button of my jeans. "Let's see just how bad you wanna be for me, sweetheart."

I grinned, a slow, deliberate curve of my lips, my confidence building with every dark, hungry look Ghost gave me. "You always run that filthy mouth," I said, dragging my nails down his chest, feeling the hard muscle tense beneath my fingertips. "Maybe it's time you shut up for once."

Ghost's smirk twitched, his grip on my hips tightening. "Oh, yeah?"

"Yeah."

I pushed him back against the couch, pinning him down, loving the way his sexy blue eyes flashed with heat and surprise.

He exhaled a rough laugh, his hands settling firmly on my waist. "Baby, you can try all you want, but we both know who's really in control here."

Challenge accepted.

I leaned down, my mouth brushing against his ear as I rolled my hips, grinding against the thick, solid length of his cock beneath me.

Ghost groaned, his fingers digging into my skin.

"That so?" I whispered, dragging my lips along the edge of his jaw and beard. "Because it feels like I'm the one calling the shots right now."

His jaw clenched, his breathing controlled, but I felt the way his body reacted to mine, the way his restraint was starting to crumble under my touch.

I kissed a slow trail down his neck, tasting him, savoring the power I had in this moment. Then I ran my tongue back up his neck in one long stroke.

"Fuck, Halston," he growled, one hand gripping the back of my neck, the other slipping beneath my waistband, his fingers ghosting along the edge of my panties.

I grabbed his wrist, halting him.

His gaze snapped to mine, wild and hungry, but I just smirked, enjoying the rare moment where Ghost wasn't the one dictating the pace. "Uh-uh," I said, my voice dripping with sweet defiance. "Not until I say so."

His eyes darkened, his nostrils flaring. "You're gonna be the death of me."

I laughed softly, then leaned in, pressing my lips to his ear, letting my breath tickle against his skin. "Then I'm doing something right."

He groaned. For once, he wasn't the one calling the shots. I was.

"Halston." He said my name—half pleasure, half warning.

I whispered against his skin. "Say my name with those pretty lips."

Ghost chuckled.

His grip tightened, his control hanging by a thread as I bit his earlobe. "Fuck me, Halston," he groaned, his head falling back.

"That's the plan."

He let out another low chuckle.

I bit his neck gently, scraping with my teeth, my lips barely grazing, teasing, feeling his heartbeat pound hard beneath my tongue. "I wanna make you lose control," I whispered, gently biting his ear, grinning as he let out a deep moan. "Make you beg for me. Make you cum so hard you forget your own name."

His fingers dug into my skin. "Jesus fucking Christ, Halston," he groaned. "Are you tryin' to wreck me?"

I leaned back, meeting his hooded gaze, letting my hands slide down his chest, over his abs, my fingers hovering just above the waistband of his jeans.

"I want you wrecked," I purred. "I want you desperate. You think you're the only one who can play this game? Baby, I can make you fucking feral."

His chest heaved, his muscles coiled tight, his hands gripping my thighs.

I reached down and pulled his shirt up. He lifted his arms for me, and I tugged it off the rest of the way, dropping it to the floor.

His breath was warm against my skin as I pressed my breasts to his face, slow and deliberate. His hands slid up my thighs, gripping harder now, digging into my flesh.

He tried to cup my breasts, but I denied him.

"Fuck, sweetheart," he groaned, his voice ragged. "You're gonna make me lose it."

"I want you undone," I whispered, my lips on his ear. "Wrecked. Mine."

He growled deep in his throat, and in a blur, his hands moved, one arm rounding my waist, the other grabbing the back of my neck as he surged upward, pressing his mouth to mine, rough and possessive.

I moaned into it, grinding down on him, feeling the hard proof of just how far gone he already was. His hands moved like he couldn't decide where to touch–my back, my ass, my hips. His hands were everywhere, all at once, like he needed more of me than he could take. And it made me crazy.

He tore his mouth away, breathing hard. "You wanna make me feral?" he growled. "You better fucking mean it, Halston. 'Cause once I break... I don't come back easy."

"Good," I breathed, my pulse pounding. "I don't want easy. I want you. Every filthy, dangerous, uncontrollable inch."

Chapter 70

He growled again. It was an honest-to-God, guttural sound, his eyes flashing something dangerous, his restraint threatening to snap like a frayed wire. "You talk a big fucking game, baby," he growled, flipping me beneath him so fast I gasped. "Now show me you can back it up."

Ghost had me pinned beneath him now, his hands tight on my wrists, pushing them above my head, his thighs on mine, the weight of his body pressing me into the cushions.

His blue eyes burned, dark and devastating, his chest heaving as he stared down at me like I had just lit a match to a fucking wildfire inside him.

I licked my lips, refusing to back down, my pulse hammering against my ribs. "I can handle whatever you throw at me, Kasper." My voice was breathless, but my eyes dared him. "Question is... Can you handle me?"

A slow, wicked smile curved his lips, and my stomach flipped at the heat in his gaze. "You wanna make me beg, baby?" He leaned in, his lips hovering just over my mouth, teasing, torturing. "You're gonna have to work a lot fucking harder than that."

I pulled up, rolling my hips into his, feeling just how hard he was for me.

Ghost groaned, his head dropping, his forehead pressing to mine. "Fuck, Halston." His grip on my wrists tightened, his fingers flexing.

"What's the matter?" I taunted, my lips grazing his jaw. "I thought you had all the control?"

His chest rumbled, his lips slanting over mine in a kiss so deep, so all-consuming, it threatened to knock the air from my lungs. I moaned into his mouth, my fingers curling against his grip, needing to touch him, to pull him closer, to feel his skin under my hands.

"You wanna take control?" His voice was rough, his breath hot against my lips. "Then do it."

He released my wrists, and before he realized what I was thinking, I pushed my hips up, shoving his body off me and off the couch to the floor, following him down, straddling him once again.

His grin was dark, proud, and fucking cocky as hell. "There she is."

I rolled my hips, watching the way his eyes fluttered shut, the way his jaw clenched tight, his fingers digging into my thighs.

I grabbed his wrists, pinning them down, just like he had pinned me.

He fucking let me take control.

"Your turn to stay put," I whispered against his lips.

Ghost's tongue flicked out, swiping my bottom lip. "Make me."

Oh, damn. The way he used that sexy tongue...

I rocked my hips, grinding against his hard cock that was still restrained in his jeans.

His jaw clenched, his breathing shallow, but that cocky smirk was still there, hanging on by a thread. "That all you got, baby?" His voice was low, challenging.

I scraped my teeth over his jawline, then kissed my way down his throat.

Ghost groaned, his hips jerking up.

I lifted up, putting space between our bodies, denying him. "Not so cocky now, are you?" I whispered against his skin.

"You're fucking evil, Tits." His voice was a low growl, but I felt the way he shuddered, the way his body responded.

I smirked, dragging my tongue over his lips. "Just returning the favor."

I slid my hand between us, palming him through his jeans, feeling just how hard he was.

Ghost sucked in a sharp breath, his hips tensing, his head tipping back, his eyes closing. "Fuck, baby."

My chest clenched. I loved when he called me baby.

I pressed harder, rubbing, teasing, watching his lips part, his chest rise and fall. His hands clenched into fists above his head. "You like this?" I whispered, brushing my lips against his. "Like me touching you?"

His blue eyes snapped open, dark and dangerous. "Why don't you find out just how much?" he challenged, his smirk returning.

I unzipped his jeans, feeling him beneath my hand, his body tensing. His eyes locked on me like I was the only thing that existed.

And, fuck if that wasn't the best feeling in the world.

I freed him from his jeans, tossing them aside. Then, I pulled his boxer briefs down, wrapping my fingers around his thick cock, stroking him, teasing him, watching his stomach tighten with every move.

Ghost let out a shuddering breath, his jaw tight as he fought for control. "You gonna play with it all night, baby?" His voice was raspy, strained, but that cocky smirk still clung to his lips.

I squeezed my fingers around him, dragging my hand up, my thumb sweeping over the head. "You're impatient," I said, leaning down, trailing my tongue along his throat.

"No, I just know you're dying to put your mouth on me."

I laughed softly, brushing my lips along his jaw, still stroking him. "Cocky," I whispered, watching his smile fade as I moved faster, tightening my grip.

Ghost groaned, his fingers digging into my hips now, his breath coming in sharp gasps. "Jesus, Tits. You're gonna make me—"

But before he could finish, I let go, pressing a kiss to his chest, his abs, moving lower.

"Fuck." His hand tangled in my hair as I took him into my mouth, swirling my tongue around the tip before sinking lower, savoring the way he shuddered beneath me. "Holy fuck…"

I worked him slow, teasing, licking, sucking, his breathing ragged, his body so tense he was shaking. I took him deeper, tightening my lips, swallowing him down, his grip tightening in my hair, his hips spasming as he fought not to lose himself too fast.

"Fuck, Halston, you're killing me." His voice was hoarse, his muscles flexing, his body trembling beneath my hands.

I hummed around him, using his own tactic against him, the vibrations making him suck in a sharp breath, his fingers tugging at my hair, his legs tensing beneath me.

I could feel the way he was unraveling, the way he was right there, on the edge of breaking completely.

"Not like this," he said. Suddenly, his hands were on me, yanking me up, flipping me onto my back. He hovered over me, his eyes dark and dangerous, his breath ragged. "If I'm cuming, I'm cuming inside you."

My stomach flipped, my pulse pounded in my ears, and my body trembled with need. "Then what the fuck are you waiting for?"

He grinned, that wicked, filthy smirk taking over his face.

He peeled my jeans and panties down and quickly discarded his boxer briefs. Before coming back to me, he grabbed a condom and rolled it on.

He was back on me, covering my body with his. In one motion, he parted my thighs and slid into me.

I arched beneath him, crying out, my body already raw with pleasure.

"I want you like this," he growled. "Open. Moaning. Mine."

I gasped, my fingers digging into his back as he set a punishing rhythm. His mouth dragged up my throat to my lips.

"Where's that control, baby?" His voice was ragged, breathless, his hands gripping my thighs, pushing deeper into me, making me feel every inch of him.

I moved with him, lifting my hips, matching his pace, taking everything he gave. My body was on fire, my mind a complete blur of pleasure and heat.

His fingers found that perfect spot between us, circling with ruthless precision.

Ghost gritted his teeth, his body trembling against mine. "Fuck, baby, cum for me."

I did. I came screaming his name.

Ghost's grip was unrelenting as he drove into me, bringing his own release, stroke after stroke, until he finally slowed to a stop.

He let out a rough laugh, dragging a hand through his sweat-dampened hair. "That was fucking unfair."

I smirked, trailing my fingers down his chest, still reeling from the high.

His eyes met mine, dark and highly amused. "Jen was wrong about you."

"She was? About what?"

His lips curved into a smug grin. "She thought you wouldn't know what to do with someone like me."

My eyes widened as I sat up. "You heard that? We weren't even in the warehouse."

His grin widened. "We all did."

He brushed a strand of hair off my face. "And I can say confidently that you don't have any weaknesses in the bedroom."

I laughed, shaking my head. "Wow. Was that a compliment?"

Ghost smiled. "It was."

I grinned, running a hand down his chest, feeling the heat still radiating off him. "The stone man is turning into a real boy," I teased.

Ghost chuckled, a devastating grin on his lips, the one that always turned my insides molten.

"You realize you called me baby?" I asked then, my voice teasing. "Several times."

He didn't answer right away. Instead, he tilted his head, studying me, his fingers trailing along my bare thigh, setting my skin on fire. "Do you realize you only ever call me Kasper when I'm fucking you?"

A fire shot through me at his filthy words. He was right. I only ever called him by his real name when we were tangled up like this, when I was gasping for air, completely at his mercy. "You said not to call you that in front of other people. So, I only call you it when we're alone, Kasper," I said, dragging out his name.

Ghost hummed, trailing his fingers higher, teasing the sensitive skin at the crease of my hip, making me shiver. "You're becoming more cocky like me every day."

I smirked. "And do you like that?" I asked, my voice low, filled with the same seductive edge he always used on me.

Ghost's eyes darkened, his smirk turning downright sinful. "It's hot as fuck."

Then he rolled on top of me again, pressing down on me, his mouth capturing mine in a deep, slow kiss that made my toes curl, my stomach clench, and my entire body melt into his.

His lips moved down my throat, his teeth grazing, his beard tickling my skin just enough to make me squirm. "My little sexual deviant."

I laughed, breathless, as his mouth continued its path downward.

"You like that?" he asked, his voice rough, his breath hot against my skin.

"Yeah, I like that."

Ghost chuckled, his tongue flicking out, tasting me, making my hips arch involuntarily beneath him. "I like that you admit it now."

I let out a soft, shuddering breath, my body responding to every little thing he did. "You corrupted me."

His grin turned wicked. Leaning in, he brushed his lips over mine, his voice a low, gravelly whisper. "I'm seriously thinking about fucking corrupting you again."

I moaned loudly and flicked his lips with my tongue. "Do your worst, Kasper. Wreck me. Or are you all mouth tonight?"

"That's it," he said, his voice dropping, making me laugh as he whispered. "You've done it now. Round two, baby. Let's see if you're still talkin' shit when I make you cum on my mouth."

Chapter 71

"So, you're liking it here?" I asked one of Ghost's new hires.

He was young, maybe early twenties, just a few years younger than me, with sandy blonde hair, and a bright-eyed eagerness about him that made me smile.

"Oh, yeah!" he said enthusiastically, his eyes lighting up. "It's been amazing. I mean, I've worked at a couple of smaller places before, but nothing like this. The guys have been teaching me a ton, Ghost especially. He's a beast, man. He knows everything."

I laughed, shaking my head. "Yeah, he has a way of making sure you learn real quick."

The kid nodded, his expression full of pure admiration, like he was talking about some kind of legendary cowboy, not the grumpy, foul-mouthed, sex-on-legs man who barely tolerated social interaction.

It was endearing, really, the way he saw Ghost.

"Fucking cozy?" The sharp, deadly voice cut through the morning air like a blade.

I jumped, surprised, spinning around to see Ghost as he closed the last few steps between us. His blue eyes blazed with something dangerous. His shoulders were tense, his jaw clenched tightly, and the look on his face? Pure, unfiltered anger.

The kid beside me froze like a deer caught in headlights. He looked at Ghost, then at me, then back at Ghost, like he suddenly regretted ever opening his mouth.

"What the hell is your problem?"

Ghost ignored me. His gaze locked onto the poor guy like he was mentally deciding how many bones to break.

The kid took a slow step back, clearly getting the hint. "Uh... I should, uh... go check on the horses." He mumbled before turning and practically jogging toward the stables.

I turned back to Ghost, planting a hand on my hip, scowling up at him. "Are you serious right now?"

His nostrils flared, his eyes still dark, his body tense. He said nothing else, just turned away, his mood shifting in that unpredictable way it always did.

Oh, for fuck's sake. I went after him.

"Was that necessary?" I called as he walked toward the barn.

Ghost didn't stop. "What?"

I gritted my teeth, catching up to him. "Yelling at us when we didn't do anything, scaring that poor kid like that."

He snorted, shaking his head. "Really? Because when people jump, it usually means they're doing something they shouldn't be."

I rolled my eyes. "Or it means someone came up behind you and shouted, scaring the hell out of you."

Ghost didn't respond.

I reached out, grabbing his arm, forcing him to stop just inside the barn. "I was asking him how he liked working on the ranch. He was just being nice by answering my question."

Ghost turned to face me fully now, his blue eyes still angry. "When a man is nice, he's usually trying to get in your pants."

I folded my arms, raising a brow. "So what?"

"You just jump at the first motherfucker who gives you a little attention?" His voice was low, controlled, but there was fire beneath it.

"Oh, fuck off, Ghost," I growled, pushing off his chest.

His hands shot out, gripping my hips, yanking me into him. "That what you want, Tits? You want some dumbass kid with a hero complex?" His voice was rough, demanding, pissed.

I swallowed hard, my heart pounding. I should have shoved him away from me and told him to go to hell.

But instead, I felt that familiar heat shoot up my spine, the same one that always hit me when Ghost got like this. His anger was always laced with sexual heat. The man could turn me from angry to lustful in a split second. And he was holding my hips the way I couldn't help but like. Possessive, like he owned them.

Then he spoke again, his words holding an edge of something dangerous. "I won't let you walk all over me. No woman will ever make a fool of me again."

There it was. That undercurrent of something unspoken, the reason he was the way he was. The reason he kept me at arm's length. The reason for his brutal mood swings. He'd been burned. Badly. And obviously by the ex Henry had mentioned.

I exhaled, trying to keep my frustration in check. "I don't know who you're referring to, but it's not me." My gaze was hard, unwavering. "I've done nothing to hurt you. Don't you think I should get the benefit of the doubt instead of making me pay for your last relationship?"

Ghost watched me, his jaw clenched.

I tried to reassure him. "I'm not flirting with anyone but you, Ghost. I don't want some kid. I just want you. We were talking. Nothing more."

His jaw flexed slightly. "It looked like a lot more."

My eyes held his gaze. "You sound jealous. And you make sure to tell me every time we're together that I'm not your girlfriend."

Ghost's lips curled slightly. "Trust me, I am far from jealous. And you're not my girlfriend."

It stung, but not as much as it would have before. It was so obvious he was fighting inner demons. "Well, thanks for the reminder," I said, trying to step back, trying to pull away. He was constantly trying to hurt me when he got angry.

But Ghost didn't let me go. His voice dropped lower, sharper. "I don't like liars."

I snapped my head back toward him, offended as hell. "I don't like liars either. And I'm no liar."

Ghost watched me, his gaze intense, like he was testing me, pushing me, waiting to see if I'd break.

I didn't.

Instead, I stepped closer, meeting his stare head-on as I gave him hell. "I've only slept with you. You're the only one I want to sleep with. Hell, you're all I think about most of the time," I growled. "And the only time I ever lied to you was when I said I didn't like your vulgar mouth. Because I do. I really do. It turns me the fuck on."

Something in his blue eyes shifted. Then he kissed me. Hard. His hands gripped my waist harder, pulling me against him, his mouth hot and unrelenting, his tongue sweeping against mine with delicious, toe-curling precision.

I let out a small moan, my arms going up around his neck, my body already burning for him. Damn him. He always did this. He wrecked me senseless.

And I let him. Every. Damn. Time.

Chapter 72

G host kissed me good, turned me on, then released me. "Now stop distracting me. I have work to do."

I turned to leave, but I could still hear the anger in his voice. He wasn't over it yet. We hadn't resolved anything. And by now, I was starting to understand his mood swings, starting to see through his bullshit defenses.

At the last second, I stopped and turned back and lifted my shirt, flashing my tits at him. No bra.

Ghost stared completely stunned, his entire body going still. Then he laughed. A real, genuine laugh, deep and unguarded.

I grinned. "You can still laugh."

He shook his head, rubbing a hand down his face and over his beard. "Damn it. You make me want to."

I beamed, my heart swelling in my chest. I knew I probably looked like a lovesick fool, but I didn't care. For better or worse, I was seriously in love with this man. This stubborn, closed-off, impossible man.

Ghost was still watching me, his chest rising and falling a little faster than before. I think he was waiting to see what I would do next. So, I was going to give him something to watch.

Stepping closer, I reached for his waistband.

His brows lifted slightly. "What are you doing?"

I smirked. "You think you're getting away after turning me on with that kiss?" I pulled at the button, unzipped his jeans, and slid his boxer briefs down just enough until he sprang free, already hard in my hand.

Ghost let out a deep, guttural groan, his hand immediately tangling in my hair as I sank to my knees before him. "Fuck, Halston."

The way he said my name, his voice rough with need, I loved it.

"I love how silky smooth the tip is." A little precum squirted out, and I licked it, looking up at him, my eyes teasing him.

He growled, his chest vibrating against me. "You're all fucking kinds of sexy."

I took him into my mouth, slow at first, savoring the way he shuddered against me, his fingers tightening in my hair.

He whispered my name.

Then, I took him all the way down, as far as I could until he hit the back of my throat, earning a groan from him. Again and again, I swallowed him down and sucked him up, faster and faster.

Ghost let out a ragged breath, his entire body tense with need. His jaw tightened, his blue eyes burning into mine, wild and ravenous.

And as he tensed and made a rough sound, I pulled up, taking my mouth off him, before he got to the point of no return.

His voice was a low growl, full of frustration and lust-drunk approval. "Fucking cruel, Tits. You don't stop a man when he's that close unless you're begging to be punished for it."

A wicked smile tugged at my lips as I slowly, deliberately, licked a long, teasing line up his cock, my tongue swirling around the sensitive head before trailing back down, savoring him like I had all the time in the world, like he was a delicious lollipop I was enjoying.

Ghost took a sharp breath, his hands twitching like he was about to grab me and force me to finish what I started. "Jesus fuck," he hissed, his head tipping back against the cabinet, his breath unsteady. "You trying to kill me, baby?"

I hummed against him, then placed a teasing kiss to the tip, my hands running up his thighs as he met my gaze again. "Wouldn't dream of it." My voice was syrupy sweet, but we both knew the truth. I was absolutely torturing him. Because watching him was torching me inside.

I wrapped my lips around him again and took him deep, swallowing him down as far as I could again, my hands gripping his hips as I worked him, sucking him harder, faster, deeper.

Ghost let out a rough, broken groan, his hands flying back to my hair, tangling his fingers in the strands, guiding me, trying to control the pace. He was losing it, unraveling in my mouth.

"Goddamn it, Halston," he growled, his voice hoarse and desperate.

His hips rolled into me, his fingers tightened, his muscles strained, and I knew he was close.

"Fuck. Don't stop this time. Take it, baby. Take every fucking drop."

The command sent a rush of heat straight through me, my body aching with need. I didn't stop. He gave in completely, his entire body shaking, his groan filthy as he found his release.

Even then, I didn't let up, savoring every last drop, swallowing him down until he was completely spent.

When I finally pulled back, my breath shallow, I wiped my mouth with the back of my hand and met his gaze, watching the way he stared down at me.

A slow smirk spread across his lips as he exhaled, running a shaky hand through his hair. "Well, shit." His voice was rough.

I arched a brow, mock-innocent, licking my lips just to tease him. "What?"

Ghost let out a deep, satisfied chuckle, his grip tightening in my hair as he tilted my head back further, forcing me to look up at him. "That mouth, Tits." His eyes darkened, sinful and wicked. "I might be fucking addicted."

Standing, I smiled, happy I'd sufficiently wrecked him.

Ghost zipped up and adjusted himself, his breathing still ragged. He exhaled slowly. "I really have to get back to work."

I nodded, satisfied that his sour mood had vanished. "Okay. I'll get out of your way."

Even though I wanted to linger, wanted to see if he'd pull me close, I forced myself to stop that train of thought. It wasn't about me. He had things to do, and I respected that.

So I stepped back, turning away to leave, to let him have his space.

Then he smacked me on my ass, making me yelp.

I looked back to see that cocky grin and laughed.

I took a walk so I wouldn't be tempted to follow him around just so I could keep staring at his beautiful body and sexy smile. Those deep blue eyes could undo me with one look.

As I made my way out of the barn and away from Ghost, I glanced back to see that Lulu was following me as usual, which made me laugh.

What caught me off guard and made my eyes widen? Ghost's dogs left where they had been sitting and started following me too.

I fought the urge to say anything out loud, afraid that if I acknowledged it, they'd change their minds and go back to him.

I bit my lip, pretending I wasn't bursting with excitement inside. This was... big. Ghost's dogs followed no one but him. And now, they'd chosen to follow me.

A warm feeling spread through me.

Was this how it felt to be truly accepted into his world?

Chapter 73

The minute I walked in, I knew this was a mistake.

The event was packed. Loud. Flashy. A promotional stunt meant to put all eyes on Ghost. And judging by the sheer number of women here, it was working.

Ghost was at the center of it all, sitting at a long table with his name plastered behind him, posing for pictures, signing merch, and being swarmed by women.

Candace, his social media manager, was on her phone, snapping content for his pages, recording videos, taking behind-the-scenes footage. This was good PR, good for business.

Bad for my fucking sanity.

Cameras flashed. A sea of fight fans flooded the venue, hyping him up. Ghost was the main attraction. And the man who made it all happen stood in the middle of it.

The high roller. Sleek suit. Fake charm. That snake-like smile.

I hated him.

Candace gave me a friendly smile as I walked past, but I barely acknowledged it. Because my focus was locked on Ghost. He was in the middle of it all, playing his part perfectly.

He was posing for pictures, shaking hands, doing interviews.

"Jesus," Niki muttered, sipping her drink as she watched the spectacle unfold.

I said nothing. I was too busy watching these women hang all over him, their hands lingering when they touched his arms, his chest. Watching them press in too close, their flirty little giggles filling the air as they posed for photos, some even posing in his lap, sneaking in a quick kiss on his cheek.

I clenched my jaw, my fingers tightening around my drink. It was fucking excruciating.

And Ghost? He was eating it up.

Not in an obvious way, but he didn't look bothered by it. He was relaxed, letting it happen, letting them touch him, letting them grab his arm, his shoulders, some even getting bold enough to run their hands down his chest.

I wanted to break every single one of their fingers. But I couldn't, because I wasn't his girlfriend. I had no right to be mad. But oh, I was. Fury boiled under my skin, hot and suffocating.

"Is it just me," Josh said, leaning toward Drew, "or are these chicks being really fucking aggressive?"

Drew grunted. "You ever been around a fighter? Women flock to them. They love the hype, the muscles, the danger. It's a whole thing."

"Yeah, well," Niki muttered, eyeing me carefully, "not all of us are enjoying the show."

I hadn't told Niki that Ghost and I had even kissed. It wasn't my right to. And I knew if I told anyone and Ghost found out, it would be over. But I knew she at least knew I liked him. She saw my white-knuckled grip on my drink, saw the way my eyes hadn't left Ghost in over an hour.

But I wasn't gonna make a scene. Not when Candace was snapping pictures, hyping up his social media. Not when another woman slid into his lap like she fucking belonged there. I was determined not to ruin his night, even if it was torturing me.

But I sure as hell didn't need to stand there and watch it any longer.

I set my drink down so hard it sloshed over the rim. "I need some air," I said, turning away before I lost my damn mind.

I was on the balcony taking in the cool breeze when he stepped out on the balcony for a quick five-minute break.

"Ghost."

He turned at the sound of my voice, looking like trouble, like every bad decision I wanted to make all over again.

"What's up, Tits?" he drawled, cocking his head.

I stopped two feet in front of him, arms crossed, fury vibrating off me. "Are you kidding me?"

Ghost raised an eyebrow. "Am I supposed to know what you're talking about?"

"I just sat through two hours of you getting mauled by half the female population of this city, and now you're gonna act like nothing happened?"

Ghost chuckled. The fucker chuckled.

"Aw, sweetheart," he said, stepping closer, his voice teasing, "are you jealous?"

I bristled. "You fucking know I am."

He smirked.

My fists clenched. "I'm serious, Ghost. You had women all over you."

He shrugged, completely fucking undisturbed. "Comes with the job."

Oh, I was gonna kill him.

"Oh, it 'comes with the job'?" I repeated, my voice sharp. "You know what doesn't come with the job? Letting women sit in your fucking lap. Letting them put their hands all over you while you just sit there and smile like it's the best part of your damn day!"

Ghost's smirk widened like he was enjoying this, like he loved the way I was unraveling over him. "You know what's funny?" he said, stepping closer, invading my space, his eyes locked on mine.

I swallowed, refusing to back up. "What?" I snapped.

Ghost's voice dropped, low and smooth. "You sat there for two hours, watching, seething. But you didn't leave."

My breath caught in my throat.

He grinned. "You stayed. Watched me. And got pissed." He leaned in slightly, his lips just inches from mine. "And that tells me everything I need to know."

I hated how his voice slid over me, like velvet, like a fucking spell, turning my anger into heat. I glared at him, my heart pounding. "And what exactly do you think you know, Ghost?"

His eyes darkened. "That if I touched you right now, you'd let me."

I pulled in a shaky breath. He wasn't wrong.

I clenched my jaw. "Fuck you."

"That's what I was hoping you'd say, sweetheart."

He smiled that slow, cocky as hell grin like he'd won, like he thought he had the last word.

Not this time.

I wasn't letting it slide. Not when he had me so wound up I could barely breathe. Not when he was standing there with that cocky smirk, like he had me.

I stepped forward, closing the distance between us.

Ghost stopped mid-step, his eyes flickering with surprise as I leaned in close. "Yeah?" I whispered, my voice teasing. "Why? You wanna fuck me right here? Right now?"

His smirk faltered.

Ghost's jaw tightened, his muscles tensing. His hands clenched like he wanted to grab me, pull me in, and take exactly what I was offering.

Good. If I had to be turned on and frustrated, then so did he.

Before he could say a word, before he could recover, I grabbed his face, pulled his mouth down to mine, and kissed him like I wanted to ruin him. My tongue swept into his mouth, claiming, devouring, sliding against his, slow and demanding.

I felt the exact moment he lost control, his hands flying to my waist, pulling my body against him, his groan vibrating against my lips.

For one brief second, I let him have it, let him grip me, pull me in, kiss me like he needed it to survive.

Then I broke away, panting, my lips tingling.

Ghost's grip tightened, his pupils wide, his chest rising and falling fast.

He reached for me again, hungry, but I shoved his hands away, my lips taking on a smirk of my own. "Oh, no," I whispered.

Ghost shuddered, his breath shaky.

I leaned up on my toes, my hands pressing against his chest. "While those women are crawling all over you," I purred, "I want you to think about that kiss. I want you to think about these lips." I dragged my thumb across his lower lip, teasing, enjoying the way his lips vibrated with his deep groan.

I rubbed him through his jeans, slow and torturous, feeling how hard he was.

His body tensed.

"Think about how wet this pussy gets when you're close," I whispered.

Ghost's head fell back, a rough sound escaping his throat, his control hanging by a shred.

Then, just like he always did to me, I pulled away.

As I turned to walk away, feeling damn proud of myself, I barely made it two steps before Ghost's voice rumbled behind me, low and full of frustration. "That," he growled, his voice tight, "was fucked up, sweetheart."

I stopped and looked back. "You know where to find me when you want more, Kasper."

He was standing there, with his jaw tight, like it was taking everything in him not to grab me and drag me back to him.

His crystal blue eyes burned into mine, a mix of heat, hunger, and pure, raw need. "You're a tease."

It was glorious.

I shot him a smirk, slow and taunting, my voice syrupy sweet. "Welcome to my world, Ghost."

Then, I left the balcony. Leaving him hard as fuck, frustrated as hell, and completely wrecked.

Chapter 74

I stepped into Ghost's house, shaking off the cold that clung to my skin.

The smell of coffee filled the space, but it was the sight in the kitchen that had my chest tightening.

Lulu's bowls had been moved inside.

Not just her bowls. Her bed was there too, tucked neatly in the corner.

I stared at it, my stomach flipping. Ghost had brought her inside. I shouldn't have been so affected by that. It was just a cat bed, just a couple of stainless steel bowls on the floor. But the gesture did something to me.

I exhaled slowly, pushing past it as I set my bag down and moved to refill her food. Lulu brushed up against my leg, purring like she knew I needed a distraction.

I scratched behind her ears. "You've been promoted to house cat because your owner is secretly a softie... for you, anyway."

Ghost hadn't texted or called me last night. Nothing, just radio silence. And yeah, I knew I wasn't his girlfriend, but I'd all but begged him to find me after the event. No, I hadn't said the exact words, but it was implied that I wanted him to come find me after he was done. I'd practically promised him sex. Ghost was usually the smartest guy in the room. Did he not get that? If he had done that to me and I was the one posing for pictures last night, I would have shown up at his place for the main event. I made it obvious that I wanted him.

Maybe he was just tired of fucking me? It was bound to happen.

I grabbed my bag again and moved toward the door. I just needed to leave before I ran into him. I had no desire to see him right now.

But just as my hand hit the doorknob, the sky cracked open. Heavy rain slammed against the windows. It was the kind of storm that made driving a terrible idea.

Shit. I groaned, tilting my head back. Of course. The universe hated me.

I had no choice but to wait it out.

I clenched my jaw and set my bag back down.

That's when I heard footsteps on the porch. Then the door swung open, and Ghost walked in soaked to the damn bone. Water dripped from his hair, his shirt plastered to his chest, the fabric clinging to every defined muscle like some kind of cruel, wet dream.

I swallowed hard. Jesus.

His eyes landed on me instantly.

"I fed Lulu. I was just leaving," I blurted.

Ghost stepped fully inside, shaking the rain out of his hair. "I think you should wait out the rain."

My eyes narrowed. "I'll take my chances."

Ghost let out a breath like he was trying not to get irritated. "You left without saying anything."

I crossed my arms, keeping my gaze locked on the door. "Yeah, well... I didn't feel like watching that circus anymore."

Ghost sighed, moving toward me. He let his gaze drag over me. Then he let out a low chuckle, shaking his head. "You're somethin' else, Tits."

I ignored the way my heart slammed against my ribs when he said it. Ignored everything.

When I turned to step past him, his wet, calloused fingers wrapped around my wrist. I yanked my wrist free before he could say anything else. I wasn't giving in this time.

I reached for my bag and pulled out my laptop, dropping it onto the counter with a little too much force. "If I'm stuck here, I might as well get some work done," I said, flipping it open. "I'll head out as soon as the rain clears."

I could feel him watching me, standing there in his soaked clothes, dripping onto the kitchen floor, making it really damn difficult to focus on my screen. I kept my eyes trained on the glowing display, pretending he wasn't a wet, shirt-clinging, muscle-packed distraction standing right in my peripheral vision.

"Hey, if you wanna come over here and help me get dry, sweetheart, just say the word."

I gritted my teeth, refusing to acknowledge the visual that sentence just put in my head. Then the bastard peeled off his shirt. I heard the fabric hit the chair, and I knew his chest was glistening from the rain.

I ignored the heat that took over my body.

Ghost grabbed a towel and slowly dragged it over his chest, his stomach, soaking up the water, knowing damn well I was struggling. "You're quiet," he mused. "Normally, you'd have something smart to say."

I clicked my mouse aggressively, pretending to focus. "Normally, you're not half-naked and dripping wet in my personal space."

Ghost leaned against the counter, too damn close, his arms crossed, his tattooed body still on full display. "You don't like it?" he drawled with smugness in his voice.

I ignored him.

Ghost stepped around the counter. "Let me get this straight," he drawled, his voice thick with that infuriating, cocky tone. "You're just gonna sit here like we're business associates?"

I didn't look at him. "Yep," I said, concentrating on my email.

Ghost let out a low chuckle, shaking his head. "Damn, sweetheart. You're really gonna ice me out?"

I finally glanced up, arching a brow. "Yes."

His lips held that smirk that always got me into trouble. "Bullshit."

I clicked my tongue, refocusing on my screen.

I left the event in a good mood last night. I had turned the tables on him, flipped the script, left Ghost exactly how he'd spent all those nights leaving me. Wrecked and wanting. For once, I had the upper hand. So I waited. Waited for him to call. Waited for him to show up at my house, looking like sin, throwing me against the door, his hands in my hair, his mouth on mine, picking up exactly where we left off.

But the call never came. And neither did he. I stared at my phone, but it never went off. Nothing. Not a text. Not a missed call. And as the hours ticked by, that good mood? It fucking disappeared.

Ghost folded his arms across his chest as he stared at me. "I'm clueless here, Tits. Are you gonna tell me why you're pissed?"

Oh, my God. I wanted to yell at him. I wanted to punch him in the damn gut, exactly how I felt when he never showed last night.

I finally looked up at him. "How are you that clueless?"

The man literally looked lost. His expression showed he didn't have a clue what I was angry about. "Enlighten me, sweetheart."

My nostrils flared. "You left the event last night and you couldn't call me? Text me? You sure as hell didn't show up at my place."

Ghost watched me, tilting his head slightly. "You expected me to show up at your house?"

I let out an angry breath, my blood boiling. "Are you fucking kidding me? What do you think that was last night? I didn't just kiss you for fun, Ghost."

He smirked. The smug bastard smirked.

"No?" he mused. "Because it sure as hell looked like you were having fun to me."

I was one second away from punching him in the throat.

I glared at him, crossing my arms tighter. "I'm serious."

His smirk faded slightly. "I had shit to handle."

"What shit?"

Ghost exhaled, running a hand through his wet, messy hair, looking almost irritated. "There was an issue at the ranch," he said. "One of the new foals got tangled in a fence line. I didn't get back to the house until late."

I hesitated. I believed him. But I was still mad. Because he could have called me. He could have sent a single damn text. Instead, he left me wondering. Waiting. "Whatever."

I turned to walk away, but he caught my wrist, his grip firm but gentle. "You're still pissed," he said, watching me closely.

"No shit." I glared at him.

A beat of silence passed between us.

"You really wanted me to come over, huh?"

I yanked my wrist free, heat burning up my neck. "Go to hell."

Ghost grinned. "Nah, sweetheart. You'd miss me too much."

I flipped him off and walked away, refusing to let him see the truth written all over my damn face.

Chapter 75

The rain hammered against the windows; the wind howling outside as if it was trying to tear through the walls.

I sat at the kitchen island, my laptop in front of me, trying to focus on the design for a jewelry store logo on my design software. I experimented with fonts, adjusting the lettering to something elegant, bold, something that matched the style and prestige of the jewelry store.

I was deep in the zone, chewing my bottom lip, when Ghost walked back into the room in clean, dry blue jeans. He was shirtless, his chest still damp from his shower, his jeans slung low on his hips, showing off the deep V-line, looking like every filthy thought I refused to have about him come to life.

I swallowed. Hard.

Ghost ran a hand through his freshly washed hair. "Fucking storm's worse than I thought. I think you might be spending the night, Tits."

I stared. I couldn't help it. I hated that his very existence sent heat shooting up my spine, rolling through my entire body. I wanted to

WRECK ME 423

shove him against the damn counter and rip those jeans right the fuck off.

I was way too aware of him now, of the way his muscles flexed as he tossed the towel onto the back of a chair, completely oblivious of the fact that he was standing in just his low-slung jeans, his snap unfastened, driving me completely insane.

"You—" My voice caught, my throat suddenly too dry to function. "You look—" I coughed, then reached for my water, taking a long swallow.

Ghost's lips curled with that infuriating, cocky smirk. "Like something you wanna put your mouth on?"

My breath caught. Unfortunately, it was while I was trying to take a drink. I coughed up the water, spitting it all over the floor and my shirt.

Ghost gave a fully amused laugh.

I shot him a glare, but it fell short because I couldn't stop coughing.

"Jesus. Should I put my shirt on, sweetheart?"

I could hear the smugness in his tone, and that only pissed me off more. I finally got my coughing under control. "Yes," I snapped. "Please do."

Ghost grinned, making absolutely zero effort to move. Instead, he reached for the towel from the chair, slowly dragging it across his chest, over his abs, soaking up the last of the water.

A whimper threatened to escape, but I held on to it.

I glued my eyes to my screen, pretending I wasn't dying inside, that my thighs weren't tight with tension, that I wasn't imagining the weight of his body on top of mine, his hard chest pinning me down...

No. Nope. We weren't going there.

Ghost was enjoying this too much. I needed to shut it down. "You know what's funny?" I said, keeping my voice even. "For a guy who's always saying he doesn't do relationships, you sure love flirting with me."

Ghost made a noise in his throat, a deep, satisfied hum. "You call it flirting."

"What would you call it?"

His eyes burned into mine, full of heat. "Foreplay."

A sharp jolt pulsed through me. Jesus. "You really are a menace," I told him, turning back to my work.

I was two seconds away from giving in, from yanking him down and kissing him stupid.

But then his phone buzzed.

Ghost exhaled sharply, still staring at me as he pulled it from his back pocket. His jaw tightened when he saw the name on the screen. "Shit. I gotta take this."

And just like that, he was gone. He took the call as he headed down the hall to his room. And I let out a shaky breath, pressing my palms to the counter. Holy. Hell. I had been seconds away from making a mistake. But no matter how much I wanted him, I was still pissed at him. He was supposed to give in to me, not the other way around. But the man constantly wrecked me.

I grabbed my laptop again, forcing myself to focus. But it was useless because all I could think about was him. The way his voice dropped when he said foreplay.

He came back down the hall. "You hungry?"

"No," I said, staring at the screen, but not really seeing the words. I could see him out of the corner of my eye. He was just watching me, and he looked entirely too good. And I was entirely too pissed to care. Except I really did care.

I slammed the laptop shut and looked up at him, my patience officially gone. "Did you even think about that kiss last night?"

Ghost's brows lifted, amused, but his gaze sharpened. He took his time answering, like he was rolling my words over in his head. Then he sighed, shaking his head slightly. "Tits, I thought about that kiss the rest of the damn night."

My heart jumped at that.

I schooled my expression. "Then why the hell didn't you come to my house?" I challenged, my anger still simmering. "Why didn't you—" I snapped my mouth shut, cutting myself off before I said something embarrassing. Sometimes it felt like he didn't even give a fuck about me. He made me feel vulnerable. I felt like I was always chasing him. And he was just fucking me because I was there, always making myself available to him.

Ghost exhaled heavily, rubbing a hand down his beard, coming closer. "I didn't even finish the damn event," he admitted. "Henry called. I had to rush to the ranch. I was out there working 'til late in the freezing cold. And you wanna know something?"

I swallowed, my pulse kicking up at the way his voice dropped, gravelly.

"That kiss?" He grinned. "It kept me warm."

Damn him. Damn him to hell.

I hated how my body reacted, how my stomach flipped, how the heat that had been burning in anger suddenly shifted, twisted into something else entirely. Something needy and dangerous.

But I wasn't done being mad. "You still could've called," I said, trying to hold on to my frustration.

Ghost let out a quiet laugh. "And what? You would've answered? Judging at how pissed you are, I don't think you would have."

I didn't go to bed until after one. But who knows what time he finished work? If he had called me after that, I probably wouldn't have answered. I was already beyond pissed by the time I went to sleep.

Ghost let that settle between us for a beat before he stepped in even closer, close enough that I groaned when the scent of body wash, and pure fucking trouble wrapped around me.

His voice was low, deep. "And no, I didn't realize you wanted me to come over."

I clenched my jaw, refusing to react.

His lips curved. "But if I hadn't had to get to the ranch, I would've happily come over, sweetheart." He paused, his blue eyes holding mine, heat simmering beneath the teasing. "You just had to say the word."

I swallowed hard, my throat dry.

Then, smug as hell, he added, "I don't read minds, Tits. Next time, just fucking tell me to come over and fuck you."

Every muscle in my body clenched. I was hot. Furious. Wrecked. My thighs pressed together on instinct, and the bastard caught it. His gaze flicked lower for a split second before lifting again, his smug smile widening.

I wanted to slap him. I wanted to grab his face and kiss the smug right off of him.

I was so pissed. I'd dropped all the clues, and I still couldn't get him to fucking bend. That was the problem with Ghost. He was too goddamn strong. And worst of all? He knew it. I was constantly teetering on the edge, always wondering if I said something wrong, if I did something wrong, that he would drop me. And living on the edge was frigging exhausting.

So, I did the only thing I could do. I snatched my laptop, opened it back up, and pointedly ignored him, acting like his words, his presence, his entire existence didn't just set me completely on fire.

Ghost chuckled. "You're damn sexy when you're pissed, sweetheart."

And then he walked away. Leaving me to burn.

Chapter 76

Ghost had always been persistent, and tonight was no different.

He made conversation, made jokes, even cooked dinner, which was something I should've appreciated, but I couldn't bring myself to react. So we ate mostly in silence.

The storm outside had only gotten worse. I should have left hours ago, but the weather had other plans.

When Ghost finished eating, he leaned back in his chair, watching me, like he was waiting for something. No doubt, for me to break, to give in to him.

I ignored him.

Finally, he sighed. "You can't leave in this."

I stabbed at my food with my fork, pretending like that wasn't exactly what I was planning.

"Too dangerous," he added, nodding toward the windows. "Storm's just gettin' started."

I inhaled slowly, biting back my frustration, because I knew he was right, but I didn't want to be stuck here with him at the moment. "Fine."

A slow grin spread across his face. "Good girl."

I clenched my jaw, ignoring the way my pulse kicked up at those two words. Setting my fork down, I pushed back from the table, leveling him with a look.

I cleared the table and washed the dishes. Because I appreciated him cooking, even if I didn't want to say it.

Drying my hands on the hand towel on the sink, I asked, "Which room do you want me in?"

"Mine." It was a command, low and confident, mixed with heat, like he was daring me to say yes.

I swallowed hard, forcing myself to play it cool. "Not happening."

His brows lifted. "You sure about that?"

I was not sure of anything at this point. But I had to hold my ground. "I'll take a spare room," I said firmly, grabbing my laptop, heading out of the kitchen before he could change my mind.

I stood in the guest bathroom, my hair damp. The shower was supposed to calm me down, to wash away the tension, but it only made it worse. It gave me too much quiet time to think, and all I could think about was Ghost. His hands. His mouth. The way he wrecked me every time we were together.

I let out a frustrated sigh, running my fingers through my damp hair. I needed sleep. I needed to not think about Ghost.

I stepped out of the bathroom, wearing one of his old T-shirts and a pair of sweatpants rolled at my hips several times to pull the length up. But they were still too big for me because they were his, and I hadn't exactly planned on spending the night.

Ghost was leaning against the doorframe, his blue eyes watching me like a hunter tracking his prey. His shirtless, gloriously beautiful body was on full display, his sweatpants hanging low on his hips, his tattoos standing out against his golden skin.

He looked like sin. And I was one second away from committing it.

I swallowed hard, gripping the edge of the towel I was using to dry my hair. "Why are you standing there?"

Ghost grinned, like he wanted to make me suffer. "Came to tuck you in."

Heat flared through me. I forced a snort, acting uninterested. "Yeah, not happening."

Ghost tilted his head, stepping closer.

I lifted a warning hand, stepping back. "Don't."

His grin deepened. "Don't what?"

"Don't cross that threshold."

"You don't trust me?" he asked, watching me closely.

"I don't trust myself." The words slipped out before I could stop them.

Shit.

Ghost's lips parted, his expression shifting into something even more dangerous.

I cursed myself. Stupid. Stupid. Stupid.

His voice dropped lower, deeper. "You want me to leave?"

Yes. No. I had no fucking clue anymore.

Ghost let the silence stretch, reading me like an open book. Then he made it worse. "You sure you don't wanna sleep in my bed, sweetheart?"

My stomach clenched.

He smiled. "You looked real good in it last time."

I exhaled sharply, my legs going weak, my brain calling it quits at the memory of exactly how I'd felt in his bed. Under him. Writhing.

Ghost chuckled, his voice a low, sinful rumble. "You still thinking about it?"

I snapped my gaze back to his, narrowing my eyes. "I hate you."

His grin turned wicked. "You keep saying that, sweetheart. And yet, you keep letting me fuck you."

Before I could cuss him out, he turned around and walked away. Leaving me wet, turned on, and absolutely furious.

I threw my towel at the door. Bastard.

I shut off the light, pulled off my borrowed sweatpants, and got in bed. The low lights that ran down the length of the hallway gave the bedroom a soft glow, so it wasn't totally dark since I'd left the door open.

The storm had only gotten worse. The wind howled, rattling the windows, and the rain pounded against the glass, relentless. Every few seconds, the sky would explode with a violent streak of lightning.

I hated storms, always had. It didn't matter how old I got; something about the way they ripped through the sky, the way the thunder boomed so loud it shook the walls, unnerved me.

I pulled my knees to my chest, staring at the dark window, waiting. Praying the next lightning strike wouldn't be as bad.

Then lightning lit up the entire room, casting eerie shadows that danced along the walls. I barely had time to brace before...

Boom.

The thunder slammed into me like a physical force, so close, so loud and sudden that I let out an involuntary scream, my heart slamming against my ribs.

And then, from down the hall, I heard laughter. Deep. Low. Knowing. That bastard. He knew he had me.

I sat there fuming, my pulse still racing, my pride bruised. For a solid thirty seconds, I tried to convince myself to stay in this bed, to not give him the satisfaction of winning.

But then another clap of thunder rocked the house, and I was off the bed and out the door.

I stormed into his room, the smell of him immediately surrounding me, the familiar mix of body wash and Ghost himself.

He was already waiting, leaning back against the pillows, shirtless, looking so damn smug it made me want to punch him.

"Don't you dare smirk."

Ghost put his hands up, all innocent. "I would never."

I narrowed my eyes, but I was too rattled to argue.

Without another word, I climbed into his bed, sitting up against the pillows. "Don't cross to my side," I warned.

Ghost tilted his head, watching me with a lazy, amused grin. "Wouldn't dream of it, sweetheart."

I was about to relax, thinking he might actually behave.

But then he shot me a wink, his voice dropping to that deep, lethal drawl that turned my brain to white noise. "I'm a gentleman." He let that hang for a second. Then, with a smirk that should be illegal, he added, "Until you beg me to fuck you. Then I'm an entirely different kind of monster."

Heat flooded my body so fast my throat went dry. My panties? Done for.

Chapter 77

I clamped my lips shut and slid down in the bed, refusing to give him a reaction.

I could feel the weight of his smirk, the way his body tensed like he was barely restraining himself from pushing the game further.

He arched a brow, his eyes immediately dropping to my legs, his tongue sliding across his lips. "Sweetheart, if you wanted me to keep my hands to myself, you shouldn't have worn that in here."

I followed his gaze, only to realize... Shit. In my haste to escape the terrifying fucking thunderstorm, I'd completely forgotten to put the sweatpants I borrowed back on. I was sitting there in nothing but a thin tank top and a pair of lace panties.

That smug smile spread across his face.

I yanked the blankets up, covering myself.

He laughed, his gaze still locked on me, and I could tell he was enjoying every second of my misery. "You were in such a hurry to get to my bed, you forgot your pants."

I shot him a glare. "You wish."

Ghost's grin turned wicked. "Or did you come in here like that to get me hard?"

I felt a rush of heat flood my face and other places. I tried to swallow it down. "I came in here because I hate thunderstorms."

"Right. So it has nothing to do with the fact that you're all but naked in my bed right now?"

I rolled my eyes, pretending like my body wasn't currently betraying me by wanting him. "If you don't stop talking like that—"

Ghost cut me off. "You'll take your shirt off and show me that lace bra, too? Please do, sweetheart."

I narrowed my eyes at him. "How do you know my bra is lace?"

Ghost shrugged, looking entirely too satisfied with himself. "I'm just assumin', Tits. Figured it matched your panties."

The way the word 'panties' rolled off his tongue like filthy silk had no business being that hot. Everything sounded hot and obscene coming out of his beautiful mouth.

I lifted my chin, fighting my own grin. "It does match."

Ghost's eyes darkened. His fingers twitched against the sheets, like he was physically restraining himself from grabbing me to find out for himself.

Then, just to fuck with him, I added, "Black lace. See-through."

Ghost's entire body tensed, his jaw going tight, his muscles visibly flexing beneath the blanket. And then he groaned. A deep, guttural, involuntary sound that shot straight between my legs.

And just like that, the tables had turned. I felt a hint of satisfaction. He wasn't the only one who could tease.

His hands clenched the sheets, his jaw tightening. "You are such a fuckin' problem for me, Tits."

I bit my lip, trying to suppress my smirk. "Am I?"

His blue eyes held mine in place. "Yeah." His voice dropped lower, thick with heat. "Because now, all I can think about is making sure those pretty lace panties don't match for long."

I took a sharp breath. Oh. Fuck. He did not.

It took me a second to regain my wits, and I pushed back. "I said it matched. I didn't say I had it on."

Ghost went still. His eyes shifted to something dangerous, something carnal.

He exhaled a slow, rough breath. "You're really playin' with fire, sweetheart." His voice was low, raw, like the restraint was physically killing him.

I pretended he wasn't torching me right now. His southern drawl was so sexy when it kicked in. I lifted a shoulder, feigning innocence. "Am I?"

Ghost's leaned toward me. "You better pray I never find out if you're lyin'," he said, his voice dropping to a lethal whisper.

I swallowed hard, my stomach flipping, because fuck.

The thought of him finding out made my thighs press together under the covers.

He noticed. His smirk turned wicked, his eyes burning with heat. "You're breathin' too fast, Tits." He tilted his head, his voice smooth as silk. "You gettin' worked up?"

I scowled. "No."

He chuckled. "You just can't stop lyin', can you?"

Then, just to make it worse, just to ruin me, he leaned in close, his breath whispering against my jaw. "When I finally take those panties off you, sweetheart, I'm gonna make sure you regret every single time you teased me."

I barely bit back the whimper clawing at my throat.

Ghost grinned. Like he fucking won.

My entire body felt like it was on fire, and Ghost wasn't even touching me. He didn't have to. The way his voice dipped, the way his eyes dragged over me like he was already peeling off my clothes. It was enough to set every nerve ending ablaze.

I forced myself to act like his mere presence didn't set me on fire. "You're all talk, Ghost."

He smirked, and I knew he could see right through my bullshit. "Yeah?" His hand swept down his hard chest, drawing my attention. "Then why are your thighs pressed together, sweetheart?"

He knew what he was doing to me, and he was so damn smug about it.

I flipped onto my side, facing away from him, but the second I did, I felt the bed shift.

I tensed as his voice brushed against my ear. "What's wrong, Tits? You afraid to look at me?"

I clenched my jaw, refusing to answer.

"Tell me somethin'," he whispered. "That little kiss you left me with last night... was that an invitation?"

I swallowed hard. Then, I told him how it was. "It was an invitation. Last night. You fucked that up."

Ghost chuckled.

He let the silence stretch, letting me feel the weight of his presence behind me, the heat of his body warming the space between us. Then, he sighed like I was the one frustrating him. "You know, you shouldn't tease me like that if you're not ready for what comes next."

I rolled back over, narrowing my eyes at him. "You mean the part where I leave you wrecked and turned on for once?" I lifted a brow. "How'd that feel, by the way?"

He grinned, shaking his head. "Cute, sweetheart. Real cute."

I smirked. "Is that a hint of frustration in your voice?"

His eyes darkened. "You think this is frustrating?"

Before I could react, before I could even blink, Ghost moved. He rolled, shifting fast, pinning me on my back, one of his forearms bracing against the mattress beside my head, his body so damn close it stole the breath straight from my lungs.

"This," he whispered, his lips just inches from mine, his breath warm on my lips, teasing. "This is frustrating."

I swallowed hard, my pulse hammering.

He dragged his fingers down the edge of the blanket, toying with the fabric. "You really wanna play this game, sweetheart?"

I hated it. I was two seconds away from losing it completely, from grabbing him and pulling him down on top of me. But I only hated it because he always won. I felt like I had no control in this... whatever this was between us.

His lips brushed my jaw. "Careful, Tits. You're not the only one who knows how to tease."

I let out a shaky breath, my entire body on fire, but I refused to break. Not tonight. Not when he was already so wrecked for me.

So instead, I lifted my chin, staring him down. "Then I guess we'll see who cracks first."

Ghost exhaled a rough, frustrated laugh, then pushed off me as he rolled back onto his side of the bed.

And just like that, we were back where we started. The tension was thick enough to suffocate. A battle of who would give in first.

I pulled the blanket up to my chin, swallowing back the heat clawing its way through me. But Ghost just had his hands behind his head, all casual and relaxed, grinning like a fucking menace.

This was going to be a long night.

That was the last thought that went through my head before my eyes closed.

Chapter 78

S leep barely had a chance to settle over me.

    One minute, I was staring at the ceiling, my body still burning from Ghost's last taunt.

The next I was waking up tangled in him.

I blinked my eyes open, my brain struggling to register what had happened. I was on his side of the bed, wrapped around him. My thigh was draped over his, my cheek against his chest, his heat sinking into me like a drug.

His arm was around me, holding me there.

My heart slammed against my ribs as I tried to process it, trying to remember when I had crossed the damn line.

A deep chuckle rumbled through his chest. "Look who couldn't stay on her side."

I froze. He was awake, watching me. "You—" My voice came out rough, breathless, busted as hell.

Ghost's voice was pure satisfaction. "Not even thirty minutes, sweetheart. I'm flattered."

Heat flooded my body, my face burning with embarrassment, with irritation, with need.

I tried to pull away, to reclaim whatever dignity I had left, but Ghost wouldn't let me. The second I moved, his grip tightened, keeping me right where I was. "Ghost—"

"Shhh," he whispered, his voice low, sexy. His hand slid up my spine, teasing, until his fingers tangled in my hair, tilting my face up just slightly until our eyes met. "Now that you're here... might as well stop fighting it."

I swallowed hard, my pulse out of control, my body vibrating beneath his touch. "I wasn't fighting anything."

Ghost arched a brow. "No? Then why is your heart racing, sweetheart?"

His hand was splayed across my back, his fingers brushing the exposed skin beneath my shirt.

Ghost exhaled slowly, his fingers drifting from my hair, tracing my jaw, my lips.

His smirk faded, his eyes turning serious, hungry. His fingers trailed lower, barely brushing the neckline of my shirt. "Tell me to stop, Halston. I promise I will."

He dragged his thumb across my bottom lip. My lips parted, a shaky breath escaping. "I don't want you to."

A grin spread across his lips. "That's what I thought."

He kissed me slow and deep. His hand slid down my spine, his palm settling on the small of my back, pulling me fully against him.

Ghost's lips moved over mine, his tongue slipping past my lips, his body rolling, shifting on top of mine.

"Kasper," I whispered, needy, breathless.

He growled against my mouth, his grip possessive. His hips rolled, grinding into me, sending shockwaves of pleasure through my body.

I gasped, arching into him, my body begging for more.

He gently bit my bottom lip, smirking. "How bad do you want it, sweetheart?"

"Shut up and take your pants off."

Ghost laughed, low and sinful.

He hovered over me, his breath hot against my lips.

I reached down, grabbed the hem of my shirt, and pulled it over my head, tossing it aside.

His gaze raked over me, his eyes burning with something primal. His voice was rough, strained when he finally spoke. "You look so fucking good under me, sweetheart."

I took hold of his face, planting a soft kiss on his lips.

His hands slid down my thighs, his fingers hooking under the waistband of my panties.

I shivered as he dragged them down my legs, his touch featherlight and torturous.

His fingers brushed between my thighs, and he stilled. His eyes snapped back up to mine, and his smirk turned downright wicked. "You're already soaked."

I swallowed hard, my face burning.

His thumb traced a slow, teasing circle against me, sending fire shooting through my core. I gasped.

Ghost chuckled, his voice brimming with satisfaction. "Goddamn, Halston. You're fucking drenched for me."

I glared, my body burning with need, with frustration, with pure fucking want. "You teased me all fucking day, Ghost. What did you expect?"

His smirk widened, his fingers dipping lower, dragging against my wet center, teasing me, making me writhe beneath him. "I like when you admit that I make you fucking wet."

I whimpered, desperation clawing through me. "Kasper—"

"I wanna hear you beg for it, sweetheart," he whispered, his lips brushing against my jaw, my neck, his voice pure destruction to my sensibility.

I let out a frustrated growl, my hips rolling into him.

He laughed, low and dark. Then he sat up, gripping the waistband of his boxer briefs, and quickly discarded them.

I inhaled deeply, my eyes dropping between us, my anticipation fucking killing me.

His voice was wicked, cocky as hell. "Like what you see?"

My throat was too dry to answer. Because, fuck yes, I did. Every inch of him was hard, thick, and ready. And I was aching for it. For him. For everything we were about to do.

Ghost leaned in, brushing his lips over mine, his voice a whisper against my mouth. "Be a good girl and spread your legs for me."

Ghost's words sent a violent shudder down my spine, my entire body lighting up like a live wire. I didn't hesitate. I spread my legs, and his smirk deepened, his hands gripping my thighs.

"Fuck," he breathed, his voice dropping to something almost animalistic. "You're so ready for me, aren't you?"

I nodded, writhing, my nails digging into his arms. "Yes. Kasper, please..."

Ghost gripped himself, teasing me, sliding his cock against me, getting it wet and ready.

I moaned, my head pressing back, my body desperate, aching, on the verge of losing control.

"I love hearing those pretty sounds, Halston."

He let his tip just barely slip inside, which sent me into a moan, anticipating, wanting, needing.

His breath was hot and ragged against my neck as he thrust deep, burying himself inside me. "Holy fuck," he groaned, his hands gripping my hips, holding me still as if he didn't want to move at all.

Then he froze.

Ghost froze inside me, his jaw clenching, his body tight as a damn wire about to snap. "Fuck," he said, with a ragged breath, his grip on my thighs tightening.

I looked up at him, barely processing the shift in his expression before he let out a rough laugh, frustrated, teetering on the edge of control.

"See what you do to me, Tits?" His voice was thick with heat. "You make me so fucking desperate for you, I forgot the goddamn condom."

My stomach clenched hard, a fresh wave of heat rolling through me, my breath catching at the way he said it, like it was my fault, like I had ruined him. God, I loved hearing that.

Ghost shook his head, his blue eyes darkening, fucking feral as he slid his fingers up my thigh, his hand cupping my ass, pressing me even closer to him. "I don't forget shit, Halston. Ever." His lips brushed my jaw, sending a shudder straight through me. "But you? You make me lose my fucking mind."

I swallowed hard, my pulse racing, every nerve in my body on fire for him. Then I whispered, "I'm on birth control."

Ghost stilled, his grip tightening, his breath choppy against my skin. "You gonna let me cum inside you?" His voice was rough, practically a growl, his control shredding more by the second.

A shockwave of heat rolled through me, my stomach clenching hard at his words. "Yeah," I breathed, my pulse pounding.

Ghost let out a low, wrecked groan, his body trembling. "Fuck, Halston," he said, his voice a soft, sinful whisper, his mouth skimming my jaw. His fingers spread my thighs wider, pushing deeper. "You're gonna let me fill this pretty pussy up? Just take every fucking drop?"

A shaky moan ripped from my throat, my whole body arching against him, melting for him. "Yes," I gasped. "I want it. I want you."

Ghost groaned, his head dropping to my shoulder as he stilled, buried deep inside me, his breathing ragged. "Jesus Christ, baby. You feel so fucking good."

I whimpered, already pulsing around him, already spiraling, coming undone.

"Move," I begged, my fingers gripping his biceps. "Kasper, please—"

He let out a rough chuckle. It was dark, hungry, filled with pure, raw satisfaction. "You want me to fuck you, sweetheart?"

I nodded frantically, gasping when he pulled out halfway, only to slam back inside me, stretching me, owning me, taking me apart piece by piece.

"Like that?" he taunted, his rhythm slow, teasing, torturous, his thick cock dragging against every nerve, every sensitive spot.

"Yes!" I cried out, my fingers tangling in his hair. "More," I whispered, shameless, breathless, desperate.

Ghost growled, his hands gripping my hips tight, holding me in place as he picked up his pace, fucking me deep, relentless.

Each thrust sent shockwaves of pleasure crashing through me, my body burning, my mind whiting out with pure, uncontrollable bliss.

"You take me so fucking well," Ghost panted, watching me, his blue eyes wild. "Like you were made for me."

I was close. So fucking close.

He reached between us, his fingers finding my clit, circling it, stroking it, pushing me over the fucking edge.

I shattered, screaming his name, my nails biting into his shoulders, my body shaking as waves of pleasure slammed into me, one after another.

Ghost didn't slow down. He fucked me straight through my orgasm, full speed, dragging the pleasure out, heightening it. He buried himself again and again, groaning my name as he let go inside me, his body trembling, his lips crushing against mine as he gave me everything he had left to give.

He slowed to a stop, his breath ragged, choppy.

Ghost was the first to move. He pulled back just enough to look at me, his eyes softening, his fingers brushing my hair out of my face. "You good?"

I let out a breathless laugh, still trying to regain my senses. "Yeah. Really good."

His lips curled into a satisfied smirk. "You're welcome."

I rolled my eyes. "You're such an ass."

He chuckled, pressing a kiss to my lips before rolling off me, pulling me into his chest. "Go to sleep, sweetheart," he said against my hair. "You're gonna need the rest."

My stomach tightened, my entire body still humming. Because I knew exactly what that meant.

Ghost was far from done with me. And I was perfectly okay with that.

Chapter 79

The buzz of Ghost's phone cut through the quiet of the bedroom.

I stirred, watching as he sat up, grabbing his phone off the nightstand. "Yeah?" His voice was rough, sleep-heavy. "Shit. Alright. I'll be there."

He let out a sigh, rubbing a hand through his beard before throwing the covers off and swinging his legs over the side of the bed.

I pushed up on my elbows. "What's wrong?"

Ghost stood, already pulling his jeans back on, his muscles shifting under the dim glow of the hallway lighting.

"Just something I need to check on outside," he said, grabbing his boots. "Nothing to worry about."

"At this hour? In the middle of a storm?"

He shot me a small, amused smirk. "It's a ranch, sweetheart. It doesn't run on a nine-to-five schedule."

I sat all the way up now, my fingers twisting in the sheets, uneasy. "Be careful, okay?"

His smirk faded just slightly, his gaze softening. "Always."

He grabbed a black t-shirt, pulled it on, then leaned down, brushing a quick, warm kiss against my forehead

I tried to go back to sleep. I really did.

But the rain pounded against the windows, and my mind wouldn't stop spinning, worrying, picturing all kinds of ridiculous scenarios in which Ghost somehow ended up stranded or hurt.

I wished I didn't care so much. I wanted to be able to tell him how I felt, but I knew I couldn't.

After what felt like forever, the front door creaked open, and I immediately sat up, straining to listen. A door shut. Heavy footsteps sounded through the house.

Then Ghost appeared. Rain dripped from his clothes, his black T-shirt clinging to every inch of hard muscle, his hair damp, messy, his eyes locking onto me immediately. "Did you wait up?"

"I wanted to make sure you made it in safely."

Ghost smiled, peeling off his wet shirt, his abs flexing. "Be careful, Tits. I might start to think you're catching feelings for me."

I snorted, forcing out a laugh. "You wish."

He just chuckled, shaking his head as he kicked off his boots. "I'm hitting the shower."

I nodded. My gaze stayed locked on him as he disappeared into the bathroom.

The second the door shut, my mind spiraled. Ghost. Naked. Wet. Standing under the spray of hot water.

I was losing my goddamn mind.

I threw off the covers before I could talk myself out of it, and then I headed across the floor to the bathroom.

I pushed the door open.

Ghost was standing under the spray, his head tilted down, his hands braced against the wall, the muscles of his back flexing as water poured over him.

I swallowed hard, my stomach tightening.

He must have heard me, because without turning around, he said, "Couldn't sleep?"

I stepped inside, letting the door click shut behind me. "Something like that."

Ghost finally turned, his eyes raking over me, his expression darkening with hunger. "Fuck," he groaned. "Look at you."

I stepped closer, completely bare, completely his, my fingers trailing up his wet chest, feeling the warmth of his skin beneath the water.

His hands gripped my waist, pulling me close. I gasped at the feel of his already hard cock pressing into my stomach.

"Round two, baby?" he asked, his lips ghosting along my jawline.

I tilted my head, letting him trail kisses down my neck, my pulse thundering. "Yes, please."

Ghost growled, lifting me against the shower wall, kissing me hard, his hands wandering, taking, owning.

The moment Ghost pinned me against the shower wall, I knew I was done for.

His hands roamed my body, wet and slick from the steaming water, his grip firm, his mouth devouring mine.

His fingers dug into my thighs, spreading them wider, his hard cock pressing against my core.

I whimpered against his lips, rocking against him, needing more.

"So fucking desperate for me, huh?" he whispered, his teeth grazing my bottom lip, tugging, his voice pure sex. "Can't get enough, can you?"

My hips shifted against his in torturous friction. "Never."

A low, dark chuckle rumbled through his chest like he was pleased with my answer.

My body clenched in anticipation.

His hand slipped between us, his fingers sliding right over my wetness, teasing, his blue eyes burning into mine with pure primal satisfaction. "Jesus, baby," he groaned.

I bit my lip. "You feel how soaked I am?" I whispered, stealing his line, rolling my hips into his hand. "That's all for you."

Ghost's jaw tightened, a sharp groan slipping from his lips.

Then, in one swift movement, he slid deep inside me, pressing me into the tiles.

I cried out, my fingers gripping his shoulders, digging into the hard muscle there.

"Fuck, Halston," he growled.

I clenched around him, rocking my hips just right, feeling every inch of him.

"You're so fucking hard, Kasper," I panted, licking the water from my lips, watching the way his eyes darkened at my words. "You feel so good inside me. You always do."

Ghost let out a deep, guttural curse, gripping my hips tighter, his thrusts turning brutal, relentless. "Say that shit again."

I grinned through the pleasure, barely able to get the words out between moans. "I love the way you feel inside me, so hard."

His fingers dug into my ass, his thrusts turning punishing, his teeth gritting like he was barely holding on. "Fuck, baby," he groaned, slamming into me harder, making my entire body tremble against the tiles.

I moaned shamelessly, rolling my hips to meet every thrust, my legs wrapped tight around his waist.

I was gone. Completely fucking gone.

"You like watching me lose my mind over this tight little pussy, don't you?" he growled, his lips trailing down my neck, my shoulder, biting and sucking his mark into my skin.

"Yes," I gasped, clenching around him, feeling my release building, ready to explode. "God yes, Kasper. Don't stop."

"Not until you cum, baby," he groaned, thrusting harder, faster, chasing it with me. His breathing was rough, uneven, his body tensing beneath my hands.

I shattered.

A sharp cry tore from my throat, my entire body convulsing around him, waves of pleasure slamming into me.

Ghost found his release, his groan vibrating against my skin, his hips rolling into mine again and again. He buried himself deep, pulsing inside me until he was spent.

I grinned, tracing my fingers down his still-heaving chest.

Ghost let out a deep, satisfied chuckle, pressing a slow, lingering kiss to my lips. "We're never gonna sleep if you keep looking at me like that, Tits."

Chapter 80

The text came out of nowhere.

Yacht party. Tonight at 9.

I didn't need to guess who it was from. The high roller, the man in the suit who had been circling Ghost like a vulture, testing him, pushing him.

I wasn't stupid. This wasn't a simple invitation for drinks and small talk.

But if he thought I was going to let him toy with Ghost without a fight? He had another thing coming.

The yacht loomed in front of me, massive, lit up against the dark water like a floating kingdom. Laughter and clinking glasses echoed from the upper deck, the air thick with money, power, and something darker lurking beneath the surface.

I stepped onto the gangway, my heels clicking against the polished wood, and the second I reached the top, there he was.

The high roller stood at the entrance, a crystal tumbler of whiskey in hand, his smirk planted on his lips like a devil's invitation. "Ah," he mused, swirling his drink. "You actually came. And don't you clean up nicely?"

I narrowed my eyes as his sleazy gaze roamed over me in the body-hugging black dress. "Only to tell you to leave Ghost the hell alone."

He chuckled. "It's not about leaving him alone. It's about testing him. Pushing him past his limits."

I clenched my teeth. "You think you own him now?"

"Everything has a price," he said smoothly, stepping closer, lowering his voice. "Even men like Ghost. I just needed to know if he was worth it."

I held my glare steady. "Ghost isn't for sale."

His smirk widened. "No? Then why is he on my yacht right now?"

I turned so fast my head spun.

Ghost was at the entrance, his sharp eyes scanning the crowd, his expression controlled.

My stomach twisted.

He hadn't told me about a fight tonight. Not a word. Not a message. And that wasn't like him.

I went to every single one of his fights. That was our unspoken thing. No matter how bad the day, how rough things got, I was there. He always made sure I knew when he had a fight. But this... this felt different.

This wasn't his usual underground scene. This wasn't for pride or release or even for money.

This was for him.

The man in the suit. The puppet master, with the whiskey and the smirk.

These fights weren't about survival. They were about ownership. About pushing Ghost, controlling him, branding him.

And the worst part?

Ghost walked into it. Willingly.

My heart thudded against my ribs. What the hell was going on in his head?

The announcer's voice boomed over the speakers. "Ladies and gentlemen, we have a special surprise tonight!"

The crowd erupted in cheers.

"In this corner, our undefeated champion... Ghost!"

The roar of the crowd was deafening.

"And in the other corner..."

My stomach plummeted as a fucking beast of a man stepped onto the fight platform in the center of the deck. He was huge, built like a tank, his body scarred from too many battles.

"Meet KING. The man who's never been knocked out!"

The high roller turned to me, humor flooding his eyes. "I had to make it interesting."

I had to stop myself from lunging at him. "You set him up."

He tilted his glass toward me. "Of course. That's what I do."

Ghost stepped onto the platform, rolling his shoulders, shaking out his hands.

King cracked his knuckles, grinning like a predator.

The announcer dropped his arm. "FIGHT!"

The yacht exploded with noise as the two men circled each other.

King swung first, hard, brutal. But Ghost ducked, slipping under the punch like smoke, countering with a sharp hook to the ribs. The impact echoed, and for a second, King didn't move.

He laughed. "You're fast. But I like a challenge."

Ghost smirked. "Let's see how you like getting your ass kicked."

King lunged, trying to grab him, but Ghost was faster. He spun out, landed a brutal kick to the knee, then another sharp elbow to the side of King's head.

The crowd went wild.

King staggered but didn't drop.

Ghost circled around, but the second his gaze landed on me, something shifted. A flicker of confusion, a question in his eyes.

King swung, and Ghost pulled back, but his fist clipped him before he was clear.

I could see he'd rung Ghost's bell, and it was my fault. Seeing me there caught him off guard. I wasn't supposed to know about this fight tonight, obviously, because he hadn't invited me. The damn high roller planned this to rattle Ghost, to test him.

Ghost hit him with a jab, then ducked a right cross.

He was tough. But Ghost was relentless.

With a swift fake, Ghost feigned left, making King lower his guard, then, Ghost spun, launching a savage spinning back kick straight to his face.

The impact was sickening. King hit the deck hard, his body crumpling like a sack of bricks.

Ghost won. Again.

And the high roller was grinning.

Ghost didn't wait for the announcement. He stepped off the platform, his fists bloodied, his breath ragged.

The high roller clapped, his smirk widening. "Now that..." He exhaled, shaking his head. "That was a fight."

Ghost didn't react. Didn't move.

"You ready to fight for me exclusively? No outside fights? I think we could benefit from each other."

Silence stretched between them.

Ghost's gaze slid to me.

I was still standing there, my heart hammering, my nails digging into my palms.

Ghost turned back to the high roller. "That so?" His voice was calm. Controlled.

"I think we could do some damage together," the high roller said.

"What the fuck is she doing here?" Ghost asked, his voice low but lethal. "You invite her?"

The high roller gave a lazy shrug, sipping his whiskey. "I thought it'd be good for her to see what you're made of."

Ghost's jaw ticked. "Pull this shit again, and you'll be sorry."

The high roller smirked without a care. "I'll get in touch with your media manager. We'll get something on the books to promote your next fight."

Then he turned to me. "I told you everything has a price."

I glared, my stomach twisting with fury. "And I told you to leave him alone."

He just laughed, disappearing into the crowd.

Ghost grabbed my wrist, pulling me away, into the lower deck of the yacht.

And the second the door clicked shut behind us, he was on me.

His hands gripped my waist, his body pressing me hard against the cabin wall, his breathing still ragged from the fight.

I gasped, my pulse skyrocketing, my mind struggling to catch up.

"You shouldn't be here," he growled, his voice low, dark, dripping with raw need.

I couldn't focus on his anger. Not when his hands were everywhere, his body so close I could feel the heat radiating off him, his muscles still tense, vibrating from the fight.

"I came to—"

"To what?" he cut me off, his lips hovering dangerously close to mine, his blue eyes burning into me. "To save me? To tell that motherfucker to leave me alone?"

"Yeah, actually," I shot back, breathless, my hands against his chest, feeling the rapid pounding of his heart beneath my palms.

He let out a sharp laugh. "You're insane," he said. "You drive me fucking insane."

His hands tightened on my hips, pressing me harder against the wall. I could barely think, barely breathe. The electricity between us was unbearable, like a live wire, sparking, growing hotter by the second.

"I can't fucking stand it," he bit out, his voice hoarse, like he was fighting himself.

"Stand what?" I whispered, my own resolve crumbling.

Ghost's hands trailed up my thighs, gripping my ass, yanking me against him.

I let out a sharp gasp. I felt how hard he was, his entire body tense with restraint. "Wanting you," he said, his voice nothing but gravel. "Wanting to rip this fucking dress off you and claim you, own you."

My stomach plummeted straight into a fiery pit of need. His lips brushed my jaw, his breath hot, sending a shiver down my spine.

"Fuck," he groaned. "You have no idea what you do to me."

I turned my head slightly, my lips barely grazing his.

And that was all it took. Ghost snapped.

His mouth took possession of mine, his hands grabbing my thighs, lifting me as he set me on the nearest surface. A desk, a dresser—I didn't even know. I didn't care. All I could focus on was him. His hands ripping at the hem of my dress, pushing it up my thighs, his mouth devouring mine, his tongue sliding deep, owning me in a way that sent every nerve in my body into overdrive.

"You don't think I see it?" he bit out between kisses, his voice dripping with frustration.

"See what?" I gasped, my body on fire.

"You want this as bad as I do. Every time." His hand slipped between us, shoving my panties aside. The heat of his fingers teased me before pushing inside.

My head dropped back, a sharp cry slipping from my lips.

"Fuck," he groaned, watching me, his gaze dark, intense. "So fucking lost in you, Halston."

I moaned, rocking against his hand, begging silently for more, but Ghost wasn't having it.

He withdrew his fingers and removed my panties. Pulling me into him, he buried himself inside me.

I cried out, my body going electric at the sudden feel of him, the way he consumed me.

Ghost fucked me like he was losing his goddamn mind. It was hard, fast, desperate. Like he had been starving for this. "Is this how you like it?" he gritted out, his teeth clenching, his pace brutal.

I could barely think, my body melting, unraveling, breaking apart.

"Tell me," he growled, pulling me against him with every thrust, forcing me to take every inch.

"Yes," I gasped, my voice raw, wrecked, needy. "Yes, Ghost. Fuck yes."

He let out a dark, satisfied groan, his mouth taking possession of mine, swallowing my moans as he drove me closer to the edge.

He tore his mouth from mine. "You're mine, Halston. Say it," he growled low.

I was panting, coming apart at the seams. "I'm yours," I gasped.

"Fucking right you are," he said, driving into me again and again.

And when I shattered, my entire body trembling in his arms, he didn't stop. Didn't slow. He fucked me through it, his own release following mine, his breath ragged, his groans low as he buried himself deep again and again, finally slowing to a stop.

We stayed there, our bodies still joined, our breathing heavy, the only sound in the room, the slow, satisfied hum of the yacht rocking beneath us.

Then Ghost pulled back. "Goddamn, Halston. I think you fucking wrecked me."

I gave a small laugh, and he softly kissed my lips.

Nothing else was said. Nothing needed to be said.

Because whatever this was, it wasn't just sex anymore. It was desperation bordering on addiction.

Chapter 81

M usic floated from the stage set up near the center of the festival. It was bluesy and raw, the kind that made you sway without thinking about it.

Ghost and I sat across from each other at a wooden picnic table, a plastic tray piled high with crawfish between us. A bucket of ice sat in the center of the table, stuffed with cold beer bottles.

He had on a backward ball cap, and I couldn't stop looking at him. It didn't matter if he was in jeans, sweats, a cowboy hat, or a ball cap. The man was sinfully gorgeous.

"You got some on your face," I said, pointing at a spot to the side of his lip.

"Yeah?" he asked, grinning. "You gonna wipe it for me or just stare?"

I tossed a napkin at him. "Do it yourself, caveman."

He laughed, wiping his mouth, then grabbed another crawfish and cracked it like a pro.

He brought the shell to his lips and sucked the head like it was second nature.

I scrunched my nose. "How can you do that?"

"That's how you get all the flavor, sweetheart." He smirked, licking his lips.

"Still..." I said, shaking my head and taking another pull on my beer.

He leaned in, his voice rough. "You know from experience that I can suck the flavor out of anything. Especially when it's dripping and begging for attention."

I choked on my beer.

He just grinned and reached for another crawfish, completely smug. "Still grossed out?" he asked, glancing at me sideways.

My body was on fire. "Keep that up and I'm coming across the table for you."

"Across the table. On my fingers. In my mouth. On my cock. It's all good with me, sweetheart."

That picture undid me.

He winked.

I stood and rounded the table. Throwing my leg over him, I straddled his thighs right there on the bench with no mind to the tons of people around us. "What did I say?"

He laughed. "Don't threaten me with a good time, baby."

I smiled, then kissed him, my tongue sliding in to rub against his, the fire of crawfish spices hitting my tongue as he wrapped his arms around me, pressing me to him.

I pulled back to look at him. He was watching me with those beautiful, baby blue eyes, a devilish grin on his face. "People are staring."

I shrugged. "Let em."

He laughed. "You wouldn't have said that a few months ago."

I smiled, tugging gently on his beard. "Yeah, well... a few months ago, I wasn't completely obsessed with the way you kiss. How hot your body is against mine, how good your cock feels between my legs."

His grin deepened, cocky and dangerous. "Sweetheart, you keep saying shit like that and I'm gonna skip the truck and take you right here on this picnic table."

I leaned in, my lips brushing his ear. "Will you pin me down and make me scream just the way you like me to?"

He laughed low and dark, his arm tightening around my waist. "You keep tempting me like that, and I'm gonna forget where we are and make the whole damn festival hear what kind of sounds I can pull out of you."

Heat shot through me, my breath catching in my throat.

"Yeah?" I asked, my tone a challenge.

"You'll be begging, sweetheart. Begging me not to stop while the band plays on."

I bit my bottom lip, my pulse kicking up like a drumline in my chest. "I'm begging you now, Kasper."

He leaned in, brushing his mouth against my jaw. "Careful what you're asking for, Halston. I'm not shy."

Without warning, he grabbed me by the hips and lifted me from his lap, setting me on the tabletop in front of him.

He called my bluff and spread my legs wider, standing between my thighs.

I immediately caved and climbed around him, jumping back down off the table, making him laugh as I made my way back to my side of the table.

"You're not quite ready for exhibition displays, sweetheart."

I smiled at him across the table. "I guess not."

He gave a soft chuckle. "Proud of you, though."

"Yeah?"

He nodded, his eyes sparkling with mischief. "Yeah. A few months ago, you would've blushed, stammered, and damn near passed out if I even suggested half the shit you just said."

I laughed. He wasn't wrong.

Ghost leaned in a little, dropping his voice just low enough to make my breath catch. "Now you're whispering filthy things in my ear like you want me to ruin you in public. Makes a man feel real fuckin' lucky." Then he winked. "Keep talkin' like that, Halston, and I might just start carrying a blanket everywhere we go. Just in case."

I laughed, but a shiver ran up my spine, because it brought me back to Christmas and what he did to me on the couch, under that blanket.

And that was exactly what he wanted me to think of.

I watched him for a second, and before I could stop myself, I asked, "Would you ever consider quitting fighting?"

He froze, just for a second. Long enough for me to know he wasn't expecting that question. "Just... working the ranch full-time?"

I nodded.

"You tired of coming to my fights?"

"No, I'm tired of watching you come out of them bruised and bleeding."

Ghost was quiet, his fingers drumming lightly against his beer bottle. His gaze drifted out across the festival, but I could tell his thoughts were with me.

He leaned back in his seat a little as his eyes scanned the festival.

The live band played something slow and southern behind us, but the only sound I was really focused on was the silence stretching between us.

"I don't know if I'm ready to quit fighting," he said finally, his voice lower, more serious than before. "I think I've still got a lot of fights left in me."

I said nothing. Mostly because I didn't trust my voice not to betray the disappointment that settled in my chest.

He must've felt it though, because he looked at me, that smirk lifting the edges of his mouth. "How would I blow off steam if I quit?"

"That's what you have me for."

His grin widened. "You offering up your body to me in exchange for retiring?"

"Not in exchange," I said. "It's already yours. Whenever you want it."

His head tilted, and his eyes dragged over me in a way that lit every nerve I had on fire. "You're making me hard again over here, sweetheart."

I smiled, sipping my beer casually, like he wasn't melting me in public. "I was just asking if you might want to give your body a rest from getting pummeled."

"I do most of the pummeling."

"Fine," I said, rolling my eyes. "How about giving your fists a rest?"

He lifted a brow. "For the rest of the day?"

I sighed. "You know what I'm saying."

He chuckled low and leaned in just a little. "I do. How about I promise to be good today, and we can talk future fights another time?"

I looked at him for a second, then smiled. "Good enough."

Chapter 82

We had just enough beer in our systems to be loose and comfortable. The sun was starting to dip behind the trees. The music shifted to something faster.

"Do you ever think about... settling down and having kids someday?" The question just sort of slipped out. I hadn't planned to ask it. I didn't even know where it came from.

Ghost didn't answer right away. His whole body went still. His jaw flexed for a second.

Something in him pulled back, just slightly.

"I mean," I started, backpedaling, "you don't have to answer. I was just curious. You don't strike me as the minivan and juice box type."

He let out a low breath, then finally looked at me. "Not sure that's in the cards for me," he said, his voice quieter.

I nodded. "I guess I should have known that already by how you were at Christmas. You're so good with your family, but don't like sappy stuff like love."

He gave a small shrug, his eyes focused somewhere beyond the festival crowd. "Some things you don't talk about unless you're ready. That goes for marriage and children."

I didn't push. I wanted to, because something about the way he said it, the tightness in his voice, made me think there was a story there.

But I left it alone.

Instead, I nudged his knee under the table. "Well... I think you'd be a great dad. Terrifying, but great."

He glanced at me then, something soft flickering behind the blue in his eyes.

Then, just like that, he pulled back, his signature smirk sliding into place. "What happened to not picturing white picket fences?" he asked.

I gave a short laugh, shaking my head. "I'm not picturing anything. I was making conversation."

"Asking about children isn't conversation, sweetheart. That's biological-clock shit. You listening to that ticking already?"

"Wow, did you really just bring up my biological clock? I'm twenty-four, Ghost."

His grin widened, his pretty white teeth flashing. "I call it like I see it."

I sighed, turning away and grabbing my beer. "I'm sorry I asked you anything personal."

He laughed, low and completely unbothered. "Don't get all shy on me now, Tits. You started it."

I rolled my eyes, but a smile threatened to break out on my face.

The air between us shifted again. Lighter this time. Playful.

Exactly how Ghost liked it. Exactly how he needed it to be... when things got too close to something real.

We were still smiling at each other when a shadow passed over our table. Then another.

I looked up and saw three guys, mid-twenties, built like they spent too much time at the gym, their shirts tight, their faces already red from too much sun and beer.

And they were staring straight at Ghost.

"Hey," the guy in the middle said, rocking on his heels, cocky smirk already in place. "You're Ghost, right?"

Ghost didn't even glance their way. Just took a pull on his beer.

The guy leaned in a little. "Didn't think you'd be the type to come out to festivals. Thought you were too busy beating the shit outta people."

Still nothing from Ghost.

I watched him across the table, trying to warn him off. "Please," I said. "Don't let them get to you."

That's when he finally looked up at the guy. Then at me.

And without a word, he leaned across the table and kissed me, deep, like he hadn't just been challenged. Like I was the only thing that mattered.

When he pulled back, he looked at the guys and said, "I'm just trying to enjoy my day out."

The guy scoffed. "Whipped already? Damn. Didn't think Aureus had it in him."

Ghost just raised an eyebrow, not biting. "Sorry, man. I promised her I'd behave today."

"Pussy," one of the others muttered.

Ghost laughed. He actually laughed. "That the best you got?"

I could tell he wasn't mad. Not yet. But the guys weren't backing down.

"Figures. Big bad fighter can't even throw hands when his girl's watching."

I stiffened, watching, waiting. Eventually, they were going to push him too far.

He stood slowly, setting his beer down. "We're leaving."

I'd just made it to his side of the table when the guy muttered something else, something about him being all bark now that he had a leash on.

And that's when I saw the shift. The quiet edge of Ghost slipping away.

I squeezed his hand. "Don't."

He looked at me, and for a second, I thought maybe he'd listen.

Then a shout broke out behind us.

I turned just in time to see one of the guys swing.

Ghost moved fast. He blocked the hit, grabbed the guy's arm, twisted it, and threw him to the ground. But the other two jumped in, trying to pin him.

It turned into chaos, with bodies flying, people yelling, beer cups toppling. One guy had Ghost's arm. The other got in a hit.

That's when I snapped. Three to one was bullshit.

I climbed onto the table and leapt onto the nearest guy's back. My arms went around his neck into a headlock, just like Ghost had shown me. My legs wrapped around his waist. "Let. Him. Go!"

He stumbled, trying to shake me off, but I clung to him, applying pressure to his throat to give Ghost a chance to take out the other two.

The third guy let go of Ghost to come after me.

Big mistake.

Ghost surged forward, slamming his fist into the guy's jaw and he dropped.

The guy holding me yanked me off his friend, grabbing my arm hard as I stumbled back.

Ghost was there. He pulled the guy away from me, landing a punch to his gut and a quick jab to the jaw, sending him sprawling into the dirt.

The third guy had already taken off running.

When it was finally over, Ghost turned to me, breathing hard. "You okay?"

I nodded, even though my adrenaline was still peaking. "Yeah."

His hands ran over my arms, checking for bruises. His eyes scanned every inch. Only when he was sure I was good did he finally breathe.

"Are you fucking insane?" he asked, his eyes blazing with something wild.

"Excuse me?"

"Jumpin' on that guy's back like a damn koala on Red Bull. You tryin' to get yourself killed, Tits?"

"You looked like you needed rescuing."

Ghost leaned in, kissed me hard, then whispered against my lips, "Next time, sweetheart... just bring the truck. I'll do the fighting."

"It was an unfair fight," I said, my arms crossing defensively over my chest.

An incredulous laugh slipped out. "And you thought jumping on some guy's back like a goddamn leech was gonna even things out?"

I shrugged. "I just wanted to distract him so you could break loose. And you did."

Ghost shook his head, a muscle ticking in his jaw. He took a step closer, towering over me, that restless energy rolling off him in waves.

"Do you hear yourself right now?" he asked, his voice tight. "Just because you've had a few self-defense lessons with me doesn't mean you jump on the biggest bastard and run with it."

Before I could answer, he reached out and gripped my face gently but firmly, tilting my chin up so our eyes locked. "It was stupid, Halston." The disappointment, the fear, the anger–it was all right there in his voice and his eyes. "Don't ever do something so reckless again. You understand me?"

I nodded, the best I could, with his fingers still cradling my jaw.

"It's not that I don't think you're capable," he continued, softer now, but still deadly serious, "but that guy probably weighed three times what you do. You're strong, yeah. You're smart. But physics doesn't give a fuck about that."

I nodded again, smaller this time, feeling the heat of him, the steady press of his thumb against my cheek.

His voice dropped to almost a whisper. "I can't watch you get hurt, sweetheart. Not because of me."

I closed my eyes, breathing him in, feeling the ragged pulse of emotion between us.

When he finally let me go, stepping back half a step, his jaw was still tight. "Next time?" he said, his voice rough. "Let me protect you. That's my job. You hear me?"

I nodded, this time stronger, my heart pounding.

Because under all the anger, under all the roughness, Ghost wasn't just claiming responsibility. He was claiming me.

And God help me, I wanted to be his to protect.

Chapter 83

The fight was being held at an abandoned warehouse on the outskirts of town, just past the old train tracks.

The kind of place that had been forgotten, with rusted metal beams, broken windows, and graffiti-covered walls.

It was bigger than the last venue, with a makeshift cage set up in the center, surrounded by rows of mismatched chairs and crates, where people crowded in close, hungry for blood, for violence, for the thrill of the underground.

The lighting was dim, mostly from industrial floodlights and flickering neon signs, casting eerie shadows that made the place feel even more lawless. The floors were concrete, stained and scuffed from years of use as a factory. But now it was the latest illegal fight club in the city.

It was louder here, the echoes of shouts and jeers bouncing off the high, cavernous ceilings.

And tonight, Ghost was in his element.

The energy of the underground fights was always electric with crowds pressed tight, shouting, fists pumping as Ghost squared off in the ring.

I was watching with Drew, Josh, and Niki, our drinks in hand, the bass of the music vibrating under our feet.

The fight was intense. Ghost's opponent was strong and fast, but he wasn't Ghost. Every movement Ghost made was controlled, calculated, and brutal. His fists connected with precision, his body moving like it was built for this, and maybe it was. I knew how good he was, knew he hadn't lost, but I still felt my pulse spike every time he took a hit.

Then, chaos erupted in the crowd.

It started with two guys shouting and shoving. The energy of the crowd turned from thrilled to aggressive in seconds, and suddenly, people were swinging. Bodies collided, shouts turned to curses, and before I could register it, the crowd surged violently, sending a domino effect rippling through the space.

I got caught in the crush. Someone backed into me hard, knocking the air from my lungs. I staggered, trying to regain my footing, but then caught a hard elbow right in my face.

My head snapped back, pain exploding along my mouth and chin, with the metallic taste of blood on my tongue. My knees buckled, and I hit the ground, my hands bracing against the hard concrete.

Ghost's voice rang out loud, sharp, full of fury, echoing off the cavernous ceilings. "Hey!"

The entire room froze like the air had been sucked out of it.

Ghost wasn't in the ring anymore. He was here in the crowd, pushing through. His fight wasn't over, but he'd left it.

I blinked rapidly, my vision swimming as I felt Drew and Josh helping me to my feet, but my attention locked onto the absolute rage in Ghost's eyes as he shoved his way through the stunned crowd.

He didn't mask it. Didn't play it cool. Ghost was livid.

The guy who had thrown the elbow was already backing up, his hands raised in surrender, but Ghost was on him in seconds. He didn't throw a punch. He grabbed the guy by the collar and yanked him forward until their faces were just inches apart, danger coiled tight in his voice. "You just hit my woman."

My woman. The words slammed into my chest with as much force as that elbow had.

The guy stammered something about it being an accident, about the fight getting out of control, but Ghost wasn't interested in excuses.

His grip tightened.

"Ghost!" My voice was loud, firm. "It was an accident."

My words made it through, thankfully. Ghost shoved him back hard enough to send him stumbling, then turned, his eyes zeroing in on me.

He was in front of me in two strides, his hands already on me, my face, my chin, tilting it up to survey the damage. And just like that, his fury was gone. Replaced with concern. Real, raw, unfiltered concern.

"Jesus, Halston," he whispered, his thumb grazing the cut on my swollen lip.

I winced.

His entire body tensed. His jaw clenched. "He got you good. You're bleeding."

I swallowed, trying to ignore the fact that his hands were still on me, gripping me like he didn't trust me to stay upright. "It's just a split lip," I said, my voice hoarse.

His hands dropped to my shoulders, my arms, like he needed to check for more damage, like he needed proof that I was really okay.

"I'm fine, Ghost," I reassured him. The guy had definitely rung my bell, and my mouth was throbbing, but I didn't say it. I didn't want him to worry more.

His nostrils flared. He didn't like that answer.

He exhaled sharply, pressing his forehead against mine for the briefest second, his grip still locked onto me. I had never seen him like this. It wasn't like the festival where he was pissed at me for interfering. Ghost was clearly rattled. Ghost never showed weakness. But tonight? He didn't care who saw. Not our friends. Not the entire goddamn crowd that was still watching, whispering.

Because right now, I was the only thing that mattered, and that tore at my heart.

Ghost laughed, but it wasn't his usual cocky, self-assured laugh. It was something deeper, rougher, something edged with reluctance. His hand was still gripping my chin like he wasn't ready to let go.

His blue eyes held mine, searching, lingering. "You're okay?"

"I'm fine," I assured him. "But you have a fight to finish."

He exhaled sharply, his grip tightening for just a second before he finally let me go, shaking his head like he couldn't believe I was sending him back into that cage. "You're bossy as hell, you know that?"

I smirked, ignoring the way my stomach flipped at the fact that he was still standing so damn close. "People paid to see you beat the shit out of someone tonight."

His lips curled, but there was something in his eyes, raw and unguarded, before he covered it up with his usual smirk. "Yeah, yeah."

He took a step back, rolling his shoulders, his focus shifting. Game face back on. "Stay put. And don't go picking any more fights while I'm busy handling mine."

"I can't promise anything," I shot back as I watched him turn with a chuckle.

As Ghost disappeared back toward the cage, I turned—and immediately met the wide-eyed stares of Drew, Josh, and Niki.

Drew's mouth was literally open.

Josh blinked as if he were trying to reboot his brain.

Niki just stared at me, her beer halfway to her lips, completely forgotten.

None of them said a word. Not at first.

Then Drew leaned in, his voice low, like he was afraid to break whatever fragile alternate reality we'd just stepped into. "Did he just call you his woman?"

I lifted a shoulder in the most casual shrug I could manage, even though my lip was throbbing and my insides were still rattling like a shaken soda can. "Guess so."

Josh blinked again. "So... all that fighting? The yelling? The 'shut up, Ghost' and 'you're disgusting, Ghost' and 'I would never touch you if you were the last man on earth, Ghost'—that was just... what? Foreplay?"

I sipped my drink, then winced. "Apparently."

Niki smirked. "You really had them fooled," she said, nodding toward the guys. "I saw the way you were looking at him during that promo event. All those girls hanging on him? You were two seconds from launching one into a display table."

I opened my mouth to argue, then closed it again.

Because... she wasn't wrong.

Niki just grinned wider and took a long drink from her cup like she'd been waiting for this moment all along.

The second he stepped back into the cage, the entire crowd went insane, the energy shifting. Ghost was back, and he was pissed.

His opponent barely had time to register what was happening before Ghost was on him, unleashing hell.

And as I stood there, watching him fight, one thing was crystal clear.

Ghost had shown his hand tonight. And there was no taking it back.

Chapter 84

Ghost's knuckles were bruised, his body tense, his jaw tight as he drove.

The night air was thick with silence, the weight of everything that had happened still pressing down on us.

I was staring out the window. He hadn't said much since the fight, but I could feel his edgy mood.

Then, we turned onto a familiar road. "Uh... Ghost?" I glanced at him. "This isn't the way to my house."

His fingers flexed on the wheel, but his voice was steady, unyielding. "No, it's the way to mine."

I stared at him. "I see that. Why are we at your house?"

Ghost exhaled sharply, like the question annoyed him. "Because you're sleeping here tonight." He pulled into the driveway and punched in the code.

I let out a breath of laughter, trying to read his expression. "I am?"

He slid into his usual space, throwing the truck into park before cutting me a sidelong glance. "Yeah. I need to keep an eye on you, make sure you don't have a concussion or some shit."

I gave a small laugh. "I don't have a concussion."

He ignored me, already getting out of the truck.

I rolled my eyes, but deep down, a warmth settled in my chest. This wasn't about a concussion. This was about him seeing me on the ground tonight, hurt, vulnerable, something he clearly couldn't handle.

I got out of the truck, and the second my door shut, Ghost was there, his large, calloused hand gripping mine. I nearly tripped over my own feet. Ghost never held hands. Gripping my wrist was the closest he ever came.

He didn't even look at me as he led me toward the house, his grip firm, like I might try to slip away.

As we stepped inside, the house was dark and quiet, the soft hum of the fridge the only sound as he pulled me toward his bedroom.

Ghost turned. He yanked my sweater up over my head.

His scent wrapped around me like a vise. My breath caught. "Whoa—"

"Relax." His voice was lower now, with that husky drawl. "Not tryin' to fuck you, Tits. Just gettin' you comfortable."

I swallowed, my pulse flickering wildly. "I wasn't complaining. You just caught me off guard." I never complained when he touched me. The heat I felt around him was always electric, consuming.

He gave a chuckle as he undid my jeans, pushing them down my legs, his fingers brushing against my skin just enough to make me ache.

I stepped out of them, left in nothing but my underwear and a T-shirt.

Ghost barely looked at me. Instead, he pulled the blankets back and guided me into the bed with a hand at my waist, his touch oddly gentle.

He reached for the hem of his own shirt, pulling it over his head in one swift motion.

My mouth went dry, and my pulse kicked up a notch.

He was already shoving his jeans down, leaving him in just his black boxer briefs, his broad, powerful frame a wall of muscle, tattoos and scars.

I was still watching him when he climbed into bed, shifting back against the pillows before tugging me into his arms, pulling me against him, pressing me into his very warm and hard chest.

He wasn't trying to fuck me. He was just... holding me. And something about that wrecked me.

His warmth surrounded me, his heartbeat steady beneath my cheek.

He let out a slow breath, his voice rough, strained. "You scared the shit out of me tonight, Halston."

I pressed my face into his chest, my throat tightening. "I could tell." It was the only time since meeting him that he let his guard down, showing his hand in public, without making it a joke.

For a long moment, he just held me. Saying nothing. Just breathing. Then his voice came out low, raw. "Sometimes I feel like I'm drowning, and you're the only thing saving me."

I froze, my breath catching in my throat. Because Ghost never said things like that. He never admitted needing anyone. But right now, he was saying it to me. Ghost had said a lot of things to me before. He'd said filthy things, cocky things, things that made me blush and burn and want him in ways I'd never wanted anyone.

But this was different. This was raw, unguarded Ghost. A glimpse of something deeper beneath the hard, untouchable exterior.

I didn't know what to say. So, for a moment, I just stayed still, absorbing the weight of his words, the quiet confession that felt heavier than anything he'd ever spoken aloud. His arms were tight around me, his grip firm, unrelenting, like he was afraid I'd slip away if he let go. It all meant more to me than I could express.

"Ghost..." My voice came out strangled, my chest tightening. I cleared my throat.

He exhaled, his breath warm against my shoulder. "Forget I said anything."

I pulled up. "No."

His fingers stilled. "No?"

I tilted my chin up, meeting his gaze. "No. I'm not forgetting it. I heard you."

His jaw tensed. "Don't make it a thing, Halston."

"It is a thing." I exhaled. "And you don't have to pretend it's not. And you don't get to take it back. I won't let you."

For a long moment, we just stared at each other.

His eyes held mine, and for once, they weren't teasing or wicked or full of some dirty joke he was about to whisper in my ear.

They were just... open. Exposed.

I reached up, running my fingers along his jaw, feeling the thickness of his beard, the tension coiled beneath his skin.

Then his grip on me shifted, one large hand sliding up to tangle in my hair, the other pressing flat against my lower back, pulling me even closer.

His lips hovered near mine, his voice rough, like gravel. "You wanna save me, Tits?" He smirked faintly, but there was no humor in his eyes.

I swallowed hard, my eyes locked on his beautiful blue eyes. "Yes."

Ghost exhaled, his thumb brushing absently against my hip, my ribs, the side of my breast.

Then, his lips ghosted along my jaw, my cheek, before landing on my mouth.

The kiss was slow. Deep. Consuming.

Chapter 85

I kissed him back, pressing my lips softly against his, slowly devouring him, ignoring the pain in my cut lip.

I wanted to drown in him.

I gave a soft nibble on his lip, pulling back slightly, my eyes locked onto his.

Ghost groaned, his fingers tightening on my hips, his jaw clenching like he was holding himself back. "Your kiss drives me fucking mad."

I smiled. "Good. Because yours makes me crazy wet," I whispered against his lips.

He growled low. "Fuck, Halston."

The air was thick with warmth from the way he was looking at me, from the undeniable pull that had always been there but had never felt quite like this before.

Ghost shifted, rolling me onto my back. He hovered above me, his breath slow and controlled, but his eyes... God, his eyes. They were burning into me, searching, needing, wanting.

Reaching between us, he helped me off with my shirt. Then I slid his boxer briefs off his hips and down his legs.

Ghost returned the favor by hooking his fingers into the waistband of my panties and pulling them down my thighs. Once they were off, he made his way back up my legs, his hands sliding up, his mouth kissing, licking, causing me to moan loudly with consuming need.

He dragged my hands above my head, our fingers locked together, his grip firm, grounding me in place as he nudged my thighs open with his knee.

I opened them wide for him, my breath hitching, my chest heaving already.

He pushed his cock in, slowly sinking into me.

I moaned, my head tilting back, my body melting into his.

The sensation was all-consuming.

Ghost let out a deep groan, his breath mingling with mine, our bodies moving in perfect sync.

His hips rolled slowly, and I raised mine to meet his.

I arched beneath him, his name slipping past my lips as he captured my mouth in a slow, toe-curling kiss, one that sent a pulse of heat through every inch of me.

I had never felt this connected to anyone before.

He could feel it too. I could tell in the way he held me, in the way he threaded his fingers tighter with mine, in the way he whispered against my lips.

I moaned into his mouth, my legs tightening around him, my body responding in ways I couldn't control.

He groaned, his lips moving down my throat, his hands gripping mine tightly. I never wanted him to let go. Because this was different. This was Ghost giving me something he didn't give to anyone else. I could feel it in every way tonight.

Our breaths tangled. Our bodies moved in a rhythm that didn't rush, didn't chase—just felt. Every slow thrust, every whisper of skin against skin, made it clearer.

This wasn't about fucking.

It was about something else. Something neither of us had the courage to name out loud.

His hands stayed locked in mine, his body heavy and warm on top of me, grounding me, wrecking me in the most tender way possible. I felt everything—every inch of him, every beat of his heart, every unspoken truth passed through his touch.

"Halston..." he whispered, his voice hoarse, like he had something more to say but couldn't quite get it out.

So instead, he kissed me again. Slow. Deep. Reverent.

And in that kiss, I heard it. Felt it.

I came with his name on my lips, my body arching into his, my heart somehow splitting wide open and healing at the same time.

He followed right after, groaning deep into my mouth as he buried himself inside me, spilling everything he'd been holding back.

For a moment, the world stilled.

Then, with his face buried in the crook of my neck, his weight draped over me like a promise, he exhaled.

Not the cocky kind. Not the arrogant kind. A quiet one.

We stayed like that, tangled and spent, the only sounds between us our breaths and the fading echo of something that felt suspiciously like more.

Chapter 86

I spent the night at Ghost's house.

The next day, we stayed in bed, talking, laughing, wrapped in warm sheets.

It was odd and amazing at the same time. It was like we had somehow stepped into an alternate reality where Ghost let me stay. Where he let himself be soft with me.

Eventually, we got up.

I sat at the counter, watching as he moved around the kitchen, effortlessly putting together eggs, bacon, and toast.

"I love that you cook." I said, stealing a piece of bacon off his plate.

Ghost shot me a look. "I realized women find it sexy."

I snorted. "Right. So you're just doing this to seduce me?"

He smirked. "Is it working?"

"The bacon helps."

He chuckled, setting a plate in front of me before grabbing his coffee and sitting down beside me.

When we were done eating, I sighed, setting my cup down. "I should probably find Lulu."

We let her out to run off some energy early this morning.

Ghost nodded, finishing the last of his food before standing to clear the plates. "I'll find Lulu. You can stay inside."

Something warm settled in my chest. "Thank you. That's very sweet of you."

He paused, arching a brow at me. "Don't spread that shit around. I have a reputation to protect."

I laughed, and before I could say anything else, he leaned in and gave me a quick kiss on the lips.

Ghost went outside, and I stood near the window, watching him, watching the way he bent down to see if Lulu was under the shed, calling her. She ran out and twined around his legs. He picked her up and carried her back toward the house.

This man. This gruff, impossible man. He was so much more than he let people see.

When he came back inside and set the cat down, I kissed him. My hands gripped his shirt, my lips lingering on his for way longer than necessary.

He didn't pull away. If anything, he kissed me deeper.

We spent the rest of the morning being lazy, cuddled up on the couch, my head resting against his chest, his arm draped casually around me.

The dogs and Lulu were curled up in their beds.

I let out a contented sigh, closing my eyes, soaking in the quiet comfort of it all.

Then Ghost's phone rang.

He groaned, grabbing it from the coffee table, answering without even looking. "Why are you calling me? Did you get the tractor stuck again?"

I smirked, my eyes still closed, expecting Henry's usual gruff response.

But instead, I felt Ghost go completely still beneath me. His entire body went rigid, his muscles tightening like steel, the warmth that had been there just seconds ago vanishing into thin air.

I sat up, my stomach twisting immediately. Something was wrong. Really wrong.

Ghost slowly lowered his phone, staring at it for a moment like he was processing something. He hung up.

"Ghost." My voice was soft, cautious, but urgent. "What is it?"

He didn't respond immediately.

Then finally, his blue eyes flitted up to mine, unreadable, but hard. "My ex, Alesandra, is at the gate."

My stomach dropped. I didn't know the story, but I knew she was the cause of Ghost's jealous and untrusting behavior.

Suddenly, the warmth of the morning, of the fire, of his arms around me felt a million miles away.

His ex was back. And he had to be feeling some kind of way about it, but he wasn't saying anything.

Ghost stood abruptly, his body tense, his movements tight and controlled as he walked toward his room.

I followed silently, not saying anything, not pushing him, because I knew that if he wanted to talk, he would.

I knew we were both thinking a million things.

Inside his room, Ghost moved with purpose, grabbing a pair of jeans and pulling them on, his expression unreadable, closed-off. "I have to go outside and talk to her."

I nodded, watching him closely. "Okay."

He zipped his jeans, grabbed a plain white T-shirt, pulling it over his muscular frame, the fabric stretching slightly over his shoulders before settling into place. He grabbed his black boots and sat on the edge of the bed to put them on.

I just watched him. Saying nothing. Not because I didn't want to. But because I didn't know what to say. I knew nothing about the situation outside. I didn't know why Alesandra was here. Did she want something from him? Was she here to try to get back with him?

All I knew was that dread was spiraling deep in my stomach, spreading like a slow, creeping fire. Ghost was already guarded enough. He was just barely letting down his guard with me. If she was back to do it again? If she wrecked all this progress he'd made, I didn't know if he'd ever let anyone close to him again. Not even me.

He was gone for less than ten minutes. But in that time, my entire world started to unravel.

When he came back inside, his expression was unreadable, his jaw tight, his hands flexing at his sides. "She wants to have dinner to talk."

My stomach twisted violently. I swallowed, trying to keep my voice steady. "What did you say?"

Ghost exhaled, his blue eyes meeting mine. "I said yes."

I felt it then. That gut-wrenching feeling. Like I had just been punched in the stomach, like the air had been stolen from my lungs, like the ground beneath me had suddenly turned to quicksand.

Chapter 87

He was pacing.

Slow, methodical strides back and forth across the living room, his jaw tight, his shoulders locked. I didn't say anything. I just watched him, the tension in his body coiled tight. Whatever Alesandra being here had stirred up, it wasn't small. It was big. Bigger than I'd realized.

I needed to bring him back down. To do something.

So I quietly turned and walked down the hall, into his bedroom, flicking on the light in the bathroom. I started the water, adjusting the temperature until it was just right, then added a bit of soap, letting the tub fill. I folded a towel and set it on the edge of the tub, then stood there for a second, breathing in the steam.

Then I went back for him.

He didn't notice me at first—still caught in that loop, still pacing—but when I stepped in front of him and gently reached for his hand, his eyes snapped to mine.

I didn't speak. I just tugged.

And somehow, he followed.

Inside the bathroom, the room was warm and filled with the scent of eucalyptus from the soap. The bath was nearly full. I turned off the tap and looked up at him.

Ghost stood there, still tense, still wired.

"Let me help you relax," I whispered.

I stepped closer and reached for the hem of his shirt, sliding it up slowly, over those rigid abs, over his chest, and then off over his head. His arms dropped back to his sides as if he'd let go of the weight for just a moment.

I kissed his chest, right over his heart, then unbuttoned his jeans. He didn't move. Didn't help. Didn't resist.

I tugged them down, then hooked my fingers into his boxer briefs and slid those down, too.

He stood naked in front of me, exposed in every way—not just physically, but emotionally, too. And still, he said nothing.

I stood and pressed a kiss to his sternum, letting my hands trail slowly down his arms. "Get in," I whispered, guiding him gently.

Ghost stepped into the water like he was moving through molasses—slow, unsure. But once he sank into the warmth, I saw his shoulders finally fall. His eyes closed. His chest rose and fell just a little easier.

I stripped down and stepped in behind him, nestling him between my legs and pulling him back against me. I reached for the washcloth and dipped it into the water, then ran it gently across his skin—his shoulders, his arms, his back.

He didn't speak. But he didn't need to.

Because right now, I was speaking with my hands. With my presence. Holding him together when he was coming apart inside.

"I just want to help you breathe," I whispered, running the cloth slowly over his back. "That's all."

He didn't say anything, but he let me. His shoulders relaxed just a little as I washed him. I pressed kisses to his spine. Ran the cloth over his arms and down his chest.

When I was done, I set the cloth aside and began massaging his shoulders, my fingers pressing into the knots there, the silent pressure inside him breaking my heart. He was holding so much—like always—but tonight it felt heavier.

And after a long silence, when his breath finally evened out, his voice broke through the steam like a ghost of itself. "We were married."

His voice was flat, careful, like each word had been chosen from behind a wall he didn't want anyone to scale.

My breath caught. I stayed still, my hands resting lightly on his shoulders. Not pushing, not asking. Just listening.

"We'd been trying to get pregnant. For almost two years."

His voice dropped slightly, the water lapping gently around us as he leaned back into me, just a little.

"She insisted I get my sperm count tested. Took months to get the appointment. Weeks more to get the results."

I could feel the pain bleeding through the careful calm in his tone. I slid my arms around him from behind, pressing a kiss to the back of his neck, grounding him. Letting him go on.

"Before I even got the results back... she got pregnant. I was over the moon. I was gonna be a father." He gave a rough, hollow laugh. "Doctor called and told me to come in. Sat me down and explained I'd probably never be able to father children. Said it was from a high school football injury. Blunt testicular trauma."

My stomach twisted.

Ghost went still. So still, it was like he'd frozen.

"I told him he was wrong. I laughed at him. Told him my wife was already pregnant."

He exhaled sharply, bitterly.

"But when I told her what the doctor said... I saw it. The guilt. Right there on her face."

I swallowed hard.

"She said she got frustrated. Got drunk. Slept with someone else. That he was the father."

The silence stretched, deafening and raw. I pressed my cheek against his back again, holding him tighter. Tears pricked my eyes.

"She wanted me to raise the kid with her. Said the guy wanted nothing to do with it. Said she was sorry. That it was a mistake. That she loved me."

He shook his head.

"I threw her out. She backed her car into the front gate and took out my sign. Said it was an accident, but I knew better. She was pissed because I wouldn't forgive her."

He let out a long, steady breath, like every word was a wound being reopened. "She let me believe it. She let me look like a fool."

His body tensed in the water.

"I've never hated anyone more than I hated her at that moment."

I wrapped my arms around him fully now, holding on like maybe I could take some of the weight from him.

"For a fleeting moment," he whispered, his voice cracking just slightly, "I had a wife and a child. For one brief moment, I had everything. But everything I thought I had was never really mine. Not the baby. Not even her."

I kissed his shoulder. His jaw. His temple.

Then I whispered against his skin, "I'm here. And I'm not going anywhere."

He didn't answer.

But he leaned back against me. And this time, he let himself breathe.

Chapter 88

The drive to Ghost's house was the longest I'd ever taken.

I knew where I was going, but my hands trembled on the wheel. I didn't know what was coming, but my heart was already preparing for the worst.

He called me this morning and told me he needed to talk. And I had hoped, prayed, that maybe it wasn't what I thought it was. Maybe he realized something last night. Maybe after everything, he had changed his mind and cancelled his dinner plans with her.

But deep down, a tiny voice whispered something else.

I gripped the steering wheel tighter, my stomach in knots.

This was Alesandra, the woman who had shattered him. The woman who had torn out his heart and left him bleeding. And yet, he had agreed so easily to have dinner with her.

I parked outside his house, staring at the familiar outline of the place that had begun to feel like home.

I let out a slow breath as I walked up to the house.

Ghost was waiting inside, standing near the fireplace. His blue eyes swung to mine, guarded, serious.

My heart clenched. Not the way it did when he smirked at me, when his voice dropped to that low, teasing tone that always made my knees weak. This time, it clenched with the fear that I was about to lose him.

And he hadn't even spoken yet.

"Hey," I said softly, my voice carefully neutral.

"Hey," he responded, just as quietly.

I swallowed hard. "So. What happened?"

Ghost exhaled, dragging a hand through his hair. "We talked."

The words sat heavy between us.

"She apologized for everything." His voice was steady, like he had rehearsed this already, or he'd been thinking about it a lot. "Told me she regretted what she did. She knows she hurt me. And she asked if we could be friends again. That maybe, eventually, we could... build on that."

I couldn't breathe. Because this was my worst fear never even realized.

I had finally broken through his walls, finally gotten close enough to touch the parts of him he refused to show. And now it felt like he was slipping away again.

"Right," I said, forcing a nod, pretending my chest wasn't ripping in half. "And what did you say?"

Ghost's eyes darkened with something I couldn't place. "I told her I needed some time to think. Some space to figure stuff out."

Space.

My stomach dropped, and my breath caught, my pulse pounding so loudly I couldn't hear anything else. This was it. This was where I lost him. He wouldn't have told her that if he weren't thinking about it. He would have turned her down right there.

"Halston," he said, stepping toward me, his voice soft, almost hesitant, like he knew what he was about to say was unfair. "I just need some time."

I nodded, swallowing the burn in my throat. "Time from me?" I managed to choke out.

"From everyone. I need some time to myself to figure some things out."

"How much time?" I asked, my voice steady, though my insides were shaking.

Ghost exhaled, shaking his head. "I don't know yet."

I don't know yet. The words carved through me like a knife. He was considering letting in the woman who'd broken him. Which meant I wasn't enough.

I knew this would happen. I knew he was never going to let me in all the way. I knew it. And still... it felt like I was dying.

I forced a smile, pretending it didn't matter, pretending this conversation wasn't ripping my heart out with every word he spoke. "Understand what you're asking me," I said quietly, not able to stop my voice from quivering. "You want me to take a step back, so you can contemplate some sort of a relationship with a woman who cheated on you and got pregnant with someone else's baby. A woman you kicked out of your life."

Ghost clenched his jaw, but I didn't stop.

Damn it all if tears didn't start falling. I couldn't stop them. My attempt to be strong was weakening quickly.

"You want me to wait around while you figure out if she still has a place in your life?" I let out a humorless laugh. "Do I mean so little to you? Do I mean anything to you?"

Ghost's gaze flickered, something flashing across his expression. "I need time to figure that out," he admitted, stepping toward me.

I froze. I fucking froze. Because that sentence right there shattered everything. All the nights we had spent together. All the kisses, the teasing, the moments when I thought I had him. All the times he held me close, like I was the only thing anchoring him.

It was all just... uncertain to him. Something to figure out.

I blinked rapidly, but I couldn't stop the tears. They just kept coming. My heart felt like it was cracked down the center, leaving an empty, gaping hole.

I turned away, swallowing hard, forcing the pain down, locking it up. He didn't deserve to see it. He didn't deserve to know how badly he just broke me.

"The fact that you need time to figure out if I mean anything to you," I whispered, my throat tight, "tells me I already have my answer."

"Halston, that's not fair."

I looked back at him, my chest tight, my voice low, angry now. "You're damn right, Ghost. It's not fair."

I barely made it to the door before I heard his footsteps behind me. "Halston, wait."

He reached for my arm, but I pulled away, my chest tight, my throat burning.

He grabbed my face in his hands, and even though I wanted to pull away again, I didn't. "I'm all fucked up in the head. I need to sort it all out," he said, wiping my tears away with his thumbs.

Silent tears continued to fall, but I didn't cry outright. I held it back. I wanted to scream and cry and tell him he was an asshole for breaking my heart like this.

"Tell me something, Ghost. If she wasn't back, would you need to be taking this break from me right now?"

Ghost's jaw flexed, his thumbs still resting gently on my damp cheeks. His eyes searched mine like he was looking for a version of me that wouldn't hate him for what he was about to say.

And then, quietly, honestly, he nodded. "Yeah. Yes."

Before I could pull away, he continued, his voice low, rough around the edges. "It's not just her, Halston. It's not just about her being back." He paused, swallowing hard. "The last few days... the crawfish festival, the fights, seeing you hurt. It threw me for a loop." He was still holding my face. "You got under my skin, sweetheart. But now?" He shook his head. "Now it's something else. And I don't know what the hell to do with that."

My breath caught in my throat, and I tried to swallow it down.

"I haven't let anyone matter in a long time," he said. "I've never wanted someone to matter. Not like this."

I stared up at him, trying to keep it together, but my throat was so tight with a full-out cry trying to break free. My chest ached with every breath.

"So yeah," he finished, quieter now. "Even if she hadn't come back... I still would've needed a minute. Not to decide between you and her. But to deal with the fact that I'm fucking terrified of what you're starting to mean to me."

His voice cracked on that last line, and all that cocky bravado was gone. No smirks. No teasing. Just Ghost—raw, unsure, and standing on the edge of something real.

And all I could do was stand there... trying to figure out if the ache in my chest was from hope or heartbreak. Because what he was confessing had me turned inside out.

"Fine." The word tasted like acid on my tongue, but I said it nicely because even though I felt like he was asking me the impossible right now, he wasn't being an ass about it. And even though it felt like I was breaking inside, he had every right to feel the way he did.

I pulled my keys from my pocket, my hands shaking.

Ghost exhaled sharply, running a hand through his hair, looking frustrated, but not as wrecked as I felt. "Please understand, Halston. I do feel something for you. I just don't know exactly what that is."

The words hit harder than I expected. Then, I let out a slow breath, forcing myself to smile, even though it felt nothing like one. "You got your space, Ghost." I grabbed my bag, gripping the strap tight enough to turn my knuckles white. "I'm just not sure how I'll feel by the time you make your choice."

His jaw clenched, his blue eyes storming with something he refused to say out loud. "Halston."

I didn't stay to hear any more. I walked out, stepping into the cool air, feeling the ache in my chest expand with every step I took.

I walked away. Because I refused to let him see me fall apart any more than I already had. Because if I didn't, I was going to break in front of him, and maybe even beg him not to leave me.

I would give him his space. But I wasn't lying when I told him I wasn't sure how I'd feel by the time he made his decision.

Chapter 89

It hit hard around three in the afternoon on day five.

The grief, the hurt, the betrayal.

All of it slammed into me while I sat on the couch with my laptop open, trying to work on a new logo for a tattoo shop. That was my latest client. I had work to do, but instead, I was staring at the screen, unable to think, let alone work.

This was how I spent my week. Every day, I tried to work, tried to push through the pain, but I ended up breaking down. Today, it just hit me the hardest.

My fingers hovered over the keys as hot, stupid tears blurred my vision. My chest was tight, my throat raw.

I didn't even realize I was crying until a tear dropped onto the back of my hand.

And once it started, I couldn't stop it.

I dropped my head into my hands, sobbing into my palms like a girl who'd been sucker-punched by someone she trusted. Because I had.

I'd let him in. I'd opened myself up to a man who was emotionally unavailable and reckless with my heart.

I had ignored every warning sign, every sarcastic deflection, every time he pulled away when things got too deep, every time he let me get close and then slammed the door in my face.

But God, when he let his guard down, when he looked at me like I was the only person on earth who ever saw him clearly, those were the moments that wrecked me. Those were the ones I clung to like they meant something.

Because they did.

To me, they meant everything.

I'd memorized every detail of him. The way he ran a hand down his face when he was frustrated. The way he flexed his jaw when he was about to say something he didn't want to. That rough, vulgar mouth of his that somehow still knew how to make me feel cherished. The stupidly hot smirk he gave me when he was trying not to laugh. The quiet moments when his voice dropped, and he'd say my name like it meant something to him.

I loved him.

And he wasn't sure if I mattered to him.

That realization cut so deep I had to close my laptop and shove it off my lap before I shattered it.

I wiped my face with the sleeve of my hoodie and curled up on the couch like a pathetic disaster.

I hated feeling this way. I hated being this girl. The one who let someone wreck her. The one who waited.

No. No, I wasn't going to be that girl.

I stood, pacing the living room, letting the pain twist inside of me until something else started to build. Something hotter. Stronger. Louder.

Anger.

It rolled through me like a storm. Because I didn't deserve this. I didn't deserve to be benched while he decided if I was worthy of his love, like some option on a list. I wasn't second place to some ghost from his past.

I had stood by him, watched him fight, watched him bleed. And I was there when he needed someone. I let him see parts of me I'd never shared with anyone and didn't hold back, not once.

So why the hell was I the one sitting here in pieces? If he didn't know what he wanted, that was his problem. But I did. I wanted more. And I deserved more.

I took a shaky breath, wiped the remaining tears from my face, and opened my laptop.

The screen glowed with the half-finished design for the tattoo shop logo with jagged lines, ink splatters, a bold gothic font I hadn't quite settled on yet. It was moody. Dark. A little aggressive. Just like the man who'd inspired it.

I clenched my jaw and clicked into the project.

I was going to push the hurt down and push on. Because Ghost might have needed space to figure out what I meant to him, but I wasn't going to cry about it anymore.

I adjusted angles. Sharpened edges. Tweaked colors. I didn't stop to feel or spiral or hope. I poured every ounce of emotion into the design, letting it bleed through every stroke and shadow.

This was my armor now.

And no one was going to break me.

Chapter 90

When Niki texted me earlier, telling me we were going out to blow off steam, I didn't question it. Didn't overthink.

I should have.

Because the second I stepped into the bar, I saw Ghost. I realized that this wasn't just a bar. It was a fight venue.

Shit. I should have asked questions, but I didn't.

My pulse kicked up, a sharp breath catching in my throat. Fuck.

But I just stood there, aching. Because there he was. The man I loved. And I couldn't have him.

Before I could spiral any further, Ghost turned, his blue eyes locking onto mine across the room.

I inhaled a sharp breath, my chest tight. It had been seven days. Seven agonizing, silent days since he told me he needed space. And I'd given it to him. Now that I'd gotten distance from the situation, now that I wasn't so emotional, I wasn't about to beg for someone who was deciding if I was worth it.

But now I was here. And he looked pissed.

I could see it in the way his jaw clenched, his hands flexing at his sides. The way his eyes darkened the second he spotted me.

Niki leaned in, oblivious to the fucking war brewing inside of me. "Glad you finally got off your ass and came out with us. We were starting to think you were gonna die alone."

I ignored her, watching Ghost like he was a loaded gun.

He turned away, barely sparing me another glance. Instead, he tipped his chin to Josh and Drew, who were already drinking at the bar, rejoining their conversation.

So that was it? He wasn't going to say anything? Just act like I wasn't here? Fine.

I turned to Niki, pasting on a smile. "Buy me a drink, bestie."

She grinned. "Now we're talking."

We made our way to the bar, sliding onto stools as the bartender approached. The music pulsed through the venue, the air thick with anticipation.

"Ghost's fight is happening soon," Niki said.

"I came because I thought we were hanging out at a bar. I didn't realize it was one of his fights."

"So, he won't care."

"He asked for space, Niki. Now, I look like a desperate bitch who can't stay away from him."

"I'll tell him I invited you."

"Please don't," I said, letting out a loud, frustrated breath. "Just get us some alcohol."

She laughed. "You got it."

Niki ordered for us.

I could see Ghost staring at me from across the bar again. He still looked pissed. What the fuck ever. Let him stay on his side of the venue and I'd stay on mine. He did look really good though, in a black t-shirt that stretched over his broad chest, faded blue jeans, and his sexy motorcycle boots.

God, I missed him. I missed our talks and flirting with him, and I missed his beautiful blue eyes burning into me, his sexy hands on my body... I missed—

No, not going there.

I grabbed my shot, tipped it back, and let the burn settle in my throat.

I raised a hand, signaling the bartender for another.

Niki nudged my elbow, the corners of her mouth curling into a grin. "Okay, listen. We're not doing the sad-girl thing all night. Let's drink, people-watch, and scout this place for someone hot enough to distract you."

I let out a laugh, shaking my head. "I don't want a guy, Niki."

"Why not? A little flirtation could be fun."

"Because I've got enough man troubles. I don't need another one added to the list."

She sighed dramatically. "Ugh, fine. But if you change your mind, that guy by the jukebox in the tight blue tee? Built like a brick wall. We could get him to buy us drinks just by making eye contact."

I glanced over and immediately looked away. "Nope. Absolutely not."

"Okay, but the offer stands." She lifted her glass. "Until then, you're stuck with me and vodka."

"Honestly? Best combo I've had all week."

She smiled, softer now. "Good. Because I'm here for whatever you need tonight. If that means we drink, talk shit, and pretend Ghost doesn't exist, I'm game."

"Thanks," I said quietly, grateful.

She bumped her shoulder against mine. "Anytime. Now drink up, bitch. And don't look back at him, because he's still watching."

I downed my drink. Of course he was.

Just as I started to feel a little lighter, a little looser, a guy slid onto the stool beside me, catching me off guard.

Niki, however, was highly amused. "Well, hello there," she said, sipping her drink, her eyes twinkling with mischief.

The guy had dark hair. He was a little too clean-cut. He flashed me a smug, easy grin. It was the kind of confidence that came from a man who had never been told no in his life. "Couldn't help but notice you sitting here," he said smoothly, his attention fully on me.

I gave him a tight smile, already bored.

But I didn't tell him to leave. Because I could feel Ghost watching. And I was suddenly fucking pissed. I know he asked for space, but could he not come over and just acknowledge I existed?

"Had to come over before someone else did."

"That so?" I said.

"Yeah." He leaned in, letting his arm stretch out along the bar like he was claiming the space. "A girl like you shouldn't be sitting alone."

I arched a brow and motioned to Niki. "I'm not alone."

He smirked, completely ignoring Niki's presence. "You know what I mean."

I let the silence stretch. Let Ghost see. I wasn't flirting. But I wasn't sending the guy away either. Because if Ghost wanted his space, he could fucking have it. Petty? Yeah. Yeah, it was. But I hadn't heard word one from him in a week, and the longer I sat there thinking about it, the more frustrated I became. I wasn't going to sit here like some pathetic, heartbroken idiot while he acted like he wasn't destroying me.

The guy took my silence as encouragement, scooting in closer, his knee brushing mine. "Tell me, do you believe in love at first sight, or should I walk by again?"

Niki snorted into her drink.

I sighed. Jesus.

Before I could figure out how to shake him without making a scene, the guy went rigid, his eyes darting over my shoulder.

And I knew Ghost must be coming.

Then, I heard Ghost's voice. Low. Lethal. Territorial. "Mind moving, bud?"

The guy swallowed hard. "We're just talking."

Ghost's jaw hardened. "You got two seconds to get the fuck up before I move you myself."

The guy hesitated. Stupid move.

Ghost reached out, grabbing the guy by the collar, and hauled him up off the stool.

"Jesus, okay, okay!" the guy choked out, holding his hands up. "Relax, man."

Ghost looked far from relaxed. He looked like he was two seconds from ending this guy's entire existence.

The guy stumbled back, adjusting his shirt with an offended huff before turning to me. "You should really learn how to pick 'em better," he said.

Ghost took a step forward, but I shot up from my seat, pressing a hand to his chest before he could follow through. "Not worth it," I said, my voice clipped.

Ghost's heated glare stayed on the guy, but after a long, tense moment, he exhaled sharply and let the guy walk away.

I turned back to Ghost, my pulse pounding.

His blue eyes burned into mine, but they weren't furious anymore. They were something worse. Something darker.

Chapter 91

H e shot me a look. "Follow me."

With a quick look at Niki, I did. I followed him through the thick crowd, my heart pounding, my emotions teetering on the edge of exploding.

He led me into a hallway, away from the chaos, away from prying eyes.

And then, just as I was about to demand why the hell he was even acknowledging me now, he turned sharply, his voice low but firm. "Why are you here?"

I gave a tight, bitter smile. "I'm doing good. Thanks for asking. How about you, Ghost? How's your week been? Get enough space? Work through all your life-altering decisions?"

His jaw flexed. "That's not what I meant—"

"No, I'm sure it's not," I cut in, folding my arms. "But you don't get to vanish for a week, ignore me completely, and then bark at me for showing up somewhere I didn't even know you'd be. You wanted

space? You got it. But don't act like I'm crashing your sacred medita-
tion retreat."

His eyes narrowed, and his voice dropped lower, rougher. "You
think you're funny? Standing at the bar with some pretty boy while
I'm across the room watching it?"

"Watching it? You didn't even say hi."

"Because I didn't want to lose my shit in front of a crowd," he
growled. "You looked real comfortable with him."

I stepped closer, my heart pounding. "Oh, so you get to decide my
life now? You needed space, remember? Or is it only space when you're
the one doing the walking?"

"I needed time to think, not a front-row seat to you flirting with the
next warm body that walked up."

"Well, maybe if you'd sent a single damn text, you wouldn't be
wondering who I was talking to."

He stared at me, breathing hard, his hands clenched at his sides like
he didn't trust what they'd do next.

"Niki invited me out, Ghost. I didn't know this was one of your
fights. I wasn't even going to talk to you, since you obviously weren't
going to talk to me. You're the one that pulled me aside."

His jaw flexed. "I told you I needed space."

Seven days of silence. Seven days of wondering if I mattered. Seven
days of waiting for a decision that shouldn't have even been a decision.
And he had the audacity to say that to me?

"So take it," I spat. "I didn't ask you to approach me."

"You had to know coming here would upset me. Then, you're
flirting with some guy. To what? Make me jealous?"

That was it. That was the moment I snapped.

"I wasn't flirting with anyone. And I didn't realize that I couldn't
hang out with my friends when they were at your fight." My tone was

razor sharp, my anger rising like a tidal wave. "Why don't you just give me a list of rules so I know exactly what I can and cannot do? Or better yet, why don't you tattoo the list right on my ass? Since you seem to think you own it, anyway."

His eyes darkened, his nostrils flaring. "Watch it, Halston."

"Or what?" I challenged, stepping closer, tilting my chin up. "You gonna kick me out of your life for good this time? Just say the word, Ghost. Make your damn decision. Because I am so fucking sick of this game already."

His jaw tightened so hard I thought he'd crack a tooth.

Then he grabbed my arm and yanked me into the public restroom, slamming the door shut behind us.

We stood there, chests heaving, rage radiating between us like wildfire.

His eyes held mine, his fists clenched. "Stop making this so goddamn hard on me," he growled.

I let out a bitter laugh, shaking my head. "Hard on you? This is hard on you? Are you fucking kidding me, Ghost? I'm the one waiting for you to decide if I'm worth—"

"Just give me space!" he snapped, cutting me off, causing me to jump.

"Understand this! I need to see if I have feelings for you—" He exhaled sharply, his eyes blazing. "—or if I'm just addicted to fucking you!"

The second the words left his mouth, they hung there between us.

And then, like a shockwave, they hit me with pure, unrelenting heat. A fire lit up inside me, the words triggering something dark and desperate.

Ghost saw it. His blue eyes flashed, his breath hitching for a second before something feral took over.

Then he was on me.

His hands gripped me like a lifeline, like he was drowning in his own fucking torment, as he kissed me, his mouth taking absolute possession of mine.

There was no talking, no teasing, no playful banter, just raw, carnal hunger.

He growled, shoving my skirt up around my waist, gripping my thighs so hard I was sure I'd have bruises. Then he ripped my underwear clean off my body, the fabric snapping in his hands.

"Ghost," I gasped, already lost, already melting into him.

He turned me, pressing me hard against the door, his body covering mine, his heat searing through me. He unzipped and pulled his boxer briefs down just enough to spring free.

Gripping my hips, he slid inside me, making me moan.

He didn't slow down. He didn't hesitate as he drove into me, his hands digging into my hips, his breath ragged against my ear, his teeth nipping at my neck as he pounded into me like he couldn't control himself anymore. Like he'd needed this for too damn long.

I was grabbing at the door, my cries of pleasure echoing off the metal as he pushed me toward the edge, his rhythm relentless.

Over and over again, he drove into me, fucking me senseless.

I slammed a hand against the metal door, the intense pleasure tearing through me violently as his hips rolled over and over.

Gasps shot out of me while the pressure built, clawing at me from the inside.

And when I shattered, when I came so hard I couldn't breathe, he allowed himself to follow, his body shaking against mine, a deep, guttural curse ripping from his throat.

For a long second, we just stood there, his body pressed tightly against mine.

My forehead was still pressed to the door, my body still trembling, his hands gripping my waist like he couldn't let go.

He exhaled sharply, dragged a hand through his hair, and pulled up his jeans, zipping them.

And just like that. Reality slammed back into him, into us, into the mess we had just made.

His entire body tensed. His jaw locked. "Motherfucker," he growled.

And without another word, he turned and walked out, leaving me standing there alone in the bathroom.

I sucked in a shaky breath, my chest still heaving, my legs barely holding me up.

I locked the door, pressing my back against it.

I broke down. Tears spilled down my cheeks; the ache inside me was too much to contain. Because I needed him. God, I needed him. But it wasn't up to me. It was up to him.

And right now, I felt like I'd already lost him.

Chapter 92

The neon sign above the dive bar flickered, barely hanging on to life, casting a red glow over the sidewalk as we approached.

The Rusty Note wasn't much to look at, but Niki swore by their strong drinks and chaotic open mic nights.

Inside, people were already buzzed, cheering on some guy in a flannel shirt doing an emotional and terrible rendition of "Tennessee Whiskey."

"This is my penance," Niki said, as we slid into a booth near the back. "For not telling you that was Ghost's fight last week. I officially suck, and this is me making it up to you with tequila and karaoke."

I raised a brow. "Karaoke?"

"Hell yeah. We're singing tonight. I already picked our songs."

"You what?"

"Don't worry, I got the classics. I'm not throwing you to the wolves with some sad breakup song. We're going in hot early with Britney. Maybe some Shania if we're drunk enough."

I gave her a skeptical look. "We're definitely going to be drunk enough."

We ordered two rounds back-to-back. Shots first. Cocktails after. It wasn't long before we were laughing loud enough to get looks from the next table over, singing along with every bad performer and heckling each other like we were at a roast.

When our names were finally called, we stumbled toward the stage, drinks in hand, Niki giggling and dragging me by the wrist.

The music started, and I nearly choked laughing when "Man! I Feel Like A Woman" blared through the speakers.

We belted out the lyrics like we were headlining Madison Square Garden, dancing, twirling, and high-kicking across the tiny stage. A guy in the front row handed Niki a rose made out of a napkin. She took it, kissed his cheek, and winked.

"You're trouble," I said in between verses.

"Good trouble," she shot back, her hips swaying.

After that, we barely sat down. We kept drinking and singing.

A table of guys near the back started buying us rounds, one of them even getting up to sing Usher just to impress us, which he wasn't bad at.

One of them leaned over and said, "If either of you is single, I'm free next Friday."

Niki laughed and tossed her hair back. "Sorry, handsome. We're both taken. But your confidence is sexy."

I grinned and chimed in, "Yeah, you're definitely the bravest guy in here."

The night blurred into dancing with strangers, more singing, and taking selfies we'd cringe at tomorrow.

Someone handed Niki a cowboy hat, which she wore for a full hour without questioning it.

By the time we finally left, the bar was closing down, and we were clinging to each other as we wandered into the quiet night air, arm in arm.

"We killed it," Niki said, her heels clicking against the pavement. "That Shania performance? Legendary."

"We're icons," I said, slurring a little, trying not to trip on the curb. "Drunken, chaotic icons."

We started singing again, off-key, loud, and without a care in the world. People across the street turned to stare as we shouted the chorus of "Since U Been Gone," but we just sang louder, middle fingers in the air, laughing like idiots.

"Where are we going?" I finally asked, panting between fits of giggles.

Niki squinted dramatically at the horizon, then shrugged. "Do you want to hit up another bar?"

I blinked. "Don't you think we've had enough?"

She shook her head with a grin. "No."

And we both burst into laughter so loud it echoed off the buildings, stumbling down the sidewalk like two girls who didn't have a care in the world. Just for tonight we had each other and a shit ton of alcohol, and I hadn't thought about Ghost... much.

We'd barely made it two blocks down the street when we heard music thumping, people laughing, the unmistakable beat of a rooftop party in full swing. Light spilled over the edge of the building like it was calling us.

Niki looked at me, her eyes bright and wicked. "Tell me you hear that."

I smirked. "I hear it. I'm just trying to decide how dangerous it is to climb a fire escape in heels."

"We've done worse."

And that was all it took.

Laughing, half-drunk, and high on the chaos of the night, we found the fire escape ladder and started our way up, giggling like two teenagers sneaking out past curfew.

When we reached the rooftop, it was like stepping into another world. There were twinkling string lights, loud music, bodies pressed close together, red cups and cocktail trays floating between clusters of people.

"We're in," Niki whispered like we'd just broken into a vault.

We barely made it ten feet in before we snagged drinks from a passing tray with no hesitation, no shame. Whoever's party this was, they obviously had money. They weren't going to miss a little bit of alcohol.

I was halfway through a cup when a guy stumbled backward into me, hard, the cold contents of my drink sloshing down the front of my shirt. "Oh, what the hell—"

I looked up just as he turned around, his eyes wide and apologetic.

He was tall. Cute. Messy dark hair. Big, broad shoulders. Not Ghost-cute, but... still something. "Shit, I am so sorry," he said, flustered.

Niki cackled behind me. "This looks familiar."

I wiped at my soaked shirt. "Doesn't it?" I muttered, shooting her a look.

The guy was still apologizing when a woman stormed up beside him, her voice like a blade cutting through our conversation. "Seriously, Van? You're just going to walk away while I'm talking?"

He winced. "It's not the time, Lily."

"Is that your girlfriend?" I asked, more amused than anything.

"Unfortunately," he said.

The girl gasped. "You asshole!"

I laughed. "You're funny," I told him, already enjoying the show.

He smiled, flustered, but flattered. And that was apparently the last straw.

"Are you fucking flirting with this slut right in front of me?" she screeched.

I blinked, then burst out laughing. Niki joined in, snorting into her drink.

I wasn't sure how I got caught up in this, but I was beyond buzzed, soaked, and still riding the high of a perfect disaster. So I leaned in, tilted my head, and looked her dead in the eye. "I just gave him a blowjob in the bathroom, so I guess slut is fair."

Niki nearly choked on her drink, her eyes going wide. "Oh my God," she whispered, stunned and delighted.

Lily lost her mind. "We're finished, Van. Lose my number!" she shrieked, shoving him hard before storming off in a cloud of rage and glitter.

Van turned to me, slack-jawed, then laughed, shaking his head. "Was I high? 'Cause damn. I think I'd remember that."

I smirked. "You're welcome."

"She thinks you really blew me."

I nodded. "Yep. Next girl you date? Make sure she's not such a bitch."

He laughed again, full-on now. "Who are you?"

I slid an arm around Niki's shoulder and grinned. "Just a girl trying to have a little fun. Hanging out with her best friend. Drowning heartbreak in alcohol and reckless decisions."

He motioned to someone across the party. A tray of shots arrived like magic.

We each grabbed one. Van raised his glass toward me. "To reckless decisions," he said, grinning at me like the devil.

We downed them, then high-fived like idiots.

The rest of the night blurred into music and dancing. Niki and I hung out with Van and his friends, laughing, playing drinking games, and shamelessly flirting just for the hell of it.

Every time a guy leaned in a little too close and flirted, one of us would grin and say, "We're taken. But keep trying."

We were loud. We were drunk. And for the first time in two weeks, I felt free of stress.

We collapsed onto a patio couch tucked in the corner of the rooftop, the string lights above us casting a golden glow over our flushed, sweaty, completely trashed faces.

"Selfie time," Niki declared, pulling out her phone and scooting closer. We leaned in, cheeks pressed, grinning like fools.

Then, we pulled Van into the next one, then another guy from their group who had been trying and failing to balance a beer can on his head.

Niki scrolled through the photos, snorting. "We look like absolute chaos."

"Hot chaos," I corrected, tossing my hair dramatically.

She laughed and tapped a few buttons. "Sending these to Josh."

A few seconds later, her phone buzzed. Josh sent back **You two look trashed.**

She turned the screen toward me. I burst out laughing. "He's not wrong."

Niki giggled and fired back a reply. **We are trashed.**

We burst out laughing again. My cheeks hurt from how much we'd been smiling tonight.

Her phone buzzed again. **I'm coming to pick you up.**

"Boo," I groaned, flopping back against the couch. "We were just getting warmed up."

"I know," Niki pouted. "Party pooper."

But neither of us really argued. We were sticky with sweat, our feet hurt, and I was starting to feel the world tilt sideways when I stood too fast.

"I guess we should head down to the sidewalk and wait for him," she said, already wobbling toward the fire escape.

I sighed, standing with a stretch. "Probably."

Before we left, I pulled her into a warm, tight hug, swaying from the alcohol. "Thanks," I whispered against her shoulder. "For the best night I've had in a while."

She hugged me tighter. "What are best friends for?"

We stumbled down the fire escape, heels in hand, laughter echoing behind us as we made our way back into the real world, just a little lighter, a little louder, and a lot drunker than we'd started.

Chapter 93

B y the time I got home, my feet were throbbing, my throat was sore from screaming Shania lyrics, and my body was buzzing with alcohol and adrenaline.

I dropped my keys on the counter, kicked off my heels, and stripped off my sticky, rum-soaked clothes on the way to the bathroom.

The hot water felt like salvation. I stood under the spray, letting it beat against my skin as my head tilted back, eyes closed. I washed away the sweat, the glitter, the lipstick smudges, and the fake confidence.

By the time I stepped out, towel-drying my hair and pulling on a shirt, the high from the night had started to fade.

The house was quiet. Too quiet. No singing. No tequila-fueled giggles. Just the soft hum of the fridge and the echo of my own thoughts.

I grabbed a glass of water, gulped it down, and then crawled into bed. The sheets were cool, the pillowcase soft against my still-damp skin.

But my mind didn't quiet. It never did when it came to him.

Ghost.

God, I hated how fast the memories came. The way he looked at me when no one else was around. The sarcasm, that vulgar mouth, that stupid, cocky smirk.

I missed the way he held me, like he couldn't bear the thought of letting go. Like I meant more than just release.

I stared up at the ceiling, blinking into the darkness.

I wanted to call him. I wanted to text him. I wanted to drive over to his place and crawl into his bed again, tangle myself in his sheets and pretend none of the shit between us had ever happened.

But I couldn't.

Because he was the one who pushed me away. The one who said he needed space. And even now, even after everything, he hadn't called.

I curled onto my side, pulling the blanket up over my shoulder, wrapping it tight like it could protect me from the hollow ache in my chest.

The night had been exactly what I needed.

But now... Now I was just a girl in a dark room, missing a man I wasn't even sure missed me back.

Sleep wasn't happening.

I stared into the darkness for another few minutes, my chest heavy, my heart loud in the silence.

Then something sparked.

I sat up slowly, tugging the blanket tighter around me. My laptop was still on the nightstand. I pulled it into my lap, opened the lid, and stared at the blinking cursor on the screen.

The tattoo shop logo. I'd been stuck on it for days. Nothing felt right. Nothing screamed at me.

But now...

Something shifted. Maybe it was the leftover buzz in my veins or the raw ache of missing Ghost, but suddenly, I could see it—what the logo needed.

It had to be bold. Gritty. Unapologetic. But there had to be precision to it too. Like Ghost. Rough around the edges, but sharp. Intense.

I started tapping away, sketching out a few new concepts. Something black and stark, maybe with a hint of red. Clean lines. Ink-drenched grit. The kind of logo that would look just as good burned into skin as it would across a window decal or a merch drop.

Rebellious Ink was going to love it.

It was 3:42 a.m. before I stopped.

And even though I was exhausted and still nursing a hole in my chest where Ghost used to be, I felt a flicker of something steady settle in my bones.

I wasn't going to fall apart. Not tonight, anyway.

I closed the laptop and set it on the nightstand beside the bed, laying back against the pillows.

Maybe he didn't want me anymore. But he still had a piece of me.

And I'd just turned it into something damn beautiful.

Chapter 94

The sleek black sedan rolled up to the curb.

I was walking from my car to the house when the back door swung open, revealing a man in a perfectly tailored suit. "Get in."

I recognized him as one of the high roller's men. "Not happening."

The man sighed, shaking his head. "My employer insists."

Before I could turn away, two massive men in dark suits stepped forward, their grips firm as they grabbed my arms.

Panic shot through me like lightning. "Let me go!"

"Don't make a scene," one of them warned, his voice low and cold.

And just like that, I was forced into the car, the door slamming shut beside me.

By the time the car pulled up to the venue, my heart was slamming against my ribs.

As I was led inside, I heard the roar of the crowd. I realized I must be at one of Ghost's fights.

Son of a bitch. Could I seriously not escape people dragging me to his fights?

And then, I saw Ghost. His movements were sharp, precise, dangerous. He possessed the kind of controlled violence that made men fear him. I knew this wasn't some reckless fight. This was an audition, another test of sorts. A high-stakes demonstration to prove he was the best of the best. His opponent was twice his size, swinging brutal, heavy fists. But Ghost was too fast. He dodged effortlessly, countering with a devastating knee to the ribs, following it up with a vicious right hook that sent the man staggering.

I was immediately irritated. He was still fighting for the sleazebag high roller.

Whatever. It wasn't my business any longer.

I struggled in the guard's grip. "Let go!" They didn't budge.

I felt the weight of a hand land casually on my shoulder. The high roller stood beside me, his smirk lazy, pleased. "He's something else, isn't he?"

"Why the hell am I here?"

"Because I needed to see something about your boy." He took a slow sip of his whiskey, his eyes never leaving the fight. "I needed to know what he's really made of. What he's willing to fight for."

Before I could respond, his arm slid around my shoulders. I froze, my entire body going ice cold. "I wonder what happens when a man with nothing to lose suddenly finds something worth fighting for."

My spine went stiff, my jaw locking tight. I turned my head, leveling him with a glare. "As usual, asshole, you're off base. He broke up with me. He's probably moved on already."

The high roller chuckled, low and knowing. "Oh, beautiful. Is that what you think?" He tilted his head, watching me. "Tell me, then... why does he look like he's ready to burn the world down over you?"

Before I could snap back, Ghost's eyes were on me.

And for a second, the whole damn world stopped.

His gaze roamed over me, taking in every detail. And then some-thing in his face shifted. The darkness there deepened. And he fucking snapped. Ghost had already been dominating the fight, but now? He was a blur of raw, vicious power. He hit him with a fist, then a knee, followed by an elbow. And he ended it with a spin kick to his head.

His opponent collapsed.

The crowd went insane.

The ref tried to grab Ghost's hand to announce his victory. But Ghost wasn't hanging around for his victory applause.

He was coming for us. His eyes were locked on the high roller.

The high roller's guards tensed, ready. They tried to grab him, but he easily kneed one in the gut, and the other caught an uppercut.

Ghost didn't stop. Didn't slow. He walked right up to the high roller, getting in his face. His voice was low, cold, deadly. "Get your fucking hands off her."

The high roller's smirk barely faltered. "Relax. It's just business."

Ghost's entire body coiled tight with restraint. "You brought her here to get to me." His voice was lethal. "I warned you. This was your last fucking mistake."

The high roller took another sip of whiskey. "Come on, Ghost. You, of all people, should understand leverage."

"Leverage? You didn't need to fuck with me. All you needed to do was keep lining up fights. You fucked up."

Ghost leaned in. His breath was steady, but the rage in his voice was barely contained. "You think dragging her here makes you smart?" His voice dropped lower. "You think using her makes you powerful? It makes you a dead man."

"I was just testing you."

Ghost's voice went flat. "Our arrangement is off."

The high roller's smirk finally dropped. "Now, wait a damn minute—"

"No!" His tone cut sharp. "We're done. Whatever you thought this was? It ends now."

The rest of the room dropped into silence.

The high roller set his drink down, his jaw tightening. "Be careful, son. You don't wanna make an enemy out of me."

"Don't fucking threaten me. I promise you, you'll regret it." Ghost took another step closer until he was in the man's face, his voice sharp, deliberate, final. "You will leave her alone. Because if you ever touch her again, if you even look at her again..." His blue eyes were cold, lethal, filled with something that should have scared the hell out of anyone with a brain. "I will bury you so fucking deep they'll forget you ever existed."

The high roller held his gaze, but I saw the flicker, the moment where he realized just how badly he had miscalculated.

Ghost wasn't his pawn. And I wasn't his bargaining chip.

"Come on, Halston." Ghost's voice was gravel and grit, rough from the fight, rough from everything that had gone down. "We're leaving."

I didn't argue. Not this time. Not after what just happened.

I took his outstretched hand, walking beside him, my pulse still pounding, my heart still wrecked from the weight of everything that had just happened.

The high roller didn't stop us. Because he knew the truth. Ghost wasn't a man to be owned. And he sure as hell wasn't a man to be fucked with.

We stepped outside, and Ghost walked me straight to his truck, pulled open the door, and gestured inside. "Get in."

I hesitated.

His jaw flexed, and then his voice dropped, softer, but still edged with something sharp. "Please, sweetheart."

That broke me. I climbed in.

The drive was quiet.

I stole a glance at him, his knuckles still raw from the fight, his jaw still clenched tight, his eyes focusing on the road.

I should've been mad at him. I was. But something about tonight had shifted something in my chest. He could've let the high roller play his game. He could've kept the deal, taken the money. But the second I got dragged into it? It was over. Ghost didn't let people use him. But just as important? He didn't let people use me.

Ghost finally spoke. "Josh sent me the selfies."

My head snapped toward him. "What?"

He kept his eyes on the road, his lips twitching like he wasn't sure if he should smirk or frown. "You and Niki. Singing into a beer bottle. One where you had a slice of pizza in one hand and a shot in the other like a goddamn champion." He glanced over at me, just for a second. "Looked like you were having a good time."

I let out a soft laugh, brushing my fingers against my knee. "She took me out to help me drown my..." I trailed off, my throat tightening as I looked out the window, then back at him. "To distract me."

His knuckles flexed on the steering wheel, his eyes darkening as he stared forward again. "I'm glad you had fun," he said, but his voice was quieter now. Careful. Like every word was being filtered through something he didn't want me to see.

"We did," I replied, just as softly.

Silence settled again, but this time it was heavier.

I turned toward him, watching the sharp cut of his jaw, the quiet tension in his shoulders. "You don't sound happy about that." I knew as soon as the words were out that I was fishing for something from him. Some sign that he was missing me as much as I was missing him.

He let out a breath, finally looking at me again. "I'm glad you had fun," he said honestly. "But I hate that I'm the reason you needed to be distracted in the first place."

The truth of it hung between us. But that answer was far from what I had hoped to hear from him. "Not as sorry as I am," I said truthfully.

His hand tightened on the wheel again, and his jaw clenched like he was fighting the urge to say something more.

When we finally pulled up to my house, Ghost killed the engine, sitting there for a long beat, his hands still gripping the wheel.

I reached for the door handle, my fingers brushing the cool metal. "Thanks for the ride," I said, trying to sound casual. Like my heart wasn't hammering against my ribs. Like tonight hadn't cracked something open inside me.

But before I could step out, his hand shot out, wrapping around my wrist.

I froze. Heat shot through me like a live wire, flatlining every rational thought I'd had.

He didn't speak. Just held me there, his grip firm but gentle, his thumb brushing over my wrist, steady, soothing. A complete contradiction to everything else about him.

I swallowed hard. "Ghost."

His blue eyes met mine. They were intense and unreadable. "Please don't hate me, Halston," he said, his voice rough, low, barely above a whisper. It wasn't a demand. It was a plea.

I exhaled, the weight of everything we'd been through pressing heavy against my chest. Those words, the look in his eyes, threatened to break me. "I don't hate you, Ghost," I said softly.

Because how could I?

How could I hate a man who had just gone full beast mode to protect me? A man who had just shown me I meant something to him, even though I didn't know exactly what that was, even though he obviously still didn't either.

Still caught in the moment, I reached out and cupped his cheek, my fingers sliding along the edge of his jaw. My thumb brushed over the coarse hairs of his beard, and he leaned into my touch.

His hand landed on top of mine, big and warm.

Tears stung my eyes, and a lump formed in my throat. I knew I had to get out of there before I started crying again.

So, I did the only thing I could do.

I slipped my hand out of his, my heart twisting as I opened the door. I stepped out into the cool night air before I said or did something stupid.

And as I shut the door behind me, I didn't look back. Because if I did, I might've climbed back in.

Chapter 95

G host finally texted me.

After ending his ties to the high roller, it was another week of silence.

I stared at the message for a long time, my heart pounding, my chest tight with emotions I wasn't ready to name.

Come over.

No phone call. No explanation. Just come over.

And like an idiot, I went.

The second I pulled up to the ranch, confusion settled into my chest. The gates were wide open, which was unusual in itself. And there were cars everywhere.

What the hell was this?

I opened the door, stepping into the house, my eyes scanning the crowd.

Loud music pulsed through the air. People were laughing, drinking, and moving around like this was some celebration. A goddamn party. Since when did Ghost have parties?

I clenched my jaw, my frustration rising fast. Seriously? After not hearing from him, after he asked for space, after he made it clear that he needed time to figure out what I meant to him. He finally reaches out and invites me to a fucking party? Unbelievable.

I took a deep breath, forcing myself to keep my composure as I moved through the party.

That's when I saw the banner. It was Henry's birthday.

I said hi to Ghost's guys, keeping my voice light, even though my blood was simmering beneath the surface. Henry was by the kitchen with a drink in his hand. I hugged him and wished him a happy birthday.

I found Drew, Niki, and Josh. We exchanged greetings and talked for a few minutes, all the while pretending I wasn't fuming inside.

I even went to Ghost's room to look for him and found the dogs and Lulu, crouching down to pet them, letting their warm presence calm me just a little. But it wasn't working. Because the longer I was here, the more I realized Ghost had avoided me for another week, then invited me here like nothing had happened. Like I was just another guest at his party.

I still hadn't seen him. I had no idea where he was right now. But when I found him? He was going to get an earful.

I moved through the house, pushing my way through the crowd of people drinking, laughing, having the time of their lives. While my insides burned with frustration, confusion, and heartbreak.

People were dancing, drinking, and celebrating.

And I wanted to scream.

I moved from room to room, my pulse hammering, my chest tightening with every second that passed without finding him.

As I stepped out of a back bedroom, back into the hallway...

I froze.

Because there he was. Standing in the kitchen. He hadn't been there on my way in. But then I noticed he wasn't alone. He was talking to a woman with long black hair. And I already knew who she was.

Alesandra.

A rush of emotions hit me all at once, pulling me from one end of the spectrum to the other. Shock. Pain. Anger. Heartache. Because why the hell was she here? He needed space from both of us, and now we were both here. Why? So he could choose between us?

Nothing, and I mean nothing, prepared me for what happened next.

As I stood there watching him, frozen in place, Alesandra leaned in and kissed him.

What was left of my heart cracked wide open right there in the middle of that crowded kitchen, with the music still blaring, people still laughing, the party still going on like I wasn't dying inside.

Ghost kissed the woman who destroyed him. And in doing so, he destroyed me, too.

Then it hit me. Hard. He'd made his choice. He'd picked her. And he'd called me here to tell me that.

I didn't stay to watch.

I moved through the crowd as fast as I could, my stomach twisting so violently I thought I might throw up.

The second I stepped outside, I sucked in the cold night air, but it did nothing to calm the storm raging inside me. I had spent so much time being patient, so much time waiting for him to figure out what I meant to him. Three fucking weeks.

And now? I had my answer. And it wrecked me.

I sucked in a sharp breath, falling to my knees, trying to force the ache in my chest to settle.

I wiped at my tears, trying to steady my shaking hands, my stomach still twisting from what I had just witnessed inside that house. I had given Ghost everything. My patience. My time. My heart. And he had shoved it all back in my face. No wonder he'd asked me not to hate him. He'd made his choice. And I was such a fool.

And then, a voice came from behind me, smug, dripping with satisfaction. It made my blood run hot. "It hurts when someone betrays you, doesn't it?"

I turned, my breath catching in my throat.

Jen.

Standing there with her arms folded, a self-satisfied smirk twisting her perfect lips.

"What the hell are you doing here?" I snapped, my fists clenching as I made it to my feet.

She shrugged, all feigned innocence. "Alesandra invited me... after I called her and told her that Ghost missed her."

My eyes widened, the realization slamming into me like a freight train. But my shock quickly morphed into something darker. Something deadly. "You fucking did this?" My voice came out low, lethal. "You invited that woman back into his life to hurt me?"

Her smirk widened, her head tilting in mock amusement. "I told you I'd take him from you." She sighed dramatically, inspecting her perfectly manicured nails. "Since he turned me down, I had to get creative."

A slow, deadly silence stretched between us.

Rage unlike anything I'd ever known poured through me. It burned hot and consuming, flooding my veins like liquid fire, sending every single self-defense move Ghost had ever taught me racing through my head. I fought every primal instinct screaming at me to beat the shit out of her where she stood. I had never hated anyone like I hated her at that moment.

My gaze drifted. My eyes caught sight of something lying against the wall next to the open garage. A tire iron. Cold, heavy, solid metal.

My pulse hammered in my ears, my vision turning sharp and dangerous.

"You shouldn't have crossed me," Jen said, cutting her eyes at me.

I looked back at Jen, my lips curling, my voice deadly calm. My eyes flicked back to the tire iron, then bounced back to her. "No. You really shouldn't have crossed me."

Chapter 96

I rushed her. Jen jumped back, her eyes wide with fear as I brushed past her, my heels crunching against the gravel driveway.

I didn't look at her. Didn't say a word. Because tunnel vision had taken over.

I grabbed the tire iron, my grip tight, knuckles white, my breath ragged with rage as I whirled around.

Jen screamed and took off running as I started toward her.

And she should have. Because I was blind with fury, my pulse hammering like a war drum, my entire body electric with adrenaline-fueled insanity as I lifted the tire iron high and brought it crashing down on the hood of her car.

Once.

The metal dented with a sickening crunch, but it wasn't enough.

Twice.

The impact rattled up my arms, but still, it wasn't enough. Not for what she had done. Not for what she had taken from me.

Plastic and paint cracked under my next swing, the left headlight shattering into shards of plastic. That was for her, for the shitty excuse of a friend she had been, for every petty dig, every manipulation.

I swung again, taking out the right headlight. That was for Drew, for the way she had used him, broken him, made him believe she loved him when all she ever loved was herself.

I rounded the car, stopping by the side mirror, my breath ragged, my vision swimming in pure rage. I brought the tire iron down onto the windshield. Again and again. Each hit sent cracks spidering across the glass, the thick layers of safety glass splintering beneath my force.

That was for Ghost. For his inability to commit, for casting me aside like I was nothing when I had been the only damn person who ever truly cared about him. For choosing to chase after a woman who had gutted him, instead of the one who would have never done him wrong.

My heart pounded in my ears, and it was all I could hear.

I lifted the tire iron again, slamming it down harder, my arms shaking with the force of my fury. That was for every night of passion we shared, for every moment he made me feel special, only to throw it all away like it had meant nothing to him, for every time I had lost a little more of my heart to him.

I raised the tire iron again, my mind a whirlwind of chaos. Because for the first time in my life, I wasn't holding back for anyone.

I was mid-swing, ready to bring the tire iron down again to take out her side mirror, when muscular arms wrapped around me from behind, yanking the tire iron from my grip with ease. "Halston!" Ghost's voice sounded like he was underwater. "Halston!"

I fought, thrashing, kicking, my rage still white-hot and all-consuming. But Ghost crushed me to him, holding me so tight I could barely move. "I fucking hate her!" I snarled, still struggling. But I was no match for him.

He turned me to him, bear-hugging me into submission, his lips brushing my temple as he spoke in a low, calming voice. "I know, sweetheart. Calm down."

Sweetheart.

Something about the way he said it, about the way he held me, so secure, so grounding, made the last of my energy drain from my body. I stopped fighting. Stopped struggling. I went limp, exhaustion hitting me.

Ghost adjusted his hold, supporting my weight as my chest heaved from exertion. "Take some deep breaths," he whispered.

The rage started to clear, and suddenly, I could hear everything around me. That's when I realized we weren't alone. People were talking. There were whispers and gasps.

"Holy shit!"

"Damn!"

"She fucked that car up!"

Ghost didn't let me go. Instead, he cupped my face, forcing me to look at him. His blue eyes searched mine, his brows furrowed with concern. "Are you okay?" he asked.

I took a deep breath and let it out, my pulse still pounding in my ears, but the fire inside me was tamped down. I nodded. "Better."

Ghost let out a low laugh, shaking his head, looking from the destroyed car back to me. "I fucking bet."

Before I could respond, a shrill voice cut through the night. "I'm calling the cops!"

I turned to see Jen standing there. Her face was twisted in rage, her phone already in her hand. "I'm having you arrested!" she shrieked.

I tilted my head, my expression blank. "I couldn't give a shit less." And I meant it.

I did feel better.

Ghost exhaled sharply, his arm still wrapped loosely around my waist. "Don't call the cops," he told her, his voice firm.

Jen stared at him, furious. "She destroyed my fucking car!"

"You deserved it, you bitch." I said with a shrug.

"Fuck you!" she screeched. "That's it!"

"I said stop, Jen!" Ghost snapped, his tone sharp, cutting through the chaos like a blade.

She hesitated, her fingers hovering over her screen, her eyes flashing with defiance.

Ghost let out a long breath. "I'll pay for the damages. Plus extra."

I jerked back, spinning to face him. "I'd rather go to jail."

Jen let out a vicious laugh. "Fine with me, bitch!"

I lunged at her, and she screamed, scrambling backwards. But Ghost yanked me back against his chest, his arms locking around me again. "Halston, you have to calm down."

I huffed, trying to cross my arms over my chest, but Ghost had me pinned to him. "I am calm." My tone betrayed me, though. It was still sharp, still pissed. "I'd rather go to jail than give in to that bitch."

Ghost turned me to face him fully, his hands gripping my shoulders, his voice serious. "Don't fight me on this."

I narrowed my eyes at him, my voice low but furious. "I don't want you paying for my shit."

His jaw clenched, but he didn't let go of me. "Halston, trust me, you don't want to go to jail. You're being stubborn now, but the minute they slap on those cuffs, reality will sink in, and you will wish you'd taken me up on my offer."

I gritted my teeth, my whole body still tense. "Maybe you're right. Maybe not."

"I am." His voice was firm.

I took a deep breath, forcing myself to focus, to think clearly. But my anger wasn't going anywhere.

I turned back to Jen, glaring, my voice cold, sharp, lethal. "She split us up, Ghost." I kept going, my voice quieter now, but no less deadly. "Jen is the one who called Alesandra and told her you missed her. She's the reason she showed back up in your life."

Ghost's entire body went rigid.

"She caused this chaos to get back at me because I stood up for Drew and broke them up. And because you wanted me and turned her down."

Ghost's eyes snapped to Jen, disbelief flashing over his features before twisting into something lethal. "You did that shit?"

Jen lifted her chin, still trying to act like she was in control. "Damn right I did."

Ghost took a deep breath, then motioned to Henry, his expression cold. "Pay that bitch and get her off my property."

Henry grinned, cracking his knuckles. "It'd be my pleasure." He grabbed Jen by the arm, leading her toward the gate.

The second his hands were on her, the entire crowd went crazy cheering, hooting, hollering.

"Get the fuck off me!" Jen screamed. "I don't want to be here, anyway!"

Ghost stood beside me, his body vibrating with tension, but his eyes never leaving me.

I exhaled, shaking my head, my hands still tingling from the rush of adrenaline.

"Now I see why you fucked up her car."

I shot him raised brows. "She had it coming."

"Kasper."

Ghost and I both turned at the sound of her voice. Alesandra.

She stood there, with her long black hair perfectly in place, her trim figure in a blue dress. Her eyes were wide with concern. "What happened?" she asked.

But my attention wasn't on her words. It was on the way she said his name. Kasper. Like his mother, like his grandmother. Like she still belonged in his life, still had the right to call him that.

And God, it hurt. It felt like a knife straight to my chest. Because she knew him in a way he was never going to allow me to know him. She had won.

Ghost exhaled, his voice steady, even. "It was an accident," he explained to her.

Alesandra's eyes darted to the car, her lips parting in shock. "Oh, my God! That car!"

Ghost let out a frustrated breath, rubbing a hand over his face. "I'll explain in a minute. I need to talk to Halston."

I swallowed, trying to contain the burning ache in my chest. My voice came out icy, detached. A brittle layer of calm stretched over the chaos inside me. "No need."

Ghost's jaw tightened.

I crossed my arms. "I'll find a way to pay you back for the car."

Ghost sighed. "I'm not worried about that."

"Well, I am. It was my fault... not that I regret it, but I did it. Besides, I don't want to owe you anything," I said, my words taking on a sharp, angry tone.

His blue eyes locked onto mine, something tightening in his expression. "Halston, come on. I'm trying here."

Trying? Maybe it was too little too late.

Before I could respond, Alesandra spoke again, her impatience showing. "Kasper."

My stomach twisted, the blade digging deeper, sharper. I laughed, but it was a bitter, hollow sound. "Go, Kasper," I mocked, my voice thick with anger, with hurt, with something I couldn't even name anymore. "I'm done here."

I turned on my heel, unwilling to be second place to a woman who had already broken him once before.

"Halston, I need to talk to you."

Every time he said my name, it was another stab in my heart. I wanted to fold myself into his arms. Wanted to let him fix this before it broke beyond repair. But he wasn't mine. He never had been.

Ghost reached for my arm, his touch just missing me as I pulled away. "You got her." I turned, my voice steady, final. "That's what you wanted."

Then, before he could stop me again, before he could wreck me even further... I walked away.

Chapter 97

I kept busy.

I worked. I hung out with my friends, laughed at their jokes, played along, pretended like I was okay.

But inside? I was dying.

Ghost had torn me apart, and the worst part was he didn't even know it. Because I wouldn't let him see. I wouldn't give him the satisfaction of knowing how much it was killing me to be without him. I wouldn't show him I was completely shattered inside, that I felt like I was walking around in a body that no longer belonged to me.

So I kept my head up, kept my shoulders back, and refused to break where anyone could see. Especially not where it could get back to him.

But in the quiet moments, when the world stopped moving, when I was alone at night in my bed, staring at the ceiling, that's when it hurt the most, that's when I let the tears fall. That's when I would reach for my phone, my heart pounding, my fingers hovering over his name.

The unread messages piled up. The missed calls. So many times he'd tried to reach me. And I ignored every single one. He'd even shown up at my house. But I refused to open the door. I pretended I wasn't home. Not because I didn't want to answer. I wanted to talk to him. I wanted to hear his voice. But I was too weak. I couldn't hear him ask me if we could still be friends. There was no way I could handle that gracefully.

I didn't know if I could survive him again.

I pulled up to the warehouse, parking under the streetlamp. It was already late, and I took comfort in the fact that I would be well lit when getting in my car later.

Niki invited me out to a rave with her, Drew, and Josh.

The warehouse was packed with bodies moving, neon lights flashing, and the air was thick with vapor from a fog machine. The bass pounded through the walls, vibrating beneath my feet.

I shouldn't have come. I knew I wasn't ready for a night out.

As I searched the crowd of dancing bodies for my friends, I immediately felt out of place. I wasn't in the mood to be here.

I stiffened the moment I saw him across the room, my breath hitching in my throat.

Ghost.

His tall, broad, inked body was impossible to ignore, even in a crowd this size. His blue eyes zeroed in on mine, pinning me in place like a damn target.

My stomach dropped.

I turned away. If he was here, it meant that Niki fucking lied to me. I'd said I would come only if Ghost wasn't invited. My friends swore up and down that they hadn't called him, that they respected my decision to let his calls go unanswered.

Lying assholes.

I grabbed a random guy's hand, pulling him onto the dance floor, doing whatever it took to put distance between me and the past.

But the past had other plans.

"Can I cut in?"

I stiffened. He made his way around to face me, his voice wrecking me all over again. "No," I said without hesitation.

Ghost sighed. "I deserve that."

"You deserve a lot more than that."

He gave a small, rueful smile. "True. I was an ass."

I let out a harsh laugh, shaking my head. "Fucking understatement of the year."

Before I could stop him, Ghost turned to the guy I was dancing with, his gaze dark and unyielding. "Appreciate you keeping my girl entertained, but your services are no longer needed."

The guy hesitated, his brows furrowing. "Uh, man, she said—"

"She also said no to me, and here I am."

"Dude, she grabbed me," the guy said.

Ghost tilted his head, his expression deceptively calm. "You really wanna test who she's walking away with?"

The guy held up his hands, taking a step back. "Didn't realize this was a whole situation."

"It's not," I snapped, glaring at Ghost as the guy walked away.

"It is," Ghost corrected, stepping into my space, placing my hands around his neck, pulling me against him by grabbing my hips.

Everything in me went electric, my body betraying me, my heart beating out a traitorous rhythm. I wanted to kiss him, punch him, cry into his chest, scream at him until he hurt the way I hurt.

Instead, I pushed him back, putting space between us, because if I didn't, I would lose myself in him all over again.

Ghost sighed, rubbing a hand down his face and beard. "I know you got my calls, my texts, my messages through Niki."

"I did," I said.

"Don't be mad at her, okay? I asked Niki to invite you so I could talk to you. Since you wouldn't answer me."

I sighed. "I'm not mad at her. I'm mad at you."

He let out a loud exhale. "I've been trying to tell you that I realized in the last couple of weeks that I more than like you."

My eyes narrowed, my anger boiling over. "What the fuck does that mean?"

Ghost hesitated. "It means I'd like to go back to what we had."

A sound came out of me somewhere between a laugh and a growl. The rage was blinding, raw, almost too much. "Now that you've had your fill of fucking her?"

A collective gasp rippled through the crowd around us, but I didn't care.

"I didn't fuck her," Ghost said, his voice firm. "I meant it when I said I needed space from everyone."

I laughed, bitter and broken. "I saw you kiss her, Ghost."

"At my party?" he asked, his brows dipped down. "I didn't know you were in the house. I texted you to come over, but I didn't see you until you went apeshit on Jen's car."

I clenched my jaw, my throat tightening. "I wanted to talk to you. In a stupid moment of weakness, I was going to ask if you'd had enough space because, as much as I pretended I was okay, I was dying without you."

He reached for me, but I jerked away. "I walked into the kitchen to see you kissing that... woman."

Ghost sighed, stepping closer, his voice calmer, softer, measured. "She kissed me. I didn't kiss her. The time I took was to figure out what I felt for you, and to see if I still felt anything for her. I don't. And I told her that. It took being around her to realize that I had let her go a long time ago."

My heart leaped, but I forced it back down, shoving it into the locked box where it belonged.

"I knew I didn't want her back even before you fucked up Jen's car. That's why I texted you to come over. I wanted to tell you everything. I didn't even invite her to the party; she just showed up. I was about to tell Alesandra it was time for her to leave for good when she kissed me. Next thing I know, Josh is running in telling me you'd gone crazy."

"So that's it? You wanted one last kiss to be sure? And now you think we can just go back?"

Ghost ran a hand through his hair, frustration bleeding through his voice. "You're not listening to me, Halston. I didn't initiate the kiss. She did. But the second her lips touched mine, I told her it wasn't going to happen. I knew I didn't want her. Because she wasn't you."

His words hit me like a sledgehammer. I stared at him, my chest rising and falling too fast, my heart a fucking wreck in my ribcage. "And what? You expect me to just believe that?"

His jaw clenched. "Yeah. I do."

I shook my head, swallowing my pride, my pain, my broken heart. "How do I know you're telling the truth? That you didn't sleep with her?"

Ghost's eyes flashed, his jaw tightening. "I don't lie. I hate liars. You know that. I will always tell you the truth."

I inhaled deeply, exhaling slowly. I believed him. "It doesn't matter."

"What do you mean?"

I lifted my chin, forcing the words out. "Seeing you with her made me realize I wouldn't be okay with our arrangement, not anymore. I don't want you to be with other women."

Ghost hesitated, then exhaled, rubbing a hand down his beard. "I haven't actually been with anyone else since I met you. You were always hanging around my place, pulling me in with your pretty blue eyes and sexy smile. You took up rent in my head. I couldn't think of anyone but you."

I let out a sharp breath, my eyes burning. Fuck. Fuck, fuck, fuck. He was making some really good points and seriously weakening my already flimsy defenses when it came to him. "You don't get to just decide now that you're done with her and I should forgive you."

"I'm not asking for forgiveness." Ghost's voice was low and thick.

"Then what the hell are you asking for?"

"You."

The word hung between us, heavy, final.

I sucked in a shaky breath, my hands trembling at my sides. It was all I'd wanted to hear for weeks. But I was too hurt to listen right now. "You can't just say that, Ghost."

"Why not? You want me to pretend like I don't feel it?" He stepped closer, his hands twitching like he wanted to grab me, hold me down, make me listen. "I want you back in my life, Halston."

"I don't know what I want anymore." My voice cracked. Goddammit.

Ghost exhaled sharply, rubbing a rough hand over his jaw. "Then let me remind you."

He didn't wait for permission.

Ghost grabbed my waist, pulling me hard against him. His mouth crushed mine hungrily, heat, frustration, and desperation controlling the kiss.

I should have stopped him. Should have pushed him away. But I didn't. The moment his hands gripped my hips, the moment his tongue slid against mine, slow, claiming. I fucking melted.

I knew I would never stop wanting him.

Ghost pulled back just enough to let me breathe, his forehead still resting against mine, his hands gripping my waist. His blue eyes burned into me, searching, waiting.

I swallowed hard, my pulse a wreck, my mind spinning. Fuck, I couldn't think when he was this close.

I'm not gonna lie. I wanted him. I wanted to climb him right then and there and give the rave-goers a show. Ghost had that effect on me, and he had ever since I met him. But he also broke something inside me, and I wasn't sure I could forgive him for that.

I licked my lips, trying to steady my breath. "I need time, Ghost."

His jaw tightened.

I felt the tension ripple through his body, felt the way his fingers tightened on my hips, like he wanted to argue.

But he didn't.

Instead, he exhaled sharply, stepping back, his hands falling away from my body, leaving me cold.

His expression was unreadable, but his voice was rough when he finally said, "I fucking hate it, Tits." His voice was laced with frustration and heat. "But I get it."

I let out a breath I didn't realize I was holding.

Ghost wasn't the kind of man who waited. He was the kind who took, demanded, and consumed.

But he wasn't fighting me on this. He was letting me go. For now.

He ran a hand through his hair, exhaling sharply before shaking his head. "You really are a pain in my ass."

I forced a small smile. "So are you."

Ghost stepped back again, shoving his hands into his pockets like he had to physically restrain himself from reaching for me. "Take your time, sweetheart." His lips curved, but it wasn't his usual cocky grin.

It was something else. Something that made my stomach twist. "But don't take too long."

Then, without another word, I turned and walked away.

Chapter 98

It'd been weeks since I had walked away from Ghost.

Weeks since I had shut the door on him, on everything we were, everything we could have been. And I was still trying to convince myself it was the right thing to do.

I called Henry on impulse, needing to know, needing to hear something about him.

"How's Lulu?" I asked, keeping my voice casual, like I wasn't dying inside.

"She's good." Henry's voice was gruff but kind. "You don't have to worry. Ghost is feeding her. She's won her place inside. He won't throw her back out."

I exhaled slowly, something in my chest tightening. No matter how stubborn he could be, how emotionally unavailable the man was, he wasn't cruel. He would never let Lulu starve. And he hadn't cast her out either.

Still, the knowledge that he was taking care of something I loved, even when I wasn't there, sent a fresh wave of ache through me.

Henry hesitated. "How are you?"

I let out a short laugh, shaking my head. "I don't know."

And that was the truth. I didn't know whether I had made the right choice. I didn't know if I should have fought harder, stayed longer, held on tighter. I didn't know if walking away from Ghost had been necessary. Or if it had been the biggest mistake of my life.

I swallowed. "And Ghost?"

Henry sighed. "Keeping busy." There was a pause, a hesitation, before Henry finally said what I wasn't prepared to hear. "He's been entering three to four fights a week. It's like he's punishing himself by letting people beat on him."

My stomach twisted violently.

I closed my eyes, pressing my fingers against my forehead, trying to breathe through the sudden tightness in my chest.

Ghost was hurting. And instead of facing it, instead of talking, instead of dealing with it, he was throwing himself into fight after fight, letting people hurt him, letting them take out the pain he couldn't express.

He was self-destructing. And I had been so sure he didn't really care, so convinced that he was fine without me.

But now? Now, I wasn't so sure. The endless loop of 'what-ifs' weighed down on me.

Women obsess and overthink everything. We replay moments over and over, turning them inside out, upside down, analyzing every single word, every single action, every single second. Could I have said this? Should I have said that? Done that?

It would rip my heart out to show up somewhere and see him with someone else. Because I couldn't handle watching him move on while I still felt like I was drowning in him.

I let him go because I was too angry and hurt to take him back.

But wasn't being without him ripping my heart out even more?

Then a realization hit. Was I just punishing him for hurting me? Was I so angry at him for hurting me I wanted to hurt him, to make him suffer the way he made me suffer? It was just the pain talking. It had been childish of me to want to hurt him. And now, the thought of him suffering was like a brutal stab to the heart.

I shot up out of my seat and hurried to dress.

The underground arena buzzed with energy, the crowd alive, voices roaring as Ghost's fight unfolded before me.

I said hi to my friends, playing it cool, pretending like I wasn't on the verge of falling apart just being near him again.

Ghost took a few hits, his head snapping back slightly, but he shook it off, his movements swift, calculated. And in the next moment, he landed a spinning back kick to his opponent's head.

He won, and the crowd exploded.

He took his lap and made his way through the crowd.

That was when some random blonde appeared. She was beautiful, beaming as she threw her arms around him. "You're the best!" she squealed, clinging to him.

My stomach clenched, but Ghost simply muttered, "Thank you," then walked away from her.

My heart was pounding with anticipation.

His eyes landed on me.

He froze, his blue eyes wide, his body tensing slightly like he wasn't sure if I was real. "Halston."

I tilted my head, letting my lips curl into a smirk.

And then, in the middle of the arena, in front of everyone, I yelled, "Nice cock!"

His jaw dropped. "What?"

I could feel my friends staring at me, probably wondering if I had completely lost my mind.

Oh, I definitely had.

I doubled down.

"Nice cock!" I repeated, enunciating, so he was sure not to misunderstand this time. Surveying the crowd, I asked, "Which one of you does he belong to?"

Ghost's brows furrowed, confusion flickering across his face.

I shrugged and kept going. "I've got some free time if you wanna go bang one out in my car."

Ghost's mouth twitched, and then a grin spread across his face, his entire demeanor shifting. "That's repulsive."

I laughed, arching a brow. "Really? That usually works."

Ghost chuckled, his hands finding my waist, his lips just inches from mine. "The vulgar things that come out of that mouth, Tits."

"You like?" I asked with a sly smirk.

"I love," he said just before he kissed me.

The crowd went wild, cheers and whistles filling the air.

Ghost pulled back just slightly, his eyes still locked onto mine, his hands firm on my waist, like he was afraid to let go. "I wasn't sure I was ever gonna see you again," he admitted.

I swallowed, my arms around his neck, gripping onto him like he was the only thing keeping me upright. "I wanted to stay away," I whispered. "To show you that I'm better off without you. But I'm not. Having you in my life the way we were is so much better than not having you in my life. Fuck my stupid pride. I love you, Kasper."

I kissed him again, slow and deep, letting it back my words up.

When I pulled away, his expression softened, his jaw relaxed, and something in his blue eyes shifted. "Halston—"

I shook my head, cutting him off. "You don't have to say anything."

"But I do," he admitted. "I've been going through it all in my head for weeks, sorting it out. What I wanted to tell you the night of the party." His blue eyes searched mine. "I told you I needed space to figure out if I had feelings for you... or if I was just addicted to fucking you."

My heart lurched.

"The sex was so fucking insane, I started thinking maybe that was all it was." His eyes burned into me, his voice tight, low, like the memory alone was enough to ruin him all over again. "I've never had a woman who makes me feel the way you do. Never had someone completely wreck me like that."

Heat flared inside me. I swallowed hard, my pulse hammering in my throat.

"But you wanna know the part that really fucked me up, sweetheart?" His voice dropped to a low, devastating rasp, the kind that reduced me to nothing but heat and desperation.

I exhaled shakily. "What?"

Ghost smirked, his voice soft. "It wasn't just the sex that wrecked me." His fingers tightened on my hips. "It was you," he admitted, his voice rough. "You, sitting in my bed after. You, sleeping next to me, wrapped around me like you fucking belonged there."

My breath caught in my throat.

"I realized real fast it wasn't just about how good you feel when I'm inside you, or how fucking tight you are when you're cuming around me," he said, his voice sending a violent shiver down my spine. "It was about how I felt when I woke up and you weren't there."

That did something to me.

He ran a hand down his beard, shaking his head. "I needed space, Tits. And I took it. But all it did was prove what I already fucking knew."

I stared up at him, my heart in my throat. "And what's that?"

Ghost stepped into me again, so close I could feel the heat radiating off his body. His fingers brushed my jaw, tilting my face up to his. "That I don't just want you in my bed," he whispered, his voice thick. "I want you, period."

I took a deep breath, blinking fast as my chest tightened.

"You had my attention the first time you turned me down at the fight," he continued, his voice low, raw, stripped down to the bone. "And the more I got to know you, the more you got under my skin. When you got my dogs to follow you, you stole my heart, Tits."

A laugh bubbled out of me, even as tears slipped down my cheeks.

Ghost wiped them away with the pads of his thumbs, his touch so gentle it made my heart ache. "I love you, Halston." His voice dropped even lower, rough with emotion. "What do you say we make this thing official?"

My heart soared, my chest tight with happiness I hadn't allowed myself to feel until now. I let out a breathless laugh, nodding. "You're all in? I'm all in."

He smiled. "Only way I want it."

And then, he kissed me, his tongue stroking mine slowly as he took his time wrecking me with his kiss.

We finally pulled apart, and I realized our friends were staring at us.

Ghost didn't hesitate. He looked right at them and said, "Yes. We're together."

Josh put up his hands. "Cool, man."

Drew smirked. "Welcome to the club."

Niki grinned, shaking her head. "It's about time."

They laughed.

Ghost grabbed me again, kissing me deep, sealing whatever was left between us with nothing but heat, want, and something that finally felt like forever.

The End

Content Warning & Spoilers

S teamy Warning
This book contains mature themes and explicit content intended for adult readers (18+). Reader discretion is advised.

Graphic sexual content (explicit language, multiple detailed sex scenes)

Profanity and vulgar dialogue (including dirty talk)

Underground fighting violence (including blood, injuries, and high-stakes tension)

Mentions of trauma and past abuse (verbal/emotional)

Possessive male behavior and dominant tendencies

Dubious emotional boundaries and morally grey choices

Casual discussion and use of alcohol and suggestive behavior

Death of a secondary character

About the Author

A.J. Blaze writes spicy chaos and happily ever afters with extra heat. Her books feature hot men, smart women, and scenes that'll make you blush in public. With explosive chemistry, sharp banter, and enough steam to fog up your screen, her stories are bold, dirty, and impossible to put down. If you like your romance a little wild and a lot filthy... welcome home.

When she's not writing scenes that could make a nun blush, she's sipping vanilla chai tea lattes, dreaming up morally gray heartthrobs, and pretending her characters actually listen to her.

Welcome to your next obsession.

Spoiler: it's filthy.

A Note from A.J.

Thank you so much for purchasing and reading my book! I put my heart and soul into my stories, and your support means everything to me.

Before you go... Please consider letting me know what you thought about the book, as it helps readers find their next romantic entanglement, and it helps me to reach more readers like you. Thank you!

www.ingramcontent.com/pod-product-compliance
Lightning Source LLC
Chambersburg PA
CBHW021939110726
47901CB00003B/896